Linda Gillard lives on the Black Isle in the Scottish Highlands and has been an actress, journalist and teacher. She's the author of six novels, including STAR GAZING which was short-listed in 2009 for *Romantic Novel of the Year* and *The Robin Jenkins Literary Award*, for writing that promotes the Scottish landscape.

HOUSE OF SILENCE became a Kindle bestseller and was selected by Amazon as one of their Top Ten *Best of 2011* in the Indie Author category.

Linda's latest novel, THE GLASS GUARDIAN is a supernatural love story set on the Isle of Skye.

Also by Linda Gillard

Emotional Geology
A Lifetime Burning
Star Gazing
Untying the Knot
The Glass Guardian

www.lindagillard.co.uk

HOUSE OF SILENCE

Linda Gillard

First published as a Kindle e-book in 2011
This paperback edition 2012

Copyright © 2011 Linda Gillard

ISBN 978-1479237081

Cover design by Nicola Coffield

www.lindagillard.co.uk

For my mother, Margaret,
who loves a mystery.

A Beginning

Chapter One

Gwen

I used to wonder if Alfie chose me because I was an orphan and an only child. Was that part of the attraction? I came unencumbered, with no family.

We were kindred spirits in a way. Detached, self-centred, yet both obsessed with the past. *Our* past. The difference was, I had no family and Alfie did. He had a family – a large one – but mostly he behaved as if he didn't, as if he wanted no part of them, however much they might want a piece of him.

As a lonely child, then a solitary adolescent, I used to fantasise about having a family – a *proper* family, teeming with rowdy siblings, jolly aunts and uncles and of course doting parents. Alfie had that. But I suspect his fantasy was that they had all died, leaving him in peace as sole owner and occupier of Creake Hall.

It was a macabre joke we shared: that he lived on grim expectations. I used to chide him for his callousness and he would get angry, which was unlike him. He'd say, 'You have no bloody idea, Gwen! You don't know how much *they* expect of *me*.'

And it was true. I had absolutely no idea.

It's Gwen. Short for Guinevere.

Don't ask.

I was conceived, so I was told, at Glastonbury, foisted by father unknown on a semi-comatose mother. Sasha (she always insisted I call her that) must have done one line of coke too many. Sasha always said she had little recollection of my father but claimed my conception had been historic in all senses, that she had felt a deep, *deep* connection to the past (if not my father, whom she never saw again.)

To my eternal embarrassment, she named me Guinevere which was mercifully shortened to Gwen and sometimes, when she was having a stab at being maternal, Gwenny. But never Ginny. Ginny was the pet name (I use the term advisedly) of one of my dipsomaniac aunt's monstrous and much-loved Persian cats. There were three: Whisky, Vodka and Gin. Aunt Samantha had a quirky sense of humour when she was sober, which wasn't often.

Aunt Sam did booze, Sasha did drugs and my Uncle Frank did men – boys, if he could get them. This unholy trinity went down like ninepins in the '90s, martyrs to over-indulgence. All three died tragically young of, respectively, cirrhosis of the liver, a drug overdose and AIDS.

As for me, I'm allergic to alcohol and worry a lot about my pension. If she were alive, Sasha would have said this was unnatural in one so young. (Twenty-six, but people say I look older. I certainly feel older.) My mother, fond as she was of clichés, would have said, "Eat, drink and be merry, for tomorrow we die!" And Sasha did. I wouldn't describe myself as the ambitious type, but I do aim to live longer than my mother. If I make it to thirty-five, I'll have achieved that modest goal.

So it's Gwen, not Guinevere. That's one of the few things my mother and I agreed about. Names are destiny. So you might be surprised to learn that, despite the name and a genetic pre-disposition to excess, my friends describe me as frighteningly sensible, not at all the sort of woman who'd fall for an actor. And his home. And his family.

But Sasha would have understood. So, bless them, would Aunt Sam and Uncle Frank. They would all have cheered me on from the sidelines, for it would appear family is destiny too.

Even when you haven't got one.

Alfie Donovan wasn't my type. Given my limited experience with the opposite sex, I'm not sure I can presume to say I *have* a type. *Male, sober, solvent and heterosexual* would be at the top of my wish-list, with *tall, dark and handsome* not far behind. I don't claim to be original. At five feet nine myself, I think I can be forgiven for giving short-arses a wide berth. Uncle Frank used to claim, "It's all the same when you're lying down, sweetheart," but his powers of discrimination declined in later years. (Or, as he liked to put it, he developed "more catholic tastes".) Alfie was no taller than me. He was blond and funny-looking. Literally. His face made me laugh. His letterbox grin made a grey day suddenly sunny. Old ladies smiled at him for no reason and babies in buggies would crane their necks and stare, fascinated. Alfie's face was so mobile, so expressive, he could talk with it without opening his mouth. A roll of his eloquent brown eyes spoke volumes. He could crack you up with a look, hint at filthy *double entendres* with the hoist of an eyebrow. But handsome? No, never. His was a striking face, a memorable face, and – though I didn't realise it at first – it was also a familiar face.

I'm talking about Alfie as if he's dead... He isn't, of course. Not exactly.

But something died. Some*body*.

~~~

A man dressed in breeches, topcoat and elaborate cravat strode along the gravel path. He came to a halt in front of a wooden bench and addressed its occupant, a young woman in jeans and a man's linen shirt, her head bent over a spiral-bound notebook.

'Excuse me.'

She peered up at him, shielding her eyes against the sun, and cast a professional eye over his appearance, from carefully arranged blond curls to immaculate riding boots – only a size eight by her estimation. He was slender and pale and looked very hot. Smiling, he said, 'You're Wardrobe, aren't you?'

She didn't return the smile. 'Well, I don't actually have a pair of wooden doors, but thanks to an exhaustive training and a couple of years in the rag trade, I have been known to

3

work wonders with a safety pin.'

His large brown eyes rolled heavenwards. 'Music to my ears! You see, I've got a problem with my breeches.'

She turned back to her notebook. 'They're meant to be tight. Caroline's a stickler for authenticity – didn't they warn you? Don't expect to breathe and don't even think about sitting down. If you get tired, you have to lean against the fireplace. Decoratively.'

'Oh, absolutely! Understood. No, this is more serious than breathing problems. Especially from Caroline's point of view. My breeches are falling down.'

She looked up. 'What do you mean, falling down?'

'Travelling earthwards. I think I might have lost a button—' He flicked the cascade of lace at his throat. 'But I can't see past this sodding cravat. I can feel them slipping down. I know I'm not imagining it. One of the extras – who's already shown an unhealthy interest in my arse – referred to me as "droopy drawers" when he thought I was out of earshot. One of your safety pins might just save the day. And my face. Or rather arse.'

Suppressing a smile, the girl shut her notebook, stood up and said, 'Follow me.' She led him away from the mêlée of actors and technicians to a secluded part of the shrubbery. Turning to face him, she said, 'Undo your waistcoat. And please try not to destroy your cravat!' She bent down and examined his costume. 'Oh, I see your problem. You've lost a button at the waist. Have you put on weight since you were fitted for these?'

He gasped. 'My, that was tactful! I thought you wardrobe ladies were meant to be the soul of discretion, masking the numbers on your tape measure with a carefully placed thumb to avoid damaging fragile egos.'

'Oh yes, we do that for *stars*. And some of us will do it for nobodies. We don't do it for people who address us as pieces of furniture. We're funny that way.'

'Sorry, I was a bit stressed. I'll address you as anything you like – your majesty – if you'll fix me up. You see, if they ever finish with those bloody lights, we get to shoot the one and only scene in which I have to do some acting, as opposed

4

to propping up fireplaces. Decoratively. So I'd like to look my best. Please. *Ma'am.'*

'I see.' She produced a small tin from the breast pocket of her linen shirt and extracted a safety pin. 'Stand still. *Very* still.' She knelt in front of him and slipped her hand inside the waistband of his breeches.

He looked down, bemused, at the top of her shining dark head, now on a level with his crotch. 'Well, let's hope there are no paparazzi behind me, lurking in the shrubbery with a telephoto lens. I can see the headline now... *Blow-job in the bushes: BBC's desperate attempt to boost ratings with Regency sex romp.'*

Unperturbed, she stood up and examined her handiwork. 'OK, you're done. You won't be able to pee in a hurry, though.'

'*Pee?* My dear, we have catheters sewn into our breeches, didn't you know?' He noted with satisfaction that she was now avoiding his eye in an attempt not to smile. The corners of her mouth twitched as she let the curtain of her hair fall forward to hide her face. He pressed home his advantage. 'What's your name – er, your royal highness?'

'Gwen Rowland.'

'Well, Gwen, I'll save you the embarrassment of admitting you haven't the faintest idea who I am. Don't worry, you're not the only one. The director's either forgotten my name or doesn't recognise me in costume.'

'Could be all the weight you've put on, I suppose.'

The eyes that now met his conveyed both challenge and mischief. From a distance, he'd thought she hadn't looked all that attractive, but at close quarters the reluctant curve of that pretty mouth, the provocation in those blue eyes meant he was enjoying this more than he'd expected. 'You know, I *like* you, Gwen, I really do. I suppose it would be too much to hope the feeling was mutual?'

She shook her head. 'Far too much. But I might like you better if I knew your name.'

'I doubt it. My name's Alfie. Alfie Donovan. I'm a nobody. Playing a nobody. The youngest brother. A tousle-haired tearaway. It's a speciality of mine. So...' He stood back to let her admire him. 'You reckon I'll survive Caroline's scrutiny?'

5

'Turn round and let me see... Yes, you'll do. No-one's going to call *you* droopy drawers. But you might find your arse on the receiving end of more unwanted attentions now.'

'That wouldn't include yours by any chance?'

She fixed him with a look. 'As well as covering up tell-tale numbers on tape measures, we're trained to rebuff sexual advances from artistes who think they can take advantage of an intimate working relationship.'

'Is that so? I see what you mean about the training being exhaustive. How very disappointing. I *was* going to ask – politely – if you'd have dinner with me. In about three weeks time when we've finished shooting this bloody scene. I wonder – if I *had* asked – what you would have said?'

'I might have said yes. Though I'm not sure someone with a weight problem should really be dining out.'

He beamed at her. 'Gwen, you are a delight! *Please* have dinner with me. Or rather, please let me watch you eat dinner. I'll just toy with a breadstick.'

She folded her arms. 'OK, I give in. You've worn me down. A girl can stand only so much relentless charm. Is this what they teach you at drama school nowadays? Come and find me when you're through. You might want some help getting out of those breeches.' She grinned, then turned and walked away, leaving him temporarily bereft of words.

He watched her long-legged stride and the way her thick, dark hair swung from side to side in time with her step. He called out after her, 'You know, you just made my day!'

Laughing, she turned back, executed a mock curtsey, then continued on her way.

Gwen

Alfie had various alternative titles for our Regency epic (which he described as 'based on an original idea rejected by Jane Austen'). One was *Age and Avarice*, another *Plots and Plausibility* and, at the end of a long and trying day, when filming hadn't gone well and we were considering more sensible ways of earning a living, *Fees and Feasibility*.

Alfie and I shared a passion for the novel on which the

series was loosely based, so I thought his cynicism justified. The screenwriter who'd adapted the book had changed the plot, the characters and the ending and he'd set it ten years later (because the costumes were prettier). Apart from those minor alterations, he claimed, it was *totally* faithful to the original. There were those who said the sex scenes were gratuitous and inappropriate, but as the director repeatedly informed the cast, this was to be a Jane Austen for the twenty-first century. Sex scenes were apparently what Jane herself would have written if she'd had a free hand. And, I added privately, if she hadn't been a spinster. And a virgin. And disinclined to write a scene in which no female character appeared, on the grounds that she, Jane, had no idea how men talked to each other when ladies weren't present.

Or, as Alfie put it, much more succinctly, *Sperm and Spuriousness.*

We were filming on location in Sussex. Alfie lived in London and I shared a flat in Brighton with two other girls. We decided to have dinner in Brighton and Alfie said he would get the train back to Victoria. He wasn't staying in digs for the shoot and said he always went home if he possibly could. He lived alone in a basement flat in Highbury. His mother had bought it for a song years ago to use as her pied-à-terre in town, although Alfie suspected it had actually served as a love-nest. It was now worth a small fortune. Alfie said knowing he was perceived as a man of property had proved cold comfort when he'd been burgled (twice) and mugged (once) on his own very expensive doorstep.

He gave me all this information, partly to entertain, but also, I suspect, to let me know he didn't expect me to offer him a bed – shared or spare – after our meal. Alfie let me understand right from the start that he was a private person, that he was territorial. At first I thought it must have something to do with being a member of a large family. I now know going to ground in that gloomy basement was the only way he could switch off. Only when he closed his own front door could he stop performing. He said, if he didn't spend some time alone, every day, he forgot who he really was.

I used to dismiss some of the things Alfie said as hyperbole, the camp exaggerations of an actor and *raconteur*, but I came to realise that truth was vitally important to him. Paradoxically perhaps for an actor who spent his life pretending, Alfie rarely told lies. It was a point of honour with him. More than anything, he wanted to be taken seriously.

~~~

Gwen glanced up from her menu and studied Alfie as he read the wine list. He wore a white T-shirt underneath a fawn linen suit. Both revealed his weight problem to be imaginary. His hair, like the suit, was fashionably rumpled, the Byronic curls no longer in evidence. He looked up and said, 'So what are you having?'

'The sea bass, I think.'

'Snap. How do you like your wine?'

'Not at all. I'm allergic to alcohol.'

'How tragic.'

'Not really. I had a very dear aunt who was an alcoholic, so the attraction of booze always escaped me.'

' "Was"? Is she an ex-alcoholic?'

'No,' Gwen replied, not looking up from her menu. 'An ex-person.'

Alfie didn't answer immediately, then said softly, 'Alcoholism is a *bugger*, isn't it? Children have no idea what's going on. Or what to *do*.' Gwen said nothing and continued to stare fixedly at her menu. Alfie took the hint. 'Well, I'm going to have a glass – possibly two – of *sauvignon blanc*. Would you like some mineral water? Sparkling?'

'Yes, please,' she replied, relieved at the change of subject. As he ordered for them, Gwen resumed her study of Alfie. He definitely wasn't handsome, but he was appealing. Sexy in a quirky, boyish sort of way. She had to admit, he was definitely growing on her.

When the waiter had gone, Alfie leaned across the table

and said, 'If you're going to make me the object of scrutiny, I shall have to ask if you're mentally undressing me and if so, is it for professional purposes or just for pleasure?'

She laughed. 'The conceit of the man! Just listen to him!'

He feigned surprise. 'I thought a degree of familiarity was appropriate when addressing an attractive woman who's already had her hand down my trousers.'

'For professional purposes *only.*'

He inclined his head and narrowed his eyes. 'So – why the fixed gaze? The puzzled look?'

'I thought I was being quite discreet.'

'You were, but I'm observant. One of the tools of my tawdry trade.'

Gwen had a moment to consider her reply as the waiter brought their drinks. When he retreated she said, 'I was watching you and thinking you look familiar somehow. But I'm sure I've never met you. I think if I had, I'd have remembered.'

Alfie waved a dismissive hand. 'Oh, everyone thinks they know me. They do in a way. A *version* of me. A younger version.'

'What do you mean? Were you a child actor?'

'No, but a child actor has played me.'

'I don't understand. Are you famous then?'

'No, unfortunately. But my alter ego is.'

'You have a twin?'

'No, though you're getting close.'

'Oh, Alfie, stop being mysterious! Please explain. Why do I feel as if I know you?'

He sighed. 'Probably because you've seen photos of me in magazines and newspapers. You might also have seen a documentary about my mother – who *is* famous. She was filmed explaining – at interminable length – how I was her muse. What she didn't mention was that I'm also the wellspring of her considerable income. The goose that laid the golden egg. Or should that be gander?' He shrugged and poured them both some mineral water. 'A biological impossibility... But then so am I.'

'Alfie, who the hell *are* you?'

'Tom, Dick and Harry.'

'*What?*'

'I was the inspiration. The books were based on me. My mother created one of the great characters of twentieth-century children's fiction and she based him on me.'

'Oh! You mean *Tom Dickon Harry!*'

'That's what I said.'

'So your mother is Rachael Holbrook?'

'Yes. She married twice. Her second husband was called Alfred Donovan, after whom I had the misfortune to be named. I was the fifth and final child, the longed-for son after four disappointing daughters.'

'So Tom Dickon Harry was a real boy?'

'No, not really. But my mother claimed I was the inspiration for him and the media have pandered to that fantasy. It's good copy. A feel-good family story about a gifted but long-neglected author making a comeback in middle-age with a new character who captures everyone's imagination, appeals to boys, girls, parents, teachers, librarians, *everyone.* Everybody loves Tom Dickon Harry and many have profited from him. Booksellers love him because every year they can bank on shifting shed-loads of the new TDH, as it's known in the trade. Publishers love him because he's made children's fiction fashionable and lucrative. Librarians and teachers love him because he doesn't indulge in anti-social behaviour and talks in polysyllables. Boys love him because he's the friend they've always wanted: reliable, resourceful, a good person to have around when you're in a tight spot. And girls love him because he's a hero in miniature: brave, kind, funny and not bad-looking for a twelve year-old. Tom Dickon Harry is human,' said Alfie, shaking out his napkin as food was set before them, 'But he's not *real.*'

'And... TDH is you?'

'No, Gwen, I am TDH. In the minds of millions of readers. The documentary was made ten years ago but they repeat it now and again on daytime TV and every time Rae brings out another book, they run a picture of me alongside one of the illustrations in the new book, pointing out how I've aged while good old TDH stays forever young. It's the reverse of

Dorian Gray. I get older and more raddled, but my pen-portrait in the attic remains ever pure and youthful.'

'You sound bitter.'

'Do I? I shouldn't be. TDH has paid for almost everything I own. But he's also responsible for the non-event that has been my acting career. Maybe I'd have been a nonentity anyway, who knows? It's hard to say. But some years ago I accepted that all the time I was perceived by casting directors as an ageing schoolboy, I wasn't going to be offered Hamlet. Heroes of any kind, in fact. I'm TDH. I even *look* like TDH because he's based on me. So I'm doomed to toil away in the theatrical ghetto of younger sons and heroes' sidekicks. My destiny is to play Buttons to some taller guy's Prince Charming.'

'You *are* bitter.'

'No, frustrated! I'm a better actor than people realise. But I can't get anyone to take me seriously. I'm famous as Rae Holbrook's son, as the inspiration for TDH. She's Frankenstein and I'm her monster.' He shook his head. 'That's a lot of baggage to carry into an audition.'

'But I thought children of the famous got breaks because of their connections?'

'We do. We get the breaks and we have impressive address books, but few of us make it big. People will talk to me at parties. TDH is an ice-breaker because everyone has read at least one of the books – Rae's been writing them for twenty years. There's now a generation of readers introducing them to their own children. But the thinking goes like this: TDH occupies a place in the popular mind as an archetypal boy hero. White, middle-class, rather old-fashioned. The product of a middle-aged mind struggling to get to grips with the gross materialism of the '80s and coming up with a boy hero who's a refugee from the pages of John Buchan. Curiously dated, but also timeless. When the first book was published people described it as "an instant classic" and they were right. It was. Now when people meet me, they compare me with *their* idea of TDH. Whether I disappoint – and surely I must! – isn't really the point. Casting directors decide that I'm so associated with TDH, no-one is going to believe me as Henry V or Heathcliff, because I'm TDH! It's easier, safer, to cast someone else.'

'But – well, forgive me if this sounds a bit harsh—'

'No, go on. Put the boot in.' He grinned. 'I love it when you're mean to me.'

'Maybe you don't get those parts because you just aren't right for them.'

'Good point. Do you know what one of my tutors said at drama school? She said I had a face more suited to radio.'

'What a bitch!'

'Not really. Just a hard-nosed professional. And as it happens, I like doing radio. I can be tall, dark and handsome on radio. My voice is flexible and versatile and I'm a good mimic. I can do any accent you care to name if you give me half an hour with a demo tape – Russian, Iranian, Cumbrian... The last one's the hardest, by the way. Voice-overs and radio pay the bills, so I can't complain. But the problem is, my voice doesn't really go with my cheeky face, does it? Or the seven-stone weakling physique.'

'Oh, come off it! Just because you're not tall—'

'You should have seen me before I joined the gym. They used to call me Tom Thumb. The thing about the casting game is, you never know why you don't get parts. My agent used to call and say, "Sorry, Alfie love. No dice. They saw the part as older." Or younger. Or taller. Or Asian. Or any of the things I'm not, that TDH is not. Now she just sends me for TDH parts.'

'What are they exactly?'

'Young Oxbridge dons, toffs in Agatha Christie, chick-flick eye candy, assorted younger sons and ne'er-do-well nephews. I am perennially puerile. My earning capacity depends on my continuing ability to play overgrown schoolboys and I'm thirty next year. God forbid I should ever lose my hair! The work would dry up altogether.'

'I can see it must be very frustrating for you.'

'Humiliating, frankly. Oh, Rae will see I'm all right for cash. Or my sister Vivien will – she holds the purse strings. But I really would prefer to be independent. Of all of them.'

Scowling, Alfie lifted his glass and swallowed a mouthful of wine. 'I suppose I could always earn a crust on the after-dinner speaker circuit, talking about what it was like growing up as a childhood icon.'

'What *was* it like?'

He laughed. 'Don't remember! I was too busy trying to be a normal boy. But I'm sure I could improvise something over the port. Anyway,' he said, pushing his empty soup plate aside, 'I was raised by my father. I didn't even know all the TDH stuff was going on.'

'Really?'

'Oh yes. I didn't have to contend with being a Living Legend until they made the documentary. I was eighteen.'

'So your parents had divorced?'

'Yes, a few years after I was born. Rae wasn't the maternal type and she was pushing fifty. So I went to live with my father. Then I was packed off to boarding school and just saw my family in the holidays.'

'So you're saying your mother created a boy hero and based him on a child she didn't actually know?'

'Yes. That's exactly what I'm saying. My dear mother's a fraud. Being an impostor is one of the few things we have in common. TDH's childhood was supposed to be based on mine, his character based on mine. But when Rae Holbrook wrote those books, I wasn't actually around.'

'So TDH is just a figment of her imagination?'

'Precisely! And if, by common consent, I am TDH, what does that make *me*? A figment of a figment... More water?'

'Thanks.' She watched as he refilled her glass. 'It's quite a story.'

'No happy ending, I'm afraid.'

'Your mother sounds extraordinary. I'd be really interested to meet her.'

Alfie shook his head and intoned solemnly, 'Over my dead body.'

Gwen

Alfie appeared to have inherited his mother's talent for words. One of his many verbal flights of fancy was *The Short*

Life and Lamentable Death of Tom Dickon Harry, a theme he'd return to often and with relish. He'd pleaded with Rae to kill off her creation and when she'd refused, he'd devised his own story – several in fact – in which TDH met a variety of gruesome ends. There was to be no ambiguous tumbling over the Reichenbach Falls for TDH, no possibility of a comeback. Alfie murdered his *alter ego* in cold blood, sending him to a watery grave, tossing him into an erupting volcano, blowing him to bits with a bomb. Alfie's disposal of TDH was vengeful and very final. I don't doubt it was also therapeutic.

He was right. He *was* a much better actor than anyone gave him credit for. But he knew how good he was and that knowledge contributed to his bitterness. He didn't want fame. In a way he already had that. Minor celebrity status anyway. What he wanted was recognition. He wanted his talent to be recognised and he wanted to be appreciated for *himself*. He hated being thought of as someone's son, or worse – an ageing Peter Pan, frozen in time, forever on the cusp between boyhood and adolescence. He used to say, if only his mother had allowed Tom Dickon Harry to grow up with the books, his life would have been more bearable.

TDH was Alfie's shadow, attached to him and a version of him, but a distorted one. The only way he could be rid of that shadow was to stay out of the limelight, keep a low profile – things an actor would find hard to do, even if they didn't constitute professional suicide.

On that first evening together we sat talking in the restaurant until it seemed too late for Alfie to think about returning to London. He insisted on paying for dinner, claiming the pittance he was paid was probably more than the pittance I was paid. He insisted too on waiting with me for a taxi. There was something oddly appealing about the way he coupled courteous behaviour with scurrilous talk.

'You could stay, you know. I really don't mind.'

'Wouldn't dream of imposing.'

'It wouldn't be an imposition. I mean... no strings. You could have the sofa. I wasn't assuming that you'd want – I meant, I didn't—' As I ground to an embarrassed halt he leaned forward and kissed me.

'My return to town should not be read as a reluctance to consummate our relationship. And if you were to put your hand down my trousers *now*, you'd perceive the truth of that.' He kissed me again. 'Another time. There will be another time, won't there? I've got to be on the set at 9.00am tomorrow – costumed, made-up, coiffed and looking fresh as a daisy. Make-up will have to use industrial-strength concealer on the bags under my eyes.'

'So stay over.'

'No. I like to sleep in my own bed. Not necessarily alone, you understand. Will you be on the set tomorrow?'

'Yes.'

'And the day after?'

'Yes.'

'You'll be around for a while, I hope?'

'Yes.'

'Good.'

Alfie stepped out into the road suddenly and hailed a passing taxi. It slewed to a halt and he opened the door for me. I kissed him on the cheek and climbed in. By the time I'd given the driver my address and looked round to wave goodbye, Alfie was gone. As the taxi drove away we overtook him, his hands in his pockets, his head bowed. Pale-faced, pale-haired under the street-lights, he looked slight and insubstantial, like a ghost.

I didn't see much of Alfie in the next few weeks. We were sometimes on set together, but his filming schedule was punishing and my hours were long, so there wasn't much time or energy left over for socialising. We had a tacit agreement that the friendship that *might* become a relationship was on hold until we could give it our full attention. At least, I think that's what was going on. We flirted, touched, kissed in snatched moments of privacy, but Alfie put no pressure on me to go up to London with him and he never accepted my invitation to stay over in Brighton, even though it was pretty clear I was no longer offering him the sofa.

It was an odd sort of courtship – and *courtship* is what it felt like, not just because he was in Regency get-up most of the time we spent together. Alfie's verbal seduction of me left me in no doubt that his mind and feelings were engaged, even if for the moment his body wasn't. I had a sense of his attention being lavished on me and I watched him to see if he treated everyone in this way. He didn't. He was friendly, funny, respectful to the director and experienced members of the cast and crew, but with me he was more open, somehow vulnerable. I can't think of a better word to describe it. I just had a sense of Alfie being *himself* with me. Except that he wasn't really. It was so obviously a performance for my benefit: entertaining, endearing, apparently sincere but also self-consciously charming. The contradictions were what made him so intriguing. And so infuriating.

When I look back now, it seems to me that the best and most convincing performance I ever saw Alfie give was off-camera. As himself.

It was the performance of a lifetime.

Chapter Two

Gwen

It probably sounds as if I was a pushover, besotted from the outset. Maybe I was. I was certainly pretending, to myself and to Alfie, that I *wasn't*.

When I said I didn't have much experience with men, I wasn't referring to a lack of interest in them, nor to an unprepossessing appearance. (I gather I'm attractive to men. Slim, but not skinny, with shiny, straight, dark hair, as featured in shampoo commercials.) My meagre love life was a result of caution on my part and cowardice on men's. They found me challenging. I just wasn't "girly". I didn't wear make-up. I didn't wear fashionable clothes, preferring vintage and second-hand clothing. I didn't wear heels. Not a feminist statement, or even a fashion statement. If you're 5' 9" and single, you'd have to be supermodel-confident to think you could wear heels and still have a good chance of pulling.

To make matters worse, I was intelligent and articulate. Not exactly self-confident, but I was at least capable. A "coper". With a family like mine you learn to cope at an early age. You accept that sometimes you are effectively the head of the household, or at least the most responsible member. I earned my own living and I was pursuing a career. I wasn't killing time until I could bury myself alive with babies and soft furnishings. But nor was I a girl-about-town, clubbing, drinking, sexually adventurous. I liked sewing, reading, tending my houseplants, pottering about in flea markets and Oxfam shops. I enjoyed old black and white movies and I listened to Radio 4. On the basis of all this, more than one ex-boyfriend had described me as "seriously weird".

The reasons for my eccentricity are not hard to fathom. I'd seen, in gruesome detail, where partying got you: drunk, diseased and dead. No wonder then if I chose to err on the side of caution. From my "weird" point of view, Alfie had a lot going for him. He drank very little. As far as I could tell, he didn't do drugs. He seemed thoroughly heterosexual despite numerous, sometimes pressing invitations to widen his sexual horizons. But he wasn't a womaniser. An incorrigible flirt maybe, but older women were more often favoured than young. The more senior the *grande dame*, the more likely she was to receive his attentions. I observed him at a party meeting Dame Judi Dench for the first time. When she moved on to the next group of guests, he turned back to me looking slightly dazed. He looked down at the hand she'd shaken and claimed he wouldn't wash for a week. Was the reverence real? I think so, but you could never tell with Alfie.

He wasn't the slightest bit threatening, to me or anyone, nor did he seem to feel threatened by me. If anything, I think he found my foibles amusing. We were a couple of oddities. By the time we finally slept together – both stone cold sober – we were already friends. We felt safe with each other. I think we both realised that even if the sex was a disaster, we would try again because we liked each other.

But sex wasn't a disaster. Far from it. Alfie was as kind, attentive and funny in bed as out of it and, I have to say, he looked a good deal better with his kit off than on. I told him so and he said, 'Damn. I've always suspected that. I look taller naked, don't I?' For some reason he did. His was a slender, wiry frame, more muscle than flesh, thanks to his assiduous working out at the gym. Naked, he put me in mind of one of Leonardo's anatomical drawings, where you're aware of the body as a machine, how it's put together, how all the different bits work. When I was an art student we had to do a lot of drawing in our foundation year. Even though textiles were my first love, I enjoyed the challenge of figure drawing, trying to convey the body beneath the clothes, the structure that supported them. Although you couldn't see much of the body in my sketches, I wanted the viewer to have a sense it was there.

That's how it was with Alfie once our relationship became sexual. I was always aware of the body beneath the clothes, the steel behind the softness, another Alfie, rather different from the one he presented to the world. Alfie stripped for action was Alfie stripped in more senses than one. Divested of clothing, he looked older, tougher, harder. Instead of the Bambi brown eyes and the soft blond hair that said, "Ruffle me", I was aware of sinew and bone. The contrast was perplexing, but also exciting.

Dressed or undressed, Alfie was gorgeous. As he himself put it on one of the many occasions I had trouble keeping my hands off him, 'Admit it, Gwen – you don't stand a chance. I'm sex on legs.' Then he grinned and added, '*Short* ones.'

So everything was going really well.

Until I mentioned Christmas.

~~~

Turning the pages of a Sunday colour supplement, Gwen glanced up at Alfie as he finished the last of his breakfast, then said, with studied nonchalance, 'How would you feel about spending Christmas and New Year in Scotland? I've got the use of a flat in Edinburgh. A friend's going ski-ing and she's happy for me to keep the place warm for her.' Alfie froze, a piece of toast poised in mid-air. She added, a little uncertainly, 'It was just a thought. Hogmanay's great fun. It's bigger than Christmas up there. They have a big festival in Edinburgh.'

He sighed, leaned across the table and poured more coffee. 'I have to spend Christmas with my family, I'm afraid.'

'Really? The way you talk about them – or rather *don't* talk about them – I thought they'd be the last people you'd want to spend Christmas with.'

'Well, yes, that's true. But I still have to go. Christmas is the only time I *do* go. I see everybody and get it all over with. It's a yearly ritual. And I'm the sacrificial victim.'

'Oh.' Gwen bent her head over her magazine again.

'Couldn't you ask someone else? It sounds like it would be fun.'

'Everybody spends Christmas with their family or partners. And if they don't, they book holidays. I can't think of anyone I could ask. And I don't want to stay in Edinburgh on my own. Not at Hogmanay anyway. It's a sociable time... Don't worry. I shouldn't have mentioned it. I just sort of assumed we'd spend Christmas together. Sorry.'

'No need to apologise.' Alfie swallowed some coffee and shook out his newspaper, scowling. 'I'd much rather spend Christmas with you than my bloody family.'

After a moment, Gwen looked up and said, 'Could I come with you?'

'To Creake Hall?'

'Yes. I'd be interested to meet your family. And from what you've said about the house, it sounds as if there'd be plenty of room.'

'I don't think that would be a very good idea, Gwen.'

'We wouldn't have to share a room. I realise your mother might not approve.'

'No, it's not that. In any case, Rae doesn't actually do Christmas. She rarely emerges from her room. One is given an *audience*.'

'Then surely she'd hardly miss you if you didn't go?'

He shook his head. 'It's a point of honour. I go because... well, because I've always gone. Because Rae wouldn't understand if I didn't go. Because Viv thinks it's important that I go. And because Hattie likes to see me. And I'm quite fond of Hattie. The ties that bind, Gwen... It's all pretty intense. I don't think you'd enjoy it.'

'I don't think I'll particularly enjoy Christmas on my own. My flatmates won't be here and Brighton in December is beyond bracing. '

'This is beginning to sound like emotional blackmail.'

'Well, it's also sounding as if you really don't want me around.'

'It's not that.'

'What is it then?'

'It's difficult to explain.'

'Try.'

'I'm a different person with my family.'

'Isn't everyone? We revert to an earlier childhood self, usually a self we've consciously rejected. I do realise the

20

whole thing would be a performance.'

Alfie regarded her, his expression grave. 'Do you?'

'Well, that's the nature of families, isn't it? Everyone trying to accommodate everyone else. Struggling to like people they'd normally cross the road to avoid. Trying hard not to dig up buried hatchets.'

'For an orphan, you seem to know a lot about families.'

'My mother came from a dysfunctional family. I never got to meet my grandparents because they would have nothing to do with her. I think she ran away from home when she was sixteen, gave herself a new name, a new life. Or maybe they threw her out. I gather they were very religious. They'd have seen Sasha was going the same way as her older brother and sister. Fast track to Hell.'

Alfie smiled. 'And you think *my* family sounds interesting?'

'I know about families, I just don't *do* families. Maybe if I came to Norfolk with you, you might actually enjoy the festivities more. I could lighten the conversational load. Mothers usually like talking to their sons' girlfriends.'

'Rae wouldn't. She hasn't really taken on board that I'm a man. I'll always be a boy to her. And Rae dictates the terms. I don't really have any choice but to play up to that. It's what she expects. And wants.'

'It's very good of you, Alfie.'

'What is?'

'To give up your Christmas to spend time with them. When it's clear you hate every minute of it.'

'I owe them.'

'What do you owe them?'

'It's hard to explain.'

'You keep saying that! I don't think one owes family anything. It's just an accident of birth and at some point in their teens, most kids realise they've been born into the wrong family. It's nice if families are friends, if they love each other, but mostly they don't. And why should they, if they have nothing in common but blood?'

'Why indeed? Self-interest, perhaps? Or just survival. The tribal instinct, wanting to belong. Wanting to be loved, even where one can't love... Do you really think it's better to have no-one?'

'I have no-one, so I don't ask the question.'

'That's one of things I admire about you, Gwen. Your pragmatism. There's no nonsense with you, is there? So what will you do?'

'For Christmas?'

'Yes.'

'Eat too much and watch old Morecambe and Wise DVDs, I expect.' She tossed the magazine onto the floor where it joined a pile of discarded newsprint. 'No, I'll volunteer to do a stint at St Patrick's.'

'What's that?' Alfie frowned. 'Sounds suspiciously worthy. I think you're about to ratchet up the guilt factor.'

'St Patrick's is the night shelter in Brighton. I've done it before. It's good fun. And more meaningful than stuffing yourself till you can't move.'

Alfie assumed a tragic expression. 'You're breaking my heart.' She hurled a cushion at him. He fielded it and said, 'No, seriously!'

'I didn't mean to sound holier-than-thou, it's just that... well, I like to keep *busy* at Christmas.'

Alfie tossed the cushion back on to the sofa. 'Something tells me there's something you're not telling me.'

Gwen fixed him with a look. 'You mean like all the stuff *you're* not telling *me*?'

Alfie avoided her eye and folded his newspaper. 'Come on, spill the beans. You know I can see right through your Plucky Little Gwen routine.'

She drew her legs up to her chest and circled them with her arms. 'It's an anniversary,' she said quietly.

'Of?'

'My mother's death.'

'Oh. I see. I'm sorry.'

'She died of a drugs overdose in 1994. On Christmas Eve.'

'Oh, *shit*.'

'Exactly.'

'Was it suicide?'

'No. It must have been her Christmas present to herself.

22

Or a present from her dealer boyfriend. An overly generous one.'

Alfie didn't reply, then his expression changed. With a sharp intake of breath he said, 'You didn't get up on Christmas morning and—'

She nodded without looking at him. 'I knew something was wrong as soon as I woke up. There was no stocking at the end of the bed. She always left me one, even though I was too old to believe in Father Christmas.'

'Bloody hell, Gwen... Were you on your own?'

'Yes. I rang for an ambulance. Then I rang my aunt.'

'The drunk?'

She shrugged. 'I didn't have too many options.'

'How old were you?'

'Twelve.'

'*Christ*, Gwen!'

'Can we change the subject, please? I just wanted you to realise that I wasn't doing the clingy girlfriend thing, I was just hoping that – I mean, I really wanted to spend Christmas with *you*. I didn't care where. Or how. I just wanted to wake up on Christmas morning and find *you* at the end of the bed. I haven't told you about Sasha to make you feel awful, I've told you because... well, I just wanted you to know. What Christmas means to me. Will *always* mean to me.'

He sat down beside her on the sofa and put his arm round her shoulders. 'I'm really glad you told me. And... I'm honoured that you did.'

She rubbed her nose with the back of her hand, blinking hard. 'St Patrick's is good fun actually. We have a laugh. And it's a wonderful antidote to self-pity. Which is just what I need at Christmas.'

'Maybe I need a dose of St Patrick's too... Look, Gwen, if I took you to Creake Hall you'd have to promise me you wouldn't ask any questions or ask me to explain anything. You'd just have to take everything and everyone as you found them. Some of them will be glad of the distraction of a new face. Others might resent it. I just don't know, I've never taken anyone home before. It's uncharted territory.'

'Alfie, I really appreciate the offer, but if your family are likely to resent an outsider—'

'No, it's not that. They aren't the problem, it's *me* that's the problem, wanting to keep my bloody life compartmentalised. I really don't think you'll like the person I am with my family, the person I have to become. Famous son of the even more famous Rachael Holbrook. It's just a performance. I'd want you to remember that.'

'Of course. You're sure they won't mind?'

'They'll be fine. Anyway, they don't get to vote. I'm the Young Master. When the Prodigal returns, everyone has to jump to it. I could probably exercise some sort of *droit du seigneur* with the local girls, but I've never actually tried.' He sighed. 'I suppose I'll have to scrap that idea now if you're going to be there, keeping an eye on me.' She threw her arms round his neck and kissed him. 'Just come with low expectations, Gwen – of me and my family.'

'I'll prepare myself for the second-worst Christmas I've ever had.'

'I doubt you'll be disappointed.'

'Thank you, Alfie.'

'What for? Your second-worst Christmas?'

'No, for lending me your family.'

'Take them! *Please!* I have absolutely no use for them. I only wish,' he added ruefully, 'they had no use for me.'

Chapter Three

Rae

Dahlias... So it must be autumn.

Red, orange, burgundy... and that frightful acid yellow. They must go. Vivien will have to tell him. Tell the gardener. What *is* his name? *Tyler.* That's it. Tell Tyler that the lemon is quite wrong. What can he have been thinking of? I must write a note for Viv and she can give it to... to the gardener. Tyler. Yes, that's his name.

The apples will be ready. And the pears. They must be stored properly. The Newton Wonders keep very well if they're stored correctly. It will be a good crop, there's been plenty of rain.

Rain, rain go away. Come again another day...

I hear it on the roof, rapping on the window panes, cascading from an overflowing gutter. It must be blocked. He needs to look at it. *Tyler...* I can see him down there in the garden, tidying the beds. And not before time, they look a mess! There are so many jobs to be done at this time of year, so many things to think about, my head spins! There's no room for stories now. Not any more. The stories have gone...

He'll be home for Christmas. Alfie. As usual. We'll have Newton Wonders and some of the Coxes. With the Stilton and port. Alfie likes a glass of port. Just like his father! But Freddie won't be there. Freddie's gone.

I *think* Freddie's gone... Yes, he went away a long time ago.

I think he's dead. He is, I'm sure of it. Freddie went away. And then he died...

Vivien said I drove him away, but I don't remember. He took Alfie with him. Viv said it was all for the best. Alfie went away to school – to a *good* school – and he was very happy. We had letters telling us how happy he was. I have them somewhere. In one of these drawers, I forget which. Vivien would know. She tidies my desk and keeps things safe for me.

Freddie died...

He must have been old, I suppose. Like me.

But Alfie didn't die, I'm sure he didn't. I'm *practically* sure... No, Alfie didn't die because he's coming home for Christmas! Which must be soon. Where's my diary? I know it's here somewhere. Vivien leaves the diary open for me, on top of my desk, and she marks it so I know what day it is. And which month. But I know it's September – I can see the blackberries!

He needs to pick them. Tyler. Harriet can help. That's a job she can do. Make herself useful, get out in the fresh air. It's September, so the blackberries must be picked and bottled.

No... We don't do that any more. What *do* we do with them? Ah, yes, we *freeze* them! Vivien freezes the blackberries and we have blackberry and apple pie...

A was an Apple Pie, B bit it, C cut it...

Bramleys of course, nothing better. We have blackberry and apple pie at Christmas because it's Alfie's favourite. Christmas Pie!

He put in a thumb and pulled out a plum –

No, that's not right... *Blackberries*. We have blackberries. I must remind Vivien. She must tell him, tell Tyler, to pick all the blackberries before the birds get them.

Blackbird Pie! *That's* what Alfie used to call it!

Four and twenty blackbirds baked in a pie. When the pie was opened –

Why is my drawer open? Did *I* open it? Was I looking for something? I must have been. Something important... It was to do with Alfie coming home. He'll be home soon. At Christmas. We'll all be together again. The family. All of us. All the girls and little Alfie. I must ask Viv to get him a present... A new jersey. He'll have grown. Boys are always growing. Always eating and always growing! He'll need a new jersey, a warm one, for the winter. And it's nearly winter now. The apples are ripe and the leaves are turning. Tyler will burn all the dead leaves. If I open the window I'll smell the smoke and I'll know it's November, almost December. And then it will be Christmas and Alfie will be home. We'll have Blackbird Pie and Viv and Hattie will decorate the house with holly and ivy and there'll be a big log fire...

When?

When will that be? Say the bells of Stepney...

When is Alfie coming home?

I'm sure I don't know, says the great bell of Bow...

At Christmas. That's soon... Where's my diary? Vivien always leaves it where I can find it. She crosses out the days so I know where I am. And how long it will be till he comes, till Alfie comes home. He's very good, he comes every year. At Christmas. It's more than we could expect. Under the circumstances. The boy is very busy, Vivien says. He's an actor. But he always makes the effort to come and see us. At Christmas.

Ah, *here* it is! My diary. Viv has marked it for me. Today is September 19th. A Friday. It says here – where are my glasses? I put them down somewhere. I can never find my – ah, here they are! It says here – she's written it down for me – that it's ninety-six days to go. Ninety-six days till Alfie comes home. Less than a hundred! Not long now. The time soon goes...

Tyler is cutting some dahlias. I don't want any in here. I don't like them. Horrid vulgar flowers. Freddie grew them. They were his favourites. He liked big blowsy flowers. What happened to the asters, I wonder? They used to look like a purple cloud at the back of the border. We used to have asters, I'm sure, when Alfie was a boy...

Ninety-six.

Why did that number just come into my head? Is it 1996? That was a long time ago, surely? Alfie would have been – let me see now – seventeen. Seventeen! Oh, no, there I go again... It's silly to cry! Why, after all these years?...

Ninety-six.

I know that number is important, but I can't remember why. It's exasperating! Vivien has no idea... But she's very good, she marks my diary for me and tidies my desk and

27

leaves it so I can find everything. If I should want to write, everything is here, ready for me. A place for everything and everything in its place. Always the same. That's how I know where I am. Every day. Every year. Every Christmas, it's the same. We have Coxes and Newton Wonders with the Stilton and the port. Alfie likes port. It won't be long now. It says so here, in my diary. Ninety-six days till Christmas.

Ninety-six! That was the number! I *knew* it was important! Ninety-six days till Alfie comes home! Not long now. Not really...

I shouldn't have cried, I know I shouldn't, but I get so confused! And I don't remember *why* I cry! Vivien says, it's because I'm old. I don't remember how old. But I think I must be old... I look old. But I don't *feel* old. The time just goes...

Where does it go? When we've finished with it? Where does time go? I give the old diaries and calendars to Hattie to cut up for her patchwork, but where does the *time* go?...

I'll ask Vivien. She'll know. And if she doesn't, she'll find out for me. Where time goes. I know it bothers her too. She says so. She says, 'Where *does* the time go?' That's what she says. She says, 'I must be getting old, Rae. Where *does* the time go?'

I don't know. Vivien doesn't know either.

But I know you can't get it back. That's what Alfie said. When he came home for Christmas – was it last year? Or was it in 1996? We played *Charades*. And *Monopoly*. It was such fun! And Alfie said – what was it he said now? I try very hard to remember the things he says. Sometimes I ask Vivien to write them down for me so I can remember them. Alfie said... ah, yes, he said he was *making up for lost time*.

The time *is* lost. Lost to me...

So are the stories now. Even Alfie's. I've forgotten it.

I've forgotten now what it is that I don't remember... What I *mustn't* remember... It's all for the best, Viv says. But I don't remember why...

I wish Vivien would come. I'm so tired.

I wish Alfie would come... He'll be home soon. For Christmas. As usual...

Where *does* the time go?

~~~

Vivien sat at the kitchen table, her legs extended towards the Aga, warming her frozen toes. To hell with chilblains. She'd come in from the garden an hour ago but still didn't feel warm enough to remove her coat. And it was only October. The cold would get worse.

She hadn't minded so much when she was young. Perhaps it wasn't so cold then? It must have been. The planet was warming up, they said. Though not this particular corner of north Norfolk, with nothing between the coast and the Arctic to deflect bitter north winds. How had they managed all those years without central heating? Admittedly fires were always lit then and there were more bodies to warm the place up, children running about and dogs that could be trained to sit on your toes.

Vivien looked down at the pair of West Highland terriers dozing in front of the Aga, side by side, one old, one young. Harris and Lewis. In perpetuity. Rae believed them to be the same dogs, after all these years. When the original Harris had died, Rae (who still had her wits about her in those days but was too distressed to think of a new name) called the replacement pup Harris. By the time Lewis died, Rae didn't know what year it was, let alone the age of the dogs, so it was agreed that while she was alive, there should always be two dogs. Two Westies: one called Harris and the other, Lewis. It made everything simpler and it reduced the number of awkward questions Vivien had to answer.

She gazed fondly at the dogs, spread out in front of the Aga like a grubby sheepskin rug. Harris made a high-pitched whimpering noise and let out a shuddering sigh. Doggy dream-time, she supposed. Picking up a pen, Vivien pulled a spiral-bound notebook towards her. She kept one in every room, even the loo. It was the only way to keep on top of things, keep track of her ideas, of all that needed to be done, especially at this time of year.

She opened the notebook and looked down at a list headed *TO DO*.

Chiropodist (Rae)
Collect prescription
Make Xmas puddings
Make mincemeat?

Turning her mind back to the garden, she added to the list.

Store/check apples & pears (Tyler)
Clear gutters (T)
Lift dahlias. (Scrap yellow)
Asters?? (Ask T)
Plant bulbs in orchard. (More crocus?)
Order seed

Where *were* the seed catalogues? She was getting as bad as Rae. She'd put them somewhere safe so they wouldn't be turfed out with the junk mail. She could order online of course but she liked to sit by the fire with her feet up and a cup of tea, studying the catalogues. She loved them. The promise of spring. A new start. Renewal. Regeneration. All those big, hopeful words. Colour and bounty were crammed into the gaudy pages of those little booklets and she still got excited when, every autumn, they landed on the doormat. After all these years...

She remembered Deborah playing with Harriet on a wet winter's day when Rae was pregnant for the last time and couldn't be bothered with her six year-old daughter. Deborah, by then a student teacher, was helping Hattie cut out pictures of flowers from old seed catalogues, showing her how to stick them down and make a picture of a summer garden, a picture for Rae, who never showed the slightest interest, in that or anything Harriet made, then or since. Rae cared for nothing apart from the birth of the baby she knew by then would be a son. But Deborah was patient and loving. She mothered Harriet. And Vivien mothered Rae. Everyone had rallied round. Even Frances.

Vivien turned over a new page in her notebook, headed it *TDH*, then wrote:

Update website – cover (& blurb?) for TDH & the
Crystalline Cave
Type up synopsis & draft chapters of TDH & the Fortress
of Fear

She looked up from the page. Was that a good title? It was rather similar to *TDH and the Tower of Terror*. But that was ten years old. There was a different generation of readers now. For some reason the publishers insisted on alliterative titles and it was becoming increasingly difficult to come up with new ones. *Fortress of Fear* would have to do for now. She would try to discuss it with Rae, ask if she had any strong feelings on the matter.

Vivien shivered. The sun had set and the temperature had dropped perceptibly. Turning back to her TO DO list, she peered at it in the fading light, then glanced up at the calendar hanging on the wall. With a sigh, she wrote

Buy Xmas presents
Order cards to be printed (100?)

Thank God for self-adhesive stamps. Hattie would do the honours. She liked stamps and, impervious to their vulgarity, she especially liked the Christmas issues. Would this Christmas see Hattie's *magnum opus*, the Postage Stamp quilt – now ten years in the making – finished at last? And who would be the lucky recipient? Rae? Possibly. More probably Alfie, poor chap.

Vivien studied her list again and wrote

Confirm Xmas arrangements with A

She knew Alfie could be relied upon. He hadn't let them down in ten years. Nevertheless, she took her pen and drew a heavy line underneath the last item on her list. It was best to be on the safe side. Christmas was always something of a nightmare with Alfie, but it would be even more of a nightmare without him.

~

As Deborah wrapped the twenty-fifth copy of *Tom Dickon Harry and the Puzzling Pyramid* she reflected, as she did every Christmas, that although her pupils would undoubtedly rather have had sweets, giving them a book as an end-of-term gift at least ensured there was some chance they might read over the holidays. Her conscience gave her a pang as she thought of the pupils who would find the text challenging and the few who wouldn't be able to read it at all, but they'd all enjoy the quirky line drawings and a sense of belonging to the pack.

In any case, it all depended what you meant by *reading*. One creatively illiterate girl often asked to "read" to Deborah and always chose a book so linguistically demanding, it remained effectively closed to her. But seated at Deborah's side, Stacey would improvise fluently and without pause on a theme suggested to her by the book's illustrations plus the few words she could recognise. She even managed to recite in the same sing-song voice adopted by struggling readers. It was a *tour de force.* Deborah never failed to remark that she'd enjoyed hearing Stacey "read" to her, which was quite true. The poor girl couldn't read but, my goodness, she could tell a story! Stacey would certainly enjoy reading her copy of *Tom Dickon Harry and the Puzzling Pyramid.* She might even improve on the original.

Christmas just wasn't Christmas without books, Deborah told herself, then thought of the incongruity of books in a Bethlehem stable. With a smile she visualised a board book for the infant Jesus (*Where Did I Come From, Mummy?*), then as He grew older and developed reading stamina, a graphic novel (*Herod: Slayer of Innocents*). Before she knew it, the words *Tom Dickon Harry and the Mighty Messiah* had popped into her head.

She was tired. It had been a long and difficult term and she needed to rest. Instead there was the family Christmas at Creake Hall. She hoped Fanny wouldn't bring that man. Rae would find it very unsettling. You couldn't expect Rae to keep up with Fan's frequent changes of personnel. It was bad enough with Rae asking every year where *Bryan* was. Deborah's husband had been gone five years now, so she assumed her mother would never adjust to the split. The thing about Christmas – Christmas at Creake Hall anyway – was that it should always be the same. Predictable. No-one wanted any surprises unless they came gift-wrapped. Deborah decided she'd have a quiet word with Fanny, who could be perfectly reasonable if she put her mind to it. It was a question of catching her at the right moment. Before she downed the third martini.

Blessed are the peacemakers...

Is that what I am, thought Deborah. Or is that what Alfie is? She reached for the twenty-sixth copy of TDH, wondering if the reel of Sellotape would hold out. He was such a nice boy. So talented. He deserved to do well. She followed his career, saved the cuttings and made a little scrapbook for Rae every year as a Christmas gift. It would be rather thin this year. Alfie didn't seem to work quite as much as he used to, which was a bit worrying.

Wrapping the twenty-seventh copy, Deborah turned her mind to end-of-term projects. She was damned if they were going to sit around watching DVDs for the last week of term, especially not movies her pupils brought in (some of which were rated 18). Nor was she prepared to watch pop DVDs that seemed derived in style and content from soft-core porn. Not that she'd ever viewed any porn, but that's what they said in the staff-room. When she'd cleared out the last of Bryan's stuff, she'd found some DVDs and, seeing the lurid covers, the flesh and the leather, she'd thought at first they must be Heavy Metal. (Bryan liked to think of himself as an old Rocker and treasured his vinyl collection of Black Sabbath albums.)

But they weren't Heavy Metal. And she hadn't watched them.

If only he'd *said*. She'd had no idea Bryan was unhappy. She was broad-minded. Heaven knows, you had to be working in a place like this, where small pupils gave you too much information about their parents' domestic arrangements, even their sexual habits. If only Bryan had *talked* to her, instead of just clearing off. But Fanny said that was men for you. They weren't interested in working things out, only working things off.

With tears now pricking her eyes, Deborah looked up from copy number twenty-eight and gazed round the room at the mural her class had made representing *The Twelve Days of Christmas*, that hymn to materialism, over-indulgence and Beckham-style extravagance. Perhaps there was an end-of-term maths project there? A bit of number fun. How many gifts did her true love actually send on the twelfth day? And – as an extension activity for the brighter ones – how many presents had she received cumulatively over the twelve-day period? How many hens, ducks, geese, etc were there? The class could draw a bar chart to record this, then when everyone was exhausted, they could colour it in mindlessly, in Christmas colours.

She wondered if there were any gold crayons left or whether Leanne O'Leary had stolen them all. Leanne's mum's boyfriend was a local fence, to whom the light-fingered Leanne appeared to be apprenticed, but Deborah imagined there was a limited market for gold crayons. Now glitter glue – *that* was a different matter. But she kept the glitter glue under lock and key with the other valuables.

Reaching for the final copy of TDH, Deborah longed for rest. For silence. For blankness.

Blessed are the peacemakers for they shall be called the children of God.

That was it. That was your reward. You were called "a child of God". It didn't seem a lot. Not much of an incentive. You'd have a hard time selling *that* to Leanne O'Leary.

Oh well. There was nothing Deborah wanted for Christmas anyway. She'd even stopped wanting Bryan back. She just wanted peace. Peace and goodwill towards men. And her sisters. And her mother. And Alfie.

Was it really such a lot to ask?

~

From: Frances Judd fcjudd@googlemail.com
Sent: 12 December 2008 20:33:10
To: alfiedonovan@hotmail.com
Subject: Xmas comes but once a year

Ciao Alfredo!

It's that time of year again! :-(Just wanted
to say looking forward to seeing you. I'll be
there on Xmas Eve – and not a moment before –
and I may bring a man. If so, it won't be my
husband. Mike and I have gone our separate
ways. *(Quelle surprise!)* Didn't bother to
update you, thought it could wait till Xmas
when we can have a good old gossip.

If I do bring a man, he'll be called <u>Mark</u>.
Confusing, I know, but be an angel and try not
to call him Mike. This one's quite sweet and
quite rich and let's face it, darling, I'm not
getting any younger. I've warned him about The
Addams Family – esp. my irritating (but
adorable) kid brother – but it would be nice if
for once the clan didn't live down to my
expectations.

Saw photo of you in the *Telegraph* mag with some
anorexic floozie falling out of her dress. Will
somebody please tell me what is erotic about
<u>ribs</u>? She looked like a joint of beef. Nice pic
of you though. But did my eyes deceive me, or
did I spot some silver threads among the gold?…
Your Sexy Schoolboy days are surely numbered,
sweetie. Does *Grecian 2000* come in Golden
Blond, I wonder? ;-)

Your fan,

Fan
XXX

~

35

Hattie sat by the sitting-room fire, her workbox at her feet, her embroidery hoop on her lap, executing the final stitches in a labour of love: a sampler she'd designed herself using coloured pencils and graph paper. She'd studied faded family heirlooms beforehand and, taking her lead from them, had included her full name, *Harriet Susan Donovan* and her date of birth, *April 21st 1973*. She'd attempted to depict a view of Creake Hall but the finished result, necessarily simplified, resembled a dolls' house. Resembling dolls were four female figures standing in a line, descending in height. At the end of what looked something like a bus queue was a doll's doll: a much smaller, trousered figure holding the hand of the smallest female. The two smallest figures were extravagantly yellow-haired. The other three were dark. (Hattie had originally attempted portraits of Harris and Lewis but the white dogs were almost invisible against a neutral background, so she'd unpicked them, feeling faintly guilty about this act of artistic elimination.)

Hattie wondered if she should tone down the bright hair of the figure representing herself. Her hair, blonde when she was a child, had faded to an ashy light brown but her curls were still copious and unruly. She no longer plaited her hair but left it loose or held it back with an elastic band.

She decided to leave the abundant yellow hair of her childhood self. She was not after all aiming at photographic reproduction – accuracy of any kind, in fact. That was Fanny's job. In Hattie's picture the house and figures merely formed a frame for her text: a rhyme she'd known for many years, a ditty of uncertain origin, one that she'd perhaps learned from her father or grandmother or some other long-dead, half-remembered relation. Hattie had always liked the rhyme even when she hadn't really understood what it meant. When she was old enough to appreciate its meaning, she adopted it as a personal mantra, a comforting incantation.

She'd intended to give Alfie the postage stamp quilt for Christmas this year until she'd overheard Vivien talking about it on the phone to Deborah. Viv had laughed and her words had made Hattie re-consider. She'd decided she would save the quilt until she found a more suitable recipient, although she had no idea who that could possibly be. Hattie rarely met new people and the family never seemed to expand, only contract as one brother-in-law after another disappeared from the scene.

Short of time and daylight hours, Hattie had hit upon the idea of making a sampler for Alfie. It would be a small item and he could hang it on the wall in his flat. Or not. Since Hattie had never been invited to visit Alfie's home, she would never know if he displayed her gift. But even if he chose not to, she thought he might appreciate the sentiments behind it. Alfie was clever and he loved words. He of all people would appreciate that the expression of her gratitude must remain coded.

Hattie picked up a pair of tiny silver scissors in the shape of a bird and snipped the thread with the bird's long beak. She released the canvas from its frame and spread it out on her lap. Though she'd long known them by heart, she read the lines over and smiled as she wondered what Alfie would make of them.

If you your lips would keep from slips,
Five things observe with care:
Of whom you speak, to whom you speak,
And how and when and where.

If you your ears would save from jeers,
These things keep meekly hid:
Myself and me, and my and mine,
And how I do and did.

Chapter Four

Gwen

If Alfie's family objected to an extra houseguest I didn't get to hear about it. We set off from London by car on December 23rd. Alfie drove and once we got north of Fakenham, the Norfolk landscape began to roll out in front of us like a carpet in an empty room: flat, at times almost featureless, apart from hedgerows and an occasional windmill. The grey sky looked vast and cold as we drew nearer to the coast and I noticed Alfie take a firmer grip of the wheel as the wind began to buffet the car.

He'd insisted I would need thermal underwear for our trip and informed me, with a sad shake of his head, that sexual congress was unlikely to take place over the holiday period as we'd be wearing so many clothes, we wouldn't be able to get near each other, and if we did, the intense cold would have shrunk his member beyond usefulness. I took no notice of any of this, used as I was to sea air and Alfie's tendency to exaggerate, but I'd packed fleece pyjamas, some serious Norwegian socks and a selection of warm jumpers. Alfie assured me it would be necessary at night to wear all these garments simultaneously.

'And don't, whatever you do, get out of bed in the morning and step onto the lino in bare feet! It will be freezing and your skin will adhere to the floor. Then we'll have to send for Tyler and his trusty blow torch to thaw you out.

'Tyler?'

'Handyman-gardener. Viv's right hand man.'

'But not Viv's—'

'Oh no, *definitely* not. I've always suspected Vivien is of the Sapphic persuasion, if she's anything at all. She's lived at Creake Hall all her life, so her private parts have probably atrophied with the cold anyway. Viv's certainly never shown any interest in men. Apart from Tyler, but theirs is a communion of the spirit. They share a passion for gardening but not – as far as I know – each other. But you never can tell. They say you have to watch the quiet ones, and Tyler is *very* quiet.'

'Are you going to fill me in on the rest of the family before we get there? You haven't really said much.'

'I told you what to buy them for Christmas.'

'That didn't tell me much about them as people. As your *family*.

'You want me to dish the dirt, you mean?'

'No! I just meant I'd like to know a bit more... Though dirt is always fun.'

'I can see I'm having a corrupting influence on you, Gwen.'

'Oh, I never believe anything you tell me, on principle. But I'm sure an account of your family would be very entertaining, even it *is* a pack of lies. Which I assume it would be.'

'Me, tell lies? I'll have you know, I have a scrupulous regard for truth, just a rather cavalier attitude to the English language.'

'The facts, Alfie. Just give me the facts.'

He raised one hand from the wheel and affirmed, 'I swear to tell the truth, the whole truth and,' with a sidelong glance at me and a crooked smile, 'nothing like the truth... I am the fifth child and only son of Rachael Holbrook, reclusive children's author. Seventy-two. Eccentric. Difficult. Lucid on the page, rarely in person. She keeps to her room and communicates with the outside world through an intermediary: her eldest daughter, Vivien, fifty-one. She looks older, but then poor Viv has led a dog's life. Except that the Holbrook dogs – two West Highland terriers called Harris and Lewis – are spoiled rotten and actually lead the life of Reilly. Who *was* Reilly, by the way? I've always wondered.'

'I think it comes from an old music hall song... Mind that pheasant!'

We were off the main road now and Alfie negotiated the

winding country lanes too fast for comfort, but with considerable panache. He continued in declamatory style. 'Viv is secretary, PA, nurse, confidante, whipping boy, chief cook and bottle-washer to my mother. Viv runs the house, the garden and the gardener, for which she receives few thanks, but is allowed to live at Creake Hall, the only home she's ever known. Vivien is the possessor of a fine brain and, I suspect, some writing talent, which Rae has done her best to discourage, there being room for only one writer in the Holbrook household.

'Strangely, Vivien loves her mother, but that love is unrequited. Rae has no time for her eldest daughter. For *any* of her daughters, in fact. They are all bitter disappointments to her, for the simple reason they are *daughters*. Rae wanted a son and she made five attempts to produce one. The longed-for son and heir finally arrived – unexpectedly and some weeks premature – in 1979 when Rae was forty-three. Time had finally run out for her, so if she treats me as her little miracle, you must make allowances. She'd given up hope, you see. Resigned herself to the inevitable when – at the eleventh hour – I appeared on the scene, validating two marriages, five pregnancies and a stalled writing career. Eventually I became the muse, the consolation prize for four dull daughters and two dead husbands – one of whom was a bore and the other a philanderer.' Alfie swerved suddenly to avoid another pheasant bent on suicide. 'As you can imagine, the weight of responsibility lay heavy on my tiny shoulders. They're a lot broader now, but my burden seems to have increased. Like that saint, the one who carries the child across the river. Which one *is* that?'

'Saint Christopher.'

'Gwen, you are a mine of useless information. I insist you're on my team for *Trivial Pursuit*. Saint Christopher! That's the one. Wading across the river carrying a little child who gets heavier and heavier and turns out to be Jesus Christ, bearing all the sins of the world. That's me, carrying that little bastard, Tom Dickon Harry. He started out as a boy but now he's bigger than me and I'm very, *very* weary. Frankly, I'd like to dump him in the river and leave the precocious little sod to drown, but for Rae's sake – and my sisters' – I curb my murderous tendencies.'

'You're too good to be true, Alfie.'

'Like Deborah. It must run in the family.'

'Deborah?'

'Deb is the nicest of my sisters. She's also the dullest. The two characteristics are possibly connected. Deb is Deputy Head in a dustbin primary school in Great Yarmouth and she's there till she retires now. She'll never make it to Head. She's forty-eight and been passed over so many times, she's given up applying. So she's stuck, dodging the flying flak, but maintaining her relentless enthusiasm. Though the last time I saw her, the smile had become a bit fixed.'

'Is she married?'

'Only to the job. She was married to boring Bryan – a social worker, even duller than Deb – till he upped and did a runner with his Tai Chi teacher, twenty years younger. Usual story. So we don't talk about Bryan.'

'Any kids?'

'A son, Daniel, doing VSO. You see, altruism *does* run in the family. Daniel won't be home for Christmas, so Deb will be thoroughly miserable, but she'll put a brave face on it and organise the parlour games. You have been warned. Actually, you'll be a nice distraction for her. She likes young people and she'll like you. You might even like her.' Alfie paused and sighed. 'Deb deserves to be liked, but somehow I never quite manage it.'

'Didn't you like her even when you were a boy?'

He paused to consider. 'She was eighteen or nineteen when I was born. By the time I was old enough to register her existence, she was away at university. Our paths barely crossed. And I only lived at home for the first five years of my life. Rae's second husband, Alfred left her and took me with him.'

'Rae just let you go?'

'She wasn't really in a position to object. How can I put this tactfully?... Rae has always been somewhat frail mentally. Apparently she was severely depressed after I was born. Postnatal psychosis is the medical term, I think.'

'Oh, that's nasty.'

'She was never really right after that, I gather. And the marriage breaking down didn't help.'

'Your father was the philanderer, not the bore?'

'Correct! As you're aware, I don't have a boring gene in my body. Rae put up a fight, but she wasn't fit to care for a small child and Viv didn't want to do it. So Alfred took me abroad with him, married again and my stepmother packed me off to boarding school at the earliest opportunity.'

'So who looked after Rae?'

'Vivien. Viv and Hattie were the only sisters still at home. Hat is six years older than me, so we were never exactly playmates. She lost interest in me once I started objecting to being treated as a doll. Deb – who's really into Child Protection issues – said it wasn't very OK for Hattie to keep removing my clothes and dressing me up in her old frocks. Though as I recall,' said Alfie with a swift look at me, 'I quite enjoyed all the attention. And the frocks.'

'That must have been the formative experience of your youth: poncing about in dresses. You were doomed to become an actor.'

'Indeed. And destined to have relationships with wardrobe mistresses.'

'With a penchant for removing your clothes. Tell me more about Hattie.'

'No, it's Frances next,' Alfie said firmly. 'We must be systematic, Gwen, or you'll get confused... Fanny is the youngest of my half-sisters. She's beautiful – and doesn't she know it! I suspect she became a photographer as a result of an unhealthy interest in photographs of herself. But she does have a wonderful eye. The house is full of photos, most of them taken by Fanny.'

'Is she married?'

'At the moment.'

'At the moment?'

'Yes. It's sometimes possible to catch Fan between husbands when she's briefly single, or should I say unmarried, since she has a variety of lovers, some of whom *become* husbands and some of whom she runs concurrently *with* the husbands.'

'That all sounds very complicated.'

'She has a big, fat desk diary with coded symbols to keep her life and lovers organised.'

'Children?'

'No, that's one complication Fan avoided. She's always been a career woman. That's why one marriage broke down. She's just not maternal. Like her mother before her.'

'You seem to know a lot about her private life.'

'I do. And she knows a lot about mine. In fact we've got enough dirt on each other for a lifetime's blackmail, but I'm too good-natured and she's too lazy. In any case, we *like* each other. I suppose we're close in a way. Not in age. Fanny was about fifteen when I was born. But she always took an interest in me. I was her protégé. She likes to think of herself as a talent-spotter. It was Fan who encouraged me to pursue an acting career. She took all my professional photos when I was at drama school.'

'So she's... early forties?'

'Forty-four. But looks younger. She takes good care of herself, but then she has the example of her two elder sisters as An Awful Warning. Actually Viv is very like Fanny physically. I suppose they both take after Rae. But Vivien looks like a preliminary sketch – a rather dog-eared one – for the portrait that would become Frances. Fan's features are refined and delicate versions of Viv's. You'll see what I mean when you see them side by side. You wouldn't think it possible for two women to look so similar and for one to be drop-dead gorgeous and the other to be – well, *plain*.'

'Poor Viv. Do you think she knows?'

'Oh, yes. Viv may be a desiccated old dyke, but she isn't stupid. *None* of my sisters is stupid, though Deb sometimes pretends to be, and Hattie can appear half-witted at times. No, there's little love lost between Viv and Fanny. Viv doesn't approve of Fan and Fan thinks Viv should mind her own bloody business. So Deb keeps the peace between them at Christmas. Between *everyone*. It's Deb's great talent. She should have worked for the UN. "Peaceful conflict resolution", that's her forte. And in case you didn't know, that's education-speak for what to do instead of murdering a sibling. Deb says it's more important for kids to learn conflict resolution than reading or writing. She's probably right. Let's face it, some kids will never learn to read or write, but being able to resolve their conflicts peacefully is a really useful skill. Especially in prison, which is where, Deb says, a lot of her pupils are destined to continue their education.'

'Well, despite your attempt to paint a black picture, I really like the sound of Deborah. She sounds intelligent. And a good person.'

'Yes, she is,' Alfie said gloomily. 'That must be why we don't get on.'

'What do you mean?'

'I'm allergic to do-gooders.'

'Why?'

He exhaled, as if he was tiring of his commentary. 'I think their motives are suspect. I never met one who wasn't trying to ease their own conscience.'

'There's nothing wrong with that, surely, if they actually do some good? What would Deborah have on her conscience anyway? It sounds as if she's led a blameless life.'

He turned and gave me a puzzled look. 'Do you believe *anyone* leads a blameless life, Gwen? We all have secrets. Things we've done that we wish we hadn't, things we're ashamed of. Don't *you*?' I didn't reply and turned away, to look out the window at the bleak and colourless landscape. Alfie resumed. 'Oops. I've gone too far, haven't I? Do I hear the sound of skeletons rattling in the Rowland cupboard?'

'I think the only thing I'm ashamed of is... being ashamed. I was ashamed of my family. All of them. I told you about my aunt who was a drunk. And my mother... The only other member of my not very extended family was my uncle Frank. And he was a promiscuous and predatory homosexual.'

'Oh... Well, not a lot to brag about there.'

'I loved them all dearly and they were all I had for a family, but I was terribly ashamed of them. At times I even wished them *dead*. And now they are and I'm ashamed of *me*. They did the best they could and coped in ways that worked for them. I shouldn't have set myself up as judge and jury.'

'You were just a kid, surely?'

'I suppose so. They were all dead by the time I was sixteen.'

'Gwen, cut yourself some slack. You were a *child*, for God's sake!'

'In some ways, yes. Chronologically, I was a child. In other ways I felt middle-aged. My mother used to take me out with her when she went on her thieving sprees. She thought if she had a child in tow, people would be less likely to notice her nicking stuff.'

'Probably true. What did she steal?'

'Food mostly. All her money went on drugs. So we used to do Waitrose together. Only we *really* did Waitrose. Pay for some stuff, steal more. I never went hungry. There was always food in the house, good nutritious food. It just hadn't been paid for. But in the end I couldn't eat it. I felt so ashamed. Then I thought maybe I could blackmail Sasha into coming off drugs by starving myself. So I went through an anorexic stage when I was about eleven. She didn't even notice. But Aunt Sam did. She said if I didn't eat, she'd take me to our GP and tell him my mother was a junkie and a thief, then I'd be taken into care.'

'She'd have shopped her sister?'

'Well, she threatened to. And I believed her. So I started eating again.'

'Brutal, but effective.'

'Yes, I suppose so. Aunt Sam was a tough cookie. Well, she was with half a bottle of vodka inside her... Tell me more about Harriet.'

'Batty Hattie.'

'Oh dear. As bad as that?'

'Fan coined the nickname. She's not the most politically correct of women, as you'll discover. My sister Harriet is – how shall I put it? – *eccentric*. But quite harmless. More sinned against than sinning, if you ask me. But I'm biased. Hat's extraordinarily fond of me for some reason.'

'Well, they say blood is thicker than water. She is your sister, not your half-sister.'

'Maybe that's it... She's much younger than the other

three, so she was something of an only child until I came along. Hattie was born nine years after Frances, so she never had anyone to play with. Rae regarded her as the last in a long line of disappointments – yet another baby who failed to be the longed-for son. So Hattie was pretty much neglected, I think. She grew up a bit wild and a bit... *odd*. But she wouldn't hurt a fly. Literally. She's a vegetarian and won't even kill a wasp. She helps Viv and Tyler in the garden and one of her jobs is to collect up all the snails. Viv won't use bait because it poisons the birds. Hattie's supposed to drown the snails, but she refuses.'

'What on earth does she do with them?'

'Disposes of them in hedgerows and ditches around Creake Hall. Apparently she can be seen on a summer's evening, sauntering along, like something out of Thomas Hardy, swinging her bucket, broad-casting snails. God knows what she's doing to the ecological balance of the countryside.' Alfie slowed down as we approached a crossroads. 'We're nearly there. Are you sure you're ready for this?'

'I'm looking forward to it! From what you've told me, I fully expect your family to be as entertaining – and exasperating – as you.'

'You can have too much of a good thing, you know.'

'On the contrary. As my late Uncle Frank used to say, "Too much is never enough." And believe me, *he* would know.'

Chapter Five

Gwen

I don't know what I'd been expecting. A ramshackle farmhouse. A Georgian rectory, perhaps. I certainly wasn't expecting an Elizabethan manor house, a jumble of tall, barley sugar chimneys and crow step gables, red brick walls and a battery of mullioned windows, winking at me as the car struggled up the pot-holed drive.

It was love at first sight. I knew even before I entered Creake Hall that it would be a House of Horrors, domestic, architectural and probably culinary, but I didn't care. The house spoke to me, even at a distance. It looked neglected, wounded somehow – quite possibly by its present owners. The part of me that had considered textile conservation as a more worthwhile and lucrative career roused itself and scented challenge. But I determined to keep my eyes open, my mouth shut and my itchy, exploratory fingers to myself. I was *not* on a rescue mission.

I dragged my eyes away from the chaotic roofline silhouetted against the vast Norfolk sky and, as the car came to a halt in front of a massive double oak door, I turned to speak to Alfie, my excitement bubbling over. He sat braced, both hands still gripping the wheel, his chin sunk onto his chest. It occurred to me then that perhaps I *was* on a rescue mission after all.

His head shot up, he let go of the wheel and turned to me, a bright, artificial smile plastered across his face. He said, 'Showtime, boys and girls!' then leaned over, pulled my head towards him and kissed me hard on the mouth. Almost as if he was saying goodbye.

Alfie didn't knock. It would have taken two hands to lift the iron knocker and he had a suitcase in one hand and a large bunch of flowers in the other. He set the case down, turned an iron ring and leaned against the door. It sidled open, protesting, revealing an enormous entrance hall. A gigantic dark oak table – clearly Jacobean – stood in the centre of the room, piled with unopened Christmas cards, junk mail, a flashlight, secateurs, a ball of twine, old newspapers and a pair of dog leads. In the middle of the table stood a scruffy arrangement of evergreens and berries in a jumble sale vase. Hanging from a laurel branch was one of those jokey wooden signs announcing, *I'm in the garden*, complete with robin perched on garden fork, for the benefit of those who didn't read English. In the dust beneath, someone had written *Please clean me*.

I could hear hysterical barking coming from another room and I looked around, expecting someone to appear. There was an imposing, rather forbidding oak staircase, down which you could have driven a coach and horses. (The state of the threadbare Axminster suggested a previous generation *had*.) Coats and scarves lay heaped on a carved wooden settle, together with a tartan rug which, to judge from its noisome condition, belonged to the owners of the dog leads. A welcoming light was provided by a standard lamp with an exuberantly fringed and floral shade, but the fireplace – about the size of my bathroom in Brighton – was empty. It began to dawn on me that the hall seemed scarcely any warmer than the winter's afternoon we'd left outside. I shivered and remembered Alfie's dire climatic warnings.

The paroxysms of barking continued unabated, but still no one appeared to greet us. Then from another direction – overhead, I thought – I heard footsteps moving quickly. As they reached the stairs, they broke into a heavy-footed run. A woman turned the corner of the stairs, stopped dead and cried, 'Alfie!' She galloped down the remaining flight of stairs, long corkscrew curls flying out behind her, and I feared for her safety. She jumped the last two treads and landed, knees bent like a skateboarder, feet shod in striped socks and voluminous fluffy slippers, on a rug that slid across the polished oak floorboards, bringing her to a standstill, no more than arm's reach from Alfie.

I waited for them to embrace, but instead they stood facing each other. Each waiting for the other to make the first move? I couldn't see Alfie's face, so there was no way of knowing. Eventually he extended his arm, offering her the flowers, and said, 'Merry Christmas, Hattie.'

Seizing the bouquet, she squealed, 'Ooh, *lovely!* Are they for me?' and plunged her face into the blooms. When she emerged again, her nose was freckled with dark pollen from the lilies. Alfie smiled and withdrew a handkerchief from his coat pocket. Dabbing at her face, he said, 'Yes, they are. But if anyone should ask, they're for everyone. The *family,*' he added with emphasis.

I could see no resemblance between brother and sister. Hattie's hair was mousy and her eyes were grey, whereas Alfie's were brown. She had nothing of his easy elegance or compactness of body. There was perhaps an expression in the eyes, a sadness that I occasionally saw in Alfie's – an anxiety almost, an eagerness to please. But otherwise, they were chalk and cheese.

Hattie finally registered my presence and, after regarding me for a moment, said to Alfie *sotto voce,* 'Who's your friend?'

'Didn't Viv explain? This is Gwen Rowland. She lives in Brighton. We met when I was filming in Sussex. Gwen, this is my youngest sister, Harriet Donovan.'

Hattie thrust a hand in my direction. '*Now* I remember! Gosh, I'm getting as bad as Rae! How d'you do? Viv's put you in the attic. Don't worry, it's very cosy up there and it's near the nursery, where Alfie sleeps, so if you two want to sleep together, you can.' Hattie mistook my look of blank astonishment and explained, 'There's a double bed in the attic, you see. The springs are a bit creaky but no one will hear you – we're all at the other end of the house.' She turned to Alfie. 'But *you* have to have your old room, or Rae will go mad. Well, not mad, exactly. She's not mad yet, but she gets pretty upset if we change anything, especially at Christmas, so there was no question of putting you both in the attic.' Hattie turned back to me. 'Alfie has to sleep where he's always slept, you see. House rules. And anyway, we didn't know whether you'd *want* to share a room, and Viv didn't like to ask.' She looked speculatively from Alfie to me, then back to Alfie. *'Do* you sleep together?'

With a sidelong glance at my dropped jaw, Alfie said gently, 'That's none of your business, Hat. You're making Gwen feel uncomfortable.'

Her face fell. 'Oh, sorry! Take no notice of me, Gwen. I'm a bad person. I can't do anything right. But I *mean* well.'

Alfie shrugged off his coat and threw it on to the settle. 'Be an angel, Hat, and make us some tea, would you? And could you possibly do something about those bloody dogs? Has Viv started riding to hounds now?'

'No, that's just Harris and Lewis! They're excited. We're *all* excited! It's Christmas and Alfie's home! Let's go and have some tea and mince pies. You can have mine, which are burned but homemade, or Sainsbury's, which are neither.'

Putting on a brave smile, I said, 'I think I could probably manage one of each.' Alfie shot me a grateful look.

'Good! The burned ones aren't *too* bad. Viv put so much brandy in the mincemeat, you almost don't notice,' Hattie added cheerfully. 'Take your coat off, Gwen, and come along to the kitchen. I'll get these flowers into some water and then make us a big pot of tea.' Alfie led the way and, as I fell into step beside her, Hattie said, 'You mustn't mind me! It's just that Alfie has never brought a girlfriend home before. We'd always assumed he was *gay.'*

'Hattie!' Alfie bellowed over his shoulder. *'Tea!'*

I don't know what got into me. I think I was vaguely irritated with Alfie for not hugging his sister, for refusing to show her some token of affection when she was so clearly pleased to see him. As we followed him along the corridor, I looked at Hattie meaningfully, pointed silently to Alfie's back, and mouthed, 'He isn't'. Then I winked.

Hattie clapped a hand to her mouth and giggled noisily, like a dishwasher on its drain cycle. Alfie turned round and regarded the pair of us. 'Oh, God,' he groaned. 'I can see you two are going to get on famously.'

Hattie linked her arm through mine and squeezed it. 'Oh, I do hope so!' I looked at her pollen-stained face gazing up at mine. The expression was that of a wide-eyed, eager child; the awkward, unprepossessing body that of a woman well into her thirties.

I didn't know whether to laugh or cry.

Hattie led us into a kitchen that was scarcely less palatial than the hall, but a good deal warmer. The dogs barked madly and launched themselves at us. Hattie kneeled down to make a fuss of them, ruffling the terriers' ears affectionately. 'Gwen, this is Harris and Lewis. Lewis is the bigger one with the soppy face. Harris is very old and *much* more dignified. Aren't you, Harry?'

Alfie gave up waiting and set about making tea. He was lifting the kettle off the Aga when the back door opened and a low female voice called out, 'Hattie? Are you there? Can you take Ma some tea? I forgot to take up her tray after lunch.'

'Viv, come in! Alfie's here! And Gwen. They've arrived!'

'Already? I didn't hear a car. Hang on, let me get my boots off...'

There was a scuffling sound, then a tall, middle-aged woman appeared at the kitchen door, dressed in cord trousers and a thick fleece jacket. She bore no resemblance to Alfie, nor to her half-sister. Her short, dark hair, lank with wind and damp, showed a little grey, but her brown eyes were lively and humorous. Her rangy physique – she looked tall, even in stockinged feet – conveyed an impression of energy. This, I thought, was a woman who got things done.

Vivien removed her gloves, shoved them in her pocket and extended a large hand towards me. 'Gwen! Welcome to Creake Hall! Delighted you could come. Please excuse the gardening togs. We thought you'd be here a bit later and I was trying to get some last-minute jobs done while the weather holds. Has Hattie shown you your room?'

'Not yet,' said Hattie quickly, as she set a plate of mince pies on the table. 'Alfie wanted tea.'

Vivien turned to face her brother. She didn't hug him either, just extended her hand and shook his firmly. 'Thanks for coming, Alfie. Rae will be *so* pleased to see you. She's not been too good lately. Well, it's been a difficult year... and she doesn't get any younger.'

'Nor do *we*,' said Hattie.

Vivien glared at her, then turned back to Alfie and said, 'A visit from you will buck Rae up no end.'

Alfie didn't respond, other than to change the subject. 'How's the latest book going?'

Vivien looked pleased at the enquiry. 'Oh... A lot of false starts. Rae's not really on top of it much of the time. But we'll get there in the end. Slow but sure. I think it will be a good one. Perhaps not one of her *best*...'

I could see Alfie had already lost interest so I asked, 'What's the new book called?'

'*Tom Dickon Harry and the Fortress of Fear*. Well, that's the working title.'

'Sounds too much like *Tower of Terror*', Alfie said as Hattie poured mugs of tea from an enormous brown teapot.

Vivien looked at him, eyebrows raised. 'Surprised you remember that one. It must be ten years old.'

'That was the book that came out after the documentary. It was *everywhere*,' said Alfie, gulping his tea. 'It made me famous, didn't it?'

'Well, Rae doesn't really care about titles. Not any more. That's my department. Marketing and mammon.'

'She'd be completely *lost* without you, Viv,' Hattie said, offering me the plate of mince pies. It was all too clear which were hers. I selected the least charred and put it on my plate, crumbling the pastry surreptitiously so there would be less to eat. Alfie declined – which I thought both clever and cowardly – and watched me, the corners of his mouth twitching. As soon as Hattie got up to refill the teapot, he grabbed the remains of my pie and lobbed it silently at one of the dogs who raised its head, caught and swallowed in one swift movement. As Hattie returned to the table, I made chewing motions, avoiding Alfie's eye.

'Shall I take tea up to Rae?' he asked.

Vivien helped herself to a Sainsbury mince pie. 'That's a nice idea. Thanks, Alfie. Would you go with him, Hattie? I don't think we should spring any surprises on her. Let's take things gently. While you're doing that, I'll show Gwen her room. You're in the attic, Gwen – did Hattie explain?'

'At *length*,' Alfie snapped, before I could reply. Hattie squirmed visibly.

'Actually,' I said, 'what I'd really like to do, is see some of the garden before the light goes. Is there any chance you could give me a quick tour, Vivien?'

'Call me Viv. Yes, of course! There's a lot to see but we could certainly make a start. The light's rather magical just now, with the trees silhouetted against the sky and the sun setting. Let's go and take a look! You'll need a coat. It's pretty cold out there.'

'I left mine in the hall. I won't be a minute.'

I made my way back to the hall and retrieved my coat. On the return journey I took a wrong turning and ended up in the sitting room, confronted by what appeared to be a shrine to Alfie: a collection of photographs capturing his every mood and age. I dragged myself away and retraced my steps, listening out for voices in the kitchen. As I laid my hand on the kitchen door, I heard Alfie say firmly, 'The only person likely to blow it is Fanny.' Then he added in an undertone, 'We just need to keep her off the booze.'

As I entered the kitchen, five pairs of eyes, human and canine, turned to me.

'I'm ready', I announced, buttoning up my coat.

Viv stood up and smiled. 'Right. We'll have a lightning tour.'

Hattie began to clear the table, loading crockery on to a tray. She still looked anxious. I hoped Alfie hadn't been mean to her in my brief absence. 'Delicious mince pies, Hattie,' I said. 'Thanks for going to all that trouble.'

She cast me a look of abject gratitude. 'They'd have been even nicer if I hadn't *burned* them. I'll get it right next time. I'll use the timer.'

From the back door, Viv called out, 'Take Ma her tea, Hattie. Then take Gwen's things upstairs.'

'No, really,' I protested. 'There's no need!'

'Please let me, Gwen. I like making myself useful.'

'Well, thanks very much. But don't unpack for me. I

haven't finished wrapping all my presents.'

'*Presents*? Have you brought us presents?'

'Just little ones.'

'Oh, how exciting! What did you bring *me*?'

Viv reappeared at the kitchen door, boots in hand. 'Hattie, for goodness' sake, stop badgering Gwen!' She turned to me and said, 'You really shouldn't have, you know. We didn't expect anything. We're delighted to entertain a friend of Alfie's.'

'She's more than just a *friend*,' Hattie announced, standing at the door with a tea tray, waiting for Alfie to join her.

'Hattie! That's enough!' Vivien said sharply.

'Anyway,' Hattie replied, a note of defiance in her voice. '*I've* got a present for Gwen.'

'Have you?' Viv looked surprised. Clearly not to be outdone, she said, 'As it happens, *I've* got her a little something too.'

'Well, *mine*,' said Hattie mysteriously, 'is a *big* something.'

Alfie opened the door for her and Hattie set off along the corridor, rattling crockery, triumphant.

~~~

Vivien led Gwen through a dingy lobby littered with dead leaves, dried mud and discarded boots and shoes. Once outside, she paused for a moment to allow her guest to take in the view: a formal garden divided by intersecting brick and gravel paths into a patchwork of flowerbeds edged by lavender and low box hedging.

'The structure's pretty formal, as you can see,' Vivien said as they walked across a paved area broken up by clumps of low-growing plants that Gwen thought might be herbs. 'But I like to keep the planting pretty *in*formal. The plants have to be hardy – we're not far from the coast here – and they have to earn their keep, year round.' She turned to Gwen and smiled. 'I'm ruthless! There's no room for slackers in my garden! Take this bronze fennel, for example.' Vivien stopped by a skeletal, spindly plant, almost as tall as she was, and touched the umbrella-shaped seed-heads, festooned with spiders' webs. 'It's good for flowers, for scent, for seeds – the birds love them – *and* it's good with fish! What more could you possibly want in a plant? It's one of my favourites. And it looks just as good in winter as in summer.'

As they moved along the path, Gwen said, 'I love gardens in winter. You can see the shapes more. The *structure*. I think trees are just as beautiful without their leaves, don't you?'

'Oh, yes, definitely! And there's more time to stand and stare in winter. It's the only quiet time for a gardener. A time to take stock. Plan for the future.'

'Is the garden as old as the house?'

'Bits of it are. Creake Hall was an Elizabethan manor house originally and some of the garden walls are sixteenth century. Over there – can you see? That's the original walled kitchen garden. Hattie cultivates that. We also have a gardener who helps out and does odd jobs around the house. There's always something that needs doing in a place this old. The garden went to rack and ruin while Rae was ill. She used to be a very keen gardener – it was she who taught me – but,' Vivien sighed. 'She never leaves the house now. Barely leaves her room. Observes it all from her window... And leaves me *notes*.'

Gwen glanced up at Vivien, observed her mouth set in a thin line and said, 'It must be very difficult for you and Hattie. I mean, coping with Rae... Families can be such a trial, can't they?'

'Oh, yes.' Vivien replied. 'But if you don't marry and don't have a career – well, the expectation is there. One has to do one's duty. After all, nobody *chooses* to become old and infirm, do they? Lord knows who'll look after me when I'm old and losing my marbles. Some paid stranger, I suppose. God forbid it should be Hattie!'

'What happened to Rae? Or would you rather not talk about it?'

'Oh, it's common knowledge. The papers had a field day. She had a breakdown about ten years ago. A second one. Hasn't Alfie told you about this?

'No, he hasn't.'

55

Vivien peered at Gwen in the failing light. 'What *has* he told you?'

Gwen thought of all the information Alfie had given her about his family and tried to remember something repeatable. She drew a blank and said, 'Not a lot. I know about the books of course. And how successful they are. But I don't know much about the family history. Hardly anything, in fact.'

'Well, I think all you really need to know about us as a family, Gwen, is that we're... *fragmented*. We aren't close. Never have been, never will be. Oh, I'm fond of Hattie, but she's only a half-sister and I'm old enough to be her mother. Ours is a strange relationship... We're an odd bunch of siblings altogether! The only thing we have in common is Rae. Our ambivalence towards her. And our concern for her. But since Rae's literary estate is worth millions and the house is worth another couple, concern for Rae hardly falls into the category of pure altruism. Alfie comes to see her once a year and we're all very grateful to him for that. It keeps Rae going. He's her obsession now – has been since the last breakdown. He's her precious *son*. But she was never a mother to him. Never a proper mother to any of us, if truth be told. Rae was very ill after Alfie was born and her second husband, Freddie – that's Alfie's father – looked after him, with the help of a series of nannies. Until Freddie decided he couldn't cope any longer and ran off with one of them. Taking Alfie.'

'How on earth did Rae cope with that?'

'She wasn't really living in the real world. I think her mental state insulated her against the worst of the pain. Nothing much ever got through to Rae in those days. That's one of the reasons her husband left her. In the end Rae dealt with her loss by writing.'

'The Tom Dickon Harry books?'

'Once she got going, they just poured out of her, one after another. I think she saw TDH as her son, not Alfie. TDH was somehow more *real* to her.'

'Perhaps she felt she could exercise more control over an imaginary son than a real one.'

'Yes, that's a good point. Maybe she did.'

'I don't really understand the creative process of writers, but I gather their characters can seem as real to them as actual people. Alfie says it's the same with actors. You think you're just playing a rôle, but the rôle can take you over. You *become* the part. The boundaries can become blurred.'

'Is that so? Well, Alfie would know, I suppose... Damn, that's the bell!'

'Bell?'

'That's Hattie ringing a school bell. The kind they used to have in playgrounds. It means I'm needed back at the house. I expect there's some problem with Rae. Look, do you want to carry on, on your own? You can't get lost. Just follow the path and keep turning left. You'll get back to the main entrance eventually. Don't be alarmed if you come across a man somewhere in the grounds. It's just Tyler, the gardener. He always works until it gets dark. Stop and say hello. He's not the most forthcoming of individuals, but he's a nice chap. Almost part of the family. Sure you'll be happy finding your own way back?'

'Perfectly.'

'Well, we'll send out a search party if you're not back in half an hour. I'll go and sort out Rae and get dinner started. You're not vegetarian, are you? It's not a problem if you are. Hattie is, so we always have a veggie option.'

'No, I'm as carnivorous as they come.'

'Jolly good! I'm roasting a big joint of beef. I'm hoping to lure Rae downstairs to watch Alfie carve. She thinks it's a job only a man can do properly! The poor woman's living in the Dark Ages.' Vivien shook her head. 'In more ways than one... I'll see you later, Gwen. Enjoy the rest of your walk.'

Gwen

It was so cold, the grass crackled underfoot, stiff with frost. I strolled through the garden in the fading light, preceded by the cloud of vapour emanating from my mouth. The air felt heavy and cold as I drew it into my lungs, so cold it almost hurt. Skeletal trees cast long, weird shadows across my path.

57

In the distance I could hear a cracking noise, a snapping and tearing. Something horticulturally violent. A tree or shrub being mutilated by the gardener, I supposed. As I turned the corner round a russet-leaved beech hedge, glowing in the last of the sunlight, I saw him bent low over some cut branches of holly and laurel, hacking the evergreens into pieces suitable for Christmas decorations. His white head was bare and he wore no coat, just a shapeless woollen jumper over what appeared to be another shapeless woollen jumper. Baggy cords and muddy wellingtons completed the ensemble: the last word in Designer Scarecrow.

His back was turned towards me. I doubted he'd heard my approach over the racket he was making, so I hailed him from a distance, hoping not to startle the old man. He turned slowly and easily, straightening up as he moved. Even before I saw his face, I realised I'd got it wrong. Really wrong.

He wasn't old. His hair was silver – short and sleek, moulded to his head like a cap – but from his face and the way he'd moved, I guessed he was only in his forties, mid-forties at most. As I approached, I'd scarcely adjusted to his age when I was struck by the strange beauty of his features – a beauty so odd, it seemed almost to border on ugliness. His eyes were large and sad, so dark a blue, it looked navy – almost violet as he faced the low, setting sun. His brows were black and well-defined and dark stubble shaded his jaw. His nose was too long for handsomeness but high, wide cheekbones and a full mouth compensated. Together with his height (even stooping slightly, he was considerably taller than me), the overall impression was striking, but his features seemed out of place in an English country garden. There was something other than Anglo-Saxon blood flowing in his veins. He was too tall for a Celt and his cheekbones were too wide. Despite the wellingtons and the grubby Aran sweater, Mr Tyler managed to look *exotic*.

He returned my greeting. 'And a merry Christmas to you.'

'It's Mr Tyler, isn't it?'

'No.'

'Oh, I beg your pardon. Are there two gardeners? Vivien only mentioned Mr Tyler.'

He smiled but the smile didn't reach his eyes. 'It's not *Mr* Tyler.'

'Tyler's your first name?'

'No.'

'Well, now I'm thoroughly confused. How should I address you? Or shall I just beat a retreat and pretend we never met?'

'That would be a pity.' Finally the smile reached those extraordinary eyes. 'The family call me Tyler, but it's not my name. Mrs Holbrook calls all the gardeners Tyler.'

'Is there more than one?'

'No. There's a line of succession. My predecessor was called Tyler. So was his. I presume there was once a Mr Tyler who gardened for Mrs. Holbrook, in the days when her memory was in better shape than it is now. Miss Holbrook hired me and she likes to keep things simple for her mother. Out of consideration for the old lady, I was asked to adopt the dynastic name. So the family call me Tyler. Just Tyler. No Mister.'

'Doesn't anyone use your real name?'

'I doubt anyone remembers it now. If they did, they probably wouldn't be able to pronounce it.'

'Will you tell me what it is?' He regarded me, unsmiling. I took a deep breath and said, 'My name's Guinevere Rowland... Oh, well done for not laughing! Not everyone shows so much restraint. I'm known as Gwen. I only told you my real name to explain why I'm taking such an interest in yours. It's not just nosiness.'

'I didn't suppose it was.' He leaned forward and extended a hand towards me: large, long-fingered and very cold. 'Marek Zbydniewski.'

'Oh my goodness! What a *wonderful* name. Say it again!'

He laughed then, a deep, un-English sound and his face creased into dozens of fine lines radiating from his eyes. I decided I liked him and resolved on the spot to avoid him for the rest of my stay. He showed every sign of being dangerously attractive and I, like poor old Rae, liked to keep things simple.

As he released my hand he repeated, 'Marek

Zbydniewski. At school they called me Zebedee.'

'In England?'

'Yes.'

'But you're Polish?'

'Half. Polish father, Scots mother. The two temperaments lived side by side for fifty years in semi-permanent discord. Now they slug it out in me. You're here for Christmas?'

'Yes. I'm a guest of Alfie's. I don't normally do Christmas. I've no family and my friends are always busy with theirs. I've always meant to go away and do one of those singles house parties, but I've a nasty suspicion they might just be like an extended office party, one that goes on for days and days, with matching hangover. So I usually just hole up in my flat with a lot of M & S food, a few good books and wait for it all to blow over. But I gather I'll get the works here – brandy butter, silver threepenny bits and Charades.' He smiled again and the word *mistletoe* drifted unbidden into my mind.

'Yes, the Holbrooks keep a good Christmas.'

'Do you join them? Or do you have your own family Christmas?'

'I live alone. In the old windmill.'

'*Windmill*? You're in danger now of sounding terminally picturesque.'

'It's draughty, uncomfortable and the furniture doesn't fit, but it comes with the job, so I don't complain. But picturesque it isn't.'

'So will you be joining us at Creake Hall?'

'I'm always invited for drinks on Christmas Eve. And I'll see you at lunch on Boxing Day. Vivien and Hattie do a big buffet.'

'And who gets to wash up?'

'Mrs. Colman and Mrs. Judd.'

'Named after long-dead domestics, I presume?'

'No, they're the middle sisters,' he replied, unsmiling. 'Deborah and Frances. There are four. Two married. Two didn't.'

'Well, I'll leave you to deck the halls with boughs of holly. I must go and unpack. Will I get back to the house if I continue along this path?'

'Yes. It'll take you back to the main entrance.'
'Right. I'll see you tomorrow, then.'
He didn't reply but raised a hand in farewell.

~~~

He watched as the young woman retreated. He tried to place her age. Rosy-cheeked in the cold December sunset, she'd seemed fresh-faced, girlish. But there was something knowing about the eyes. A hint of invitation. Twenty-two going on thirty-two, was his guess. Gathering up the cut greenery, he wondered when was the last time he'd seen an attractive woman, or rather *registered* one.

The holly had pierced his skin. He'd felt nothing – his hands were numb with cold, his skin hardened by manual labour – and he watched with dispassionate interest the slow seepage of blood, how it formed a scarlet bead on the heel of his hand, like a holly berry. He made a mental note (which he knew he'd ignore) to wear his gloves. He should protect his hands. There would be no work – nor any music – without them. But he liked to feel the living stuff in his hands: branches, leaves, flowers. Where was the sense in living and not feeling these things? You wouldn't play a cello with gloves on. Your fingers respond to the feel of the strings, the wood, the varnish. Touch was so important. It was something *live*. He needed that.

His blood was pooling now and forming a viscous trail. He stood very still and watched it trickle across the heel of his hand, felt his heart begin to race. He knew what was coming. He should move. Wipe away the blood, trim the holly, keep moving, think of something else, anything, before he saw, before he remembered...

Too late. There was just red in front of his eyes. Small, twisted limbs. And somebody screaming for help. *Him*.

He should wear gloves. It just wasn't worth it.

Chapter Six

As Gwen headed back she looked up towards the house silhouetted against an improbable apricot sky. Lights were on at an upstairs window. The joyous reunion of Alfie with his mother, she supposed. Gwen hoped Alfie would behave, would make an effort to be kind. She'd been disappointed and puzzled by his performance so far.

She glanced up at the window again and this time saw a figure, dark against the warm glow of the bedroom. A woman. A tall woman. Vivien? No, but similar in bearing and build. Was this Rae? The figure didn't move. Gwen was being watched, evidently. She hesitated, then raised her hand and waved. Still the woman did not move, then, eventually, as if with an effort, she lifted her hand and moved it slowly, in regal salute. Gwen remembered Alfie's words: *Rae doesn't really do Christmas. She rarely emerges from her room. One is given an audience.*

Daunted by the prospect, but buoyed up by curiosity, Gwen decided to request an audience at the earliest opportunity.

Rae

There's someone in the garden... Looking up at me. Is it Frances? No, Frances isn't tall. She's thin, but she isn't tall. And Frances never comes until Christmas Eve. That's tomorrow. Today is the twenty-third. It says so in my diary. The twenty-third is the day *Alfie* comes. He's here now. At Creake Hall. He was in the room a few moments ago. I didn't imagine it this time. I didn't need to. He was here. He took my hand and kissed me on the cheek. Then he said he loved the smell of my face powder. How it always reminded him of his childhood. And the bedtime stories. Stories about Tom...

Alfie was a sweet boy. My *only* boy. Four daughters, then a son. It was such a long wait...

That woman is still there. In the garden. She's waving at someone. Is she waving at me? But I don't know her. Should I wave back? I don't wish to seem rude. Not at Christmas. Perhaps I *do* know her. I forget so many things nowadays... Her face doesn't seem familiar. A pretty face. Very young. I was never pretty. Not even when I was young. Just tall. And capable. Like a boy. Like Vivien. She's no beauty either. Frances was the beauty, even as a child. She took after her father and Vivien took after me.

I think I ought to wave at that girl. She must be something to do with Alfie. He mentioned someone. I *think* he did... A guest. Alfie said I was to come down and meet her. This evening. I was to come down to dinner and he would carve the roast. He said it would be beef. Or did he say pork? I forget now... Alfie said he would introduce me to someone... His *girlfriend*, that was it! And her name was ... Gwyneth. No, it wasn't Gwyneth. But it was something like that.

I'm going to wave. There's no harm in waving. She looks a nice girl. And if she's Alfie's girlfriend, she *must* be a nice girl. I'm sure Alfie would want me to wave... There! Now she's smiling! What a lovely face. Poor Frances will be quite put out. She doesn't like competition. Never did.

That girl's gone now. I can hear the front door... She's coming indoors. It must have been Alfie's girlfriend.

He looked well. Very well. His hair needed cutting though. He has lovely hair – still soft as a baby's – but it was very untidy. Looked as if it hadn't seen a hairbrush for a week. She should make him cut it. That girlfriend... She had nice hair. It swung as she walked. I wish I could remember her name...

Alfie kissed me on the cheek. He said he loved the smell of my face powder. And he remembered its name! Coty. I've worn Coty face powder for – oh, how many years? Since I was eighteen. How old am I now?... I don't remember. I know I'm old. But I don't *feel* old. My mind feels old – worn out – but *I* don't. Sometimes I feel quite young. Like that young woman in the garden just now...

Gwen! That was her name – *Gwen*. Yes! Alfie's girlfriend is called Gwen. It suits her. She looks like a Gwen. Not a Gwyneth at all... Alfie doesn't look like an Alfie, but that was his father's name. Alfie's a *Tom*. That's a much better name for him.

Tom Dickon Harry. That's our little joke. A joke we share...

Alfie isn't Alfie. He's *Tom*.

~~~

'Oh, there you are!' said Hattie, descending the staircase as Gwen pushed open the front door. She ran down the last few stairs and helped Gwen with the heavy door. 'We thought you must have got lost.'

'No, I had a wander around and then stopped to have a chat with... with Tyler.'

'Chat?' Hattie's eyebrows shot up. 'You got Tyler to *chat*? Congratulations.'

'Perhaps I'm exaggerating. It wasn't exactly a *chat*. More of a verbal reconnaissance.'

'He can be hard work,' said Hattie, helping Gwen off with her coat. 'But he's very good at listening,' she added, folding Gwen's coat carefully, then casting it onto the untidy heap of coats and jackets piled on the settle. 'And gardening of course. Though I believe he had to study that. The listening comes naturally, if you ask me. But you didn't, did you? So I'll shut up. Now, I've taken your case upstairs—'

'Oh, Hattie, you needn't have done that! It was very heavy.'

'You're telling me! I can't wait to find out which of us is getting lead piping for Christmas.'

Gwen laughed. 'That makes me think of Cluedo. You know, the board game. Colonel Mustard in the library with the lead piping.'

'We play Monopoly, which Fanny always wins. Watch out – she's quite ruthless, you know. No, that's not the right word... *Tenacious*. That's what Fanny is. She acquires things – and people – and she doesn't like letting them go.'

'Alfie said he wants me in his team for Trivial Pursuit,' said Gwen, bending to remove her damp shoes.

'Won't make any difference. He'll still lose, unless he's got Deb. Deborah's team *always* wins Triv because she's a teacher and knows everything about everything. Except why Bryan left her.' Hattie took Gwen's shoes and stowed them under the settle. 'Bryan was her husband. Did a bunk,' she added, lowering her voice.

'Yes, Alfie mentioned it. Poor Deborah.'

'Whenever I feel depressed about being an ageing spinster, I just have to think about what poor Deb went through. She cried buckets, even though Bryan was *the* most boring man in the world... What was it in your case that was so heavy?'

'Books and a couple of bottles. Port for Alfie and sherry for Rae.'

Hattie's face brightened. 'What did you buy me?'

'I didn't buy you anything.'

Her face fell. 'Oh...'

'But I *have* brought you a present. It's a bit unorthodox but I think you might be pleased with it. At least, I hope you will. I took advice from Alfie, but it was my idea. And he thought it was a good one.'

'What is it?'

'Wait and see!'

'I hate surprises!'

'And I love them! The bigger the better.'

'Can I eat it?'

'No.'

'Drink it?'

'No.'

'Can I wear it?'

'Is Twenty Questions another one of your parlour games? Stop fishing, Hattie! You haven't got long to wait now anyway. Are you going to show me to my room?'

'Yes, of course!' she exclaimed, linking her arm through Gwen's. 'Sorry. I'm being a rubbish hostess, aren't I?'

'No, you're not! I feel perfectly at home already. Watch out or you'll have trouble getting rid of me.'

'No, we won't, said Hattie, looking glum. 'Alfie will drag you back to London in a couple of days. He never stays long. It's *such* a pity... Right, come with me and I'll give you a bit of a tour on the way up.'

The two women climbed the stairs, arm-in-arm. On the half-landing Gwen stopped to look at a sombre portrait of an aged Victorian gentleman. She studied it for a moment, scanning the man's features for a resemblance to Alfie and finding none.

'Who's this?'

'Sir Eglamour Slopbucket.'

'*What?*'

Hattie shrugged. 'No idea who he is, but that's what we've always called him. Don't you think it suits him? Rae named all the paintings years ago when my sisters were small, long before Alfie and I were born.'

'These are not family portraits then?'

'Oh, no! Rae bought them to furnish the house. Portraits by the pound, Alfie said, for those with more money than taste. Actually she got them in auctions and flea markets. I've always thought it was a nice idea – giving a home to unloved, unwanted portraits. We created a sort of artistic Battersea Dogs' Home, taking in other people's rejects.'

Gwen smiled and peered at another portrait: an attenuated flapper with a glazed expression, wielding a cigarette holder. 'Who's this?'

'Henrietta T.T.D'

'T.T.D?'

'Too-Too-Divine. Isn't she lovely? I wish I looked like that. Slim and elegant. Like you.'

'Well, thank you! I may be slim, but I don't think I'm elegant.'

'You are compared to *me*,' Hattie said firmly. 'This one's my favourite.' She dragged Gwen across the landing to stand before a painting of a Highland soldier with a jutting chin and dark, tragic eyes fixed on the horizon. 'When I was a girl I dreamed of marrying him. Isn't he handsome?'

'Yes, very. But he has something of a doomed look about him, doesn't he? As if he knows he won't be coming home...

What did Rae call him?'

'Captain Donald McDashing.'

'Perfect!'

'Isn't it? Rae was very clever in the old days. She was always making up stories and characters. She was more interested in her made-up people than us.'

'Really? But she must have been proud of her family, surely? I noticed there were a lot of family photos in the sitting room. I put my head round the corner when I went to get my coat.'

'There are loads of Alfie. Almost none of me. And the few of me were taken by Viv. She was sixteen when I was born and interested in photography, until she realised Fanny was better at it than her. Well, that's what Fan says. Viv loved babies and didn't mind that I was yet another girl. My parents did. *Terribly*,' she added, gazing up at the portrait.

'That must have been hard for you. I mean, as a child you couldn't have understood—'

'Oh, but I did! I understood very well! Children do. I desperately, *desperately* wanted a Barbie doll when I was little. I wanted to play with the other girls, *be* like other girls. But Rae didn't approve of Barbies. And I had hundreds of dolls to play with anyway – all my sisters' cast-offs. But when Christmas came round each year, I still asked for a Barbie doll. I never got one, so I knew what it was like to wish for something and not get it.'

'Did you ever buy one for yourself? With your pocket money?'

'Yes, I did!' Hattie's eyes lit up with mischief. 'I found one in a jumble sale when I was six and I got Viv to buy it for me. Someone had cut off most of her hair – some evil brother I expect – but I dyed what was left with ink and made her into Punk Barbie. I cut up an old pair of black leather gloves and made her an outfit held together with tiny gold safety pins. She looked terrific! But I had to keep her a secret. If Rae had found Punk Barbie, she might have thrown her away.'

Gwen sighed. 'Childhood is so painful, isn't it? People talk about it as a carefree time, but I think they just forget all the agonies and disappointments, the way women seem to forget the pain of childbirth.'

Hattie nodded. 'But some things are best forgotten. They're just too terrible to remember.' She stopped suddenly and pointed at a door. 'That's the nursery, where Alfie sleeps. Or is *supposed* to sleep,' she added, with a meaningful look at Gwen. 'And up here,' she said turning off the main passageway and ascending a narrow, winding staircase, 'is the attic, where we've put you. It's quite cosy. Not at all spooky. It's where I like to sit and sew. The light's not brilliant, but I can leave my projects spread out and come back to them whenever I want, without Viv nagging me to tidy up all the time. But don't worry – I've tidied up in your honour.'

'You really needn't have bothered, you know. I'd have loved to see some of your work. You must show me tomorrow.'

Hattie came to a halt outside a door, reached for the handle, then turned abruptly to face Gwen. 'Would you *really* like to see? Or are you just being polite? I may not be the brightest bunny in the warren, but I do know how boring and *messy* all my projects seem to other people.'

'Not to me, I can assure you! I design and sew for a living and I spend my working life surrounded by clutter. You should try spending a day on a film set – organised chaos! Creativity *is* untidy! My mother used to say, "Tidy home, boring mind." '

'Is she still alive, your mother?'

'No, long dead. I have no living relatives. None that I know of anyway.'

'Well, you're welcome to some of mine,' said Hattie, wrinkling her nose.

'Do you know, that's exactly what Alfie said!'

'Did he?'

'Oh, perhaps I shouldn't have repeated it. It wasn't a very kind thing to say, after all.'

'Alfie isn't particularly kind,' Hattie replied, matter-of-fact. 'He does his duty. And that's all we can expect of him.'

'Oh, I don't know. I think good manners dictate a bit more than just duty. Not to mention Christmas spirit.'

'No, you don't understand,' Hattie said patiently. 'It's very good of Alfie to come and see us. We don't expect any more of him.'

'Maybe you don't.' Gwen replied. 'But *I* do.'

Hattie stared at her a moment, then took her hand. 'Come on in. Let's unpack your things.'

She opened the door and turned on the light revealing a large attic room with dark oak beams and a sloping ceiling where, to judge from the brown stains on the white emulsion, the roof had once leaked. The room was furnished with a selection of pieces ranging over the last 150 years, all of them ugly, some of them chipped and scratched. The floorboards were bare apart from a few rag rugs faded to indeterminate hue and an Indian dhurrie, which Gwen identified at once as Habitat c.1980, because she'd grown up with it. There were two dormer windows, hung with gaudy patchwork hangings in place of curtains, and an exuberant hexagon quilt on the double bed.

'Grandmother's flower garden!' Gwen exclaimed, walking over to the bed and laying her hand reverently on the quilt. 'I *love* that old pattern! Oh, where did you get that green? It's very unusual. You can't get greens like that now.'

'It was a summer dress of my grandmother's. From the 1930s.'

'Thought so... These hexagons are quite small, Hattie. And you've done it all by hand. It must have taken you ages.'

'*Years*. There were times when I thought I wouldn't live long enough to finish it. Viv used to call it Hattie's Unfinished Symphony. But I did in the end. It's cheerful isn't it? I like to have it on the bed in winter because it reminds me of summer. Flowerbeds surrounded by lawn.'

'I like your big quilting stitches. They're a design feature, aren't they?'

'It's meant to look like rain coming down. You know – like stair-rods.'

'Oh yes! How clever.'

'I *can* do very small quilting stitches but I fancied a change. I called the quilt *Summer Showers*. It won second prize in a local show.'

'Congratulations. Did you make the curtains too? I love them!'

'They were going to be quilts for twin beds but I got fed up and decided to make them into curtains instead.'

'Where do you keep your other quilts? You must have more. I'd love to see them.'

'My unfinished quilts – and all the old ones, made by dead people – are in the trunk.' She pointed to a large leather trunk at the end of the bed. 'I've put all my finished quilts and my sewing things into the cupboard under the eaves, apart from some hand quilting. I left that out to do in the evenings. I like to have something to do with my hands, otherwise I'm fidgety and get on everyone's nerves. But I haven't really got time to sew at the moment. I'm supposed to be practising my piano part.'

Gwen folded back the hexagon quilt and lifted her case up onto the bed. 'Are you giving a recital?'

'Well, not exactly a *recital*. We do a little concert every Christmas Eve. It's a family tradition now. Alfie and I do Flanders and Swann and Tyler and I murder the classics.'

'Alfie *sings*?'

'Oh yes. Very well.'

Gwen unzipped her case and carefully removed some wrapped presents while Hattie watched, wide-eyed. 'What instrument does Tyler play?'

'The cello. He's very good.'

'Do your sisters take part?' Gwen shook out some clothes and Hattie indicated a rail with coat-hangers.

'Deb used to recite the odd poem, but she hasn't performed since Bryan left. We don't ever mention him, by the way. Well, *we* don't, but Rae does. She can't seem to get it into her head that Bryan isn't part of the family any more. You'll have to turn a blind eye – or rather a deaf ear – to Rae's ramblings.'

'I gathered from Tyler that Rae has a problem with names generally.'

'Yes, she does. She probably won't remember yours but you mustn't take any notice. Fanny makes things worse by bringing a different man every year – well, almost. We long ago gave up trying to get Rae to remember the name of the new incumbent. She calls them all Henry because that's what Fan's first husband was called.'

'Oh dear. That must be awkward for Frances. And her men friends.'

'Oh no, they're always very obliging once the situation's explained to them. Fan likes her men biddable, so they answer to anything. She calls them all "darling". I think that's because even *she* gets confused at times. But we have to make allowances for Rae and our visitors do too. Did Tyler tell you *his* real name?'

'Yes, he did.'

'Gosh, you must have made an impression!'

'What makes you say that?'

'Because Tyler doesn't tell anybody *anything*. He's been working for us for – oh, I don't know how long... *years*. Yet nobody knows anything about him. Well, I do, a little bit, because we're friends, but none of the others know much about him. I think Fanny tried to get him into bed once, but I suspect she failed. Either that or he was no good when she got him there.' Gwen choked suddenly and Hattie rushed to the bedside table, poured a glass of water from a carafe and handed it to her. Gwen controlled her coughing and stood blinking away tears, unable to suppress a smile. 'Anyway,' Hattie continued, 'Fan was pretty grumpy, for whatever reason. Of course, she was still married to Husband Number Two then, so that could have accounted for it, even if Tyler hadn't turned her down... Sorry – am I boring you, going on like this? I forget you won't be interested in all our *complications*. You're not family.'

'Maybe not, but I'm still interested in everything you have to say. You're good company, Hattie. We must sit and sew together and have a good old natter. Put the world to rights.'

'Did you bring some sewing?'

'I never travel anywhere without.'

'Oh, yes – let's! That would be wonderful!' said Hattie, clapping her hands.

'Did you know that in the days of the American pioneers,

it was essential for women to turn up for the communal quilting bee? If you didn't, your character would be assassinated in your absence by the assembled needlewomen.'

'Really? Just *think* of all the stories those old quilts could tell, if only they could speak!'

'I think they do tell stories, in their way. Silent stories.' Gwen removed her case from the bed and smoothed the quilt back into place, stroking Hattie's pattern of stitches. 'You just have to know how to read them.'

Chapter Seven

Gwen

Hattie said she needed to go and peel potatoes, so she left me to sort myself out. I drew the heavy patchwork curtains, shutting out the darkness. I set out my toiletries on a chest of drawers and peered at my tired face in a cracked gilt mirror. I hoped the blemishes were on the mirror's surface and not mine. Contemplating the luxury of a bath, it occurred to me that, although she'd left me towels, Hattie had neither shown me where the bathroom was, nor invited me to use it. I thought this was more likely to be a reflection of her social skills than an embargo on hot water usage. And it _was_ cold. Once you moved out of the vicinity of the Aga, the draughts made their presence felt. A chill rose up from the stone-flagged floor in the hall and lodged in the marrow of your bones.

The idea of a bath began to seem more and more appealing, so I set off down the little winding staircase with towel and toilet bag, hoping that the plumbing wouldn't prove to be Jacobean.

Well, it wasn't twenty-first century. Barely even twentieth. I found a cavernous bathroom in which you could have held a small cocktail party and still had plenty of room to circulate. There was something that I thought was probably a primitive Edwardian shower, but it might equally have been a relic from an aqueous torture chamber, so I decided to play safe and run a bath. As I contemplated the depth of the claw-footed, cast iron monstrosity, it struck me that if I wanted to be ready in time for dinner, I should have started running the water an hour ago. Nothing daunted, I turned on the mighty brass taps.

The room echoed with the distant sound of trumpeting elephants. Trumpeting elephants in pain. The pipes juddered and the wooden floorboards began to vibrate. Was this a quirk of the plumbing or was Creake Hall now the epicentre of a minor earthquake? I almost lost my nerve and turned the water off, but as steam rose from the depths of the bath, the thought of a long, hot soak proved irresistible. The herd of elephants began to retreat, the earthquake abated, until there was just the sound of water cascading into the bath. I poured in some bath oil, removed my clothes, clambered over the high side and wallowed.

Bliss... Or it was until I remembered this was Christmas. A family time. For once I was spending it with a family, but not my own. Would that make it easier or harder for me to get through the yearly ordeal of remembrance? Spending Christmas with Alfie's eccentric relations surely couldn't be any worse than spending it alone, or in the dubious company of the night shelter derelicts at St. Patrick's?

Perhaps I would have a *wonderful* time. Viv and Hattie seemed very nice and the gardener was... Was what? 'Interesting' was as far as I was prepared to commit myself. Now, if Alfie would just thaw a little towards his family, surely a good time could be had by all, even me?

A good time... My family's speciality. Burning the candle at both ends and melting it in the middle. Perhaps they were all still having a good time, wherever they were. Given their track record, presumably not Heaven. But surely the afterlife in the other place must be like one gigantic party, with people turning up unexpectedly, decidedly the worse for wear. The music would be too loud, the food would be stale and the white wine would – naturally – be warm. But Sasha, Sam and Frank would still be having a good time, of that I had no doubt.

I lay on my back and studied the ceiling, seasonably festooned with chains of dusty cobwebs. 'Merry Christmas, Sasha... Aunt Sam... Uncle Frank.' My voice sounded hollow, echoey, not like mine at all. 'I'm having a wonderful time,' I murmured. 'Wish you were here...'

~

I got out of the bath, dried my body and my eyes, got dressed and donned comfy old slippers. I went back downstairs again, heading for the warmth of the kitchen and the sound of voices.

The slippers were possibly a mistake.

Marek was at the sink, washing his hands. (I couldn't think of him as Tyler now I knew that wasn't his name.) I tried to ignore the fact I felt pleased to see him again and in better light. Such an emotion seemed quite unaccountable, so I decided not to account for it.

Viv and Hattie were preparing dinner. 'Gwen!' said Viv, smiling broadly. 'Another cup of tea? Sit down and make yourself at home. Have you met Tyler?'

'Yes. We had a chat in the garden.'

Marek twisted round from the sink to nod at me – it wasn't quite a smile – then said, 'You didn't get lost then?'

'No. I stuck to the path, as you suggested.'

'You weren't tempted to stray?' He smiled and, to my total consternation, I blushed. I turned away and sat down at the kitchen table, from where I was still able to observe him. He'd removed the scruffy woollen layers and his boots and I contemplated a tall, long-limbed frame that dwarfed even Viv as she stood beside him, beating hell out of a Yorkshire pudding batter. I couldn't imagine why I'd thought he was old. It must have been his stooping posture and the silver hair, which gleamed now under the bright kitchen lights.

Marek was washing his hands with a clinical thoroughness, scrubbing at his skin and nails with a brush. As I watched, one of his hands started to bleed. 'Oh, stop!' I exclaimed. 'You're bleeding.'

He looked up, surprised, and said, 'It's nothing. I just stabbed myself with some holly. Looks worse than it is because of the hot water.'

'When was your last tetanus?' Viv said, taking a break from her batter. 'Perhaps you should you put a plaster on it.'

'Have you got one of those Mickey Mouse jobs?' he replied.

'No, Hattie had the last of those. We're down to bog-standard Elastoplast.'

He shrugged. 'I'll pass then.'

'Serves you right if you bleed to death,' Hattie said cheerfully, as she lobbed another peeled potato into a pan.

Leaning over to grab some kitchen towel, Marek said, 'Thanks, Hattie. You're all heart.' He dried his hands with the same thoroughness with which he'd washed them. I stared, fascinated, at his long, bony fingers manipulating the bloodstained paper. I remembered Hattie had said he played the cello, that we would hear him play on Christmas Eve. I didn't actually like the cello – a mournful, depressing sound, I'd always thought, but I was prepared to admit I might have been over-hasty in my judgement. One should keep an open mind. (Though I wasn't entirely sure it should be kept as open as mine.)

Marek turned and caught me staring at him. I looked away at once and glanced round the kitchen, searching belatedly for Alfie, rather as a shipwrecked mariner might scan the horizon for land, but he was nowhere to be seen. Suddenly at my shoulder, Marek said, 'He's in the sitting room. Laying a fire.'

'Oh... Thanks,' I replied.

'Tyler, drink your tea before it gets cold,' Hattie scolded. He padded across the kitchen, sat down at the table and pulled a mug of tea towards him. Hattie offered him a plate of mince pies, her eyes watchful. The contents of the plate had been augmented with some cheese straws, too golden and uniform to have been created by Hattie.

Marek didn't even hesitate. He helped himself to one of Hattie's mince pies and disposed of it in two mouthfuls, with every appearance of relish. She looked at me over his head and grinned. I smiled back, absurdly pleased. It occurred to me – and this was not a comfortable realisation – that Marek had passed some sort of test, not just in Hattie's eyes, but mine. A test that Alfie had failed.

Hattie poured a cup of tea for me and one for Alfie. I took them and Marek held the door open for me as I left the kitchen. As I walked along the corridor, heading for the sitting room, I told myself he might not have known Hattie had made some of the mince pies. Then I admitted to myself I was clutching at straws.

Cheese straws.

Nothing Alfie had said about the strain of spending time with his family prepared me for what I saw when I walked into the sitting room. The door was ajar and he didn't hear me come in; his eyes were closed, so he didn't see me either. He'd collapsed in an armchair between the Christmas tree and a display of family photos, most of which were portraits of him and I had a moment to register the change in his appearance as he sat sprawled in the chair, looking as if he'd survived some gruelling ordeal.

He'd aged about ten years. Alfie looks boyish; when he's asleep he looks angelic, blessed as he is with unlined skin and long brown eyelashes, at odds with his fair hair. As I regarded him across the sitting room, it seemed as if the bones of his face had worn through his flesh, creating ridges and hollows I'd never noticed before, that I could have sworn didn't exist. Perhaps it was just a trick of the light. The room was illuminated only by a table lamp, the Christmas tree lights and the glow from the fire. The flames cast moving shadows over Alfie's frame, which seemed smaller and more frail than I remembered. But was that because I'd just been paying attention – possibly too much – to Marek's?

I'd just come to the conclusion that the low light must account for Alfie's transformation, when he opened his eyes, saw me and sat up like a jack-in-the-box, rearranging his features. Then I saw another transformation take place. He passed his hand over his face in a tired gesture, revealing, like a conjuror, quite a different face. The smile dazzled, his eyes creased amiably at the corners and the haggard look vanished. The only tell-tale sign of exhaustion was the way he then ran a hand through his hair, raking it back from his forehead.

I approached with my offering. 'I've brought you some tea. You look like you could use it.'

'Thanks.' He took the mug and set it down beside the photographs, where it remained untouched.

'How was Rae?'

'Oh, the usual. Maybe a bit worse. It's hard to tell. She gets emotional. And then she just rambles on.'

'Is her mind going?'

'Gone, I think. No, not *gone*. It's her memory that's affected, not her mind. She can remember tales from my childhood in minute detail – and insists on regaling me with them. But she doesn't really know who I am. Just who I *was*. She doesn't care who I am now, it's what I represent. A key to the past.'

'Is that what's so tiring?'

'Tiring?'

'When I came in you looked shattered. Is it the trips down memory lane that take it out of you?'

'Must be. That, and trying to follow her train of thought. And – well, it's all pretty *sad*. Pathetic, in fact.'

'Will she come down for dinner?'

'I doubt it. She looked tired and confused by the time I left. She sent her apologies for not greeting you and hopes you'll understand. But she'd like you to go and see her later. After dinner. If you wouldn't mind.'

'Not at all. I'm dying to meet her.'

'She takes camomile tea before bed. You could take her tray up to her.'

'I'd love to.'

'I'll come with you if you like.'

'No, I'll be fine. We'll do girl talk.'

He smiled at me gratefully – relieved, I supposed, to be spared another encounter.

I put my mug down and knelt beside the table of photographs to take a closer look. There were pictures of Alfie as a sleeping baby in a pram and as a toddler on a beach, carrying a bucket of sand; there was Alfie up a tree, distant and waving; Alfie dressed as a shepherd in a Nativity play; a formal portrait of Alfie in school uniform, looking vaguely apprehensive, or perhaps just bored. All the photographs were of Alfie as a boy; none pictured him as a teenager or a man. There were silver frames, leather frames, wooden frames – all of them dusty, as if the photos were never disturbed. I couldn't think who would touch them if Rae rarely emerged from her room and I doubted that dusting was high on Viv's agenda.

I turned to look at the adult Alfie, who, like his schoolboy self, looked slightly apprehensive, or maybe just bored.

'You were an adorable child, weren't you?'

'Oh, yes. Sickeningly lovely.'

I ignored the heavy sarcasm. 'It must have been nice growing up feeling you were so loved. So *wanted*. That you'd been the answer to someone's prayer.'

'Stop this, right now, Gwen, or I'll throw up over that nauseating display of childhood memorabilia. Rae has all those photos because I was her son *in absentia*. She never actually knew me as a boy! Freddie must have sent her photos, I suppose. I was a fantasy child, *her* fantasy child. But I assure you, I picked my nose and farted just like any normal boy.'

I picked up the photo I'd decided was my favourite. A golden-haired boy of perhaps eleven or twelve playing cricket, his eyes narrowed against the sun, leaning forward, wielding his bat awkwardly, wearing shin pads that looked far too large. Alfie looked quite the little man, but I couldn't detect in the boy's features any trace of the man he would become. I replaced the photo on the table, noticing as I did so that my fingers had left tell-tale prints in the dust on the leather frame.

'Alfie, why *do* you suffer so much when you come home?'

His eyes didn't meet mine. 'Suffer? This is nothing! Wait till the gang's all here and things really get going. Remember then that you insisted on coming, Gwen.'

'I'm having a great time! And I love my attic room. Hattie's going to show me her quilts tomorrow and we're going to have a sewing bee.' Alfie groaned in mock dismay. 'I'm looking forward to the concert too,' I added. 'I hear you're performing!'

'It's unavoidable.' He spread his hands. 'Hattie has decreed.'

79

'I can't wait.'

'Tyler's good,' he conceded. 'And Hattie's not bad. She plays better than you'd think. When all her scatter-brained energy is focussed she can be quite... *intense*. Expressive even.'

'Like her sewing.'

'How do you mean?'

'She channels her thoughts and feelings into a quilt, doesn't she? Any object that she makes. Something huge and complex like her hexagons quilt, it's like a map. A map of her mind. Or a window looking into it... I really liked it. And I really like her.'

'Thought you would. She likes you too, I can tell. But be on your guard. She'll cling. The poor girl's desperate for friends. Always has been.'

'She seems to get on with Tyler.'

'Yes, that's an odd relationship. I used to wonder if they'd been lovers. She seems quite fond of him.'

'That doesn't mean they've slept together, surely?'

'No, I just wondered. He's a weird guy. I could imagine him being Hattie's type.'

'Why do you say he's weird?'

'Have you met him yet?'

'Yes.'

'Well, don't *you* think he's weird?'

'I hadn't really thought about it. But no, he doesn't strike me as weird. A bit odd, perhaps. But he seems nice enough. He ate one of Hattie's mince pies,' I added.

'He *must* be sleeping with her, then. No other possible explanation.'

'Don't mock. It's more than either of us managed to do. I was impressed by the gesture. I think Hattie was too.'

'She would be. Little things mean a lot to her.'

'They mean a lot to me too. Viv and Hattie are being so kind. Making me feel part of the family. I'm glad I didn't listen to you and brought presents for everyone.'

'They wouldn't have expected anything, you know. Let alone generosity on your scale.'

'It's more blessed to give than to receive. Don't sneer,

Alfie! You don't realise, the downside of having no family is not just that you don't receive any presents, it's that you don't get to *give* any.'

He looked up, beyond me. I turned to see Hattie and Marek standing in the doorway. 'Rehearsal time!' Hattie announced. 'Alfie, are you going to rehearse with me, or just busk on the night? I've been practising like mad, but if you're going to do anything funny, like pauses, or knowing looks at the audience, I'd like to mark them in my score. Sorry, Gwen, talking over your head like this, but we're performing tomorrow night and I'd like at least one rehearsal with Alfie.'

'Yes, of course. That's fine. I'll clear off out of your way.'

As I turned to get up from the floor, Marek's hand was there, offering to help me. I noticed he offered his left hand and I tried to recall which one had been bleeding in the kitchen. Was he left-handed? Or was he protecting his right hand? And why the hell was I asking myself so many questions about this man?...

He said nothing as I grasped his hand and felt him brace himself to take my weight. His dark eyes watched me as I rose, rather more elegantly than I might have done unaided.

'Thanks.'

'You're welcome.' He turned away and walked to the side of the room where he opened a cello case which stood beside a baby grand piano, neither of which I'd registered in the dim light. The fire was dying down now and Alfie got up and chucked another log on. The flames flared up and cast their warm, flickering light on the photographs. My eye was drawn again to the one of Alfie playing cricket. Much as I liked it, there was something odd about it, something unsettling I couldn't place.

'Dinner at seven, Gwen,' Hattie said. 'Help yourself to a drink in the dining room. That's next door.'

'I'll go and give Vivien a hand in the kitchen.'

'Oh no, you won't! Not on your first night. Viv gave strict instructions to that effect. If you're good, we might let you unload the dishwasher tomorrow.'

'Thanks, Hattie. I'll look forward to that.'

She grinned at me. 'Now, off you go, or our performance

won't come as a wonderful surprise to you.'

'More like a terrible shock,' said Alfie under his breath, thumbing through a book of sheet music on top of the piano.

'Practice makes perfect,' was Hattie's crisp retort. As brother and sister started to wrangle, I sidled past Marek, now seated by the piano, the cello positioned between his long legs. He struck a piano key, then started to tune. I watched the glow of firelight reflected in the cello's burnished surface and wondered if the instrument was old and if it was Polish. He must have seen me looking at it and said, 'It was my grandfather's. It was given him by a famous Polish musician. He gave it to me when I was smaller than the cello. I grew,' he added simply.

'It's so beautiful,' I replied. 'Just to *look* at, it's beautiful.'

'And to hold and to touch.' He stroked the curved body of the cello. 'The wood speaks of what it's seen and heard. Then, with the addition of the bow...' He drew it across a string, making a low, mellifluous sound at almost the same pitch as his voice, 'It sings.'

He didn't look up, but seemed absorbed in the tuning of his instrument, then in warming up. For a few moments I stood and watched, fascinated, as his hand moved crab-like up and down the finger-board, then I left them all to it. It wasn't until I was on the landing, facing Sir Eglamour Slopbucket, seated at his desk, quill pen poised, that I realised what it was that had bothered me about the photo of Alfie.

The boy in the photograph was holding the cricket bat left-handed.

But Alfie was right-handed.

The Truth

Chapter Eight

Gwen

Of course, there had to be a rational explanation. Alfie must be – or at one time must have *been* – ambidextrous. Or the negative had been printed back-to-front. That seemed the most likely explanation. This thought calmed me a little, until, in my mind's eye, I saw the rest of the picture and the background against which young Alfie had been photographed. The scoreboard was visible and the numbers hadn't been reversed.

So the boy in the photograph was left-handed.

But the boy in the other photographs appeared to be *right*-handed. If memory served me – and I'd studied those photos for several minutes – the toddler carried his plastic bucket in his right hand; the boy in the tree was waving his right hand; the schoolboy actor held a shepherd's crook in his right hand. But the boy playing cricket was left handed.

There had to be an explanation.

There *had* to be.

I sat in my room brooding uselessly. Eventually I decided to go and find someone to talk to. I changed my slippers for shoes, brushed my hair and headed downstairs. As I passed the sitting room I could hear Hattie and Alfie talking – arguing, in fact, their conversation interrupted now and again by snatches of jaunty piano music. My spirits sank further.

I walked on and put my head round the dining room door. I saw a dark room, crammed with mahogany furniture, cut glass and velvet, all of it dusty-looking, as if the room was rarely used. The table was laid for five, with festive red napkins and what looked like home-made Christmas crackers. Hattie's work, no doubt. Wooden linenfold panelling surrounded an imposing stone fireplace that housed only a two-bar electric fire. Above the mantel was a dreary oil painting, dark with varnish, of a Norfolk landscape, complete with windmill.

There was a movement behind the door and I turned to see Marek in a corner of the room, shutting his cello case. My spirits lifted. He stood the case on its side in a corner, then turned and saw me. He smiled briefly and, indicating the cello, said, 'I'm leaving it here tonight. It's not worth taking it home.'

'How did your rehearsal go?' I asked, coming into the room.

'Very well. Hattie has been practising hard. Can I get you a drink?'

'Is there something non-alcoholic? I can't drink, it makes me ill.'

He went over to a sideboard and shuffled a few bottles. 'Orange juice? Tomato? There's various mixers.' He lifted the lid of a hideous plastic ice bucket, shaped like a pineapple. 'And ice.'

'I'll have an orange juice, please.'

He made my drink, then poured himself a vodka and tonic. He handed me a glass and raised his.

'Your good health,' I said and sipped my juice. There was an awkward silence, so I asked, 'What do they say in Poland?'

'*Na zdrowie!*'

This brought the conversation to a complete standstill, but Marek appeared unperturbed. Rallying, I asked, 'Do you speak Polish?'

'Yes. Though it's getting a bit rusty as all the old relatives die off. I have less reason to speak it now. Less reason to speak generally.'

I smiled at this odd remark. 'How do you mean?'

'I live alone. And I've never been much of a talker.'

He demonstrated the fact by allowing the conversation to languish again but I wasn't prepared to give up yet. I said, 'Have you always been a gardener?'

'No... But I've always been a listener.'

I was beginning to feel like Alice interviewing Humpty Dumpty. In fact I had the distinct impression that perhaps Marek was interviewing *me*. I decided to treat it as a panel game – conversational *Call my Bluff* – and struck out wildly. 'Did you listen for a living?'

He gave me a quick, shrewd look. 'Yes.' Then – reluctantly? – he added, 'I was a psychiatrist.'

'Oh...' I replied. 'I *see*.' But of course I didn't. I was so astonished, curiosity got the better of good manners. 'Why did you give it up? If you don't mind my asking, that is.'

'I think psychiatry gave up on me.' There was the brief smile again, which I was beginning to realise wasn't so much a smile, as a re-arrangement of facial muscles.

I couldn't think of an appropriate response to that, so I steered the conversation in a more general direction. 'To become a psychiatrist, you have to train as a doctor first, don't you?'

'Yes.'

'And you felt drawn towards psychiatry?'

'Yes.' He studied the contents of his glass, swallowed another mouthful and said, 'At the time it seemed like a good way to heal people. Relieve their pain. And I suppose I thought a psychiatrist would have less to do with death and dying.' He gave a faint but eloquent shrug of his shoulders. 'I was wrong.'

'You mean, because people don't get over their loss? Their grief?'

He shot me another look, of surprise this time. 'Yes. That's exactly what I meant. They carry it around with them. Grief. Guilt. Remorse... It becomes part of them. Like a cancerous growth. And it colours everything. I used to wonder if the most humane thing would be to wipe these patients' memories. Give them a clean slate.' He turned away and appeared to study the painting over the fireplace. 'But you can never make a fresh start. Not really. Memory prevents you. Perhaps that's the only blessing of old age. A failing memory.'

'Is that why you gave up psychiatry? All the grief?'

He turned back to face me, his dark eyes considering,

then they seemed to cloud. 'I gave up because I no longer felt able to help the people who came to see me. I had a string of letters after my name, but the longer I practised as a psychiatrist, the more I realised how much I didn't know, would never know. It seemed... *presumptuous* to try to heal these people when I myself was... was such a mess.'

' "Physician heal thyself", you mean?'

'I tried. And I failed.' He finished his drink and replaced the glass on the sideboard. 'I make a much better gardener than psychiatrist. Death and disease are much easier to handle in the natural world. You have lower expectations.'

'And I suppose you see the bigger picture. Not the individual.'

'Yes. And there's always something or somebody to take the blame. The weather. The nursery that sold you the plant. The pest that destroyed it. The dead and dying can be grubbed up, burned, composted. Forgotten. They don't sit there as a constant reminder of failure. You can just dig over a bed and make a fresh start. Every spring.'

'You make it sound wonderfully therapeutic.'

'I came to gardening via horticultural therapy. It's a natural anti-depressant. It gives you a stake in the future.'

'Like children. I always think looking at babies is anti-depressant. Even the ugly ones. It's hard to look at a baby – *any* small child – and not smile.' I suddenly remembered the photographs in the sitting room and despite what I'd just said, I didn't feel like smiling. Marek had subsided into silence again but I'd got the hang of this limping conversation now. I said, 'Are you staying for dinner tonight?'

'No. I was invited, but I think Viv and Hattie deserve some family time with Alfie.'

'So you're off home? To the windmill?'

'Yes.'

'Is it far?'

'No. I cycle.' He indicated the painting over the mantelpiece. 'That's a picture of Creake Hall.'

'Really? I hadn't noticed. You wouldn't believe I had an art school training, would you? Tax payers' money completely wasted.'

I approached the fireplace, stood beside Marek and peered up at the painting. 'That,' he said, pointing with a long index finger, 'is the old mill. The sails are gone now.' He turned to me and said, 'Has Viv put you in the attic bedroom?'

I was thrown by the question. I may even have blushed. 'Yes, she has,' I replied briskly. Blushing for the second time today, and in this man's presence. I was losing my grip. Either that or he'd spiked the orange juice.

'You can see the mill from up there. Look to the right. If you look beyond the mill, you can see the sea on a clear day.'

'You must have wonderful views then.'

'I do.' He paused a moment, then added, 'You must come and see them. If you have time.'

'I'll make time. I love the sea and I'd love to see inside your windmill.'

Hattie's head appeared round the door. 'Oh, good! You found someone to talk to. Dinner in ten minutes, Viv says. Help yourselves to drinks. Things are reaching a critical stage in the kitchen and I've been summoned. Is Tyler looking after you?'

'Yes, he is, thanks, Hattie. Don't worry about me. I feel quite at home.'

'Oh, Alfie said, would someone *please* pour him a large whisky. I've driven him to drink apparently.' A door banged. 'Oops – here he comes. I'm off.'

And with that she was gone, her figure replaced almost immediately by Alfie's, like a Punch and Judy show. I hurried over to the sideboard to mix him a drink.

Alfie came into the room and asked wearily, 'What's the female version of fratricide?'

'Haven't a clue,' I replied, pouring a generous measure.

'It's still fratricide,' Marek said. 'Sisters aren't deemed worthy of their own term, even when murdered.'

'I agree *entirely*,' Alfie drawled. 'It's a crime I've been contemplating, but, as they used to say in the good old days, she's not worth swinging for.' I held out the whisky glass, offering it to his left hand. 'Thank you, Gwen. You've saved my life. And probably Hattie's.'

He took it with his right.

~~~

The black sky was tinselly with stars and Capella, the brightest winter star, hung like a gold bauble. Marek buttoned up his jacket, wound a scarf round his neck and wheeled his bike down the gravel path towards the road. He'd said too much. Far too much. She was pretty, possibly attracted to him, and he'd fallen into a trap she hadn't even set. He would be on his guard next time. It would be easy to avoid being alone with her over Christmas. He just needed to remember that, however great the temptation to talk, it just wasn't worth it. No one had ever understood, *could* ever understand, and those who'd tried fell by the wayside eventually.

He knew why he'd slipped up. She was intelligent. Sensitive. She'd taken some knocks herself, evidently. He couldn't see what a woman like her was doing with a waste of space like Alfie, but that was no reason to get involved. There was no point, even though he knew from years of embarrassing, sometimes painful experience, that all he needed to do was ask a few searching questions, listen attentively to the answers and offer the odd insightful remark. That was enough. Insight wasn't even essential. Women thought you were God's gift if you simply listened. But the bright ones (and she *was* bright) could tell the difference between listening because you were interested and listening as a way of getting into their bed – a distinction that had become blurred for him once he'd given up his practice. But he did want to listen to her. And get her into bed? Yes, probably, if he was honest. And when was he not? Self-deception was a luxury long foregone.

He switched on his lights and set off. The road was icy and he cycled carefully. He looked up at the yellow beacon of Capella and wondered idly which star the three Wise Men had followed to Bethlehem.

He knew why he wanted to talk to her. It was because he'd thought she might understand. His grin was sardonic, savage in the cold moonlight. Self-deception wasn't totally a thing of the past, then. He was still more or less human.

Gwen

I barely tasted dinner. My eyes were fixed on Alfie seated opposite me, carving the joint right-handed, passing the gravy right-handed, pouring wine right-handed. Despite the festive occasion and Viv's competence as a hostess, the dinner was blighted for the others by Rae's absence and for me by my preoccupation with family snapshots. Alfie caught me staring at him and mouthed, 'You OK?' I nodded, forced a smile and turned my attention to Viv, seated by my side.

'Alfie suggested I take Rae's tea up to her after dinner. Do you think that would be a good idea? Apparently she told him she'd like me to go and see her.'

Viv's face lit up. 'Did she? Oh, that's splendid! I'm so pleased she's taking an interest. I thought she probably would, but you never can tell with Rae. We'll make up a tray for her after dinner and I'll take you up. I'll sit with you if you like – share the conversational burden. Talking to my mother can be a bit like negotiating a maze!'

'Oh, you don't need to come. I'm sure I'll manage.'

For a moment, Viv looked disappointed, or perhaps she was worried. Whatever her feelings, she soon masked them with her warm smile. 'Have some more beef, Gwen – there's loads left. And I'm sure you could manage another potato.' She served me without waiting for a reply and I remembered my mother loading my plate with food she knew I couldn't or wouldn't eat. It was how she expressed her love for me: giving me things I didn't want or need, sometimes things she'd stolen. All I actually ever wanted was for her to hold me, just sit still for a moment and hold me, but I couldn't remember her doing that. Aunt Sam gave me drunken bear hugs and Uncle Frank would sit me on his knee, but I couldn't remember Sasha holding me, couldn't remember *anyone* holding me, holding me as if I was precious, as if they never wanted to let me go. Even Alfie liked his own space in the beds we shared. He'd make enthusiastic love, cuddle and kiss me afterwards, but he'd always turn away to go to sleep.

Viv deposited another Yorkshire pudding on my plate. As I stared down at a puddle of congealing gravy, I fought back a wave of nausea and decided that I would *ask* Alfie. There was no way round it.

I had to know.

Chapter Nine

Gwen

After dinner Viv made up a tray with a pot of camomile tea and two cups. As I mounted the stairs with the tray I felt a little nervous, but mainly curious. Viv preceded me, knocked gently on her mother's door and ushered me in.

'Ma, you've got a visitor! It's Gwen, Alfie's girlfriend. Do you remember? She's brought you your tea.' Viv moved over to the bed and started to plump pillows, obscuring my view of Rae, so I had a moment to take in the room, dimly lit apart from a pool of light around the bed.

Everywhere I looked I saw flowers. Some were on the curtains and wallpaper, some were in vases. Others turned out to be pot plants. The air was scented with something heady and floral – jasmine, or perhaps gardenia – and the overall effect was like being in a conservatory. There were family photos framed on the floral walls, as well as paintings and needlework samplers, some old and faded, one of them obviously Hattie's handiwork. I glanced up and read:

The sun though hid
Is always shining
And the darkest cloud
Has a silver lining.

The stitched picture was divided into night and day. A silver-threaded moon and stars hung above a house while a gold-threaded sun, half-hidden by an ominous cloud, shone down on another version of the house. Underneath it said:

Creake Hall
Home Sweet Home.
Harriet Donovan Aged 12

The sampler hung above Rae's desk which was neatly laid out with pens, pencils, notebooks and a diary. There were several very small vases of flowers on the desk, the only one I recognised being hellebore, the Christmas rose. I could see no evidence of any work being done and there was no laptop or PC , but given Rae's age, that didn't surprise me.

When she'd helped her mother to sit upright in bed, Viv stood aside and I finally got to see Rachael Holbrook. Her hair was a dark, steely grey, cut in a sleek but school-girlish bob, pulled back from her forehead with a hair-grip. The effect was severe but quirky. Her face was long, the nose hawk-like, but patrician. It was a strong, almost masculine face, but the eyes were good: dark and lustrous like Viv's, but without her twinkling humour. Rae's eyes looked nervous, even confused. My heart went out to the old lady. She might be curious to meet her son's girlfriend, but this was evidently something of an ordeal for her.

I moved forward with the tray which Viv took from me and set down on a side table. I approached the bed which was covered with a Baltimore wedding quilt on which appliquéd roses and honeysuckle intertwined. Trying not to be distracted by the beauty of the quilt, I extended my hand. 'Mrs Holbrook, I'm so pleased to meet you! Alfie's told me such a lot about you and your wonderful books!'

The voice was querulous but clear. 'My dear, you must call me Rae. Absolutely *everybody* does. Even the gardener. We don't stand on ceremony at Creake Hall. Come and sit beside me. Let me look at you.'

Viv placed a chair behind me, touched me on the arm and whispered, 'Good luck!' She slipped out of the room and I was left alone with Rae, who lay back on her pillows and regarded me.

'Lovely! Quite lovely! My son has very good taste. I approve. Now would you be kind enough to pour the tea, my dear? Thank you so much. If I do it, I shall only slop it into the saucers.'

I poured tea into the bone china cups and handed one to Rae. Beneath the quilted bed-jacket (also floral) her hands were large and her arms sturdy. Rae's mind might be frail,

94

but her body certainly wasn't. Viv had obviously inherited her Amazonian physique from her mother.

'Now, are they looking after you? Are you enjoying yourself?' She didn't wait for an answer but continued, 'I'm so sorry I didn't come down for dinner. Alfie tried very hard to persuade me, but I simply couldn't face it. It's been an emotional day. Seeing him again... I always cry a little and then I feel unsettled afterwards. I'm happiest in my room, you see. In my own little world, with all my things around me.' She indicated the floriferous clutter with a wave of her big hand. 'Alfie said you would come up and see me. He says you're not the nervous type. Not shy... I gather you don't have any family of your own and that he's lending you his for Christmas!'

'Is that what he said?'

'Yes! I think it's a splendid idea – borrowing someone else's family! I'll be your surrogate granny if you like. I'd love another grandchild. I only have the one. Deborah's boy... I forget his name now. I think it begins with D. Like Deborah.'

'Daniel?'

'Yes, that's right! Clever girl. *Daniel*. He's my grandson.' She nodded. 'Deborah's boy... But he isn't coming for Christmas, he's abroad. Working. I forget where... But he's doing good works somewhere. Somewhere abroad... So, you poor thing, you really don't have any family?'

'No, none at all. They're all dead. I was an only child.'

'So was I! It's not much fun, is it? I was the only child of a man who wanted sons. He had no time at all for girls. Thought they were just a drain on the finances. Unless they made a good marriage, of course. Fortunately, I did. I made a *very* good marriage. Well, good for money and position. Not good for love...' Rae's eyes wandered from my face and as they did so, her voice became softer, as if she was talking to herself rather than me. 'I didn't really love Victor... But I think he might have loved me. I don't remember now... Victor wanted a son. So did my father. *He* was hoping for a grandson. As some sort of consolation prize, I suppose.' She sipped her camomile tea and sighed. 'But it wasn't to be... Victor didn't live to father a son, just the three girls. He was disappointed, of course. But I don't think he was disappointed in *me*. Not like my father! I was a source of *constant* disappointment to him. I was no good to the business and no good for breeding! Oh, he was a cruel man. Quite horrid.' Her eyes swivelled back to me and she leaned forward, suddenly conspiratorial, spilling tea into her saucer. 'Do you know, when he died I felt *relieved*? And horribly guilty, *because* I felt relieved! And because he'd gone to his grave a disappointed man. But then – and this is very wicked of me, I know – I thought he didn't *deserve* to get what he wanted out of life!' She sank back onto her pillows. 'Oh dear, I'm rambling on, aren't I? I'm sorry, my dear. So very rude of me... Are they looking after you downstairs?'

'Yes, they are. Viv and Hattie are really spoiling me. And they feel like old friends already. Hattie's great fun, isn't she? Viv took me on a little tour of the garden. Well, she started to show me round, then she had to come indoors, so I carried on exploring on my own.'

'And I saw you on your way back, didn't I? Did you see me at the window? I waved.'

'Yes, I did. I waved back at you.'

'Did you meet... the gardener?'

'Tyler? Yes, I did. He was cutting greenery to decorate the house.'

'He's a good man, Tyler. Reliable. And *traditional*. I can't abide all these exotic new flowers and shrubs you get nowadays. They look absurd in an English garden! The light is all wrong, especially in Norfolk.' Her eyes wandered off again, followed by her mind. 'Tyler must be getting on now. He's been with us for *years*. But he never seems to look any older. But, you know, I always say, gardening keeps you young. Gardeners always live to a ripe old age, have you noticed? Well into their eighties. Even nineties... I should get outdoors, I really should. Viv says, it would rejuvenate me.'

'Why don't you go out into the garden, Rae? Do you find it difficult to walk?'

'No, not particularly. I do a few tours of this room every day – and it's a big room – and I do exercises for my knees and ankles.' She pulled a wry face. 'Vivien nags me. Says I need to do them to keep my joints supple. She says you don't have to be energetic, but you do need to look after your joints when you get to my age.'

'She's right. Keeping mobile *is* important. Otherwise you seize up.'

A large hand flew up to her temple and Rae clasped her brow, her expression pained. 'Ah! That's what happened to me.'

'What?'

'My *mind* seized up. Seized up altogether.'

I was in over my head already, but floundered on. 'What happened to you?'

'I don't remember. It was a long time ago... When Alfie came to stay... When they made that film. The film for television. Everything stopped after that but I don't know why. Alfie came home... They made the film... I became very famous and we sold lots and lots of books, then... everything seized up!'

'Were you ill?'

'Suppose I must have been.' She turned and put her cup down on a bedside table. 'I simply don't remember. I stopped writing, I do remember that. I just couldn't do it any more. My mind went blank. I thought about Tom and... and then I'd get confused. And upset... So I tried *not* to think about him.'

'Tom Dickon Harry? Your creation?'

She looked at me, her eyes vague, as if she was struggling to focus. 'He seemed quite real to me... He *was* real! He was a real boy. My son. Alfie! But it was all very confusing... When they made that film...' She shook her head and looked down at her hands clasped in front of her. 'We shouldn't have done it,' she said, her voice firm now.

'Made the documentary?'

'No, we shouldn't. Frances said I would manage, that it wouldn't be as bad as I feared. But it was! It was ... *overwhelming*. There were people all over the house – everywhere! And they kept asking me questions. About Tom... About Alfie... I couldn't sleep for worrying about it all. I don't know how we all got through it! Well, I do. Tom saw me through it. He was the hero of the hour! *He* was what the film-makers were really interested in. And the viewers. They loved him. People always do, you know! That's his particular quality. His ability to be all things to all people. Well, we all see what we want to see, don't we?'

Before I could respond to this cryptic utterance, Rae was off again on another tack. 'Tell me about the garden! Did you like it?'

'Very much. It's so beautiful, even now, in the depths of winter. I think that's because the structure is so good. You have all sorts of solid, architectural things like walls and brick paths, the stone benches and statues, and of course the trees and hedges. Those are the bare bones of the garden, aren't they? They make interesting patterns, so you almost don't notice there's not much in leaf or flower at this time of year.'

'You're absolutely right! The garden was designed with winter in mind. If a garden looks good in winter, it will look good all year round. Winter is the great test!'

'Well, it certainly did look good. Viv and Tyler have done a wonderful job. I can't wait to get out there tomorrow and have another look round.'

'Get Tyler to show you the hellebores and the winter sweet. *Chimonanthus praecox.* And ask him if *Iris unguicularis* is in flower yet. They often flower before Christmas. If they are, would you pick me a few blooms – for my desk?'

And with that Rae sagged against her pillows and closed her eyes. I wondered how she was able to remember Latin botanical names but not her grandson's. I also wondered if I'd been dismissed. I leaned forward and asked softly, 'Have you finished your tea, Rae? Shall I take your cup and put it on the tray?'

She opened her eyes. 'Thank you, my dear. Leave the tray for Viv. She'll come and check up on me in a little while. But I think I'll settle down now. I'm feeling quite tired. Too much excitement for one day! And tomorrow the rest of them will arrive. We'll have a house-full. Deborah and Bryan... But not Daniel. Daniel is *abroad*, I must remember that. He won't be coming. But Frances will. She'll be here. With her husband. Now, what is his name? I get this wrong. I *think* he's called

Henry. Is that right?' She looked at me, her brow furrowed with doubt.

I trod carefully. 'I think Frances *was* married to a Henry, but I don't think she's married to him now. They divorced.'

'Really?' Rae looked aghast. 'You amaze me! Nobody tells *me* anything! Has she married again?'

'Yes, I think she did. But I'm not sure if she's bringing her husband. If she *does* bring someone, I think it's safe to say he won't be called Henry.'

'What *is* he called, then?'

'I'm told Frances calls him... darling.'

Rae blinked at me for a moment, then burst into peals of laughter. 'Oh, that's very good! *Darling*! What a good idea! That's what I should do – call everybody darling, then I won't have to remember *anyone's* name. Oh, she's a clever girl, Frances. Always was. Tom was her idea, you know! She suggested him and I said, 'Yes! Why not?'

'And that's how Tom Dickon Harry was born?'

'The word was made flesh! That's what it says in the Bible. I remember that. It's a Christmas verse, isn't it? *The word was made flesh and dwelt among us.*'

I reflected that in the case of Alfie, the flesh had existed long before the word, but Rae seemed so delighted with her biblical conceit, I let it go. 'I think I need to get to bed too. I've had a lovely day, but a tiring one.'

As I stood up to go she grasped my hand in both of hers and said, 'We've had a lovely chat, haven't we? I *did* enjoy it. I hope I didn't ramble on too much, my dear. *Did* I?' Again, she didn't wait for an answer. 'I don't think I wander quite so much when I talk to other people. I should do it more often. When I talk to myself – in my head, I mean – I get confused. There are too many thoughts... Too many years... So many things happened. And *didn't* happen... It's all too much for me to keep clear in my head. You need a brain like Frances'. She's a clever girl. Knows what she wants from life and goes out and gets it. I wish I'd been like that. Are you like that?'

The abrupt question threw me and I had no idea how to answer. Eventually I said, 'I don't think I know what I want from life, so it would be hard for me to go out and get it. Even if I did know, I'm not sure I could be that single-minded. I'm not ambitious, you see. And I'm easily distracted. I think I've got what I want, then I see something else, somebody else's life—'

'Somebody else's man?' Rae's eyes lit up with a malicious gleam.

I thought of Marek and wondered if he was somebody else's man. I answered truthfully, tiring now of this eccentric inquisition. 'The grass does sometimes look greener, doesn't it?'

'Indeed it does, my dear. Sometimes it *is* greener. *I* stole somebody else's man. I did! I wasn't a beauty, but I had my admirers! You certainly wouldn't think it to look at me now, would you? But Freddie, my second husband, he was the one for me. I knew the minute I saw him. But I was already married. And so was he. So Freddie and I had to wait. Except that we didn't. We couldn't! It was *une passion déchâinée*! That's French for we couldn't keep our hands off each other,' she explained with a wink. 'But I stayed married to Victor and he never knew about Freddie, or if he did, he never let on. Then when Victor died, Freddie got a divorce and we were free to marry. And we were very happy, for a while... Hattie was a disappointment, of course. We were both hoping for a son. But then I fell pregnant again! We were overjoyed. But afterwards... things started to go wrong. I was ill. Very ill. It was a woman's complaint. I forget now... It was all *so* dreadful.'

'Were you post-natally depressed? After the birth?'

'Perhaps I was... I was very low. And I was so tired. Tired to *death*. And Freddie just didn't understand about the baby. What man would? The baby came between us. So did my illness. I used to cry and cry. That drove him away. Freddie left me. Couldn't stand our miserable life together. He said I wasn't right in the head. Told me he was leaving me. Then I *did* go to pieces! And Freddie went abroad.'

'Taking Alfie?'

Rae looked startled and peered at me, as if surprised there was someone else in the room. 'I beg your pardon?'

'Freddie took Alfie abroad?'

'Oh... Yes. He did. He took Alfie away. I wasn't fit, they said. Not a fit mother, so Alfie had to go too. Abroad. With Freddie. And I was left with the girls. Well, they weren't girls any more, they were grown women, apart from Hattie. Vivien looked after me. And she looked after Hattie. She was very good with her. She let her help in the garden and taught her to cook and knit and sew.' Rae pointed at the sampler above her desk. 'Hattie made that for me. As a present after Freddie left.'

'That was kind – to think of making something for you when she'd been abandoned by her own father.' I looked again at the sampler and re-read the little verse. It had left me cold before, but now, seeing the sampler in its context, I was moved by a young girl's efforts to console her mother with a few trite words and coloured threads, touched by a child's simple faith that the sun, though hidden, *is* always shining.

'Hattie's clever with her hands, I'll say that for her. Her brain isn't all it might be, but she can wield a needle. And draw and paint. Left-handers often are artistic, aren't they? Freddie certainly was.'

I seized my opportunity. 'Rae, is Alfie left-handed?'

The wandering eyes focussed. 'My goodness, what a question!' She was alert now, her eyes fixed on me. 'Why ever do you ask?' Her voice sounded quite different. Sharp. Almost harsh. I felt a shiver go down my spine and experienced a sudden desire to return to the light and warmth of the sitting room fireside.

'I just wondered. As Freddie and Hattie were left-handed.' I watched and waited for her reply.

'I don't remember, I'm afraid. I only see my son once a year. And when he was a boy, there were so many years when he lived with his father. So I don't remember details. Why don't you ask Alfie?' There was something cold and flinty about her eyes now and I felt the tables had been turned. Rae was watching *me*.

'Yes, of course. I'll do that. I'll ask him.'

~

When I emerged from Rae's room, Alfie was standing at the top of the stairs. I don't know why, but I thought he looked as if he'd been there for a while.

'Alfie! Were you waiting for me?'

'No, I just came to see if you were OK. If you needed rescuing.'

'No, I'm fine. And Rae was fine too. Not nearly as difficult as I was expecting.'

'You were in there a long time.'

'Was I? I suppose I was. We had quite a nice chat. It was hard keeping up with her, but we covered a lot of ground. She's frightened, isn't she? Frightened of stepping outside that room. It's like she's trying to hold something together.'

'Her mind, I think.'

'Yes. And she thinks if she stays in that room, just thinking about the past, she'll be able to do it. It's like a kind of mental agoraphobia.' I moved away from Rae's door towards the window. Peering into the darkness, I could see nothing outside apart from the moon and one or two bright stars. I wondered if I was looking in the right direction for Marek's windmill. 'Rae talked a lot about the garden. She was quite lucid about that. I think she misses it terribly. It's so sad.' I turned back to face Alfie. 'What does Marek have to say about Rae?'

'*Marek*? Who's Marek?'

'Tyler. Marek is his real name.'

'Really? Sounds foreign. I thought he was vaguely Scots.'

'He's half Polish. Haven't you ever talked to him?'

'Can't say I have, other than to pass the time of day. Men don't ask each other questions, Gwen, they just compare notes. Anyway, how come you know so much about him? You only just met.'

I moved away from the window where I was getting cold and leaned against a radiator, warming my hands. 'We chatted in the garden. And while you were rehearsing with Hattie. He used to be a psychiatrist apparently. I wondered what he made of Rae.'

'No idea, I'm afraid. Does Viv know he was a psychiatrist?'

'I don't know. Perhaps I shouldn't have told you. He might have been speaking to me in confidence. He didn't say he was. I assumed everyone else knew.'

'Why would he confide in you?'

'He didn't confide in me! I just asked him if he'd always been a gardener. I had a feeling he hadn't.'

'Why?'

'Oh, I don't know. There was something about him that said, "Colourful Past". You can tell, can't you? Well, *I* can. Some people seem... fragile. I don't know how to describe it, really. He just didn't seem like a gardener to me. Far too deep. So I asked him what he used to do. And he told me.'

'Why did he chuck psychiatry? That must have been a good living.'

'I don't know. He was a bit vague. Disillusionment. Burnout, maybe. I didn't like to enquire... How were things downstairs?'

'We played Scrabble. One of our many ways of spending time together without actually having to communicate.'

'Who won?'

'Viv. Hattie makes up words and tries to pass them off as Anglo-Saxon and I wasn't really concentrating.' He yawned. 'I'm knackered, so I thought I'd have an early night. Two more sisters arriving tomorrow, plus this bloody concert, so I'm off to bed.' He leaned forward to kiss me. 'We'll observe the social niceties tonight, shall we? I'll sleep in the nursery and you can sleep in your romantic garret. Maybe tomorrow night?' He lifted a hand – his right – and stroked my cheek.

I decided it was now or never. Taking hold of his hand, I said, 'Alfie, you're right-handed aren't you?'

He looked surprised. 'Yes. Why do you ask?'

'I just wondered. Are you ambidextrous at all?'

He laughed and said, 'No, I'm not! Why on earth do you want to know? Have you got some athletic Kama Sutra routine lined up for tomorrow night?'

'No, of course not.'

'How disappointing. So why do you want to know?' He folded his arms, leaned back against the banister and grinned. 'Now you're looking distinctly shifty! Come on,

Gwen, spill the beans. What's all this about?'

I took a deep breath. 'There's a photograph. Downstairs. In the sitting room.'

The light wasn't good on the landing so I couldn't swear to it, but I thought Alfie turned pale. Certainly his features froze and his broad smile became fixed.

'What photograph? What are you talking about?'

'The photo of you playing cricket. You're about twelve, I think. Eleven or twelve. And you're holding a cricket bat. Left-handed.'

'*Am* I?'

'Yes, you are.'

'I wonder why? I don't remember. There must have been a reason I suppose.'

'You aren't just holding the bat, you're actually playing. You're standing in front of the wicket, waiting for the bowler.'

'Really? And I'm holding the bat left-handed?' He was silent, his head bowed in thought, then suddenly he looked up. 'Ah! That was the summer of '91. I was twelve, you're quite right. I'd broken my arm – my *right* arm – playing rugby. I fell very heavily on frozen ground – might as well have landed on concrete. While I was in plaster, I started to play some sports left-handed – table tennis, badminton. I was crap, but it meant I could run around a bit, do *some* sport. And the playing of sport was more or less a religious observance at my school. The only way you could be excused games was if you produced a death certificate – your own or a family member's.'

'So you played cricket left-handed?'

'Well, I *tried*. My arm still wasn't strong enough to play right-handed, so I gave it a go. I expect that's why someone took the photo. Plucky little Donovan making a complete prat of himself, trying to be a sporting hero. It's all coming back to me now... I was out for a duck and the games master thumped me on the back and said, "Nice try, Donovan. Nothing ventured, nothing gained." God, he was an arsehole.'

'Who took the photo?'

'Don't remember. Maybe someone took it for the school

mag. Or the school brochure. The Head liked to brag about his celebrity kids and I was one of them. Rae was already well known by '91. The first two TDHs were out by then. She donated copies to the school library. Boys used to read them by torch-light in the dorm.'

'Oh... I see.'

He laughed. 'You don't sound very convinced! What did you think? That I was some sort of impostor or something? An evil twin?'

'No, of course not! I was just puzzled, that's all. It seemed... a bit odd. But I knew there must be an explanation. I just wondered what it was.'

'You need to get to bed. My bloody mother has tired you out.'

'Do you think I should go down and say goodnight to Viv and Hattie?'

'No, don't bother. Viv was asleep on the sofa when I left and Hattie was talking about turning in soon. They'll realise Rae has taken it out of you. Go on up to bed. Big day tomorrow.'

'All right, I will then. Good night.'

'Good night.' He kissed me gently and stroked my hair. 'Just try to relax and enjoy yourself tomorrow.'

'I *am* enjoying myself. Everyone has been so kind to me. So welcoming. If I wasn't so tired, I'd be really excited about having a proper family Christmas.'

'Is that what this is?'

'Yes! I wish you could appreciate it. It's special, Alfie! A special family time, for your mother and your sisters. Do try to see things from their point of view. You're an event on their calendar.'

'A class act, in fact. Three nights only. All performances sold out.'

'Alfie, I was being serious!'

'So was I. Get to bed, Gwen. I'll see you for breakfast. Oh – don't touch the porridge if Hattie's made it.'

'How will I know if she has?'

'Stick a spoon in it. If the spoon stands up, Hattie's had a hand in its making. She has a special recipe. I believe the ingredients include eye of newt and toe of frog.'

'Thanks for the warning.'

'You're welcome. Sweet dreams.' He squeezed my hand, then turned away. I watched him amble along the corridor, his hands in his pockets. He opened a door, looked back at me and raised his hand to blow me a kiss, then disappeared.

I climbed the stairs to the attic, my heart scarcely less heavy for my conversation with Alfie. Everything he'd said was thoroughly convincing. He'd made no attempt to avoid my eye as he regaled me with his story and there was no reason to doubt anything he'd said. But I'd spent my childhood and teens sifting truth from lies, as the unholy trinity of my feckless family tried to protect me, themselves and each other from the harsh realities of life. I'd developed one hell of a crap-detector.

So as I climbed into bed and snuggled down under Hattie's patchwork quilt, I had to face the fact that I didn't believe Alfie's story.

Not a word.

~~~

Around midnight, Viv woke from her doze on the sofa, stiff and cold. She got to her feet, poked what remained of the fire until it was nothing but hot ash, then settled the fireguard in front of it. She turned out the lights and went upstairs.

Stopping at Rae's door, she listened for a moment, then knocked gently. There was no answer. She turned the handle slowly and entered. By the light of a bedside lamp she could see Rae sleeping, propped up in bed, her head on one side, her mouth slightly open. Her large, ugly hands lay on top of the quilt and twitched now and then.

Viv approached the bedside table and lifted the tea tray her mother had shared with Gwen. Rae's eyes opened and swivelled wildly round the room.

'Sorry, Ma. Did I wake you? I just came to check on you.'

'Has she gone? That girl?'

'Gwen? Yes, she went to bed. Everyone's gone to bed. It's late.'

' "Gwen", did you say?'

'Yes. That's her name.'

'I thought she told me it was Gwyneth.'

'No, it's Gwen.'

Rae made an exasperated sound and waved her hand. 'Oh, I shall never remember! I'm no good with names.'

'Gwen won't mind what you call her, Ma. People understand. We all get forgetful as we grow older.'

'Apparently Frances calls all her men "Darling"!' Rae chuckled at the memory. 'Clever girl, Frances...' Rae lowered her voice and said, '*She's* clever too.'

'Who?'

'Gwyneth.'

'*Gwen.*'

'I meant Gwen. She's clever. I could tell. She asked me questions.'

'What about?'

'Alfie.'

Vivien set the tray down again. 'Did she?'

'Yes, but I told her I couldn't remember. Well, I can't, can I? Don't remember anything. Mind like a sieve!'

'I'm sure Gwen understood, Ma.'

'*Exactly.* That's what I'm saying! She's a clever girl. So we must be careful.'

'Careful?'

'Careful when we speak about Tom.'

'*Alfie,*' Viv replied wearily.

'Yes, of course. Alfie. Is he left-handed?'

Viv blinked at the random question. 'Alfie? No, you're thinking of Freddie. Or perhaps Hattie.'

Rae wasn't listening. 'She's clever.'

'*Hattie?*'

'No, of course not! Alfie's girl... Gwen.'

'There's no point getting anxious, Ma,' said Viv, picking up the tray again. 'Let me make you some more camomile tea. It will help you sleep.'

'No, leave me alone now. I'm tired. I need to think. That girl has *confused* me,' Rae muttered as she rearranged her pillows, then lay down on her side.

'Shall I turn out your light?'

'No, leave it on. I'm thinking. Thinking about Tom... Where's my notebook?'

'In the bedside drawer. With your pencils and pens.'

'I need the light on in case a new idea comes to me. I might need to write something down.'

'Yes, of course. That would be exciting, wouldn't it?' said Viv without much enthusiasm. 'Well, I'll say goodnight now. Hope you sleep well.'

'Thank you. Goodnight.'

Viv was balancing the tray on her hip and reaching for the door handle when Rae called out. 'Vivien?'

Viv turned round, her arms aching now with the weight of the tray. 'What *is* it, Ma?'

'We must be careful.'

'I'm always careful, Ma. Goodnight.'

Chapter Ten

Gwen

I slept badly and woke early. It was still dark outside and the air in my attic room seemed very cold. I remembered a fan heater that I'd seen on the floor, plugged in and pointed thoughtfully towards the bed. I turned on the bedside light, switched on the heater, got back into bed again and waited. Alfie had exaggerated about the temperature at Creake Hall but I'd been glad of what he referred to as my passion-killer fleece pyjamas. I'd also been glad of the weight of Hattie's quilt, insulating me against the night air. I stroked the hexagons absently, then remembered she'd said there were other quilts. But where?... In the trunk at the end of the bed?

I got out of bed again, pulled on my dressing gown and slippers, directed the fan at the trunk and kneeled facing the Siroccan blast of dust and warm air. The trunk was made of battered leather and fastened with buckles. I undid these and lifted the lid with a sense of anticipation.

There were several folded quilts inside the trunk. I removed them reverently, one at a time. On top was a Log Cabin quilt made of light and dark strips of fabric, arranged in a pattern of concentric squares known as *Barn Raising*. The reds were very faded. Red dyes were unstable and faded soonest, so I assumed this quilt must be antique. I re-folded it carefully and set it aside. The next was a *Dresden Plate* design, dating from the thirties to judge from its pretty pastel fabrics. Segments of patterned fabric were arranged like slices of pie, to form circles or "plates". It was a popular design for using up big scraps. This quilt was in such good condition, I doubted it had ever been used.

At the bottom of the trunk were quilt tops that had never been finished, including one made of hundreds of equilateral triangles, a design I knew as *A Thousand Pyramids*. There was

109

no rhyme or reason to the colour scheme and, as I examined it, it dawned on me that it was a Charm quilt – every single patch was cut from a different fabric. Making such a quilt required a huge and varied collection of fabric scraps, so I wasn't surprised this one was unfinished. Hattie had probably run out of fabrics.

The quilt top was heavy because it still contained all its paper templates – triangles cut from what appeared to be letters and calendars. Some templates were pictorial, others had numbers and days of the week, but others seemed to be cut from letters written on old-fashioned notepaper. I didn't pause to examine any but caught sight of "Dear Rae" on one of them and wondered whether she'd made the quilt. But its chaotic nature suggested Hattie's handiwork to me.

As I spread out the Charm quilt on the bed, the papers crackled. I loved the motley collection of fabrics, some of which appeared to be quite old. There was a dress cotton depicting cowboys chasing Indians, which dated the fabric to the politically incorrect 1950s. There were some Laura Ashley prints in shades of purple and chocolate brown from the unfathomable seventies. Much more appealing were some eye-popping Op-Art fabrics from the sixties. All these were interspersed with a host of Liberty prints, but the gems of the collection to my mind were some coarse and colourful patches that I suspected were cut from American feed sacks, the fabric bags used for packaging dry goods, which thrifty housewives recycled during the Depression to make clothes, quilts and household goods.

I thought of the Christmas present I'd brought for Hattie and wondered if it would enable her to finish off the charm quilt. I decided I would offer to help. If we removed the paper templates, the quilt would be much lighter to handle and we could recycle them to make new patches. Working as a team, the quilt top would be finished in no time.

I folded the Charm quilt carefully and replaced it in the trunk. I felt excited about the project, impatient for Hattie to wake, so I could talk to her about it, but it was still dark outside and there was no sound of anyone up yet. I dressed and went down to the kitchen which, thanks to the Aga, was warm and welcoming. There was no sign of Harris or Lewis, so I assumed they were allowed to sleep with Viv or Hattie. While the kettle came to the boil, I stepped outside into the garden. There was a rosy glow in the east now and the heavily frosted garden looked magical, like something out of a child's story book. Silhouetted against the sky was Marek's mill and I thought I could see a light at a window. Another early riser. I was getting cold, so I went back indoors to make tea and toast and stood at the window watching dawn creep through the garden.

As I finished my tea there was still no sign of life upstairs so I decided to go for a walk. I fancied some fresh air and a bit of exercise. A restless night had left me full of aches and pains.

I put my coat on, borrowed a pair of Wellingtons and set off down the drive, towards the road.

The country lane was narrow and winding, with no pavement. Without reflective clothing I was probably taking a risk as a pedestrian, but it was so quiet, I could hear the odd vehicle as it approached, so I could withdraw prudently into the hedgerow. After a few hundred yards I came to a crossroads. I studied the fingerpost but already knew I would turn towards Marek's mill, visible above the rooftops, where I could see light from a first floor window. I crossed the road and headed for the mill.

It was black. Tarred brick, I supposed, and not at all picturesque. Aloft there was a gallery, serving as a sort of balcony, with plants in pots. Ivy was twining round the handrail and the door, for all the world as if this was some chocolate box cottage. The mill had no sails and, as a building, it looked ugly and forbidding, an ominous one-eyed giant looming over the flat landscape.

As I approached the mill, I could see the front door and a cornucopia of tubs and pots arranged on and around the steps leading up to it. Some tubs contained evergreens, some had dead-looking plants in them, but larger pots held shrubs, even a few brave flowers: some battered chrysanthemums, winter jasmine, the odd crystalline rose, frosted in bud. I looked at the array of containers and wondered how long Marek spent watering them all in a parched Norfolk summer. It would be a labour of love, I supposed, and a pleasant task on a summer's evening.

I raised my eyes to the first floor window and saw Marek standing there, silhouetted against the light from the interior. I presumed he'd seen me standing at the foot of the steps leading up to his front door. I looked around and saw that he had no immediate neighbours, just outbuildings and fields, so I lifted my head, took a deep breath and sang:

'It came upon the midnight clear,
That glorious song of old,
From angels bending near the earth
To touch their harps of gold.'

I hadn't even got to the end of the first verse before the window opened and Marek's white head appeared. His face was swarthy with black stubble, his expression grim. My heart sank to the bottom of my Wellington boots. He leaned out of the window and said, 'If I made you a cup of coffee, would you stop singing?' Then, with a piratical flash of white teeth, he grinned.

~~~

'So you weren't impressed with my "glorious song of old", then?'

'My objections were more ideological than musical. I'm an atheist. How do you like your coffee?'

Marek, barefoot and clad in pale grey jersey pyjamas, closed the door behind Gwen. She removed her Wellingtons and followed him up a staircase, passing through a utility-come-lumber room on the ground floor, his bedroom on the first, where he grabbed a dressing gown and shrugged it on, then on up to the kitchen level, where he filled a kettle and turned to Gwen, who by now was feeling breathless.

'Sit down. The sitting room is on the floor above. For the views. We'll go up when I've made coffee. Have you had breakfast?'

'I had a piece of toast before coming out. There was something soaking on the Aga that looked suspiciously like *papier mâché* but Alfie had already warned me about Hattie's porridge, so I thought I'd play safe with toast.'

'It's not that bad. Just very... *solid*. And she likes to salt it, but that doesn't bother me. I grew up on salted porridge.'

Gwen wondered when Hattie would have been making Marek breakfast and remembered Alfie's speculations of the night before.

'Did you grow up in Scotland?'

'Until I was ten. Then we moved to England where I quickly got rid of my accent. It was bad enough being called Zbydniewski. But I was good at sport, so they left me alone in the end.' He lifted the kettle and poured water into two mugs. 'Milk? Sugar?'

'Milk, no sugar, thanks. The windows face in different directions, don't they?'

'Yes.'

'What a good idea.'

'And a practical one. If the windows lined up it would create a line of weakness in the structure, so they go round in a spiral.'

Gwen surveyed the whitewashed brick walls of the kitchen. 'It's so strange being in a room with curved walls!'

'It's less obvious in here because of the kitchen units. This room feels more like a hexagon than a circle. You're more aware of the round walls upstairs. Follow me.' Marek picked up their coffee and led the way, up another staircase, into the sitting room. 'This window faces north. Bad for light, good for sea views.'

Gwen walked over to the window and, beneath a vast grey sky, saw a distant expanse of pewter sea, scalloped with white. She turned back to face Marek who was putting a log in a wood-burning stove. 'Isn't it rather dark living in a mill?' She surveyed the curved brick walls, pock-marked with age, their red expanse broken up here and there with pictures and ethnic wall-hangings.

'The dark doesn't bother me. I spend most of my working day outdoors. In the summer I'm quite glad to come home to somewhere cool and dark. Norfolk summers can be very hot.'

He sat down in an armchair and Gwen sank onto the sofa, near the stove.

'Was this a flour mill?'

'Yes. It was built in 1826 and was a working mill for about a hundred years. Then it fell into disrepair, then dereliction. A Holbrook ancestor was into preserving the local heritage and poured money into its restoration, but he died and so did his millwright. They're a scarce breed, scarcer even than thatchers. So the Holbrooks cut their losses and converted it into a dwelling. Creake Hall staff have always lived here. It's not pretty enough to let as a holiday home and it's of little historic interest because there's no working machinery. It's just a shell. But solid. And quaint. I like it. And it suits me. What I particularly like is the lack of garden. I can come home to a guilt-free zone. No weeding. No lawns to mow.'

'Just a lot of watering.'

'You noticed all the tubs? There's no outside tap, so running up and down stairs with cans keeps me fit.'

Unbidden, a memory of Marek standing at the front door in his pyjamas swam into Gwen's mind. Recalling how the pale grey jersey had clung to the curves of his chest, arms and thighs, she was in no doubt as to his levels of fitness and strength. Feeling suddenly rather warm, she acknowledged that this was nothing to do with either the coffee or the heat from the stove.

'What are you doing out so early?' Marek asked.

'No one else was up, so I thought I'd go for a walk. It was nice to have a bit of time to myself actually. And it's so beautifully quiet compared to Brighton. Brighton never sleeps. I love the buzz, but I do sometimes long for a bit of peace and quiet.'

'Do you live with Alfie?'

'No, I share a flat with two other girls. Alfie has a flat in

London. I think it belonged to Rae originally.'

'How long have you known him?'

'About five months. We met in the summer when he was filming in Sussex.'

'What do you do? You're not an actress?'

'God, no! I'm a humble wardrobe assistant. But it's interesting work. Very varied. I really enjoy it. Especially when we're on location.'

'How did you get into that line of work?'

'I went to art school to do a fashion and textiles course. I thought I'd end up working in the rag trade, but I discovered I liked old clothes much more than new. I also had a love of old textiles, so working with period costumes seemed like the ideal job for me.' Gwen sipped her coffee. 'How long have you known Alfie?'

'I wouldn't say I do know Alfie. But he's been to Creake Hall for Christmas all the years I've worked here.'

'And how long is that?'

'Five years now.'

'You're obviously happy here.'

'I suppose I must be.'

'Alfie doesn't talk much about his family and he behaves rather oddly when he's with them. It's as if there's been some big bust-up in the past. But Viv and Hattie seem so nice, so easy to get on with... I don't really understand why he's so *distant* with them.'

'He only sees them once a year.'

'Isn't that all the more reason to be friendly when he does see them?'

'Maybe. Perhaps you're right about there being some incident in the past. He seems quite angry with them.'

'*Angry?*'

'Yes. Angry with them, or about them.'

'I know he's fed up with *Tom Dickon Harry*, but I don't know why he would be angry with his sisters.'

Marek smiled. 'I take it you don't have any siblings?'

'No, no family at all. That's why I'm here. Borrowing Alfie's.'

'What happened to yours?'

Gwen hesitated, then braced herself. 'I never knew my father. Nor, for that matter, did my mother, except in the carnal sense. She died of a drugs overdose. Her sister died of drink and her brother died of AIDS. And they were the only family I ever had.'

'I see... So you'll know all about being angry with your family, then.'

'Me? No, of course not. I *loved* my family.'

'Anger isn't incompatible with love.'

'But why on earth would I be angry with them?'

'Well, for a start they failed in their duty to provide you with a sense of security and a stable home. You might also be angry with them because they put their hedonistic lifestyle before the happiness of a child... But mostly, I should imagine, you're angry because they're dead.'

'How can you be angry with someone because they *died*? That's ridiculous! None of their deaths was suicide,' she added.

'Maybe not, but they were all playing Russian roulette with their lives. I take it your uncle died of sexually-contracted AIDS. Was he gay?'

'Yes. Promiscuously so.'

'That's what I mean. It wasn't suicide, but it was suicidal. You could be angry about that. Especially when you were younger. When did you lose them?'

'They were all dead by the time I was sixteen.'

Marek winced, then said gently, 'That must have been very, very tough. I'd be surprised if you *weren't* angry with them.'

'I was grief-stricken!' Gwen exclaimed. 'Every time!'

'The two aren't mutually exclusive,' Marek replied. 'In fact they often coincide.'

'But they died *horribly*! All three of them. I'm not angry with them! I *can't* be,' Gwen said, sounding less certain now.

'All right, you're not. My apologies. I didn't mean to upset you.'

'I'm not upset!'

'Good. That's OK then. Do you want to go back to pumping me about Alfie, or shall we change the subject altogether?'

He watched as her eyes filled with tears; watched her swallow and try to blink them back; watched her compute the distance to the stairs and the likelihood of getting beyond them before the floodgates opened. He leaned forward, picked up a box of tissues from the coffee table, deposited it at her side, then leaned back again. He sat quite still, silent, his long limbs composed, and braced himself for the inundation, but she wept quietly, discreetly, with her head bowed.

He wanted to touch her, to comfort her, but old professional habits die hard and he found he could do nothing other than sit silently, attentively. Eventually, when she'd composed herself a little, he said, 'I'm very sorry for my part in that. You now have good reason to be angry with *me*.'

She shook her head. 'No, it's... it's because it's *Christmas*.'

He nodded. 'It can be a difficult time. It's all the socialising. Christmas brings us bang up against all the ways in which our families fall – or fell – short of the ideal.'

Gwen heaved a shuddering sigh and helped herself to a tissue. 'My mother died at Christmas. She overdosed on Christmas Eve. When I was twelve. I always fall apart. Every bloody year. Coming here was supposed to be a way of avoiding the crack-up.'

'Well, you haven't cracked – as you put it – in front of the family. You've been putting on a great show as the perfect guest. And it doesn't bother me. I'm used to it. You couldn't have picked a better person to crack up on. Not that I think you cracked,' he added.

'Oh, please – stop being *kind*, it just makes things worse.' And she started to cry again. He sensed then what she wanted, also finally what *he* wanted, and he moved towards her – not fast, he didn't want to startle her – and sat beside her. He took her in his arms and she sagged against him, her face pressed against his chest, as if she was trying to muffle the sound of her cries. He sat still, his arms gently but firmly enclosing her, and registered the wet warmth of her tears on his skin as they soaked into his pyjamas. He said nothing and waited.

Eventually, she withdrew from the damp depths of his clothing and grabbed another tissue. She blew her nose, sniffed several times and said, 'I'm terribly sorry.'

'What for?'

'For being such an idiot.' She pointed to the dark patch on his chest. 'And for covering you in snot.'

He looked down at the damp patch. 'These were due for the wash anyway.'

'I thought I'd got it all under control this year.'

His smile was ironical. 'That's when we're at our most vulnerable. When we think we've got everything under control. If you'd thought you were on the edge, you probably wouldn't have accepted my invitation.'

She looked puzzled. 'To have coffee?'

'To talk. We exercise more rigid self-control when we think we might be *out* of control.'

She looked up at him, her head on one side. 'Is it very exhausting being so wise?'

He laughed and she was pleased. She felt she'd regained a little ground. 'I'm not wise,' he replied, 'just a people-watcher. If you watch enough people and watch them carefully, patterns emerge. From those patterns you can glean a few truths about human behaviour. It's not wisdom, just observation. So, no, it's not exhausting, it's fascinating. Sometimes satisfying. I don't do it intentionally any more. In fact, my intention is *not* to do it, but it still happens. It's who I am. *What* I am.'

Gwen didn't reply for a few moments, then, crumpling her tissue into a ball, said, 'Do you think I *am* angry with my family?'

'I think under the circumstances that would be perfectly normal. And healthy. I think perhaps you're angry with Alfie too.'

'Why would I be angry with *Alfie*?'

'Because he has what you want – what you lost – and he isn't grateful. Maybe you think his family is wasted on him.' She looked up at him again, her face pale with shock. 'I'm just guessing.'

'No, you're not, you're mind-reading.'

'Sorry. Perhaps you're also angry with him because... well, because he isn't what you want. And you thought he was. Now I *am* guessing.'

'It isn't that, it's that he's changed! He's different here, with his family. He isn't the Alfie I know.'

'He doesn't want to be here, so he has to put on a show of filial duty. You're intuitive and you're picking up on the insincerity of that situation. It makes you feel uncomfortable.'

Gwen considered confiding further in Marek, expressing her concern about the photographs, but decided against it. It was silly. She had simply over-reacted. It was just a photograph and Alfie had explained the anomaly. To take the matter any further would feel like a betrayal. Talking about Alfie like this, to another man, to an attractive man, to an attractive man *in pyjamas*, already felt like a betrayal. Maybe it was.

She stood up. 'I think I'd better be getting back. They'll be wondering where I've got to. Thanks for the coffee. And I really am very sorry for being such a wimp.'

'Don't apologise. It was a big deal for you, not for me. You looked into the existential abyss, I got damp pyjamas. No contest.' He rose and she felt at a disadvantage in her stockinged feet, felt she might be about to cry again, but knew it could just be that she wanted to be held. He was speaking again, in that deep, reassuring voice, and she was struggling to take in his words. 'I hope you feel better for having talked. You're not a wimp, Gwen, you're processing grief. Still. It takes a long time, much longer than people think. Sometimes we think we're over the worst, we think we've finally put the past behind us, then – wham! – we run up against something, some memory, some feeling we thought we'd buried long ago and we're back where we started. The wounds are open and bleeding again. It's a cyclical process – a sort of spiral in fact – and it takes a long time to get to the end of it.'

'I thought losing my entire family in a variety of ghastly ways had made me tough.'

'It probably has. On the outside. There *is* a tough and

capable Gwen on the outside, one very together young woman who knows what she wants. But *inside*...'

'Inside, it's all mush.'

'If you say so. And the tough exterior is brittle. It doesn't take much to break it. When it cracks, the mush, as you put it, seeps out.'

'You're making me sound like a liqueur chocolate.'

'Not a bad comparison when you consider what's inside is powerful stuff.'

'So how the hell do I get rid of all this... emotional baggage?'

'There's no quick fix. In the end there's only time. Time and kindness.'

'Kindness?'

'Yes. While you're waiting for time to pass, be kind to yourself. Treat yourself as you'd treat someone who was going through a tough time, who's having trouble getting over some major loss. A bereavement. The end of a love affair. Time and kindness heal. Eventually.'

They descended the flights of stairs in silence, Gwen following Marek. As he opened the front door for her she turned and said, 'Thank you for *your* kindness. And your time. You know, I really think you should invoice me.'

He leaned against the door frame and folded his arms. 'You're very welcome to both. *Gratis*. Any time.'

She looked up at him and, with a wan smile, craned her neck to kiss him on his stubbled cheek. 'Thanks. For everything.'

'It was nothing. Come again.'

She thought he sounded as if he meant it.

It would be easy. He could see that now. The way she had clung to him. The way she had opened up to him about her pain. She was looking for something. Somebody... And it wasn't Alfie. Something had come between them. She didn't say so, but it was obvious. She was rattled. Frightened even?

He'd been right about her. The capable young professional was only half the story. Maybe not even half.

There was a little girl lost inside. Confused. Lonely. Wanting to be wanted.

He wanted her. He knew that now. And he wanted to be wanted, thought perhaps she wanted him, or would if she knew her own mind. But she would pick up eventually on the pain within him, the pain that was rotting him from the inside. What was the word she'd used? *Mush.* She would sense the rotten mush at his core and realise there was only a fragile carapace holding him together. Perhaps that was why she was attracted to him. She recognised his vulnerability and it resonated with her own.

But she was also looking for strength. A father figure maybe. The Daddy she'd never known. He could see she'd already set him on some kind of pedestal. He should just learn to shut the fuck up... But it was hard when people were hurting, when they were needy and you thought you could help. And how, for the love of God, was he to make any kind of *reparation*, if it wasn't by helping other people?...

She would have been seventeen.

Anna.

Almost a woman. He often thought about the sort of woman she would have become, but it was impossible to imagine. She would always be five. Five for all eternity, except that in his mind, she aged with every year that passed. Every year she didn't live was another year added to her *post mortem* life, the life she lived in his head, from childhood to girlhood, to womanhood.

Between memory and imagination there was no escape. It was a life sentence. It would never end, except with his death. And that was just.

A life for a life.

Chapter Eleven

Gwen

I hurried back towards Creake Hall, feeling guilty for being out so long, guiltier still for having unburdened myself to Marek. I stepped out briskly, trying to banish the memory of how I'd felt with Marek's arms round me: strangely calm, despite the emotional turbulence; safe, despite the fact I was in the arms of a strange man while my boyfriend was enjoying a lie-in.

But it wasn't really like that. Marek was just being kind. And I was just being... what? *Pathetic*. Not like myself at all. Anyone less wilting-violet than me would be hard to imagine. Ask anyone. Phlegmatic, that's me. Unflappable. Unshockable. Bomb-proof. And one stupid little photo undid all that? A photo and a few kind words from a man old enough – just – to be my father?

'Pull yourself together, Gwen.'

I actually said that. *Out loud.*

'Why? Are you falling apart? Have we got to you already?'

Startled, I turned round to see Hattie walking the dogs. (Strictly speaking, they were walking her.)

'We wondered where you'd got to. Alfie said you'd probably eaten some of my porridge, then very sensibly rung for an ambulance and been carted off to casualty. I thought you'd probably gone for a walk. It's not a bad morning for it.'

'Yes, I went for a walk. Marek – I mean, Tyler – saw me and invited me in for a cup of coffee.'

'*Did* he? You know, I'm convinced he's smitten with you, Gwen. He's behaving quite out of character.'

And so am I, I thought. Behaving out of character, that is, not smitten. I hardly know the guy. I was just upset, that's all. Very upset. About the photo, about my mother, about Alfie being bloody to his family. I'm not *smitten*. If I do remember how it felt to rest my head on Marek's chest, it's just because that sort of thing never happens to me. *I'm* the shoulder people cry on, I'm the one passing the Kleenex. That's what I do, what I've always done: mopped up other people's emotional messes. Marek just turned the tables on me, that's all.

And no one's ever done that.

Not in twenty-six years.

'Are you OK, Gwen? You've gone ever so quiet. Did I offend you, speaking about Tyler like that?'

'No, not at all. I was just thinking.' As we turned a corner, Creake Hall came into view. 'I've been thinking about those quilts in the attic.'

'Did you have a look at them?'

'Yes, I did. I got them out. I hope that was all right. I was wondering about *A Thousand Pyramids*. The unfinished quilt.'

'Oh, *that* old horror. That's one of my many UFOs.'

'UFO?'

'Unfinished objects. I gave up on that one a long time ago.'

'I really liked it. You ought to finish it.'

'I ran out of scraps. It's a Charm quilt, you see. I could send off for some packs of fabric squares to finish it off, but they wouldn't look right. Too modern. I keep going to jumble sales and car boots, hoping to find some cast-off scrap bags or dressmaker's samples. Really, what I need,' said Hattie warming to her subject, 'is for a local quilter to die and bequeath me her fabric stash.'

'I've a less drastic idea how we could finish it off and I'd love to help. I thought we could work on it together.'

'It'll take days just to remove all the papers.'

'Not if we tackle it together. We could start taking out the papers today and then tomorrow I'll tell you my idea.'

'Why can't you tell me now?'

'It's something to do with your Christmas present.'

'Ooh!' Hattie's eyes widened.

'Oh dear, now I've said too much! I'm not going to answer any more questions. Let's just get stuck in removing those papers, then we can re-use them. They should come out anyway – the ink from those letters can't be doing the fabric any good.'

'I left them in so the quilt wouldn't lose its shape. And because I hate unpicking.'

'I quite like it when it's only tacking. It's a mindless, soothing activity. I feel in need of something like that. When are Deborah and Frances due?'

'After lunch.'

'Are you busy this morning?'

'No. I've wrapped all my presents, but I dare say Viv will have some kitchen chores for me. Apart from that, we're just waiting for Fanny and Deb. Deb's driving over from Beccles and she's picking Fanny up at Norwich station. She's coming up from London by train. Minus the boyfriend, so she'll be a wet weekend,' Hattie said gloomily.

'Never mind. We've got our quilt. And the concert to look forward to. We'll have a lovely time! Alfie and Fan can be grouchy together, while we're nauseatingly full of Christmas cheer.'

'It's a deal,' said Hattie, linking her arm through mine as we strolled up the drive.

Hattie and I entered Creake Hall by the front door and while she was removing dog leads I went ahead to put the kettle on. As I approached the kitchen I could hear two voices: Viv and Alfie, sounding serious. When I opened the door, his eyes were fixed on Viv, sitting opposite, and she was staring into the depths of her coffee mug. As they both turned to me, I watched Alfie switch on the light-bulb charm.

'*There* you are! We'd given you up for lost and had just decided to distribute your Christmas presents among the poor of the parish. Where've you been?'

Viv stood up and headed for the kettle. 'Coffee, Gwen?'

'Thanks, that would be nice.' I sat down at the table, opposite Alfie. 'I just went for a walk. It was a fine morning and nobody was up, so I went off to explore.'

'Did you have fun?'

'Yes. Well, not *fun* exactly, but I had a mooch around.' I

hesitated a moment, decided I had nothing to hide, but avoided Alfie's eye. 'I saw Tyler and he invited me in to look round the mill.'

Viv set a mug of coffee in front of me. 'It's a fascinating old place, isn't it? I think in her youth Rae had ideas of being Vita Sackville-West, writing in a tower. A bolt-hole, away from the family. Then she came to her senses and got a nice comfy flat in London. But the mill's been handy for accommodating staff. Only the really hardy can stand it though. It's very cold in winter. The situation is exposed, you see. Had to be for a windmill. I've got some old photos somewhere, of when it had sails. I'll show you later. Rae's working on an idea for a TDH story that features a spooky old windmill.'

'How is she this morning?'

Viv looked at Alfie, then answered, 'Not too good. We were talking about it just before you came in.'

Alfie leaned his elbows on the table and sighed. 'I took her breakfast up and stayed for a while.'

'And?'

'She seemed pretty confused.'

'She always is after you've arrived.' Viv sounded impatient. 'She loves to see you, but you know it always upsets her. She'll soon settle down.'

'Viv, how does Rae manage to write, when she has such a struggle keeping things straight in her mind? I mean, the TDH plots are pretty complicated, aren't they, with loads of characters. How does she do it?'

Viv didn't reply, but looked at Alfie again. He leaned back in his chair and spread his hands. 'It's your call, Viv. I can vouch for Gwen. She's the soul of discretion. Wardrobe mistresses have to be. It's in the job description.'

Viv hesitated, then said, 'Rae doesn't write the TDHs, Gwen. Not any more. She writes, and she writes about TDH, but not much of it is actually publishable. Not any more.'

I stared, my coffee mug poised mid-air. 'So who writes them?'

'I do.'

'You!'

'Yes. I've written them for years. To begin with, it was something of a joint effort. I've always typed them up and I used to make a few suggestions. Rae was wonderfully inventive but she wasn't bothered about consistency, or even credibility. So I used to make sure the plots worked as a whole, that the *series* worked as a whole and that characters behaved consistently. That sort of thing matters to children. Then when she had her last breakdown—'

'Was that after the documentary?'

'Yes, eleven years ago. After that she lost it altogether. But there was no let-up in the demand for her books. If anything, the programme created a new market for them. So I stepped into the breach.' I suppose I must have looked shocked because Viv went on hurriedly, 'It's common enough in publishing. Books aren't always written by the person whose name is on the cover.'

'Does Rae know?'

'Not really. She's been told of course, but she prefers to think she writes them. It's not so much self-delusion as being *stuck*. She's stuck in the past, when she still wrote the books, so she believes the stories are hers. I talk to her about them of course, and I read her extracts. She's usually very pleased with what she hears! Perhaps that's not so very surprising,' Viv added with a gentle smile. 'I try to write how Rae would write, if she still could.'

'But isn't there a danger that she'll be exposed?'

'I don't think so. Her publishers know what's going on and they aren't going to bite the hand that feeds them. Rae doesn't give interviews any more. I answer all her fan mail and I post articles – supposedly written by her – on the website, so it's not at all obvious she isn't participating. Her readers are happy, her publisher is happy, Rae is happy and so am I!'

'But you don't get any recognition for your work.'

'I get all the fan letters from children. And quite a few adults too. They make it all worthwhile.'

'Not to mention,' said Alfie drily, 'the sizeable income.'

'Yes. It *is* considerable.'

'But it's really yours, Viv. You're the one earning it!'

She laughed. 'Only because of Ma's name! Who'd want to read a book by Vivien Holbrook? At best, it would be a novelty item, something produced by a lesser Holbrook, daughter of the famous Rachael.'

'Tell me about it,' Alfie said with a groan.

'Anyway, what would I do with more money? As it is, I decide how we spend our income. Much of it gets ploughed back into this monster of a house. Some supports Hattie and me. It also pays for Tyler. I have to have him so I can get the writing done.'

'Does Tyler know?'

'I've never told him. But he's not stupid and he knows Rae, so he's probably guessed.'

I was silent for a moment, trying to assimilate this new information. Eventually, trying not to sound too judgemental, I said, 'How do you cope with all the... *pretence*?'

'Oh, it's become a way of life now! Rae's lived in a world of make-believe for most of her adult life. It's a world we've all had to accept. Apart from Freddie, who got out because he couldn't stand it. And Alfie, of course, chooses to keep a sane distance! The rest of us chose to play Rae's games. It suited us to do so. It seemed – it still seems – the lesser of two evils. With our support Rae can just about hold things together. Hattie and I get to stay in the family home. We can keep the garden going. And I get to write.'

'Anonymously,' Alfie muttered.

Viv turned to him and spoke sharply. 'Yes. But that's not really the point, is it? The point is the *stories* and the pleasure they bring to children.' She turned back to face me and there was a sadness in her eyes I hadn't seen before. 'I never had any kids of my own, but I rather wish I had. I can't say I ever wanted a husband, but I do love children. I regret that I've never been a mother.'

'You were more of a mother to Hattie than Rae ever was,' Alfie said.

'I suppose so. Hattie was a lovable child. It wasn't difficult mothering her, it's just that Rae wasn't the maternal type. Some people just aren't. Rae wanted marriage, but she didn't want children. Well, in those days – I was born in 1957 – you didn't get to vote. Children were expected of you and most women didn't have careers. Rae didn't exactly choose motherhood. Things were all very different then.'

'Do you think she started writing to escape?'

'From the family? Oh, yes, I'm sure she did! And when she more or less turned her back on Harriet, it fell to me to look after her. So, in a way, I feel I *have* known motherhood. I might have had the best of it, in fact. The pleasure without the pain. What's more, my other children – my readers – will never grow up.'

'Like bloody Tom Dickon Harry.'

Viv looked across at Alfie with a sad smile. 'Yes, like dear old Tom. They're for ever young. As they grow up, they're replaced by the next generation, so all those letters to Rae—'

'To the author of the books, you mean,' said Alfie, interrupting.

Viv smiled at him again. 'Thank you,' she said. 'The letters are always much the same. Though nowadays, they aren't as well spelled and punctuated as they used to be! But they're always lively and affectionate and... full of *wonder*. It's an enormous pleasure and privilege to receive them. I don't ask for any more. That would be greedy.' She stood up and started clearing away the breakfast things. 'Anyway, I must go and pick some sprouts and dig up some parsnips for tomorrow's lunch. Hattie will load the dishwasher, you don't need to bother about that. Oh, and there's some vegetable soup thawing in the Aga. Help yourselves when you feel hungry. If the weather stays fine, I may stay outside and get a few chores done.'

Viv disappeared into the lobby. After a few moments we heard the back door open and close, then she walked past the window in the direction of the kitchen garden. Alfie didn't speak and neither did I. Eventually I said, 'You knew?'

'About Viv and the books? Yes, I knew. I'm family. I know all their dark secrets.'

'And they know all of yours?'

'God, I hope not. I like to think I still have some remnants of a private life. I know about them, but they don't really know about me. It's not exactly a two-way street and that's the way I prefer it. It's how I hold on to a sense of identity. Some things need to be... inviolate.'

I looked at him across the table and noticed the tension in his shoulders. He looked tired. 'You're really rather a private person, aren't you? For an actor, I mean.'

'Yes, I'm afraid I am.'

'Why are you apologising?'

'Because I think maybe you didn't realise that.' His steady gaze held mine. 'And because I think it might be a problem for you.'

I pushed my empty coffee mug away. 'Does anyone know you, Alfie? I mean, *really* know you?'

He thought for a moment, then said, 'No, I don't think so. Fanny probably knows me as well as anybody. But I wouldn't say she knows me well. Does anyone know you? The real Gwen?'

The question threw me and I hadn't realised until he asked, how I would have to answer. 'No, I don't think they do.'

'You see. We're kindred spirits.'

'But there's a difference, Alfie. A big difference. You don't want to be known. I do.'

'Why?'

I thought for a while, then said carefully, 'Because I don't think you can love someone without knowing them.'

He looked thoughtful. 'What about love at first sight? Do you believe in that?'

'Yes, I think I do. But it isn't really love, is it? It's a rapport, an intuitive understanding, perhaps just a strong sexual attraction that quickly becomes love. Until you know someone, you don't love them, you just love the *idea* of them. Something you've constructed in your head, like a character in fiction. You could be totally wrong about them.'

'You might love the fiction more than the fact, you mean?'

'Yes.'

'Is there any real harm in that? If the fiction can be sustained, I mean?' He drained his coffee cup. 'We all have fantasies, don't we?'

'I suppose there's no real harm. So long as—'

'What?'

'So long as people are aware of the boundaries.'

'Boundaries?'

'Where fact stops and fiction starts.'

'Ah!' His eyebrows rose in mock surprise. 'And do you know where *your* boundaries are, Gwen? Are they clear? Is there a line drawn between the little girl who was neglected, possibly completely screwed up by her family, and the calm, capable, socially-skilled career woman who can handle sexually importunate men with wit and aplomb?' I didn't reply, which was a mistake. He went on. 'Where do you keep *Little Gwen*, when she's not required? What sort of an emotional lead-lined box do you use to contain her? Because you don't ever let her out, do you? She was buried alive years ago, alongside the rest of your family.'

'Stop this, Alfie.'

'Why? Are your boundaries getting blurred?'

'Stop it! This isn't fair!'

'No, you're right, it's not. But I think I've made my point. Real love, Gwen – if such a thing exists – is when you love someone *despite* what you know about them. Or *don't* know about them.' He began to recite.

> *'Love is not love*
> *Which alters when it alteration finds,*
> *Or bends with the remover to remove:*
> *O no! It is an ever-fixed mark*
> *That looks on tempests and is never shaken.'*

'Is that Shakespeare?'

'Sonnet 116. And what we know about him wouldn't fill a small pamphlet. Love is unconditional, Gwen. Or should be. "Love the sinner, not the sin", and all those other worthy clichés.' He leaned across the table, his head cocked on one side, and appeared to study me. 'You think being known increases your chances of being loved, don't you? Maybe it does in your case. It would certainly increase your chances of being admired and respected. But I don't think the same can be said of me. I don't think you'd like the real me. You're beginning to see more of the real me here and you don't like it much, do you? You prefer the Alfie Donovan confection I first presented you with. Well, so do I. Which is why I didn't want to bring you to Creake Hall. I'm known here. By my family. And it isn't possible for me to pretend. Truth seeps out. Old Alfie bleeds into new. It gets... messy. Because there aren't any boundaries. Not here. Not for me. Not in the bosom of my family. No boundaries between who I am and who I was. Who I could have been. Should have been. Was I Tom?... Am I Alfie?... It's not clear, not for me.' He ran his fingers through his hair in a gesture of exasperation. 'Sorry, I know I'm not making much sense.' He reached across the table and grabbed my hand. 'Gwen, I want you to love me, but I don't want you to know me.'

I shook my head. 'That's just not possible, Alfie. Not for me.'

'No, I know.' He looked at me, his eyes defiant. 'But it's what I want.' He released my hand and leaned back in his chair. 'What do you want?'

'I don't know. To be trusted, I suppose. To feel able to trust.'

'Love comes cheaper.'

'Maybe it does. I've known love. I never doubted for a moment that my family loved me. But I didn't trust them. Any of them! I couldn't. I daren't. If you gave me a choice, Alfie, between love and trust, I'd choose trust, every time. Love you can get in the bargain basement, on special offer. Trust is much more expensive. And harder to find.'

'So...' He folded his arms and wouldn't meet my eye. 'Will you go back to shopping around?'

'I don't know. I need to think. I'm so confused by what I feel—'

'Gwen, if you knew how difficult all this was for me—'

'Exactly! If I knew how difficult it was... Tell me, Alfie! Explain! Take me into your confidence. I'm not difficult to talk to! I listen. And I don't judge. Trust me.'

'You don't know what you're asking.'

'No, I don't. But I am asking.'

'Not here, Gwen. Not now. When we're back in London,

maybe. I hear what you're saying and I understand. I do want to make our relationship work. I mean that, I really do. But it can't work here. And maybe one day I'll be able to tell you why.'

'And until then?'

'Until then, I think we just have to... play the game.'

'What game, Alfie?'

His grin was lopsided and quite mirthless. 'Charades.'

Chapter Twelve

Gwen

It was a morning for revelations.

I left Alfie clearing up the kitchen and went to find Hattie. She'd finished wrapping her presents and agreed to come up to the attic where we took out the *Thousand Pyramids* quilt, spread it over our knees and set to with a seam-ripper each. Soon the floor was littered with threads and paper triangles.

I suppose there's something about sitting in close proximity to someone, yet having no eye contact, that encourages the sharing of confidences. Friends tell you they're gay/having an affair/leaving their spouse while staring woodenly at the motorway through their car windscreen. There's something about not having to look someone in the eye that makes you brave.

I wasn't thinking about that at the time. It only occurred to me afterwards, when I thought about the conversation I'd had with Hattie, whom I'd known for just over twenty-four hours.

~~~

Without looking up from the quilt, Gwen said, 'Are you looking forward to the concert tonight?'

'Yes. Well, yes and no. I'm looking forward to it being over and everyone saying how much they enjoyed it,' said Hattie, her curly head bowed over her work.

'Will you be nervous? I'd be petrified.'

'I'm a bit nervous now, but I won't be once I start playing. There's isn't room. I shall be totally focussed on the music. And Tyler. He's a very calming influence.'

'Yes, he is, isn't he? I've noticed that. He's very *solid* somehow.' Gwen discarded a paper triangle. 'Have you always played the piano? Since you were small?'

'Always. Apparently I climbed on to the piano stool at three and demanded that someone teach me how to play.'

'You must be very good then.'

'I was. I'm not now. I don't practise. To be good you have to do hours of practice every day. I used to, but I don't now.'

'Why's that?'

'I went to music college for a year, got pregnant, had an abortion, then decided I didn't want to be a musician any more.' Gwen looked up, astonished, but Hattie's head remained bent over the quilt, her face hidden by an abundance of unruly hair. She continued to cut stitches and remove papers at speed and Gwen watched as they fluttered to the floor. Hattie continued. 'I realised I just wasn't *strong* enough, you see. I wanted to be the best, but I realised I wasn't and never would be. So I stopped *striving*. Now I just play music when I want and how I want.'

Gwen bowed her head and resumed her unpicking. 'Do you feel sad about that? Disappointed?'

'Oh, no, it was a tremendous relief! I reverted to my other love, which was sewing. All the hours I used to spend at the piano I now spend making things. I'm much happier. I'm still being creative, you see, and sewing is much less repetitive than music-making. Mind you, there's no real outlet for *passion*. Or despair, for that matter. Though I did once see a nineteenth-century widow's quilt. It was heart-breaking! It was called *Darts of Death*. There were big black arrows on a white background. Single bed size, of course. Imagine making that!... Anyway, when I feel *tumultuous*, I play Schubert. Or I go and listen to Tyler play his cello. You perhaps wouldn't think it to look at him, but that man knows about passion. I think it's his Polish blood. Well, and his Celtic blood too, I suppose. A double dose. Watch Tyler playing Bach! He bares his soul. I think that's terribly brave. I wouldn't do it, never could, and they hammered me for that at music college. Said I was *twee*. Well, I was only nineteen – what did I know of passion? Enough to get pregnant, that's all.'

Gwen was aware of the presence of a lump in her throat that made it difficult to speak. She swallowed and said, 'Do you have any other career plans? You're still quite young. Are you much older than Alfie?'

'Six years. So I'm no spring chicken,' Hattie said with a sigh. 'I teach a patchwork class locally and Viv says I could develop that. I've got City and Guilds, you see, and there's certainly the demand. But I'm not sure if I could cope with all the people, several days a week. But I'm thinking about it.'

'I think you should do it if you can. You have so much enthusiasm to share. And skill.'

'That's what Viv and Tyler say. Tyler says it would be like playing the piano. I'd be scared until I started, then I'd get so involved in the projects, I wouldn't have time to be nervous.'

'I'm sure he's right.'

'I *know* he's right. Tyler always is. He's the oracle we all consult. If ever Viv has a problem, she consults Tyler. Not just gardening problems. Things to do with the house. And Rae.'

'Viv and Tyler... they aren't an item, are they?'

'Good Lord, no!' Hattie snorted. 'I don't think Viv's interested in men *at all*, if you know what I mean. She's never talked to me about it, but she had a very close friend in the village for some years, until she died of breast cancer. Viv took it badly, so I did wonder about them.'

'Has Tyler ever been married?'

'Not that I know of.'

'Does he have a girlfriend?'

'Well, if he does, neither Viv nor I have ever heard a word about her.'

'That seems surprising, doesn't it? I mean, he's quite an attractive man, wouldn't you say? And he seems very nice. I wonder why he isn't in a relationship?'

'Well, who knows what he gets up to in his spare time? Perhaps he goes clubbing in Kings Lynn. And the Young Farmers have a disco twice a year. Perhaps he goes there to pull.'

'Do you?'

Hattie looked up sharply, then her face crumpled as she burst into giggles. 'I think I'd do better with the Saga louts at the local day centre. You know, I've always fancied learning to play bowls. But they say it's viciously competitive. Not sure I've got the requisite killer instinct.' She sat up straight and surveyed the floor. 'Oh, look at the mess we've made! You pick up the papers, I'll pick up the threads. I brought an envelope to store the templates in. It's on the bed.'

Gwen stacked the papers neatly. The templates cut from letters appeared to be from two people, one of them Alfie. Gwen could discern only two hands and she noticed Alfie's name signing off a letter, the boy's clear, bold signature nothing like his writing now.

Hattie was scraping away at the rug, trying to pick up the threads. 'Hang on a minute,' said Gwen. 'I know a better way.' She opened her sewing box, pulled out a gadget with a revolving sticky cylinder and rolled it over the rug, catching all the threads.

'What a good idea! I must get one of those.'

'It's the wardrobe mistress' standby. Removes fluff, hairs, threads and dandruff from actors' costumes. We get through reels and reels of the sticky tape.'

'Right, I'm going down to heat up some soup. We'd better have some lunch before my sisters arrive. Are you all right clearing up?'

'Yes, I've almost finished. I'll be down in a minute.'

As Hattie left the room, the draught from the door lifted the templates stacked neatly on the bed. As she kneeled on the floor, Gwen was showered with the enigmatic confetti of the past.

Gwen

I know I probably shouldn't have examined the templates. It only happened because I had to gather up the paper triangles again. I found a *Dear Ma* and a *Love from Alfie*, so there was no doubt what some of the letters were. I couldn't resist reading snippets of what I took to be Alfie's letters home from boarding school, sent to the mother from whom he'd been parted. I assumed the letters were neither particularly private nor cherished as they'd been recycled for patchwork, but I did wonder at the cold heart of a mother who could treat family letters as so much scrap paper. But then I'd never received a letter from any member of my family, apart from one from Uncle Frank when he was doing time in Wormwood Scrubs. Evidently some people didn't revere hand-written missives the way I did.

So curiosity got the better of me and I tried to decipher the triangular jigsaw pieces of Alfie's school days. Some were incomprehensible, but others were clearer and I was able to deduce little bits of information from them. From this piece:

from

play and

I call him Laurie

the play which is "Toad

Laurie is playing Badger because

and I am playing Toad. There are lots

of words to learn. Laurie and I and the boys

ice our parts together. They all think I'm very funny

I learned there was a boy called Laurie who was in the school play with Alfie, a production of *Toad of Toad Hall*. Laurie played Badger and Alfie was cast as Toad, a notion which brought a smile to my face. Later I came across an adjacent piece of the same letter:

There's not a lot of news this week apart

telling you about the Christmas

my best friend Laurence Şa

are both going to be in

Toad Hall". Hooray!

is very tall

and lots

pract

Reading this piece, I realised Laurence (or Laurie) had been Alfie's best friend.

The other letters were from Alfie's father, and were also addressed to Rae. I didn't examine these any further as it seemed an invasion of privacy, although, once again, I assumed the letters couldn't have been of a very private nature if Hattie had been given them.

I sorted the triangles into an *Alfie* pile and a *Freddie* pile and put them away in the envelope, resisting – with some difficulty – the temptation to indulge in any more detective work.

~~~

After lunch, Gwen wrapped and labelled the rest of her Christmas presents and piled them in a corner of the attic. She was on her way downstairs when she heard a whoop from Hattie and an excited cry: 'They're here! Fanny and Deb have arrived!' Harris and Lewis joined in the chorus of greeting and by the time Gwen had descended to the hall, Alfie, Viv and Hattie were assembled, Hattie looking excited, Alfie stoical, as Viv heaved open the oak door to let her sisters in.

Gwen hung back, standing on the bottom stair, her hand resting on the banister and she was able to look over the assembled heads as the two women entered. She was in no doubt as to which sister was which. Frances, enveloped in fur, her upturned collar concealing much of her face, was a head taller than her elder sister, who wore a quilted down jacket that only added to the rotundity with which Nature had already endowed her. Gwen thought of the Holbein portrait of Henry VIII in which he appeared almost as broad as he was tall.

Deborah was beaming at her siblings and laughing, her round face creased with lines. Her nose was pink with cold and she wore no make-up, apart from carelessly applied lipstick in a shade too bright to be either fashionable or becoming. Deborah hugged Viv and Hattie, then turned to Alfie. She laughed again, at nothing in particular it seemed, then thrust out a hand, saying, 'Well, here we all are again!' and shook Alfie's hand vigorously with both of hers. Alfie said, 'Hello, Deb,' and looked relieved when she let go.

Frances, still clutching her fur to her thin frame, inclined her head, unsmiling, to kiss her sisters on the cheek, announcing their names by way of greeting, as if identifying them. Taller than Alfie in perilously elegant heels, she stood and gazed at him in an appraising way. She said, 'Hello, Alfie', leaned forward and kissed him on the mouth.

Deborah laughed again and Alfie said in a low voice, 'Hello, Fan. Happy Christmas.' He turned away, saying, 'Let me introduce you to Gwen.'

'Ah yes!' said Frances brightly, peering over his shoulder. 'The girlfriend!' Gwen noticed that she didn't smile.

Stepping forward as Alfie introduced her, Gwen took Frances' cold and bony hand, heavy with jewels, and saw the beautiful grey eyes flick up and down, appraising once again. She felt uncomfortable, but assumed this was the professional photographer's eye, assessing her as a potential subject.

Frances sighed heavily, as if disappointed, and said, 'Alfie tells me you *sew*.' The remark hung in the air for a second. Before Gwen had time to respond, Frances added with a barely suppressed smirk, 'You and Hattie must have *lots* to talk about.' She wheeled round. 'Hattie, call these bloody dogs off, will you? This coat may be fake but it was still hellish expensive.'

'They're just pleased to see you, Fanny.'

'Unfortunately,' Frances sneered, 'the feeling is not mutual. Oh, God, look – I'm covered in white hairs!'

'Don't worry, Gwen has a magic sticky thing that removes hairs and fluff.'

'Thank you, darling, but I won't be letting sticky things anywhere near this coat, however magical they might be.'

Deborah, whom everyone had forgotten, stepped forward and offered her hand to Gwen. 'Delighted to meet you, Gwen! I'm Deborah. Everyone calls me Deb. I'm so glad you could join us for Christmas. When we spoke on the phone, Hattie couldn't stop talking about you. I gather you're a big hit with everyone – including Rae!'

'And especially,' said Frances smiling slyly at her brother, 'with Alfie... Will somebody please make me a pot of tea before I faint dead away? I drank something disgusting on the train which they claimed was tea, but it most certainly wasn't.'

'Yes, of course,' said Hattie, leaping forward. 'Shall I take your coat, Fanny?'

'Not unless you've had the heating overhauled. Lead me to the Aga, fill me with hot tea, *then* I might think about divesting myself of some outer garments. *Might*, I say.' Her eyes found Gwen again. 'Are you surviving the cold, Gwen? It's *appalling*, isn't it? The nights are the worst. But then...' Her lips formed a tight smile. 'I suppose you've got my little brother to keep you warm.'

There was a silence and Gwen, who was beginning to get the measure of Frances, said, 'I'm upstairs in the attic, actually. Very cosy, in fact, under Hattie's fabulous quilt. But I'm not one for feeling the cold anyway.'

'Young people don't,' Alfie said, with emphasis. He took Frances' arm, and steered her away from Gwen. 'But I believe it's one of the trials of old age.'

Frances snatched her arm away and stalked off in the direction of the kitchen, heels tapping furiously on the flagstones. 'On second thoughts, Hattie,' she called out over her shoulder, 'would you please pour me a large sherry?'

Viv turned to Alfie. '*Now* look what you've done. You're a naughty boy. We shall all suffer for that.'

He shrugged his shoulders. 'She can be as rude as she likes to me, but she's not getting her claws into Gwen.' He turned and waited for Gwen who still lingered on the stairs. 'Come and have some tea. If she gives you any more grief, Hattie will set the dogs on her, won't you, Hat?'

'Like a shot. Don't take any notice of her, Gwen. She's just jealous.'

But of what Frances might be jealous, Gwen wasn't altogether sure and Hattie didn't say.

~

Frances and Deborah had arrived bearing gifts: six bottles of champagne from Frances and a box of chocolates the size of a coffee table from Deborah. Hattie was thrilled on both counts and insisted on opening the box to see the menu, which, with mounting excitement, she proceeded to read aloud to the assembled company.

'Chocolate pornography, Deb,' said Alfie as they drank tea, seated around the kitchen table. 'Very enterprising of you. Something to please everyone.'

'Not me, darling,' said Frances, sipping black tea from a chipped Norwich City FC mug which Hattie had allocated to her as a small gesture of revenge. 'My post-Christmas diet is starting pre-Christmas, so don't offer *me* any chocs.'

'Would this be the champagne and smoked salmon diet?' Alfie enquired. 'Or are you cutting back on the calories this year and sticking to champagne?'

'You may mock, brother mine, but *some* of us are determined not to let ourselves go.'

'Fight the good fight, eh, Fan? With all thy might.'

'They say,' said Deborah, leaning over to speak to Gwen in confidential tones, 'that when a woman gets to forty, she has to choose between her face and her backside. Well, I decided to abandon both of mine as lost causes.' She burst into laughter and Gwen couldn't help joining in.

'Well, why not? I can't imagine anyone ever lies on their deathbed, moaning, "I wish I'd eaten less chocolate".'

'Quite! And now they say, it's good for you! It's anti-depressant. Really good chocolate isn't that fattening anyway.'

'And this looks *really* good!' said Hattie, ogling the contents of the box.

'Nothing's too good for my family at Christmas,' said Deborah, pressing her lips together in a thin smile, meant to forestall tears, but which was only partly successful. 'Only the best for them – and their lovely guests!' she added, patting Gwen's hand.

'Why, thank you, Deborah.'

'Deb!'

'Sorry – *Deb*. I'm thrilled to be here. I've never had a

Christmas like this before. I'm so pleased Alfie let me come. He took some persuading and I was worried I might be intruding on a family celebration.'

'Which is total rubbish,' said Hattie, breaking off from her chocolate recitation. 'Because she's a completely lovely person and I want her to stay for ever and ever. She's going to help me finish off the *Thousand Pyramids* quilt!'

'In which case,' said Frances, 'she'll *need* to stay for ever and ever. Hattie could you please stop reading from that card? You're making me feel quite nauseous.'

Oblivious, Hattie exclaimed, 'Ooh, listen to this one! "Cranberry and coconut cream enrobed in dark chocolate." *Enrobed.* Doesn't that sound wonderful? I think I'd like to be enrobed in dark chocolate. Then Harris and Lewis could lick it all off!'

Deborah burst into bright, tinkling laughter once again and Hattie and Gwen joined in. Frances stared at her sisters and their house-guest in disbelief, then turned to Alfie. 'I do believe I *am* going to be sick...'

Chapter Thirteen

Gwen

It's difficult now for me to remember all the details of Christmas Eve and Christmas Day. The jolly festivities paled into insignificance in the light of subsequent events. What I do remember about those two days concerns mainly Alfie and Marek.

By the time Marek arrived for dinner on Christmas Eve, Frances was well tanked up and I suspected she was looking for trouble. Hattie had made the mistake of asking why her sister hadn't brought her latest boyfriend and this provoked a vitriolic outburst, condemning all men as faithless time-wasters. After that, Frances poured herself another drink and settled into sullen silence, from which only Marek's arrival roused her.

Tidy and clean-shaven, he looked rather different from the previous occasions on which I'd encountered him but – I was dismayed to find – no less attractive. He was wearing a black shirt and trousers and a red silk tie. With his silver hair, the effect was startling but he looked festive in a sombre sort of way and very tall beside Alfie. Hattie was also wearing red: a vintage 1950s party dress, over which I had almost literally drooled when she came down for pre-dinner drinks. Her loose hair was brushed and shining, held back with antique combs. Her cheeks were rosy with excitement and she kept looking at Marek, smiling nervously. At one point when he was standing beside her, he said something softly which I didn't catch. After that she seemed calmer.

Marek had brought gifts for the family: a bottle of *Krupnik*, a Polish liqueur made from vodka, honey and herbs and two home-made loaves of *Strucła*, a plaited poppy seed bread. Viv fell upon these, delighted. 'Delicious! I shall serve them with the cheese board. Thank you, Tyler! Why don't you tell Gwen about the Polish Christmas Eve? I'm sure she'd be interested.'

He sat on the sofa between Frances and me. 'Christmas Eve is the big social occasion for Poles. It's known as *Wigilia*, which means vigil. There's a twelve course meal that includes no meat, but food from the forest, fields, lakes and orchards. Families sit down to eat it after the first star appears in the sky.'

'Tell her about the chairs!' Hattie exclaimed, her eyes shining.

Marek smiled at her, then turned back to me. 'On Christmas Eve my grandparents used to blow on their chairs before sitting down to supper.'

'Why?' I asked, mystified.

'There's a traditional belief that you might sit on a ghost who came to join you for supper. So you blew them away. An empty plate was also set at the table, for dead relatives.'

Frances stirred in her corner of the sofa. 'So morbid!'

Marek turned to her. 'Not really. Families tend to remember their dead at Christmas anyway. Spectres at the feast. And despite what my grandparents believed, you can't just blow them away. Poles ritualise this and include the departed formally in the celebrations.'

'I still think it's morbid,' said Frances. 'Surely if Christmas has any meaning at all, it's about celebrating a *birth*.'

'Yes, but a birth which looks forward to a very significant death. A death foretold. That's why the Wise Men brought myrrh.'

'Well, I think it's a lovely idea,' I said, 'to remember absent loved ones like that. Much better than trying to be jolly, pretending you don't miss them. Which only makes things worse.'

Marek nodded. 'Denial makes anything worse. The quickest way to process grief is always *through*, but most people go round. And it can be a long way round.'

'Right,' said Viv, getting to her feet. 'The moment of truth! Alfie, would you go upstairs and fetch Rae? Deb's been helping her get dressed and I think she should be ready now. If she throws a wobbly, don't worry too much. I can always take a tray upstairs.'

'Leave it to me,' said Alfie. 'Charming birds from the trees is one of my specialities.'

'I wish you luck,' said Frances, swallowing another mouthful of sherry. 'That old bird fell off her perch a long time ago...'

Rae joined us for dinner and Alfie escorted her into the wood-panelled dining room which was sparkling with crystal and candlelight. Viv had made a splendid arrangement of evergreens, fruits and nuts as the centre-piece of the table. 'All from the garden!' she announced proudly when I admired them. Alfie led Rae to her seat at the head of the table. She was dressed in an ageless (and no doubt aged) tweed suit which she wore with a fussy lace blouse and heavy amber beads. She was as tall as Viv and her bearing was upright, but she moved slowly, clinging to Alfie's arm.

She smiled vaguely at the assembled company, looking nervous and confused. I wondered if she remembered my name, or even who I was. Frances and Deborah sat on her left and right and Alfie sat opposite her, at the other end of the table. I was seated on Alfie's right, next to Marek and opposite Hattie (who, unless I was mistaken, blew discreetly on her chair before she sat down.) I was relieved to find myself seated so far from Frances as to make conversation almost impossible.

Viv brought in a tureen of chestnut soup which was followed by a venison casserole and Mushroom Stroganoff for Hattie. For dessert there was blackberry and apple pie ('Alfie's favourite!' Rae declared in one of her few contributions to the conversation) and Marek's *Strucla* with cheese and fruit from Creake Hall's own orchard. He identified the different varieties of apple and pear for me and insisted I try a piece of each. 'And you must have some quince paste with your cheese. Viv makes it from the Hall's quinces.'

Viv smiled at him. 'You'll find a large jar under the tree addressed to you. That should keep you going for another year.' Marek raised his glass of port to her in silent thanks. Viv looked round the table at her family and I saw her shoulders drop a little. Finally, I thought, she can relax. Everyone is here and everyone has made it to the table. Even Rae.

I glanced towards Rae's end of the table and noticed Frances toying with pieces of fruit, looking bored. Deborah was telling Rae about her son's exploits in Africa, which might have accounted for Frances' boredom. She caught my eye and made an effort to smile. Raising her voice, she said, 'Have they told you yet that you're to be subjected to Ordeal by Music? It's a Holbrook family tradition.' She refilled her wine glass, spilling a little on the cloth. 'Other families sit back and watch DVDs, but *we* have to do home-made entertainment, as if this was some Edwardian country house party,' she added with a humourless laugh.

Hattie had heard and looked uncomfortable, shifting in her seat. I noticed her eyes search for Marek's but he was talking to Deborah about African wildlife.

'I'm really looking forward to the concert,' I said, then smiled at Hattie in what I hoped was a reassuring way. 'I heard some of the rehearsal and it sounded very good.'

Hattie stood up, shaking out the voluminous skirts of her dress and leaned across the table. 'Come on, Tyler. I think we need to go and set up.'

'Yes, off you go, musicians!' said Deborah, her colour high now after several glasses of red wine. 'Fanny and I will clear away, won't we, Fan?'

Frances' reply was affirmative but unenthusiastic.

'Can I give you a hand?' I asked.

Viv stood up and started to clear plates. 'No, you go and see to the fire, Gwen. Chuck another log on if you think it needs it.'

I followed Hattie, Marek and Alfie to the sitting room, where Marek unpacked his cello and began to tune it. Hattie and Alfie discussed the running order and Alfie made a note on a scrap of paper which he placed in his jacket pocket. Rae, Viv, Deborah and Frances joined us eventually in the sitting room. With Harris and Lewis stretched out on the hearthrug, the large room seemed almost full.

I realised I was excited. I hadn't heard classical music played live since I'd been in the school choir and suffered the accompaniment of the school orchestra. But I realised I was also excited at the thought of hearing Marek play, pleased to have an excuse to watch him, unabashed, for the duration of the musical interlude. Why this prospect should seem exciting, I didn't venture to ask myself.

~~~

Seated at the piano, Hattie regarded her audience. Her mother and sisters sat comfortably ensconced in armchairs and on the sofa, drinking coffee and brandy. Alfie was seated to one side of the room, awaiting his turn. Gwen sat at one end of the sofa, in front of Marek. Waiting for him to look up, indicating he was ready, Hattie felt an attack of the jitters coming on, so she cast her eyes down and stared at the keyboard.

'Don't worry about playing the music.' Marek's voice was scarcely more than a whisper. 'Let the music play you.' She looked up but he'd already turned away and was standing, facing their audience.

'Ladies and gentlemen, we're going to begin this evening with a piece by Mendelssohn, one of his *Songs without Words*, opus. 109. After that we'll play a movement from a sonata by Rachmaninov, the *andante* from his G minor sonata, opus 19.' He sat down again and after a moment Hattie started to play.

The piece was slow and stately and the cello had a soaring, song-like melody that showed off its higher register. Gwen had expected to be transfixed by the intricate movements of Marck's long fingers and the sweeping movements of his bowing arm, but instead she found herself watching his face. It was not a face she'd seen before. Marek, whose expression was usually calm, occasionally guarded, had dropped the mask he wore to keep the world at a distance. As he played, his eyes were often closed, but when open, they seemed brighter and more alert than Gwen had ever seen them. She'd not seen him so animated, nor seen the muscles in his face working, pulling the skin taut across his wide, Slavic cheekbones. Clearly, here was a man in whom lay depths of passion – for music, at least – and that passion was normally suppressed. *Watch Tyler playing Bach,* Hattie had said. *He bares his soul...* Gwen could believe it. It seemed to her almost unseemly to watch while he appeared exposed, almost vulnerable. She shifted her eyes reluctantly to Hattie, who frowned in concentration. There was no sign now of any nervousness. She didn't look at Marek and he didn't look at her, but they kept perfect time, linked by some form of musical telepathy.

The Mendelssohn came to an end and the family applauded. On the sofa Frances stirred. She'd kicked off her high heels and curled her legs beneath her before the performance began and Gwen suspected the applause had woken her. Deborah leaned across to Rae, made some remark and Rae nodded, clapping her large hands together.

As the applause died down, Hattie started to play again. Immediately, the hairs on the back of Gwen's neck stood up as Hattie played a tune of such languid sensuousness and melodic beauty, Gwen feared she might start to cry. As Hattie settled into the tune, her face serene, a little smile playing at the corners of her mouth, Marek launched into the cello part, deep in its low register and there began a dialogue between male and female as each instrument answered the other and their voices intertwined. When the tempo changed and the music became more dramatic, Gwen felt her heart begin to pound. She realised she was forgetting to breathe.

The piece lasted six minutes. Gwen was in tears after four, no longer able to hold back the flood of emotions she felt. As the piece came to an end, culminating in a deceptively simple, almost casual little tune, she reached into a pocket for a tissue and, head bowed in shame, dabbed at her eyes while the others applauded. Oblivious to Gwen's distress, Alfie approached the piano. Marek acknowledged the applause with a nod, then laid his cello down on its side, and went to sit beside Gwen.

'What's wrong?'

'I'm so sorry! I don't know what came over me! I hope I

didn't distract you too much with my stupid blubbing. It's just that I don't think I've ever heard anything so beautiful – let alone *seen* anything so beautiful being played in front of me! I promise I'll behave for the rest of the concert. How on earth do you play something like that and not fall apart at the seams?'

Marek laid his hand briefly on hers and said, 'We do fall apart. But the music puts us back together again.'

Alfie was leaning on the piano now, talking to Hattie who was re-arranging her music. At a sign from her, he turned to his audience and said, 'And now for something completely different, as the Python boys used to say. I'm about to lower the tone of our elegant proceedings by singing a song made famous by that immortal duo, Flanders and Swann. It's Hattie's favourite and I'm singing it at her specific request, so *don't*,' said Alfie pointedly, 'blame *me*. Ladies and gentlemen, we give you... *The Warthog*.'

Relaxed, assured, with one hand laid casually on the piano, the other in his jacket pocket, Alfie sailed through the comic song, ad-libbing skilfully when Hattie lost her place in the music. He was applauded warmly, especially by Gwen who cheered. She turned round to look at a beaming Rae who was nodding at something Deborah had said. Catching sight of Gwen, Rae waved and Gwen waved back.

As Marek got up from the sofa to resume his position with the cello, Alfie took his place beside Gwen, muttering, 'Thank Christ that's over for another year. Do you think there's an interval now? I need another drink.'

'You were wonderful, Alfie! Quite hilarious. Why have you never told me you can sing?'

'Oh, there are lots of things you don't know about me, Gwen. I like to maintain a certain mystique.'

'You should definitely do a musical. You really know how to put a song across.'

'The art that conceals art, my dear. It takes hours rehearsing in front of the bathroom mirror to look that natural. Sshh! Hattie wants to speak...'

Standing beside the piano, Hattie said, 'Tyler and I are now going to play two more pieces: an arrangement he's made of a Polish Christmas carol and finally, a Serenade in A major by Josef Suk.'

Gwen managed to maintain her composure for the final items in the concert: a simple but poignant folk tune followed by a jaunty piece which showcased Hattie's playing. Gwen noticed as they played the final piece that Hattie now looked relaxed and happy and she remembered what Hattie had said about looking forward to the concert being over.

The serenade finished with a witty musical flourish from Hattie and, as the applause started, she jumped up from the piano and moved across to Marek, now standing. They took a bow together, then Marek bent to kiss her on the cheek. The applause was long. Viv and Deborah took it in turns to shout 'Bravo!' Frances sat up and applauded respectably until Hattie, giggling, announced, 'That was so much fun, I wish we could do it all over again!' whereupon Frances said, 'Well, count me out, darling. I need my bed. It's been a long day. Night night.' Picking up her shoes and empty glass, Frances left the room, pausing to give her mother a perfunctory kiss on the cheek.

'Off to bed via the drinks tray,' Hattie murmured as she closed the lid of the grand piano. She turned and caught Gwen's eye. 'Does Fanny think I'm blind? She slept through the whole thing, right under our noses! I suppose we're lucky she didn't *snore* this year.'

'Don't let her spoil it,' said Gwen. 'You were marvellous! I adored every item, but you really shone in that last piece.'

'The Suk? Yes, it's fun isn't it? I enjoy myself with that. Tyler chose all the pieces. He's really good at programme planning and his musical knowledge is encyclopaedic. We do different pieces every year. Sometimes Alfie does Noël Coward. He's a scream.' Gwen looked round for Alfie who had evidently left the room – she assumed in search of alcohol.

Marek declined Viv's offer of another drink and fastened his cello case, saying, 'I'll be getting back home now, I think. It'll be a slow walk with the cello.'

'You didn't come on your bike?' Viv asked.

'I can't cycle with the cello. The case is too big.'

'Oh, dear, I don't think anyone's sober enough to give you a lift home,' said Viv, annoyed she hadn't foreseen this eventuality.

I am,' said Gwen. 'I haven't had anything to drink. I don't think we'll get the cello in the boot of Alfie's Polo, but if someone will lend me a car—'

'There's no need! It's really not far to walk.'

Deborah, who had parted the curtains to check on the weather, said, 'I hate to tell you, Tyler, but it's actually snowing quite hard. It looks as if we're in for a white Christmas!'

Viv fished in her handbag, withdrew some keys and handed them to Gwen. 'Take my car. It's the Volvo.'

Marek protested again but Viv overruled him. 'I won't hear of you walking, not after that wonderful concert. Do you know, Gwen, they get better every year!'

'It will only take a few minutes,' said Gwen, 'and I need some air anyway. *And* I want to see the snow!' Without waiting for a reply, she headed for the hall where she pulled on her outdoor shoes and a coat. Turning, she saw Marek standing ready with his cello case.

'This is very kind of you, Gwen.'

'Not at all. It's my way of thanking you for the concert. Come on, let's see how bad the snow is.'

Gwen

The snow wasn't heavy but the wind was strong and visibility poor, so we took it very slowly. Fortunately there was little traffic on the road. Marek said nothing as we drove and I was concentrating on the bends in the unfamiliar road. When we finally drew up outside the mill neither of us had spoken for the duration of the journey.

I turned to Marek and saw his pale profile and even paler hair outlined against the car window through which I could see flurries of snow whirling in a mad dance.

'I'm sorry I made such a fool of myself at the concert. It's just that it was... a revelation to me.'

He turned his head to look at me for a moment, then

turned away again and stared through the windscreen. 'And your response was a revelation to me. It's a very long time since I saw anyone respond to music like that. It was worthy of a Pole,' he added, with a slow smile.

'Tell me, do you *feel* Polish?'

'Only when I play.'

'Maybe that's why playing is so important to you.'

'Maybe.'

After a moment, I said, 'You're different when you play.'

'How, different?'

'Oh, I don't know. You lose your cool. You're... *passionate.*'

'You can tell?' he said, still looking through the windscreen.

'It's obvious. Blindingly obvious!' I added, laughing.

He turned to look at me, regarding me steadily, unsmiling, his body quite still. I knew then what would happen. I also knew I could prevent it, by speaking or moving, by doing anything in fact, other than sitting still and waiting.

I sat still and waited.

Marek leaned across and slipped his fingers under my hair, around the curve of my neck. He pulled me gently towards him. His lips brushed mine tentatively and once he was sure I wasn't going to pull away, he kissed me properly, lingeringly, then let me go.

I opened my eyes – I didn't remember closing them – to find Marek staring at me.

'It was your Christmas present.'

'The kiss?'

'The concert. I played for you. I wanted to move you. To touch you. With the music. I was pleased I did. Merry Christmas, Gwen.' He turned away and reached for the door handle.

I laid my hand on his arm. 'Wait! When will I see – I mean, will you be coming to the Hall tomorrow?'

'No. I'm invited for lunch on Boxing Day.' After a moment he said, 'If you'd rather I didn't come, I'd understand. I can invent some indisposition.'

'No, I want you to come! I want to see you.' Silence hung

between us as the wind whistled around the car. I shivered.

'Will you spend Christmas Day alone then?'

'I always do. Alone with my ghosts. There's plenty of chairs...'

He got out of the car, retrieved the cello and walked up to the mill without looking back. Snowflakes danced wildly around him and settled on his silver hair, spectral in the faint glimmer of moonlight.

I turned on the ignition and drove back to Creake Hall.

Chapter Fourteen

Gwen

When I got back, there was no sign of any of the women. Alfie was sitting dozing by the dying embers of the fire, his head propped on his hand, his fingers buried in his tousled hair. I knew he'd waited up for me and I had a good idea why. Convinced guilt must be written all over my face, I was relieved his eyes were closed. As I stood in the open doorway, looking at him bathed in the glow of the fire and the Christmas tree lights, I felt an urge to turn tail and creep upstairs, avoiding questions, explanations and most of all Alfie's big brown eyes, always irresistible when sleepy, framed as they were by long, drooping eyelashes. I knew what would be on Alfie's mind if he woke: bed, but not sleep. And I wished to avoid that. With guilty, sinking heart, I realised I wished to avoid Alfie.

Seeking justification, my eyes turned to the childhood photos on the side table and I examined the boy cricketer again. The damned child was still left-handed. My stomach turned over. Instinct told me I was involved in something I didn't like, something I couldn't handle. I liked to keep things simple, or if not simple, then at least straightforward. I didn't do casual sex. I didn't (as a rule) even do casual kissing. Buttoned-up I may be, and that's how I prefer to keep my clothes as a rule. The person I became with Marek wasn't a Gwen that I recognised. She wasn't even someone I approved of. What murky depths had Marek stirred? And what murky depths were there to Alfie that I didn't know about, didn't even *want* to know about?

Alfie opened his eyes and I jumped. I saw it then, what I'd seen so many times before, but not registered consciously. The shutters coming down. For an instant Alfie's eyes were wide, a little confused, even vulnerable. Then they changed. A

154

light went out, a guarded look replaced the one of openness. *Prepared.* That's how he looked. His face was prepared. *Here's one I made earlier...*

'You know,' he said, sitting up in his armchair and stretching cramped limbs, 'I could never tire of looking at a face like yours.'

'A face like mine? What sort of face is that?'

He paused and seemed to choose his words carefully. 'Old-fashioned. Characterful. Ever so slightly androgynous. You're my idea of a Shakespearean heroine. Beautiful, but not girly.'

My mouth was working but words wouldn't come. Eventually I managed to say, 'You've never called me *beautiful* before.'

'Haven't I? How remiss of me. Well, there you are. You've had your Christmas present early.'

So now I'd received two early Christmas presents. Alfie's would have seemed quite wonderful had I not already been presented with the gift of Marek's playing. One man was trying to seduce me with words, the other with music, and both were succeeding. (Shakespearean heroine or slapper? You choose.)

With blithe disregard for Alfie's compliment, I changed the subject. 'You love Shakespeare, don't you?'

'Yes. With a passion. I find him bloody difficult, but I love his words. I love the sound of them, even when I don't get all the meaning. It penetrates at some gut level. Shakespeare was why I became an actor.'

I went and sat on the sofa, glad of the residual warmth from the fire. 'How old were you when you decided you wanted to be an actor?'

'I don't remember... I was in my teens. It was a school trip to Stratford and I'd never seen live theatre before. I must have been about fourteen. Maybe fifteen.'

'As old as that? I'd imagined actors grew up wanting to play kids' make-believe for the rest of their lives. Weren't you stage-struck when they cast you as the lead in school plays? I imagine that sort of thing could go to your head, especially when you're young.'

'I dare say it could, but it never happened to me.'

An alarm bell went off in my head, distant but distinct. I ignored it. (A *stupid* slapper too.)

'What didn't happen? Wanting to be an actor?'

'No, being cast in starring rôles. I wasn't exactly leading man material. Star parts went to taller, more glamorous boys than me. 'Twas ever thus.'

I could feel the triangular pieces of paper between my fingers, crisp and crackling; I could see the round childish hand; the phrases "I am playing Toad" and "they all think I am very funny." So I persevered. (*Scheming*, stupid slapper.)

'Did you *never* play a lead then? Not even when you were young? Maybe you've forgotten?'

Please, Alfie, say you've forgotten. Please don't say what I know you're going to say. Lie. *Please...*

'I'd hardly forget something like that, would I? I can remember auditioning for parts and not getting them. And being broken-hearted.' He looked puzzled. 'Why do you want to know about all this anyway?'

'Oh, no particular reason. It was just something Viv said. Or maybe it was Hattie. I must have misunderstood. I thought she said you'd had the lead in a school play.'

'How would *she* know?'

'Your letters home?'

There was an infinitesimal pause. 'Have they kept them?'

'No, I don't think so. But I understood that you'd written home about being in a play. I must have got hold of the wrong end of the stick.'

'More likely Hattie did. She said I'd written about being in a school play? Maybe I was lying. I wasn't the most truthful of children. When your parents divorce, you learn pretty fast to say what you think they want to hear. It's a survival mechanism.'

'Yes, I can understand that.'

'I was brought up to believe that honesty was important, but I could never really see the virtue in being honest if it hurt people. And truth always seemed so *relative* to me. Perhaps it wasn't surprising that I chose to make a career out of being a fake.' Alfie stared at me in silence for a moment, then said, 'What else did Hattie have to say about my childhood?'

I could have stopped there. I could have accepted that the letter home was a lie, just a child's wishful thinking, something to impress the folks back home. I could have accepted that Alfie used to lie as a boy, in the past. But not *now*. And so I continued. With my own lies.

'She was telling me about your special friend at school.'

'Oh?'

Did I imagine it? Did Alfie's nonchalant, amused look slip for a moment? There was no sign of panic, nothing so obvious, just a sense of his being suddenly alert, watching me. As I dug a verbal pit for him to fall into, I felt sick to my stomach.

'She said you had a friend. A best friend. I think she said he was called... Oliver?'

Alfie didn't miss a beat. 'She remembered old Ollie? *Amazing!* I'd almost forgotten about him! Yes, Ollie was my best mate throughout school.' Then he chuckled in the most charming and natural way. (You're good, Alfie. I had no idea *how* good.) 'We got into a lot of trouble together.'

I could almost see him trawling through the childhood memories, memories that, according to his letters, involved a boy called Laurie.

'What happened to Oliver?' I asked, casually.

'No idea. He went to university – read History at Durham, I think – and I went to RADA. We went our separate ways and lost touch.'

'What a shame.'

'Yes. He was a good bloke, old Ollie. A loyal friend. We were quite close. Fancy Hattie remembering him.'

'Your letters home must have made quite an impression on her. On everyone. They must have looked forward to hearing baby brother's news.'

'I suppose so. I didn't realise... But you say they didn't actually *keep* them?'

'No. I think they were cut up for patchwork.'

Alfie smiled. With relief? 'They would have just been duty letters to me, nothing special. I've no memory of writing them. And it would never have occurred to me there was a family hanging on my every word.'

Or a scheming slapper of a girlfriend.

Sick with fear and disgust, wanting nothing more than to sob into my pillow, I stood up and, the words almost choking me, said, 'It's late. I'm off to bed. Goodnight, Alfie.'

He was on his feet in seconds, standing too close, the big brown eyes pleading. 'Can I join you?' His hand cupped my face and he stroked my cheek with his thumb. 'The others have all gone to bed. Not that anyone really cares where I sleep. The niceties have been observed.' He grinned. I used to think it was a sexy smile.

'I'm shattered, Alfie. And not really in the mood.'

'Why's that?'

'I don't know. I'm finding it all a bit much, I suppose. Being here. All the family stuff. Frances is a bit of a cow, isn't she? She's taken an instant dislike to me, I can tell.'

'Fan disapproves of all my girlfriends, on principle. Take no notice. Look, if you're tired we could just sleep together. Have a cuddle. That would be nice... Wouldn't it?'

'Yes,' I said, thinking, 'No.'

It must have shown. He looked into my eyes. 'What's wrong, Gwen? Has something happened? Did Tyler say something to upset you?'

'No, of course not.'

'You were gone a long time.'

'I had to drive very slowly. It was snowing and visibility was poor. It was a bit nerve-wracking as I didn't know the road or the car... I think if you don't mind, Alfie, I'd rather sleep on my own. I need a bit of space.'

'You seemed to be enjoying yourself this evening.'

'I was! I'm just feeling a bit low now, that's all. You know what Christmas means to me.'

He took my hand. 'Yes, of course. I'm sorry, I should have thought. We can't really leave before Boxing Day, I'm afraid.'

'No, I wouldn't dream of it! I'll be fine, honestly. I just need to get to bed. I'm sorry for being such a bore.'

'That's OK. I'm pretty knackered too. I should probably conserve energy for the Christmas Day onslaught. Maybe we could think about leaving on Boxing Day. Make up some excuse.'

I immediately thought of Marek's invitation to lunch at Creake Hall. Before I could stop myself, I said, 'No, really, I'll be fine. We can't leave before Boxing Day's over. Viv and Hattie would be so disappointed. And I've said I'll help Hattie finish off one of her quilts. We must stay for Boxing Day.'

'Well, if you're sure?'

'Yes, I'm sure,' I lied, sure of nothing and nobody, trusting no one, aware that this was a dark and familiar place for me, the place where I'd spent all my childhood, hoping, even praying for certainties, for something I could navigate by, someone I could trust. Then, as now, I chose silence rather than confrontation. Then, as now, I chose solitude and the lonely comfort of unheard tears.

What I hated about my mother was all the lies. The lies about drugs, the lies about money, the lies about losing things that she'd sold, the lies about buying stuff she'd stolen, the lies about the lies. In the end she lied when she didn't even need to, just because she could, because she thought maybe she *should*. Defensive, tactical lying. My mother lied about her habit and out of habit, so it became my habit never to believe anything she said – especially not anything I wanted to believe.

Aunt Sam wasn't much better, promising me, as she upended the bottle, that this really was *it*, she was never, ever going to touch the stuff again. Uncle Frank at least never lied to me, only to himself, about his age, his looks, his pulling power and about the boys he said he loved, but whose names he had trouble remembering.

What was real and true in my childhood?

Me. I was real. My thoughts, my words, my feelings. I trusted those. And my trusty crap detector. I didn't lie to anyone, not even my mother when I told her I loved her. I meant it. It was true then. I loved her when she was alive. I must have, I was so terrified of losing her. It was only after she died that things changed, that my feelings changed.

159

Suddenly there was something bigger than love that I felt towards my mother.

Marek was right. It was anger.

On the eve of the anniversary of my mother's accidental death by drug overdose, I took stock.

Alfie was lying to me.

He didn't write those letters and he wasn't the boy playing cricket.

Was he Alfie? If he wasn't, who the hell was he? Did his sisters *know* he wasn't Alfie? Did his mother? Or, if he *was* Alfie, who was the boy playing cricket? Who had written those letters home from school? Had a lonely Hattie written them as some sort of game of make-believe? If she had, why had Alfie pretended to have the friend I'd invented for him? If Laurie wasn't his boyhood chum, why should Alfie pretend that "Oliver" *was*?

That surely was the most damning piece of evidence. If I could bring myself to accept Alfie's story of the broken arm, then the cricketing photo could be explained away, but why would he pretend to have a friend called Oliver, even make up a bogus university career for him?

There could be only one explanation.

Alfie believed that was what was written in the letters.

Because he didn't *know* what was written in the letters.

Because he hadn't written them.

But he wanted me to believe that he *had*.

Because he wanted me to believe that he was Alfie...

Forgive me, Uncle Frank, wherever you are, for my harsh, self-righteous, teenage judgement. I too have been sleeping with a man whose name I don't know.

~~~

There was a light tap at the bedroom door. In their respective dog baskets Harris and Lewis raised shaggy heads in unison and regarded first the door, then their mistress. Vivien sat up in bed and said, 'Who is it?'

'It's Alfie. Can I have a word?'

She laid aside her paperback and reading glasses and got out of bed, ordering the dogs to stay. Sliding her feet into slippers, she took a dressing gown from a hook on the back of the door, put it on, belted it firmly, then opened the door.

'What's the matter? Is something wrong with Rae?'

'No, it's nothing to do with Rae. Would you mind if I came in? I don't want to be overheard. Gwen has only just gone upstairs.'

'No, of course not. Come in.' Vivien turned away, gathered up a pile of gardening books and magazines from an armchair, dumped them on the floor and indicated to Alfie that he should sit. She perched on the edge of the bed, her brown eyes wide with anxiety.

Alfie sat down. After a moment he said, 'There's a problem with Gwen.'

'What sort of problem?'

'I think she suspects. *Might* suspect.'

Vivien stared at him, her lips parted in surprise, then she bowed her head. Clasping her large, bony hands, she said, 'Well, we knew it was a big risk letting her come. What's happened?'

'Nothing much, but she's asking a lot of questions. And I don't know all the answers. Were there letters home? From boarding school?'

'Yes, one a month for a few years.'

'Do they still exist?'

'I've no idea. I lost track of them years ago. I imagine Rae would have kept them. They were addressed to her. But she might have lost them. Or destroyed them when she had the last breakdown.'

'I think Hattie's been talking to Gwen about them.'

Vivien frowned. 'Why on earth would she do that?'

Alfie spread his hands. 'Why does Hattie do anything? She's taken a shine to Gwen and they're spending a lot of time together. You know how Hattie prattles on.'

Vivien shook her head. 'I can't believe Hattie would be that stupid! Even if the letters still existed, she'd know you wouldn't be familiar with the contents. What on earth is she playing at?'

'Maybe she hasn't talked about them. But maybe Gwen has seen them.'

Vivien thought for a moment, then said, 'Even if she'd found them, she doesn't strike me as the sort of girl who'd read other people's letters. Surely the most likely explanation is that Rae has talked about them.'

'Yes, that's what I thought, but Gwen said it was you or Hattie, she couldn't remember which. I knew it wouldn't be you.'

'Did you manage to talk your way out of it?'

'I think so. She mentioned some of the content of the letters, so I just improvised. Convincingly, I hope.'

Vivien was silent and appeared to study her hands folded in her lap. After a few moments she looked up into Alfie's face and said, 'You know, you *could* tell Gwen the truth. I think she could be trusted.'

'I'm sure she could. But I care enough about Gwen not to want to lose her. So I'd rather she didn't know. In any case, the fewer people who know, the better.'

'Well, obviously. But you're entitled to a life. Your own, I mean.'

'Thanks. But I think we have to accept that, to all intents and purposes, I gave that up years ago.'

Vivien flinched and her hand flew to her mouth. 'I'm so sorry... It was never meant to be like this! It was only ever meant to be a temporary measure.'

'I know. I entered into this with my eyes open, Viv. It's my own fault for bringing Gwen here. I did it against my better judgement and it was a big mistake. We'll leave on Boxing Day. We can't decently leave any sooner.'

'Rae will be quite happy with that.'

'She'll have to be.' Alfie shifted in his chair and said, 'There's something else, I'm afraid. Something you need to know... Fanny made a mistake with the photos.'

'A mistake? What do you mean?'

'The cricketing photo. In the sitting room. The boy is left-handed.'

'Surely not! Someone would have noticed!'

'Someone did. Gwen.'

'What on earth did you say?'

'I made up some rigmarole about having broken my arm. Having to play left-handed to save face with the other boys.'

'Did she believe you?'

'I'm not sure. She appeared to, but she's been a bit odd ever since. And then there was the inquisition about the letters home. It could just be coincidence. Or she could suspect. So I thought I'd better warn you.'

'Should I tell the others, do you think?'

'Can't see the point. Hattie's the one most likely to blow it now, but if you warn her something's up, she'll blab out of sheer anxiety. Leave it for now. I *think* Gwen bought my stories. If she didn't, then she's playing her own little game of deception.'

'Why would she do that?'

'I don't know. I hope because she likes the family. Because she's already fond of you and Hattie. I hope it might also be because she doesn't want to lose me.'

'Why should she have to lose you?'

Alfie shook his head. 'You don't know Gwen. She doesn't demand a lot from life, but she does insist that what she has is *real*. Her family strung her along for sixteen years. She has no time for fantasy. Or delusion. Or deceit. If I told her the truth, I'd be taking away everything I've given her. Everything I am. There would be nothing left. Nothing real anyway.'

Vivien gazed at Alfie's face, his features sharpened by strain. 'When I think how all this started, what our *motives* were—'

'There's no point feeling guilty, Viv. You couldn't have known what you were getting into. Nor could I.'

'I just hope you and Gwen manage to sort things out. I'll never forgive myself if you don't. She's a lovely girl.'

'Yes, she is.' Alfie's smile was wan. 'More than I deserve, probably. And I'm certainly less than she deserves.' He stood up and said, 'I'll let you get to sleep. It's long past midnight.'

'Is it? It's Christmas Day, then.'

'Happy Christmas, Viv.'

'Happy Christmas, Alfie.'

He walked slowly to the door, opened and closed it silently behind him. After he'd gone, Vivien sat staring at the door for some minutes, then she covered her face with her hands.

Chapter Fifteen

Gwen

I can't say Alfie didn't warn me. He promised me the second-worse Christmas of my life and that's what I got. I spent a restless night. After I'd left a disappointed Alfie to sleep alone, I lay awake turning over in my mind what I now knew – and didn't know – about the man I called Alfie. I asked myself why I hadn't confronted him with what I knew.

I hadn't challenged Alfie because I didn't want to listen to more lies; because I would have had to admit that *I'd* told lies; because even if I'd known who and what Alfie was, I wouldn't have slept with him because my lips were still conscious of Marek's. I could still feel his long fingers on the back of my neck.

I admit I hadn't exactly occupied the moral high ground in my dealings with Alfie – the man who claimed to be Alfie – but I wasn't about to leap from one man's arms into another's. Although, come to think of it, wasn't that *precisely* what I'd done? I fell asleep wondering if I'd inherited nymphomaniac tendencies from my late lamented mother. Or uncle.

When I woke after a fitful sleep, there was a curious, cold deadness in the air and a complete absence of sound. I got out of bed and looked out on to the garden. It was only just beginning to get light but I could see the snow had settled, obscuring the features of the garden. Paths had disappeared and there were now no boundaries between lawn and flowerbed, just an undulating, white expanse broken up by the dark skeletons of trees.

The garden looked beautiful. Stark, but peaceful. I decided I would like to walk in it. It was Christmas Day, after all. I showered and dressed in my warmest clothes and went quietly downstairs. As I passed the sitting room door I heard someone clearing the grate and laying a fire. Viv, probably. I hesitated, then decided to move on without making my presence known.

As I passed through the kitchen, Harris and Lewis roused themselves from their customary stupor in front of the Aga and wove around my ankles, jumping up to be petted. I grabbed a couple of dog biscuits from a packet Viv kept on the worktop and tossed them on to the floor as a decoy. In the moment's grace they gave me, I managed to get out into the lobby. I changed into wellingtons and let myself out the back door.

It was lighter now but the cold stunned like a blow. As I trod, the snow resisted my boots and crunched underfoot. I walked briskly, following the garden path I'd taken when I'd left Marek the first time and found my way back to the house. Was that only the day before yesterday? So much had happened. I'd met so many new people and, with the exception of Frances, I'd liked them all. Hattie, Viv and Marek felt like friends already, although what I felt for Marek was surely something more than friendship.

What was it? A sexual attraction undoubtedly. There was no point trying to delude myself about that. I'd sat in the car, waiting to be kissed. I'd studied him all evening at the concert, watched his hands, his eyes, the way the illuminated Christmas tree cast gaudy lights on his white hair. At the mill I'd let him take me in his arms and press me to his chest and I hadn't wanted to be released. I could still remember the graze of stubble as I'd stood on tiptoe and, thinking of his mouth, had kissed his cheek.

Some friendship.

But when had it actually started? Meeting him for the second time in the kitchen, I'd blushed. I'd watched, riveted, as his hand bled beneath the running tap. Something had already happened then, only an hour or so after we'd met.

Snow was falling again and I'd forgotten to wear a hat. I thought of turning back but decided to plod on, past beds of spindly rose bushes. I stopped to look at a frozen rosebud, dangling at the end of a blackened branch, beautiful, but dead. I walked on, feeling more and more depressed, until I

166

recognised tall beech hedges. I'd reached the clearing where Marek had been working when I first met him.

It had started *here*.

I hadn't known it, but it had started the moment I met him, the moment I looked into those unfathomable dark eyes. What had I seen? Detachment. A kind of calm. Not the sort produced by an orderly life. No, Marek's calm was the after-the-storm variety. His was the stoical grace of a survivor. If he seemed imperturbable, it was probably because he'd known great perturbation. How did I know? Because on the morning I found my mother dead on the kitchen floor, I experienced a millisecond's calm in which I realised nothing worse would ever happen to me. Then I started screaming. Nobody came because it was Christmas and our neighbours had gone on holiday, seeking winter sun. I continued to scream, hoping to wake the dead. I screamed until I was hoarse, then the calm returned and I picked up the phone. I rang for an ambulance, then I dialled Aunt Sam's number, astonished I could still remember it, even though my mother was dead.

I experienced the worst moments of my life terrified and alone. Such a thing scars you, but it also makes you strong. No, not strong. *Certain*. You're certain nothing worse can happen. Even if a similar disaster were to occur, it would have lost some of its shock value. You know you'd recognise it and think, 'I've been here before.' You'd know what to do, how to survive. You'd know that you *would* survive.

I think that's what I saw when I met Marek, although I didn't know it then. I recognised the calm certainty that life held nothing worse for him, nothing he hadn't already dealt with, nothing he couldn't handle. I don't think I'd ever seen that in a person's face before, except perhaps when I looked in the mirror.

Beyond the dark tracery of branches, I could see the mill, black against a lightening sky. I thought of Marek, alone, celebrating his solitary Polish Christmas, with only ghosts for company. And I thought of my ghosts... Uncle Frank. Aunt Sam. My mother. I brushed snowflakes and tears from my cheeks as I brushed the memories from my mind. That was the trouble. That's what got you in the end. Memories. *'You can never make a fresh start,'* Marek had said. *'Memory prevents you.'* I shivered and turned back towards the house, stepping out to get my circulation going.

I had no fears for my future, although my relationship with Alfie was a total mess, was arguably non-existent given that he appeared to be a non-person. I had no clear idea what Marek meant to me, or if I meant anything to him, but these problems lay in the future. I knew I'd find a way of sorting them out, or at least extricating myself from any awkward consequences. I was a coper. Always had been.

When it came to facing the future, I was pretty damn fearless. But facing the past? That was a different matter altogether.

~~~

When Gwen entered the kitchen she was greeted by all four sisters who wished her a merry Christmas, despite the fact that Deborah sat slumped at the kitchen table, in tears. Gwen returned their good wishes and stared at Deborah who was being comforted by Hattie. Alfie, frying bacon and eggs, registered Gwen's dismay and said, 'Don't worry, it's not bad news. Deb's son just rang from Africa to wish her a Happy Christmas.'

'Thereby assuring,' said Frances, peeling a pear, 'that she has a thoroughly *miserable* Christmas, since the mere sound of his voice sends her into floods of tears.'

Deborah raised her head from a handful of crumpled tissues and said, 'No, Fanny, you're wrong. I was thrilled to bits to hear from him. Sounding so happy and healthy! It's just that he's so far *away.'* Deborah blew her nose vigorously, turned to Gwen and smiled. 'Sorry, Gwen. I must look a proper sight!'

'Oh, don't worry about me. I know Christmas can be a very emotional time for families.' Alfie shot her a quick look and, avoiding his eye, Gwen sat down at the table. Simultaneously, a mug of coffee and a plate of bacon and eggs appeared in front of her. She looked up and beamed at the retreating backs of Alfie and Viv.

'You never stop worrying, that's the trouble,' said Deborah.

'Not even when they're twenty-two and six foot tall?' Hattie asked, squeezing her sister's hand.

'No, it's a life sentence,' Deborah replied. 'They're always your babies. And I only ever had the one, you see, so Daniel's always been very precious.'

'Where's Daniel working?' Gwen asked, lifting her coffee mug.

'In Malawi. He loves it! Says he's never been happier. And he's made lots of friends. He monitors food aid and they've given him a motorbike to help him get about. When I think of my little Dan riding round Africa on a motorbike! Well, I feel proud and terrified at the same time, if you know what I mean. Have some toast, Gwen,' said Deborah, pushing a rack towards her. 'I won't eat all this. Or rather, I *will*, but I shouldn't.'

Gwen helped herself to toast and tried to think of an intelligent question to ask about Malawi, but Deborah needed no prompting to continue. 'Young people are so brave, nowadays – well, *some* young people. I really admire them for that. Dan and I talked it all through before he applied. He knew I was worried sick but he explained it all to me. I could absolutely see his point. He said, "Look, Mum, I could commute to London, do a boring job in a nice safe office and be blown up by a terrorist bomb on the 17.50 from Liverpool Street. Or I could go to Malawi and do my bit to change the world." It's true, isn't?' Deborah exclaimed with a tearful laugh. 'So that's what he's doing. He says he wants to leave the world a better place than he found it. Isn't that marvellous?'

'You must be so proud of him,' Gwen said, buttering toast.

'Oh, I am! Terribly proud. But that doesn't stop me missing him. I'm divorced, you see, and very single. *And* I'm a teacher—'

'Deputy Head actually,' said Hattie.

'Well, yes, as it happens. So I don't have the time or energy to get out as much as I should. And when I do, it's usually with other women. Other *teachers*, in fact,' she added pulling a wry face. 'I belong to a terrific reading group – we have a great laugh! – but it's all women. These things usually are. We did have a man for a while, but he was gay and I think he felt a bit... *out* of it. So I do miss Daniel. He lived at home while he was a student, you see. I've got a tiny terraced house in Beccles. Do you know Beccles? It's a nice little town on the Norfolk/Suffolk border. Very pleasant. Dan went to UEA – that's the university in Norwich – and read Geography. He worked terribly hard and got a first! I was *so* proud. But I still worry... It's natural, isn't it? Your babies are always your babies, even when they're grown men. So when he told me he was applying for VSO in Africa... Well, you hear such horror stories, don't you? And I'm ashamed to say, I didn't even know where Malawi was before Dan said he was going to work there. My African geography is pretty vague, I'm afraid. I'm much better on India. We teach that to Year Five every year and they just love it! I've always wanted to go. In fact, that's what I plan to do when I retire. And if I can't find anyone to come with me, I'm jolly well going on my own!'

'We'll hold you to that, Deb,' said Vivien, clearing away empty plates.

'I'd come with you,' said Hattie with a sigh. 'But I *hate* curry.'

Alfie sat down beside Gwen with a plate of bacon and eggs. As he lifted his cutlery, a mobile phone rang and he cursed. 'Who the hell is ringing me on Christmas Day? It'd better be Steven Spielberg.' He went over to the worktop where he'd left his phone, looked at the display, frowned, then answered, saying, 'Hi, Kate. What's up?'

Gwen looked up and watched with a growing sense of foreboding. At a sign from Viv, Hattie picked up Alfie's plate and put it into the Aga to keep warm. Alfie said nothing more for a few moments, but his face turned pale, then looked thunderous. He closed his eyes and they remained shut. As the call went on he screwed up his eyes and said, '*Shit!*' The caller said something else, then Alfie spoke rapidly, his voice unnaturally calm.

'How much did they take? Was it just valuables or have

they cleared me out? CDs?... DVDs?... I assume the laptop went too?... Suits?... Bloody hell. Have I got *any* clothes left?... OK, well, tell the police it looks like they've taken anything of any value and it's probably the same outfit as last time. Tell them I was burgled in the exact same way seven months ago. I'd only just finished replacing everything... I know, Kate, but there's nothing I can do about those bloody French doors, other than put an iron grille across them!' Alfie was silent, clawing at his hair while he listened. 'Yes, OK, I'll drive up now... No, don't bother, just leave everything as it is. Is it snowing in London?... Well, could you do me a favour and put some cardboard or something across the doors to keep the rain out? That's a new carpet. I presume they didn't have room for that in the van... I'll get there as soon as I can. There won't be anything on the roads, so say a couple of hours... Thanks for letting me know... No, don't be ridiculous – you weren't to know! Thank God you *didn't* go down and check. These guys are obviously professionals. You might have got hurt. Look, I'd better get going. I'll see you later. 'Bye.'

Alfie switched off his phone, put it down on the kitchen table and surveyed the five anxious faces turned towards him. 'That was the woman who lives in the flat above me. As you probably gathered, I've been burgled. *Again.* So I have to go back to London to sort things out and talk to the police.'

Hattie started to cry. Deborah slid the box of tissues towards her and put an arm round her shoulders.

'I'll come back tomorrow, Hat,' Alfie said. 'As soon as I can.'

'Do you need somewhere to stay in London?' Frances asked. 'If they've trashed your place, I can give you a key to my house. There's no one there.' She looked away and prodded her untouched pear with an expression of distaste. 'Mike moved out last month. He's living with his mistress now,' she added sullenly.

There was a silence in which the sisters registered another shock. Frances had always been the one who walked away. This was the first indication that in the latest marital breakdown, she was the one who'd been abandoned.

'Thanks, Fan,' Alfie said gently. 'If the flat's not habitable,

Kate will put me up for the night. If you'll excuse me, ladies, I'd better go and break the news to Rae, then get on the road.'

'It might be easier if you leave that to me,' Viv said. 'She'll get very upset. I really think you've got enough on your plate at the moment.'

'Thanks. If you wouldn't mind, I'd really appreciate that.'

Gwen stood up. 'I'll come with you. You'll need some help tidying up.'

Hattie looked up, her face distraught. Seeing her expression, Alfie said, 'No, stay here, Gwen. I'd rather deal with it on my own. I'll be totally foul and that really isn't how I wanted you to spend your Christmas Day. Stay here and entertain the troops. Perhaps you could spend some more time with Rae. Distract her a bit.' He turned to Viv. 'I'll try to be back for Boxing Day lunch.'

'Don't worry, we'll hold it for you,' Viv said with a forced smile.

'But what about your presents?' Hattie exclaimed. 'You can't go without opening them!'

'Afraid I have to, Hat. I'll open mine tomorrow. And I'll give you mine tomorrow. You can have a two-day Christmas this year. Double the fun.'

He turned and left the kitchen. The women sat in silence, apart from Hattie who sat weeping quietly on Deborah's shoulder, then raised her head to announce tearfully, 'He didn't even eat his breakfast!' Gwen pushed her own plate away, then rose from the table and went in search of Alfie.

Gwen knocked on the door of the room known as the Nursery, a room she'd not yet seen.

'Come in.'

Alfie was packing toiletries into a bag and didn't look up until Gwen exclaimed, 'Oh my God... It's a *museum*.'

'Yes. And I'm one of the exhibits.'

The room was a good size, light and painted in cheerful blues and yellows. The walls were decorated with a series of framed fairy tale prints which Gwen recognised were by Arthur Rackham. There was a single bed in a corner, covered

172

in a bright patchwork quilt and on the bedside table stood a lamp shaped like a sailing ship and a Mickey Mouse alarm clock. Beside the bed was a bookcase full of old children's books, the kind with embossed and illustrated cloth covers and titles such as *The Boys' Book of Steamships* and *The Romance of Modern Invention*. A complete set of *Tom Dickon Harry* books in hardback and paperback occupied the top shelf.

In the centre of the room, on a faded rug, stood a wooden rocking horse, his tail and mane sadly depleted. A motley collection of soft toys in various states of decrepitude propped each other up on a chest of drawers. Numerous board games and jigsaw puzzles were stacked on open shelves and a tennis racquet, hockey stick and cricket bat protruded from an umbrella stand. In the corner of the room stood a model castle with archers on the battlements and mounted swordsmen at the drawbridge. Under the window, on top of a blanket box, stood a wooden ark surrounded by Noah, his family and numerous animals arranged in pairs. On the floor beneath, a wooden engine waited on a circular track, ready to haul six brightly painted carriages in perpetuity.

'The blanket box is also full of toys,' said Alfie. 'So's the cupboard.'

'They've kept *everything*?'

'Yes. Well, maybe not everything. I've never done a full inventory. But there's enough here to while away a wet afternoon or two, wouldn't you say?'

'Oh, Alfie, it's *horrible...* I think I'm beginning to understand.'

'Really?' he replied sharply. 'I doubt it... Some of the stuff belonged to my sisters of course, but most of it was bought for the beloved son and heir.' He zipped up his toiletries bag and put it in a holdall. 'I hope you'll be all right on your own. Don't let Fanny get to you. Just ignore her when she gets drunk. And she *will* get drunk.'

'Are you sure you don't want me to come?'

'Positive. I expect it to be a very painful experience and, as with all painful experiences, I prefer to go through it alone.

That's the way I am.'

'I *do* understand that.'

He looked at her. 'Yes, maybe you do. I'll see you tomorrow, then. Happy Christmas.' He leaned forward and kissed her on the cheek, then bent to pick up his bag. As he turned to leave, Gwen noticed a framed photograph on the bedside table, behind the clock. It was Alfie as an adult – an Alfie she recognised – but he was wearing some sort of ragged costume and his face was smeared with dirt. She picked up the photograph.

'What's this?'

'Me when I was a drama student. Final year. I was playing Edgar in *King Lear*. That's the bit where he's on the heath, pretending to be Poor Tom, barking mad. It's a terrible part. Known as "the actors' graveyard". But the critics were kind to me. Said I was very affecting.'

Gwen stared at the photo, perplexed. 'It seems out of place here. It's the only adult thing in the room.'

'That's because I brought it with me.'

'Do you always travel with it?'

'No, only when I come here. It reminds who I am. Prevents *me* from going barking mad... See you tomorrow. Look after yourself.'

After he'd gone, Gwen sat down on the bed and surveyed the room again. A grim-faced Action Man, adorned with fearsome knives and an ammunition belt, caught her eye. She couldn't imagine Alfie playing with it, then remembered that perhaps he never had. Overcome by a sudden wave of panic, she fled from the room.

Chapter Sixteen

As Vivien carved the turkey, standing in for Alfie at the head of the table, she averted her eyes from the long faces beneath tissue paper hats. Hattie sat dejected, fiddling with her napkin. Frances, her thin face pinched with tension, had already emptied her wine glass and was helping herself to the bottle of Merlot that Vivien could have sworn she'd placed far enough down the table to be out of Frances' reach. Rae sat slumped in her chair, gazing into space, apparently unaware of the cheerful remarks addressed to her by Gwen and Deborah, seated either side, trying valiantly to compensate for the absence of the guest of honour. Glancing up, Vivien saw the wreckage of her mother's hopes etched in the deep lines of her face and she looked down again quickly. Carving more turkey, she said, 'We should have asked Tyler to join us. There's a ridiculous amount of meat on this bird. Do you think it's too late to give him a ring?'

Gwen avoided Vivien's eye and offered Rae the dish of cranberry sauce. Hattie looked round the table at the glum, silent faces and said, 'I think he'd have more fun on his own, don't you?'

Frances laughed – a brittle, high-pitched sound, not altogether pleasant. 'Hattie, really, you are *priceless!*'

'Oh, come on, everyone!' said Deborah, helping herself to roast potatoes. 'I'm sure if we all make an effort, we can rise above our disappointment and have a jolly good Christmas without Alfie. After all, we managed without him for years.'

As Gwen handed the gravy boat to Deborah, she noticed Hattie's quick sidelong look at her sister and her anxious eyes. Deborah started to speak but Vivien interrupted. 'Deb's referring to all the years Alfie lived abroad with his father, Gwen. She's quite right – we're well used to family Christmases without Alfie. It's just that we enjoy them so much more when he's with us. When *all* the family are assembled. Come on, Hattie – we haven't pulled my cracker.'

Vivien flourished the cracker under Hattie's nose and they pulled it apart, spilling the contents across the table. Rae sat up with a start. She looked round the table as if searching for a face and said, 'Tom's gone?'

'Yes, Ma,' said Viv, donning her paper hat. 'He had to go back to London. To the flat. Don't you remember? I explained before lunch. He's been burgled and he has to deal with the police.'

'Alfie's gone too,' Rae said, her expression tragic.

Gwen saw the old woman's eyes fill with tears and took her hand. 'He'll be back tomorrow. As soon as he can.'

'Alfie?' Rae shook her head and her hat slid over her eyes at a rakish angle. 'No, he's gone. Gone for good.'

'*No*, Ma,' Vivien said, barely able to suppress her irritation. 'He'll be back for lunch tomorrow. He promised.'

'And you know he always keeps his promises,' Deborah added.

Rae brightened a little and straightened her hat. 'Tom's a good boy... He'll come back, won't he? Tomorrow, did you say?'

'Yes, that's right. Not long to wait.'

'And he'll have a present for you,' Gwen added, smiling.

'Won't that be exciting?' Vivien said, with forced gaiety. 'Now eat your dinner, Ma, before it gets cold. Who's for more stuffing?'

Deborah lifted her plate eagerly. 'Yes please!'

Rae looked down at her plate and murmured, 'I'm not hungry.' She turned to Gwen and inclining her head, she peered at her face and said, 'Forgive me, my dear, but I've forgotten your name. Is it... Gwyneth?'

'It's Gwen.'

'*Gwen!* Yes, of course... Well, don't worry, Gwen. Alfie will be back tomorrow. He's a good boy. He keeps his promises.' Rae lifted her knife and fork, cut herself a small piece of turkey and lifted it to her mouth. She chewed slowly and began to dissect a potato, then, suddenly defeated, laid down her cutlery with a clatter. She lifted her napkin and held it to her mouth. A faint mewing sound indicated that she'd started to cry.

'Oh, for Christ's sake!' hissed Frances. 'Do you think Tyler would mind if we descended on him for the afternoon? A troop of Polish ghosts playing Musical Chairs would be more fun than this!' She stood up, tossed her napkin on to the table and left the room, taking her wine glass with her.

It was some time before anyone spoke. Deborah picked up the slip of paper that had fallen from Vivien's cracker and unrolled it. She read it and dissolved into giggles. 'Oh, Hattie, where did you get this one? It's a cracker! Oh, I mean—' She became incoherent with laughter again and Hattie, smiling reluctantly, took the paper from her and read aloud, *'What is Santa's favourite pizza?... Deep pan, crisp and even.'*

Gwen joined in with the general laughter, glad of a moment's relaxation. Composed now, Rae looked at her daughters, smiling vaguely, unsure of the meaning of the joke. She looked down at her plate and speared a piece of potato. 'Alfie *will* come back,' she said firmly. 'Because it's Christmas.'

'Yes, Ma,' Vivien replied, her voice as frayed as her nerves. 'That's right. Alfie will be back.'

After lunch, Gwen was banished to the sitting room while the sisters cleared away. She found Frances curled up on the sofa, staring into the fire, her empty wine glass on a side table.

'They still won't let me help,' said Gwen, bending down to the log basket. 'I've been sent to tend the fire.'

Frances didn't look up. 'There's a dishwasher. Viv and Hattie will be arguing over how it should be loaded. Deb will be making an enormous pot of tea and wondering how soon she can plunder the turkey carcase for a sandwich... It's the same every Christmas. It was only ever the men who made it bearable.'

'Men?'

'Alfie. Daniel. There used to be husbands in the old days. Mine and Deborah's. Then there were lovers...' She looked up and added, with an attempt at a smile, '*Mine*, not Deborah's. Now it's just Alfie and a lot of lonely old women... Sorry, I didn't mean to include you in that. I still haven't quite adjusted to the idea of Alfie bringing a girlfriend home for Christmas. It's never happened before. He must think a lot of you. Or alternatively, he doesn't, since he's prepared to inflict his awful family on you.'

Gwen settled down on the hearthrug and watched flames stir around the new log. 'Oh, I'm used to awful families. Not that I think this one *is* awful. But I used to have one of my own. Really awful. I miss it now.'

'Did you have a black sheep?'

'We *only* had black sheep. House rules.'

Frances laughed, showing even white teeth. Gwen could see she'd once been a beauty, perhaps would be still, if her features weren't so tainted with scorn and bitterness. The cold, grey eyes were focussed now, alight with interest. 'Do tell. What did your black sheep do?'

'You name it. Drink. Drugs. Lots of sex. My aunt used to say, "If you can't have success, there's always excess." They lived life to the hilt.'

'Well, good for them!'

'Yes... They're all dead now, unfortunately.'

'Oh. I'm sorry.'

'That's OK. They died a long time ago.'

'Were they happy? Living lives of excess?'

'Oh, no, I don't think so. Briefly, perhaps. My uncle Frank was perpetually in love. Well, what he *called* love. I can't say it ever seemed to make him happy. But then he fell for some pretty unsavoury types. Male,' Gwen added. 'But I think he preferred excitement to happiness anyway. If he was ever in danger of achieving a state of contentment, Uncle Frank would sabotage himself.'

'How?'

'Oh, screwing around. Fits of obsessive jealousy. Getting himself beaten up. Messy stuff.'

'How sad... Who drank?'

'My aunt Samantha. I think there was probably an underlying mental health problem – she suffered terribly with depression – and she managed it with alcohol. Or thought she did. But it killed her in the end.'

'And who did drugs?'

'My mother. She did quite a lot of sex too. She was very beautiful and found it hard to say no. She didn't have loving parents, you see, so when she grew up and got a lot of attention from men, she didn't really know how to handle it. That's what my aunt said, anyway. Beauty was a burden for my mother and it attracted the wrong sort of men. So she lived life in the fast lane. Until she crashed.'

Frances studied the profile of the young woman who had catalogued her family tragedies calmly, without bitterness, with even a touch of irony. Despite herself, Frances was impressed. She'd wondered why Alfie had made an exception and brought Gwen to Creake Hall. When she'd met her, she'd assumed from the pretty face and figure that Alfie must be infatuated, but talking to Gwen, sensing the steel beneath the easy-going surface, Frances was forced to ask herself if, finally, at nearly thirty, Alfie had fallen in love.

It wasn't a comfortable thought. Frances didn't begrudge Alfie his happiness, it was just the sobering realisation that Alfie was no longer a boy, wasn't even really a young man any more. Alfie had grown up and moved on. Found himself a lovely girl, with brains, beauty and a kind heart. And Frances?... Frances was forty-four and about to be divorced for the third time.

If you can't have success, there's always excess.

She began to experience the gnawing hunger that was nothing to do with food; a hunger that was assuaged – briefly – by sex; a hunger that booze, in sufficient quantities, would dull for a few hours. And if she couldn't get laid, why the hell shouldn't she get drunk?

Reaching for her wine glass, Frances was about to go in search of the bottle of Merlot, when her eyes fell on Gwen, sitting on the rug, gazing into the fire, her arms looped around her knees. Frances experienced a pang of something like pity as she remembered the girl was here because she had nowhere else to spend Christmas. Eyeing her empty glass with irritation, Frances said, 'You don't drink, do you?'

'No. I tried a little social drinking at college but I was horribly ill. The doctor said it was an allergy, but I've always wondered if it was some sort of DIY aversion therapy. My system rejecting booze because I'd seen what it did to my aunt.'

'What was your aunt like when she was sober?'

'She was lovely! So much fun! But she lacked self-confidence. I think she was quite shy, actually. She was a singer. Used to play clubs and pubs. And sometimes she worked in the theatre, singing in the chorus. *Phantom of the Opera*, that sort of thing. She wasn't famous, just a jobbing singer. She used to have a drink to calm her nerves before a gig. Then she'd have two. Then there'd be drinks after the show. Other people would buy them for her and she couldn't really say no. Eventually she got it into her head that she needed booze to perform.'

'Maybe that was just her excuse. For drinking.'

'Possibly.'

'Alcoholics are so bloody devious,' Frances muttered. 'Sorry, Gwen. I didn't mean to speak ill of your aunt. I was talking generally.'

'That's OK, I quite agree. Alcoholics *are* bloody devious. They're also bloody boring. But my Aunt Sam *liked* the person she became after she'd had a few. She said, when she had a bottle of wine inside her, she became the person she'd always wanted to be.'

'But it didn't stop at one bottle. Or even two.'

'No, it didn't. And then she stopped liking the person she became. Started hating her.'

'And then she drank because she couldn't stand the monster she'd become.'

Gwen looked at Frances and hesitated before replying, 'Yes, that's right.'

Frances looked down at her manicured hands and examined the fine lines and protruding veins with loathing. There were no brown age spots yet. But they would come. She twisted the rings on her bony fingers, tugging at them viciously, then looked up at Gwen. 'And you say you miss them? This flock of black sheep?'

'Yes, I do. Very much. Especially at Christmas.'

'You must have loved them a great deal, despite their appalling habits. How very generous of you.' She hadn't meant to sound sarcastic. Why was it that even when she tried to be kind, it came out sounding callous?

'I don't think it's so very hard tolerating other people's faults,' Gwen replied. 'I mean, it's much tougher accepting your own, isn't it? Tougher still believing other people can actually accept what you can't. *Love* what you can't.'

'You think self-hatred's a cushy option, then?'

'Yes, compared to self-love, I do. The death certificates say my family died of booze, drugs and AIDS. But what really killed them all was low self-esteem.'

Frances' jaw went slack and her eyes widened with shock, as if she'd been struck.

Gwen had given a lot of thought to her Christmas gifts. She'd asked Alfie about his family, their hobbies and interests and she'd deliberated, drawing up shortlists of possible gifts until she felt certain she'd hit upon the perfect present. Alfie had teased her, saying, 'They won't go to half this trouble for you, you know. You'll be lucky to get a book token.'

'I don't want them to go to any trouble,' Gwen had replied. 'I'm the guest. I should bring gifts. And anyway, I enjoy choosing presents. It isn't a chore for me, it's fun.'

The women in the Holbrook family were delighted with their gifts. Gwen gave Vivien *The Virago Book of Women Gardeners*. Deborah received a selection of aromatherapy oils. Frances was pleased with a vintage Italian silk headscarf and Rae was touched by the gift of an Oloroso sherry – her favourite tipple. Gwen's triumph however was her present for Hattie, who unwrapped her bulky parcel eagerly, tearing at the paper like a child. Inside, she found a large plastic carrier bag sealed with Sellotape. Beside herself with excitement, she ripped at the plastic. As the bag burst open, Hattie was inundated with scraps of fabric. She squealed and fell upon them, sorting through and exclaiming.

'This is Japanese kimono silk, isn't it? And this brocade is just *gorgeous*! And look at this lace! And all the different velvets! Yummy! Gwen, where on earth did you get all these?' 'From the waste bins at the BBC. These are bits and pieces left over from making period costumes, so there are some lovely fabrics there. Most of the pieces are small, but some are a decent size. Alfie told me you did patchwork and other crafts, so I thought you might like a *de luxe* scrap bag. I tried to choose the most interesting bits, things I didn't think you'd have.'

Hattie cast the bag aside and launched herself at Gwen, flinging her arms round her neck. 'Thank you! Thank you! What a wonderful present! It couldn't have been more perfect. I shall make some splendid quilts with these!' She looked up suddenly as an idea dawned. 'I can finish the charm quilt now! We must get cracking on those paper templates later.' With that, Hattie sat cross-legged on the floor and began to sort through the pile of fabric scraps, stroking silks, velvets and satins.

She showed little interest in the rest of the present giving, until it came to her turn to distribute gifts. Hattie presented her mother with hand-knitted bed socks which, after only a cursory glance, Rae set aside. Vivien also received socks, with which she showed every appearance of being pleased. Deborah was given a fluffy knitted scarf in a vibrant shade of green that, as it was unwrapped, caused Frances to wince, but Deborah expressed delight and slung the scarf valiantly round her neck, like a feather boa. Frances' small gift turned out to be a quilted case for sunglasses and she thanked Hattie with reasonable grace, relieved not to have fared worse.

Hattie had insisted that Gwen open her present last. As Hattie hauled it out from under the Christmas tree, watched anxiously by the women, Gwen realised the rest of the family knew what the gift was and were apprehensive, even embarrassed on her behalf. She braced herself, but couldn't help feeling a thrill of excitement as she tore away paper, revealing a cardboard box that had once held a duvet.

Inside the box was a Postage Stamp quilt – a patchwork quilt made like a mosaic with tiny squares of fabric, only slightly bigger than a stamp. Gwen was familiar with the traditional design and estimated there must be three thousand pieces. Shaking out the quilt, she gasped as she realised it was double bed-sized and revised her estimate to six thousand.

Gwen clapped her hand to her mouth in shock and said, 'Hattie, you can't give me this!'

'Why not?'

'This will be a family heirloom one day. It should stay in the family.'

'But I want *you* to have it. You'll appreciate it, what went into the making of it. The family have watched me making it for years and they're all bored to tears with it. And I don't think any of them would ever *use* it. So I'd like you to have it. I think you'll look after it. Maybe,' Hattie added tentatively, 'you'll become fond of it.'

'I love it already! I can't tell you how thrilled I am! This is the best present I've *ever* had. Thank you so much!' Her eyes shining with tears, Gwen put her arms round Hattie and the two women hugged each other, while the rest of the family looked on, bemused but thankful they hadn't been the recipient of Hattie's gaudy *magnum opus*.

As Vivien collected up the discarded wrapping paper and crammed it into a bin liner, Rae turned the pages of the scrapbook Deborah had made for her, recording Alfie's performances over the last year. Frances dozed on the sofa while Deborah and Gwen helped Hattie sort her scraps into cottons suitable for the charm quilt and a pile of more exotic fabrics that she said she would use for special projects.

Deborah held up some brightly coloured satins and taffetas. 'Aren't they lovely? You know, it's never occurred to me, Hattie, but I could bring you home some scraps from school – stuff left over from making the costumes for the Christmas play. The mums make all the outfits but I could ask, if there are any scraps, could they save them for me? It was *Cinderella* this year and the costumes for the ball scene were fabulous!' She turned to Gwen. 'I just love to see the boys dressing up. The girls are used to it, of course – party frocks are nothing special to them, nor is make-up these days

– but the boys get so excited about dressing up in bright colours. Some of them get quite stage-struck. It's so sweet!'

Gwen had been enjoying sorting the fabrics and the chatty companionship of the women, when suddenly she felt her spirits plummet. It took her only a few seconds to work out why. She'd remembered Alfie's letters home from school and the lies he'd told. She got to her feet and carefully folded the postage stamp quilt. 'I'm going to take this upstairs now,' she said to the company at large, avoiding Hattie's eye. 'I think I should keep it out of the way of the fire and cups of tea. I wouldn't want it to get damaged.' She hugged the folded quilt to her chest and left the room.

Gwen spent the rest of Christmas Day removing papers from the Thousand Pyramids quilt while Hattie cut triangles from her new selection of fabrics. Rae and her daughters variously watched TV, dozed or read their new books. The atmosphere was subdued. When Gwen wondered aloud if they should ring Alfie to find out how things were at the flat, there was a long silence, eventually broken by Frances, who looked at Gwen, her expression grave, and said, 'When things go badly wrong for Alfie, he deals with it like a wounded animal. He goes to ground. He'd probably prefer to be left alone.'

There was a note of compassion in her voice that Gwen hadn't heard before. For once Frances didn't appear to be scoring points off Alfie's girlfriend. Her aim seemed to be to spare him further pain. Alfie had said Frances was the sister who knew him best and the rest of the family seemed happy to defer to her judgement. So was Gwen, who felt oddly reluctant to contact him. But the awkward questions wouldn't go away. If Frances wasn't in fact Alfie's sister, how did she know him so well? And why would Frances – hitherto the last word in selfishness – care so much about his welfare?

Gwen bade the family an early goodnight. She tidied the heap of paper triangles into their envelope, folded the Pyramids quilt top and carried them up to her attic room. Getting ready for bed, she felt relieved Christmas Day was over for another year. Things could have been a lot worse.

Though hardly for Alfie... As she lay in bed, open-eyed in the darkness, Gwen contemplated Boxing Day. Alfie would return to Creake Hall. And she would see Marek again. Both events filled her with an unsettling mixture of relief and dread. It was some time before Gwen, still perplexed, fell into an uneasy sleep.

Gwen

I woke up cold. Reaching for the quilt, I realised it had slid on to the floor. I switched on the bedside light and blinked at my watch. Not long after midnight. I got out of bed, dragged the quilt back and settled down again, shivering, but I was wide-awake now. I decided to sit up and read until I felt tired again.

There was a selection of old paperbacks on a small bookcase and my eye lit on a couple of Georgette Heyer's Regency romances – the sort of hot water bottle reads I often turned to in times of ill-health and heart-break. I turned on the fan heater and snuggled down comfortably with the gothic intrigues of *The Reluctant Widow*.

Perhaps the plot was over-familiar. My mind wandered and so did my eyes – over to the table where I'd placed the envelope containing the paper triangles. There were hundreds of them now, many cut from letters sent by Rae's estranged husband and a boy who didn't grow up to become my boyfriend. It was possible those jigsaw pieces of correspondence held answers to some of my questions. I was certain I didn't have the right to read the letters, but, on the other hand, I was equally certain I had the right to know who Alfie was, and it didn't look as if anyone in the Holbrook household was likely to inform me, least of all Alfie.

My eyes moved mechanically over a few more pages of Heyer, taking in nothing, then I shut the book and laid it aside. I got out of bed and fetched the envelope. The room was warmer now, so I switched off the heater and climbed back into bed. I tipped the contents of the envelope on to the quilt and surveyed the pieces.

There seemed no point in examining the boy's letters.

They were unlikely to tell me anything about the man who pretended to be an adult version of their author. That left Freddie's letters, so far unexamined. Freddie, Alfie's father, who left Rae and took their son to live abroad. Rae had said she'd driven him away. She'd talked without rancour of being deserted by the love of her life, of being deprived of her only son, the only child she appeared to love. Surely Freddie's letters would shed some light on the various mysteries of Creake Hall?

My last qualm of conscience was silenced by the reassuring thought that, provided I didn't refer to the contents, no one would ever know I'd read them. On this dubious moral footing, I began to scan Freddie's letters.

He didn't seem like a philanderer. There were only odd phrases of course, but reading those and exercising a little imagination, you could see that this man cared for Rae and was trying to help her recover from some serious illness or mental breakdown. He mentioned Hattie with affection and what appeared to be a sense of responsibility, but I could find nothing about Alfie until I came upon this piece:

preten

to move on

I hope that my

at least one pressure

it does Hattie no good to

to see us quarrel and since we

for ever at odds over our son, separation

"For ever at odds over our son"... It wasn't much to go on but it was evidence of sorts that Alfie himself was what had come between husband and wife.

Another piece referred to Alfie as a baby:

the

amount of

bring him back

wasn't meant to be and

pretend any more that he exi

helped you to cope but I just can't do

for your sake. The baby has come between us

"The baby has come between us"... So even as a baby, Alfie had driven a wedge between them. Why? And what did "bring him back" refer to? Freddie had taken Alfie away as a five year old, not as a baby. I read through several more pieces, then came across one which, when I read it, made me start. Papers slid off the quilt and cascaded on to the floor as I read the words written on the paper triangle I held between trembling fingers.

We must try to come to terms with

that we lost our boy and no

wishing for him will

He <u>died</u>, Rae. It

I just can't

I know it

even

"He <u>died</u>, Rae." I read the words again and then again.

There was no mistaking their meaning. Two lines above those words, Freddie had written, "we lost our boy". Their son had *died*. Not only was my boyfriend not the man he pretended to be, he was pretending to be someone who was dead, someone who had been dead for twenty years and more.

I clapped my hand to my mouth and wondered if I should rush to the bathroom before I was sick. I swallowed down a mouthful of saliva and tried to steady my breathing, staring fixedly at the scrap of paper in my hand. Then I realised I had before me two adjacent sections of letter. What looked like a tea stain had been bisected by the scissors used to cut out the triangles. I matched the two halves of the stain and read:

We must try to come to terms with the . . .

that we lost our boy and no amount of

wishing for him will bring him back

He *died*, Rae. It wasn't meant to be and

I just can't pretend any more that he exi . . .

I know it helped you to cope but I just can't do . . .

even for your sake. The baby has come between us

"I just can't pretend any more that he *exists*." That was surely the missing word? *That* was what had driven Freddie away. And he'd gone *alone*. He'd left Rae because he could no longer cope with her fantasy that their son still lived.

I don't know how long I cried or who I was crying for. I don't know if it was shock, grief or anger. Perhaps all three. When eventually I was able to stop, I reached for my phone on the bedside table and searched for Alfie's number. I stared at the illuminated screen, my thumb poised over the button, then with a strangled sob, I hurled the phone across the room.

I got out of bed, grabbed my cords and a thick jumper and dressed quickly, my body still shuddering with the aftermath of my tears. There was nowhere I could go but I was damned if I was going to spend another minute in this madhouse. I would find a hotel and bang on the door till they let me in. I dragged my case into the centre of the room and started to throw things in. I tossed aside my Christmas gifts, including the scented candles Viv had given me and her jars of home-made jam which I'd so looked forward to eating when I got back to Brighton. I looked round the room to see if I'd forgotten anything.

The Postage Stamp quilt.

How could I take it? And how could I leave it behind?... I sank down on the edge of the bed and started to cry again, cursing the day I'd met Alfie bloody Donovan and his bogus bloody family.

And then I started to panic. I felt so alone. So *completely* alone. I'd not felt so alone since that Christmas morning when it was too quiet and I'd gone downstairs, wondering why there was no stocking at the end of my bed, why Mum was up already and her bed made (which wasn't like her at all), and I'd gone into the kitchen and seen a big heap of clothes in the middle of the floor, only it wasn't a heap of clothes, it was my mother.

Panic drove me out of the attic and down the stairs. Panic drove me past the enormous front door that my fumbling hands couldn't open, drove me on through the kitchen to the back door, which I unlocked, then locked behind me. I stood outside in the snow, staring at the key, stupefied, not knowing what to do with it. I shoved it into my coat pocket and started walking fast, oblivious of the drifted snow that went up over my shoes and was soon soaking the hem of my trousers. I walked like a thing possessed, down the drive, out onto the road and turned, like an automaton, towards the mill, in search of sanity.

The Whole Truth

Chapter Seventeen

Gwen

I stood outside the mill, out of breath, my heart pounding, and looked up. There was a light on. I had three choices. I could knock on the door and hope that Marek was awake. I could walk back to Creake Hall and cry myself to sleep. Or I could stand outside the mill and wait till I died of hypothermia.

As I considered my options I became aware of mournful music in the air. Clearly, I had completely lost it and was now hallucinating. Then I realised the music was coming from inside the mill. It was Marek's cello. I listened for a minute or so, then my frozen feet carried me up the few steps to the front door and I watched as my hand lifted the doorknocker. The sound made me jump. I wanted to turn and run, but there was nowhere to run to, so I stood still and tried to think what I'd say when Marek opened the door.

When he did, I stood blinking in the light from the doorway, blinking too at the sight of his fingerless mittens and the woollen scarf wound round his neck several times. My planned introductory remarks flew out of my head and I said, 'You look like something out of Dickens.'

'And you look like you've seen the ghost of Christmas Past.'

'I think perhaps I have.'

He gazed at me for a moment, his face impassive, then stepped back. 'Come in before you keel over.' He closed the door behind me, saying, 'I won't offer to take your coat. You're not likely to get overheated.' He led the way upstairs to the sitting room. It was lit only by candles – at least twenty by my estimation – and the round, red brick walls made the room feel womb-like. There were bunches of holly and chrysanthemums in jugs scattered around the room. On the table stood a large bowl of apples, an open bottle of red wine and a dish of nuts. Shattered walnut shells littered a plate and a silver nutcracker winked at me in the candlelight. I felt momentarily cheered by the sight. The cello lay abandoned on its side beside a chair and music stand. As Marek moved around the room the candles flickered and the burnished wooden body of the instrument seemed to breathe like a living thing.

He didn't sit, nor did he invite me to. He stood watching me, waiting, his thumbs hooked in the pockets of his jeans. After a long silence, I said, 'I couldn't sleep.'

He indicated the cello with a wave of his mittened hand. 'Neither could I.'

He said nothing more and I knew he was waiting for me to explain. I was determined not to burst into tears again, so with a kind of desperate enthusiasm I said, 'Would you play to me? I stood outside listening for a while. Was it Bach?' He nodded. 'Would you carry on? Please. I think it would calm me. Help me think.'

I braced myself for questions, but none came. Relieved, I sank down on the sofa and stared at my sodden shoes. My feet were numb with cold, but I couldn't find the energy to undo my laces. When I looked up again, Marek was seated, the cello positioned between his legs. He was watching me.

'You really think this will help?'

'Yes, I do. If you wouldn't mind.'

'Do you want to know what I'm playing?'

'Yes, please.'

'I'm going to play the *Prelude* from Bach's Suite no. 2 in D minor.'

'Thank you.'

He gave me another long look, then lifted his bow. The piece was slow, stately and infinitely sad. No sooner had Marek started to play, than he appeared to tune me out. At the concert I'd had a sense that he was trying to communicate the music to us, but this time I felt I was watching something private: a meditation, a dialogue between Marek and the instrument, perhaps between Marek and Bach. It felt almost like eavesdropping. As I listened to the music, my heart rate slowed, the need to scream abated. I became engrossed in the movement of his hands and the fierce expression of concentration on his face, which softened occasionally as he lifted his head, closed his eyes and moved his lips slightly, as if he were singing with the instrument. The candlelight played on the strong bones of his face and made his skin glow. When he opened his eyes, they seemed to burn – if something so dark can be said to burn.

When, after a few minutes, the music stopped, Marek sat very still, the neck of the cello resting against his shoulder. I stared at the instrument, envious and exhausted, wishing I could do likewise. He laid his bow down on the music stand and said, 'Why have you come?'

'I needed to see you.'

'It couldn't wait till morning? Should I feel flattered?'

'Marek, Alfie's dead.'

'*What?*'

'Rae's son. Alfie. He's dead. He died years ago. There are letters written by his father. I've seen them. Alfie died as a child. As a baby, I think. So my boyfriend – my *ex*-boyfriend – is an impostor. *And they all know!* I couldn't bear to spend another minute in that house, so I came here. I'm sorry, but it's freaked me out and I didn't know where else to go.'

'I said you were welcome any time. And you are.'

'You don't seem very surprised.'

'That you came here?'

'That Alfie – *my* Alfie – is a fake.'

'There's not much you could tell me about families that would surprise me. So no, I'm not all that surprised. It explains a lot, in fact.'

'But why would anyone *do* such a thing? Why would anyone go to such lengths? I mean, how many years has this been going on? They filmed a documentary with Alfie – *my* Alfie – eleven years ago! He's been playing the part for eleven years at least! How could anyone do that? Give up their own life and assume somebody else's? And why would the family *want* him to do it? It's just... madness! But they can't *all* be mad, surely?'

'It's not necessarily madness. It might just be a communal

195

fantasy. Something they all share. When did the child die?'

'I don't know. The letter just refers to him being dead. Freddie – that was Rae's second husband – was obviously trying to get her to come to terms with it.'

'Rae didn't accept her son's death?'

'Apparently not.'

'Then the fantasy might have been going on since he died.'

I looked at Marek in disbelief. 'You mean, the boy died... and everyone carried on pretending he was *alive*? But that's insane!'

'No, not if they all know that's what they're doing. It's just collusion. On a surprising scale.'

'It's horrible! It's *sick*.'

'Well, it's certainly not healthy. But it's a way of coping. Sometimes the dead just won't lie down. They live on. In people's minds. So they're kept alive in the memory. Sometimes the dead won't even stay in the past. Children especially. The bereaved imagine the child growing up... They fantasise about what sort of person he would have become... They observe anniversaries – not just of the death, but of the birth, so the child appears to grow up. To have a *post mortem* "life".' I stared at Marek who now appeared to be talking not to me, but to himself. His eyes had clouded over, as if he wasn't seeing me any more, wasn't seeing anything. 'It's a strange sort of comfort, I suppose. And perhaps a form of punishment. For surviving.'

'Marek... you're not talking about Alfie, are you? The dead child.'

He lifted the cello away from his chest and laid it down on the floor, then he sat up slowly, placed his hands on his knees and looked at me, searching my face for something. I didn't look away, though it was hard not to. He appeared to come to some decision and, without taking his eyes from mine, said, 'I am talking about a dead child. I'm not talking about Alfie Donovan.'

'Marek, what happened to you?'

'Nothing happened to me. Something happened to somebody else.'

'What?'

'Death.'

'Would you rather not—'

'Yes, I would rather not talk about it, Gwen, but unless you leave soon, I think we could end up in bed together. If that were to happen, I'd like you to know who you'd be getting into bed with.'

'Because, of course, I *have* known who I've been sleeping with for the last five months!'

'That seems like all the more reason for me to be straight with you. I imagine you feel in need of some authenticity. Isn't that why you're here?'

'Yes... It is.'

Marek went to the table and re-filled his glass. He turned to me. 'None for you, right?'

'No, thanks.'

He sat down in an armchair and studied his glass. Eventually he drank. He still said nothing but, watching his hands, I feared for the glass. I was about to speak when Marek said in a clear voice that shattered the silence, 'I killed a child. She was called Anna. She was five years old.'

After an eternity of silence, I said, 'It was an accident?'

'Yes.'

'Was she... your daughter?'

'No.' He raised the glass to his lips and drank again. 'If she'd been my daughter it might have been easier. That would have been crime and punishment in one. Anna was just a little girl I hardly knew. A neighbour's child. In the wrong place, at the wrong time.'

I waited but when he said nothing more, I asked, 'Do you want to tell me what happened?'

'If you're prepared to listen.'

'Yes, I am.'

He stared at the wine in his glass. 'It happened in 1996. August. I was driving home. I hadn't been drinking. I wasn't using a mobile. I wasn't even talking to a passenger... I was almost home, doing about forty. And Anna ran out into the road. Right in front of me. I braked, but I didn't stand a chance. Nor did she. I hit her and she flew up into the air.

Spinning... The car was still moving and she came down on top of the bonnet. I watched it dent with her weight... Then she hit the windscreen... She looked at me through the glass. She was still alive and her eyes were open. She looked... *astonished*. The car came to a halt and she was thrown off the bonnet, on to the road. She was dead by the time they got her to hospital.'

A log shifted in the wood-burning stove and Marek turned his head towards the glow of the fire. As he continued, his face was as expressionless as his voice.

'She was being chased by a dog. Anna's older sister said she'd been teasing a neighbour's dog. It turned nasty and she ran away. The dog ran after her and Anna ran in to the road to get away... There were several witnesses and they all said there was nothing I could have done. She just... ran out in front of the car. I was exonerated from all blame.

'I knew the family slightly. My wife was a nursery teacher and taught Anna, so we used to see them at school events, sometimes at the supermarket. But I didn't know anything about her when I killed her. I couldn't even remember her name... But I know a lot about her now. I made it my business to find out... She would be seventeen now. She would have been seventeen on April 3rd. She liked swimming and ballet and had a cat called Twinkle. Her baby brother was called Andrew and her sister was called Sophie... My wife told me all this. She didn't want to, but I insisted. Sarah – my wife – knew all about Anna. And I wanted to know. I *needed* to know. And Sarah thought it might help. It didn't.' He swallowed some more wine. 'The family never spoke to us again. They moved from the area as soon as they could. I took time off work, then I went back. Too soon probably. I didn't cope well. Everyone was very understanding. Even the papers had pointed out I wasn't to blame, but I still felt guilty. Anna was dead because of me. If I'd taken a different route home, if I'd left work earlier or later, if I'd been driving slower, Anna would still be alive.

'In the end I cracked up. So did my marriage. Sarah needed to move on. She wanted kids. And I didn't. I wouldn't allow myself that. She said it was a form of self-inflicted punishment and I suppose it was, but it punished her too. I knew what I was doing to Sarah, but I couldn't face having a child. What if we'd had a daughter? What right had I to a child when I'd killed someone else's? Sarah said I was irrational. Eventually she said I was mad. I knew she was right, but it didn't affect how I felt. The only way I could live with what I'd done was to punish myself. Make sure I never forgot Anna. It felt like the least I could do. Honour her memory. Keep it alive.'

He leaned forward, set his glass down on the coffee table, then sat with his hands clasped, his shoulders hunched.

'I had a breakdown. When I recovered I knew I couldn't go back to psychiatry. I felt a fraud. So I told Sarah... She said she needed to make a fresh start too. And she'd met somebody else... I totally understood. She was only thirty-three. And she'd stood by me for four years. The split was amicable. She married again and had twins. Two boys. I re-trained as a gardener and moved to Norfolk. I met Viv at a horticultural show and we got talking. She asked me if I wanted to work at Creake Hall. It was a bigger job than I'd ever done, more responsibility, but I liked Viv and she liked me. I felt ready for a challenge. And having the mill thrown in with the job made it easier to make ends meet.'

'Does Viv know? About your past?'

'She knows I used to be a psychiatrist, nothing more. She'll have guessed about the breakdown from the gaping hole in my CV, but she probably assumes that practising psychiatry within the NHS is enough to drive a man to the brink. And I wouldn't say she was wrong... Viv doesn't ask questions. And I don't ask *them* any questions. But if the brother died and they felt they had to keep him alive somehow... well, I wouldn't be all that surprised.' He turned his head and watched a guttering candle as it flickered, then went out. 'The dead don't let go easily.' He looked at me and added, 'You know that yourself.'

The wind had got up and was howling round the mill. The candle flames shuddered in the draught from the window and another went out. When I finally spoke I was surprised to find my voice sounded quite steady – as calmly

199

dispassionate as Marek's. 'After my mother died, I used to think about how things might have turned out differently. If I'd woken up sooner... If I'd rung for the ambulance instead of screaming the place down. She seemed dead to me when I found her, but maybe she was still alive... If I'd had a nightmare on Christmas Eve and woken up and gone to find her, maybe she wouldn't have taken the drugs that killed her... In the end I felt responsible for her death – still do, in a way – simply because I didn't prevent it.'

'You were how old? Twelve?'

'Yes.'

'That's a typical reaction. A bright twelve-year-old would blame her mother or herself, not the dealer, or the culture that makes drug-taking socially acceptable in some circles. And a bright twelve-year-old with an over-developed sense of responsibility would blame herself, not her mother. But blaming yourself for her death didn't stop you feeling abandoned, did it? The usual game the mind plays in these circumstances is, "If my mother had really loved me, if I'd been *enough* for her, she wouldn't have needed the drugs." Right?'

I nodded, unable to speak.

'What the brain knows and what the heart feels, are two completely different things. Often irreconcilable. But both are true. I knew I wasn't to blame for Anna's death but I felt I should have been punished. So for years I punished myself. Now I'm on parole, I suppose, but my mind makes sure I never forget. I have flashbacks... Every April I remember Anna's birth and every July I remember her death. They're events on my calendar. She lives on in my head. Her *death* lives on in my head. It's a life sentence.'

'But that's not the whole story, is it? I mean, how many lives did you *save*?'

'What do you mean?'

'When you were a psychiatrist, how many patients did you save from suicide?'

His shrug was dismissive. 'You never know. You only know about the ones you lose. Occasionally people recover and keep in touch. Send you photos of their graduation or their kids. But most people just want to move on. They want to forget the hell they've been through. Understandably.'

'But can you try to estimate? How many lives do you *think* you saved during your working life?'

He looked at me and smiled. 'I see what you're driving at. Very clever... But you can never really say. A correct diagnosis of manic depression could save a life. ECT saves lives. A strong therapeutic relationship with a doctor can be the difference between a patient living and dying.'

'A conservative estimate, Marek. How many?'

He sighed and ran an exasperated hand over his head, leaving his short white hair standing up on end. He looked years younger, almost boyish. 'I practised for ten years. I suppose I was instrumental in saving a few lives a year.'

'Three? Five?'

'More like five. But there are so many different factors!' he added hurriedly. 'So many different agencies are involved. It's never down to one person.'

'But,' I persisted, 'your conservative estimate is that you were instrumental in saving maybe five lives a year for ten years?'

'Fifty lives don't cancel out Anna's death.'

'Of course not! But you must see her death – which wasn't your fault – in the context of the big picture. People *die*. Some take their lives, some die in accidents, like Anna, like my mother. If you *really* want to beat yourself up, you could dwell on the fact that when you gave up psychiatry, you stopped saving lives at the rate of about five a year. When did you give up?'

'Eight years ago.'

'So perhaps forty people have died as a consequence of you abandoning your work as a psychiatrist.' He opened his eyes and fixed me with a look that alarmed me, but I pressed on. 'Do you beat yourself up about that?'

'No.'

'Why not?'

'Because another psychiatrist took on my caseload. My patients weren't just abandoned.'

'But can't you see, Marek? Anna might have died in some

other way. She might have contracted meningitis. She might have been abducted by a paedophile and murdered. She might have grown up to be a junkie and died on the kitchen floor while her child slept... Life is terminal! *All* life! But your sense of guilt has blinded you to the bigger picture. You were responsible for a death *and* you've saved many lives. And improved the quality of many more. I'm not saying the books balance, but a lifetime of guilt isn't going to make them balance. It's never going to confer any kind of *meaning* on Anna's death.'

'What would?'

'*Nothing!* It was an appalling accident that wrecked several lives, including yours. You can't forget it and you shouldn't try, but you should show the same compassion to yourself that you'd show to a twelve-year-old girl who didn't wake up in time to save her mother's life. Time and kindness, Marek – you said it! That's all there is to help us get over these terrible, meaningless things. And that means being kind to *yourself*. Seeing yourself as others see you. As *I* see you.'

'And how do you see me, Gwen?'

'As a good man. An unlucky man. And a man who has suffered enough.'

He shook his head. 'There's no end to it.'

'I know. But if the wounds start to heal, there's surely no need to tear them open again. That's not heroism, that's *masochism*.'

His eyes widened and he laughed. 'You're one hell of a girl, Gwen! You take no prisoners.' He looked at me and a weary smile lingered on his lips.

'Marek, you told me your story because you thought it would make a difference. A difference to how I felt about you.'

'Does it?'

'No. None at all. If anything it makes me care even more. I hate to see you suffer like this!'

He didn't reply for a long time, then he emptied his wine glass and said, 'Thank you. I really appreciate all that you've said.' He got up and set the glass down on the table, then glanced at his watch. He turned and stood looking down at me. 'It's late. Shall I walk you back to Creake Hall?'

I looked up and stared at his face, trying to find the answer to his question, then said, 'No. I don't want to go yet.' Reaching up, I took his hand in mine. I tugged at the coarse woollen mitten, slid it off and let it fall to the floor. I pressed his warm palm against my cheek, then took his other hand and removed the second mitten. Marek said nothing and he didn't move. I rose to my feet and found myself standing very close to him, so close I could feel his breath on my face. I shrugged off my coat and let it fall back onto the sofa behind me, then I began to unwind the long woollen scarf that encircled his neck, exposing his throat, swarthy with black stubble. I dropped the scarf on to the floor and placed my palms on his chest, feeling it rise and fall as he breathed unevenly. I moved a hand to where I could feel his heart beating and laid my head on his chest.

'You're alive, Marek... And I'm alive... We've surely had enough to do with death.'

I raised my head to look at him. After a moment I felt his long fingers cradle my head, threading themselves through my hair. Then Marek bent and kissed me, a bruising kiss that knocked me off-balance, so that I might perhaps have staggered if his arms hadn't gone round me and held me tight against him, as if he never wanted to let me go.

Chapter Eighteen

Marek woke with a jolt, flinging a hand in the direction of the alarm. Lying on his back, still half-asleep, he felt confused, oppressed by a great weight on his chest. As memory returned, he lifted an exploratory hand and found the weight was Gwen's head. Her hair was spread out over his naked chest and he lay for a moment, luxuriating in the feeling and the realisation that her body lay along the length of his, pressed against him, as she clung to him even in sleep.

He moved his other hand and laid it gently on the curve of her waist, then ran his palm down over her hip and thigh. He thought of his cello and smiled into the darkness. His smile faded when he remembered Alfie. Marek had a lot to feel guilty about, but until now, sleeping with another man's woman had not been one of his sins. Whoever Alfie was, he'd known him for five years and had nothing against the man, even if he didn't particularly like him. Marek had always thought there was something insincere about Alfie, but he'd put it down to the superficiality of actors.

Apart from kissing Gwen in the car on Christmas Eve, Marek had made no attempt to seduce her. His conscience was clear about that. Even last night, when she'd indicated she didn't want to leave, he hadn't touched her. But he'd waited to be touched, knew that she would touch him. Whatever it was between them was strong and it had been strong from the very start. He could see why, now he knew more about her. She appeared to be an independent young woman. (How young? He didn't even know how old she was.) But that was only half the story. The other half was the way she held him now, like someone shipwrecked, clinging to a piece of flotsam (yes, that was a good word to describe him) as she struggled to stay afloat.

Gwen shifted in her sleep and he felt her breasts move

against his ribcage, her thigh slide against his. He tried to ignore the stirring in his groin and turned his head to look at the illuminated display on the clock: 05.30. He should get her back to Creake Hall before Viv organised a search party. He twisted so that her head rolled away and he eased himself out from under her. As she woke, she murmured and clutched at him. He thought afterwards that he'd rarely shown more self-restraint than in that moment, when his body had longed to take her again, half-sleeping. Instead, he stroked her hair and said her name softly.

'We need to get up. You have to go back. Someone will be up soon.'

She moaned and rolled towards him, but he anticipated her move and shifted across the bed. He switched on the bedside light and she groaned again, shielding her eyes. He sat up and looked down at her: her hair tangled; her eyes puffy with sleep; her forehead furrowed against the light. She was beautiful. A thought ambushed him: *I don't get this lucky.* He pushed it away and bent his head to kiss her.

'Thank you for my Christmas present.'

She smiled sleepily and stroked the silky black hair on his chest. 'You're very welcome.'

'I hope it's not going to be like one of those single-use cameras. Christmas Day only.'

'Oh, no. Hours of fun guaranteed. But some small parts,' she said, pulling him down towards her, 'are not suitable for children under three...'

Gwen

I lay in bed and watched as Marek dressed, admiring the loose, long-limbed elegance that his work clothes completely obscured. He caught me watching him and raised an eyebrow.

'That's an appraising look.'

'I'm a wardrobe mistress. I'm estimating your inside leg measurement. Force of habit.'

'Do you want breakfast before you shower?'

'No, thanks. I'll have to do breakfast when I get back to

Creake Hall. I'll eat some of Hattie's porridge as an act of contrition.' Marek sat down on the edge of the bed and appeared to study me. I pulled a face. 'And *that's* an appraising look.'

'I'm a psychiatrist. Force of habit.' He leaned forward and kissed me, then said, 'Gwen... all this has happened very fast. You might want some time to take stock. I know you think it's all over with Alfie and I understand why, but... well, you might not want to get into something else straight away.'

I laid a hand on his thigh. 'I think I already did.'

'I'm saying you can back off. I think you'll have to, until you've dealt with Alfie. And I assume you won't do that in Norfolk.'

'Not unless I have to.'

'When are you leaving?'

'Alfie said the day after Boxing Day.'

'Tomorrow, then.'

'Is it? I've lost track. I know he was keen to get away as soon as possible. So am I now. All the women in that family seem devoted to him and that doesn't seem to be an act. Once they realise I've finished with Alfie, I don't think I'll be Miss Popular any more. It's not even as if I can tell them why it's over.'

'You're referring to the false identity thing, not me?'

'Yes. It wasn't really anything to do with you, Marek. You're just an added complication.'

'Give it to me straight, Gwen. Don't feel you have to protect my fragile male ego.'

I slid the hand that rested on his thigh high enough to deter interruptions and continued. 'It was over between Alfie and me as soon as I realised he was a fake. I mean, I don't expect perfection in a guy, but pretending to be someone you're not? I don't care what the reason is, it's not OK. And what reason could there be, but money? You know, I could almost understand if it was just a part he played at Christmas, to keep some rich old lady happy. There *is* something of the tart about Alfie, now I come to think about it. And he'd be the first to admit it.'

'That might not be the cause. It could be the effect of

spending your life rôle-playing.'

'I suppose so... I do like him. I mean, I *did*. We got on really well. But now that I know... Well, the whole thing just gives me the creeps. I don't think I could bear for him to touch me now. Am I over-reacting?'

'I don't think so. You're responding to a betrayal of trust. And there's a great deal of trust implicit in a sexual relationship.'

'Is that why you told me about your past?'

'My past is me. You needed to know.'

'And Alfie's past is... completely unknown.'

'Not completely. We know that there was something about his past that made him abandon it altogether for a past that wasn't his. A better version, presumably.'

'Couldn't he be doing it just for money? Rae's seriously rich, isn't she?'

'Yes, he could, but I think there's probably more to it than that. Is money what Alfie's about?'

'No, not really.'

'What does he want most in the world?'

I thought for a moment, then said, 'Recognition. To be taken seriously as an actor. As a *good* actor.'

'Is he good?'

'Well, he fooled me! And he's fooled the world for at least eleven years. So, yes, I'd say he was bloody good.'

'So it's not likely to be about money, then.'

'But what else could it be?'

'There are three motives for human behaviour.'

'Only three?'

'Basically, yes.'

'And they are?'

'Love. Loathing. And lucre. If you don't think Alfie's doing it for the money—'

'Well, maybe he did to begin with, but he doesn't need to now. He doesn't much like the type of work he gets, but he earns a decent living and he doesn't have an expensive lifestyle.'

'Could he be doing it for love?'

'Love of whom? Rae? Hattie? Why would he love them

when they aren't even his family? Anyway, I know he doesn't love them. He treats them quite badly really. Hattie's the only one he seems fond of. He shows none of them any affection.'

'That doesn't necessarily mean there's no love.'

'I think it does with Alfie. He's quite an affectionate person. Demonstrative. In fact, that was one of the first things I noticed when we got here – how cold he was towards his sisters. It just wasn't like him. He didn't even go through the motions of brotherly love.'

'Well, that leaves loathing, then.'

'As his motive? But who does he loathe? Frances is a pain in the arse, but he actually seems to like her. The others are all so kind... and *grateful* to him. And Rae obviously dotes on him, whether she knows who he is or not. So why would he loathe any of them?'

'You're forgetting someone.'

'Someone Alfie loathes?'

Marek shrugged. 'Maybe.'

'Who?'

'Himself.'

Marek made tea while I got dressed. I struggled into my damp shoes and put on my coat and scarf. He insisted on accompanying me back to Creake Hall with a flashlight. As it was still dark outside, I didn't protest.

I followed him down the flights of stairs to the front door and stood watching while he put on his coat. 'You're coming for lunch later today, right?'

'That's the plan.'

'And when you do, we haven't seen each other since I took you home with the cello after the concert.'

'OK.'

'I'm feeling horribly guilty. Like a conspirator.'

'Gwen, we'll be the only people at Creake Hall who *aren't* party to a massive conspiracy! Are you ready?'

I lifted a long scarf from a peg and looped it over his head, then wound it round his neck several times.

He grinned at me. 'I liked it better the other way.'

208

'You'd better not smile at me like that, or our cover will be completely blown.'

As he unlocked the front door I suddenly remembered the first time he'd opened it to me, on Christmas Eve. As we stood on the top step and he closed the door behind us, I turned to him and said, 'Can I give you a word of advice?'

' "Out of the mouth of babes and sucklings..." How old *are* you, Gwen?'

'You should never ask a woman her age,' I replied, following him down the steps.

'Is that the advice?'

'No.' I took his arm and we picked our way through the snow onto the road where it was clearer. 'How old do you think I am?'

'Older than you look. Younger than you sound.'

'I'm twenty-six.'

He whistled. 'Jesus... I'm cradle-snatching.'

'But you have to admit, I'm a very mature twenty-six.'

'To the extent that you give advice to men old enough to be your father.'

'For all I know, you *are* my father.'

'Now there's a Freudian thought... I make it a rule never to sleep with people whose names I don't know.'

'What a good idea. I think I shall do that in future.'

'What was your mother called?'

'Sasha.'

Marek thought for a moment, then said, 'No, I never slept with a Sasha. I'd remember a name like that.'

'In which case, I can give you my piece of advice.'

'Go ahead. I'm braced.'

'Don't answer the door to women in your pyjamas.'

'I'm *sorry*?'

'It just isn't fair. And you can see where it all leads.'

'Those grey things? They're ancient! And completely shapeless.'

'But you, Marek, *aren't*. Just bear it in mind. You get some very odd people knocking on doors these days.'

'In the middle of the night.'

'Exactly.'

'Thanks for the warning.'

'You're welcome. And about those fingerless mittens—'

'Too provocative?'

I nodded. 'Bit of a double message. Possibly not one you intend.'

'It never crossed my mind... It's a minefield, isn't it?' He was thoughtful for a moment, then said, 'I can see a relationship with a wardrobe mistress could have wide-reaching repercussions.'

' "Clothes make the man. Naked people have little or no influence on society." '

'Who said that?'

'Mark Twain.'

'Well, you can't argue with that.'

As we approached Creake Hall, I started to feel uneasy. As if reading my mind, Marek said, 'I'll come in with you. Just to check everything's OK,' he added vaguely. 'You've got a key?'

'I put it in my coat pocket when I left.'

We stood at the back door and stamped snow off our shoes. I unlocked the door and we walked into the lobby. As we wiped our feet, Marek laid a hand on my arm and pointed to a light under the kitchen door. 'Someone's up,' he whispered.

'No, I must have left the light on. I was in an awful state when I left the house.' His arm went round my waist and he pulled me against him in a protective gesture. I held on to him for a moment, then opened the door to the kitchen, blinking against the light. As my eyes adjusted, I was horrified to see Hattie asleep at the kitchen table, her head pillowed on her arms. I turned round quickly to send Marek away but she was already stirring. 'Gwen! Where've you *been*? I was so worried about you.' She sat upright, sweeping her long curls away from her face, then smiled uncertainly. 'Tyler! What on earth are *you* doing here so early?'

He didn't answer and I watched Hattie's face as she reached her own conclusions. It wasn't a comfortable experience, for her or for me. Shocked and clearly unhappy, she said, 'Does Alfie know? About you two?'

'There was nothing to know until last night... I went to see Tyler – *Marek* – because I was very upset.'

'I know. I heard you crying when I went to the bathroom. I thought maybe you'd rung Alfie and had a row. Then I heard you get up. I didn't know whether to come and find you or not. I never know what to do when someone cries. Some people like to be left alone, don't they?' I didn't answer her question and Hattie went on. 'I came down to check up on you, but by the time I got to the kitchen, you'd gone. The light was on, so I thought you must have gone out for some fresh air or something. But I was worried, so I waited... I must have fallen asleep. What time is it now?'

Marek looked at his watch and said, 'Six-thirty'.

'Is it really? I've been asleep for hours then.' She got to her feet and stood the kettle on the hot plate, then turned round and leaned against the Aga. 'Why were you so upset, Gwen?'

I took off my coat and slung it on the back of a chair. 'I found out about Alfie.'

Hattie turned pale. Her mouth twisted and for a moment I thought she was actually going to scream. She stared at me, her eyes wild, like an animal's. It was horrible. Barely able to control her voice, she said, 'What do you mean?'

'I read Freddie's letters to Rae. The fragments sewn into the quilt top. They said that Alfie died. As a child. Freddie said that's what drove him away – Rae's fantasy that her dead son still lived.' Hattie lifted both hands and covered her mouth. I could see from her shaking body that she'd started to cry, but I was too angry to care. 'You're all in on it, aren't you? Every one of you.'

She dragged her fingers away and stood with her shoulders hunched, her fists clenched at her side. She swallowed down a sob. 'We do it... for Rae.'

'Why?'

'I can't tell you, Gwen!'

'Hattie, for five months I've been sleeping with a man who is an impostor. He's lied to me about his name, his childhood, his family – *everything*. You've *all* lied to me! This

Christmas was a lie, this whole family is a lie! You have to tell me *why*. Somebody owes me that, surely? Tell me why and then I'll leave. I'm not going to wait for Alfie. I don't want to see him ever again. I'm going to pack my things, then I'm going back to the mill. When the trains start running again, I'm going back to Brighton.'

'Please don't go, Gwen! Not yet! Please stay and explain to Alfie. He'll be so angry.'

I exploded. '*He'll* be angry? Give me strength!'

'He was so worried one of us would let the cat out of the bag! He'll think it was me, I know he will! He made us promise we wouldn't say anything in front of you. He really cares about you, Gwen. Honestly! All this *deception*, it isn't really Alfie's fault. It's mine. All of it.'

'Don't be ridiculous. Rae must have started all this when you were a small child. How can it be your fault?'

She shook her head, vehemently. 'You don't understand, it *is* my fault. They did it to spare Rae.' Her voice dropped to a whisper. 'And to spare me.'

'You're not making any sense, Hattie.'

She spoke rapidly then, the words tumbling over themselves, her eyes beseeching me to understand. 'Rae wouldn't accept that he'd died, you see. She went out of her mind! She insisted that the baby was still alive. She talked about him, she talked *to* him! She kept the nursery just as it was, with all the little baby clothes in drawers, all the toys on shelves. We had to pretend – *all* of us – because if we didn't, it would have destroyed her. She was mad with grief, Gwen! And the pretence seemed harmless. No one was being hurt. No one was being deceived, not then. We all knew what was going on. And why... My father found it very difficult apparently, but even he went along with Rae's fantasy. It just became a way of life. The doctors said Rae would recover, that she'd snap out of it eventually. But she didn't. Well, not before Freddie left her. He stuck it for five years, then he gave her an ultimatum. She must accept Alfie was dead or he would leave... But she couldn't do it! It wasn't fair to ask – she wasn't in her right mind. So my father left us... I was eleven. He asked me if I wanted to go with him, but I wanted to stay with Viv. She was really the only mother I'd ever known. She'd looked after me while Rae was ill, you see. So I chose to stay at Creake Hall. With Viv.'

'Go on,' I said, sitting at the table.

'Rae's version of what happened was that Freddie had taken Alfie to live abroad. She said Freddie believed she wasn't a fit mother, that she was too ill to be allowed to look after a small child. It was all lies of course, but we pretended it was true. For her sake. We let her play the martyr.' The kettle came to the boil. Hattie took it off the hotplate, turned back and looked at Marek, then at me, her eyes pleading. 'What else could we do?... It was another five years before Rae came out of it. One day she just started writing. A story started pouring out of her, about a twelve year-old boy, called Tom Dickon Harry. She stopped talking about Alfie. She stopped sitting in the nursery for hours, playing with the toys and talking to herself. She sat at her desk, day after day, scribbling away at this book. Then when she finished it, she started another.'

Hattie pulled out a chair and sat down at the table again, her head in her hands. 'TDH took over her life. She talked about him as if he was a real person, as if he was her *son*. But she knew he wasn't. It was just wishful thinking and she knew it. In those days she wasn't mad. But she wasn't quite sane either... When the first book was accepted for publication, she told her new editor that TDH was based on her son, who lived abroad with his father. A harmless lie, we thought. You see, no one expected the book to *sell*. It was so old-fashioned! But to everyone's surprise, it was a huge success. Word got out about Rae's "inspiration". Interviewers asked her about Alfie and she just... *lied*. Lied and lied! She had to, or she would have been discredited. So Viv took charge and tried to limit the damage. She was wonderful. She dealt with all the PR stuff. She vetted the questions put to Rae and she stopped her doing interviews in person. She even did telephone interviews herself, pretending to be Rae! We thought everything would be all right. Rae was writing all the time and answering hundreds of letters from children. The books made her so happy! And they made an awful lot of money, enough to allow us to stay on at Creake Hall, to maintain the garden and the fabric of the building.

'Then one day the BBC rang. They wanted to make a documentary. About the books. And our family. Viv was out and Rae took the call. They sold her the idea. She was going to be presented as the new Enid Blyton, only better. The film would acknowledge her position as one of Britain's foremost writers for children. Well, Rae was always susceptible to flattery. She just lapped it up. And she said *yes*. When Viv found out, she hit the roof! She said it was just impossible. The filmmakers would want to know all about Alfie, would actually want to interview him and Rae would be exposed as a fraud. Viv insisted she withdraw. But Rae wouldn't! So we had to find someone to pretend to be Alfie. Just for the documentary.'

Hattie looked up then, startled, as if she'd heard a noise. Her eyes became fearful again, but I pressed her. 'That was eleven years ago, wasn't it?'

'Yes.'

'So Alfie's been playing the part for eleven years.'

'Yes... But it was never meant to be like that!' she added hurriedly. 'Things went wrong, you see.'

'Hattie, you have to tell me – who *is* Alfie?'

She was about to reply when she suddenly turned her head and, looking over my shoulder, uttered an indeterminate cry. I wheeled round and saw Alfie standing in the kitchen doorway, his face haggard and unshaven. He didn't smile. 'Who am I, Gwen?...' His body sagged and he leaned against the doorframe. 'That's a very good question.'

'Alfie... You're back.' Hattie stood up and for a moment I thought she might throw her arms around him, but instead she said, 'I didn't hear the car... Have you slept at *all*?'

'No. By the time I'd finished clearing up, I just wanted to get away... I parked on the road. I didn't want to wake anyone. It didn't occur to me you'd organise a reception committee.' He looked at me, then at Marek. 'So tell me, Tyler, are you enjoying a nocturnal intrigue with my sister or my girlfriend?'

'She's not your sister,' I said. 'And I'm not your girlfriend.

Not any more.' Alfie flinched, almost imperceptibly. His eyes narrowed and he looked at me, his expression unfathomable. I felt frightened then, afraid of this man about whom I knew almost nothing, but anger came to my rescue. 'Who the bloody hell *are* you, Alfie?'

'Not sure I can answer that,' he said, removing his coat. He pulled out a chair and sat down. 'But I can tell you who I *was*. And *what* I was...' He paused, looked up expectantly and waited. Hattie sat but Marek didn't move from his position leaning against the kitchen worktop, his arms folded. He stood between Alfie and me and I was glad of that.

Alfie looked at me for a long moment, then leaned forward and rested his hands, loosely clasped, on the table. He appeared to study them. 'What I *was*... was unwanted. I can hardly remember my mother, but my father – if he *was* my father – certainly made an impression on me. With whatever blunt instrument came to hand. Dad was a drunk and he used to beat Mum up when he'd had a skin-full. Eventually he beat her to death. In front of me. I ran out into the street screaming for help and I didn't stop running. I never have.' After a pause Alfie said, 'I've always wondered whether he wasn't actually my father, just my mother's pimp. Money seemed to change hands frequently. It would be nice to think that bastard was no blood relation. But perhaps any father is better than none. Would you agree, Gwen?... But I digress. The man I called Dad was put away and when they found me, I was taken into care. I was fostered by a succession of worthy women, but no one ever wanted to adopt me. I wasn't surprised. I was a fat, unprepossessing child, too old to feed the fantasies of the childless. Then, in my teens, I got difficult and started throwing my considerable weight around. Chip off the old block, perhaps? At thirteen I was as tall as I am now and my foster mother couldn't do anything with me, so she asked the authorities to take me away. And they did.'

Alfie was silent. His head was bowed and I couldn't see his face, but his hands no longer looked relaxed. They remained clasped but the knuckles were white. He took a deep breath and continued. 'I was put in a children's home and there I stayed, for the rest of my childhood, surrounded by all the stories, the personalities, the triumphs and the tragedies of the children who lived there.' He looked up and smiled. 'It was a wonderful training ground for an actor, growing up with the dregs of humanity. Well, let's face it, *I* was the dregs of humanity. I dare say I might have followed in my nefarious father's footsteps, if I hadn't been sent to a good school. Just the local comprehensive, but I was bright and adaptable. I was able to associate with a different class of child there and I absorbed their accents, their lives, the way they moved, their self-confidence. I didn't have it, but I learned how to imitate it. I was a sponge. I soaked up *everything*.

'I came to the attention of the English teacher. Mrs Gower. She discovered me. She was a teacher of the old school and she set us poetry to learn by heart. I actually learned it. And *liked* it. Liked the sound of my own voice, I suspect, but my enthusiasm was duly noted by Mrs Gower and she encouraged me. And I responded... One day she took us to the theatre to see *Hamlet*. I'd never been to the theatre before and I... fell in love. With the theatre, with Shakespeare, with the idea of being an actor, of pretending to be somebody else. Which is what I did anyway, all the time. It had never occurred to me you could get paid for doing it. But here was this guy on stage, this actor, pretending to be a man who was pretending to be mad. Or was he?'

Alfie spread his hands. 'I wanted to be him. I'd spent my whole life wanting to be other boys – thinner, richer, more good-looking boys, boys with families, pets, proper homes, but now I wanted to be that man. An *actor*. I asked Mrs Gower how you got to be an actor and she told me about drama school. I said I wanted to go. She said if I worked very hard at school, I might get a grant or a scholarship. So I did. I worked so bloody hard, they said I should try for university instead, but I said I wanted to be an actor. I was going to go to drama school. And I did.

'While I was there I went to a photographer to have some publicity photos taken, the kind of mug shots you send to agents. A mate of mine recommended Frances Holbrook. Yes, our Fan... Fanny liked me. Women tend to, for some reason I've never quite fathomed. I thought Fanny was going to be like Mrs Gower. Though I could see she *wasn't* like Mrs Gower. Fanny was... beautiful. She was fifteen years older than me and glamorous and successful. Well, that's how she seemed to me at eighteen... Fanny knew all about the acting business and she said I'd definitely got something. I didn't know if she really meant it, but it was what I wanted to hear. I'd lost all the puppy fat by then, I'd got fit with fencing and weight training and I'd allowed the despised blond curls to grow. I suppose I was... presentable. Must have been. Fan made it clear what she wanted from me and I was flattered. She was gorgeous, she was useful, and she fed my fantasies of making it big. So we became lovers. Her first marriage had reached the end of its shelf life and I was Fan's bit on the side, her bit of rough. She had no idea just *how* rough... So when the BBC approached Rae about making a documentary, it was Fan who had the brainwave. That they should get someone to impersonate Alfie Donovan. It was a mad idea, but who was to know? Alfie was supposed to have lived abroad with his father for many years. No one knew him in Norfolk and no one had ever known that the baby died because Rae had gone into seclusion and refused all visitors.

'Fan was worried that my mates at drama school would recognise me and blow the whistle, but I told her I'd always been vague about my background. I'd never talked about my parents – too ashamed of them – and I'd certainly never told anyone I was brought up by foster parents, who dumped me in a children's home when they'd had enough. No, I'd maintained an air of mystery, along with a classless accent. For all my fellow students knew, I could have been anybody. I mean, if you'd been christened "Alfred Donovan", wouldn't *you* have changed your name?...

'I was perfect for the part. Or I was by the time Fan and Viv had finished coaching me. I even looked a bit like some of the fake photos Fanny had taken for Rae, to flesh out Alfie's childhood. We agreed a fee and a yearly retainer, which bought my silence as well as my performance for the cameras. Everybody was happy. Nervous, but happy.

'But things didn't go quite as planned. I wasn't allowed to retreat into obscurity. The documentary got a lot of attention. So did Rae's books. Tom Dickon Harry became a craze with kids, a household name. I got phone calls from journalists asking for interviews, which I refused. But then I started getting calls from casting people who'd seen the documentary. It was one thing turning down money for interviews – though that *did* hurt – but I wasn't going to turn down work offers, or meetings that might lead to work offers.

'There was an added complication, a serious one that no one could have foreseen. The filming upset Rae badly. Or maybe it was me, my performance as Alfie. She'd seemed thrilled with me at the time, but she became unstable again and cracked up badly after the documentary was filmed. By the time it was shown on TV, Rae actually believed the script! She believed I *was* Alfie, the son who'd died. So the family did what they'd always done... They played along with poor old Rae's fantasies. She was no longer capable of writing a shopping list, let alone another TDH instalment. It was clear Viv was going to have to step into the breach. What was one deception more or less? So when Rae insisted that Alfie would be coming home for Christmas... Well, Fanny can be very persuasive. Alfie came home.'

He leaned back in his chair. Under the harsh fluorescent light, he looked hollow-eyed with exhaustion. 'I took Alfie's name as my Equity name. I adopted Creake Hall as my nominal home and the Holbrooks as my surrogate family. Viv gave me the use of Rae's London flat, for which I agreed to visit once a year to act out the Alfie charade for Rae. I've done that for eleven years. So to answer your question, Gwen, "Who am I?"... There are three of us. "Alfie" is a set of triplets. There's the man I pretend to be. There's the man I was – though I don't remember much about him now. And then there's little Alfred himself. The late lamented, dear departed. Except that he never really *was*, was he? He was never loved, never even *known*. Baby Alfred never achieved boyhood, let alone manhood. That was the book Rae didn't write, couldn't even bear to think about: *Tom Dickon Harry and the Boy Who Never Was.'*

Alfie looked at me then, his brown eyes dull and hard, like stones. I'd expected to see remorse or sadness. Self-pity perhaps. All I saw was emptiness. 'I didn't have much of a childhood. Not the kind you enshrine in photo albums anyway. So I stole someone else's. And made it mine.' He shrugged. 'Where was the harm? Alfred John Donovan was dead. He died as a baby. I stole a childhood that never happened, one that might have been, but sadly, never was. The worst you can say about me, surely, is that I'm some sort of... *grave robber.'*

In the long silence that followed, no one moved. When I found my voice I said, 'What is – what *was* your real name?'

His sudden mirthless smile was shocking. 'Darling, I thought you'd never ask! It's Tom. No, really! Thomas Wilson. If poor little Alfie had lived, I would have remained Tom Wilson, a struggling actor, wondering whether to change my name to something more stylish, more memorable. Wondering whether to play up my dismal, deprived background or keep it under wraps, along with my Geordie accent. Didn't want to be typecast as a car-stealing, joy-riding, crack-dealing yob, did I? Though that might have made more demands on me as an actor than playing the middle-class tossers and all-round wastes of space that have been my speciality.'

I found myself unable to meet his eye. Instead, I looked up at Marek, but he was watching Hattie who was fidgeting with her dressing gown, pulling at a button, as if she was trying to unpick it with her fingers. Marek didn't take his eyes off her. He watched as if he was waiting for something and I thought he looked afraid, afraid for Hattie. I sensed he was about to move towards her, when she suddenly announced, 'The baby didn't die.'

Alfie turned on her then, his uncanny composure gone. He leaned across the table and spat out the words. 'Of course he died! For God's sake, Hat – that's why I'm here! Why I bloody *exist.'*

'I meant – the baby didn't *die.'* She lifted her head, opened her mouth to speak, but appeared to lose her nerve.

She looked quickly at me, then at Marek, her eyes wide with terror and then her chin sank on to her chest. Looking like a shame-faced child, she murmured, 'The baby didn't die... He was murdered... I did it. I killed Alfie.'

Nothing But The Truth

Chapter Nineteen

Gwen

Hattie fled from the kitchen. We heard her footsteps pound up the stairs, then a door banged. Marek looked a question at me and I nodded. He strode across the kitchen and out into the hall. I supposed if anyone knew how to deal with Hattie now, it would be Marek.

I turned to look at Alfie, slumped in his chair on the other side of the table. He was white-faced and his eyes were unfocussed. He levelled his gaze at me and, with a visible effort, said, 'Gwen, I swear to you, I had absolutely no idea.'

'I know.'

'I'd do a lot of things for money, but covering up murder isn't one of them. I assumed it had been a childhood illness. Cot death or something. I never asked and Fanny never said.'

Neither of us spoke for a few moments, then I said, 'Do you think it's possible Hattie's lying?'

'Why would she lie?'

'I don't know. To get attention?'

'Bit of a drastic way to steal the limelight, isn't it? She looked to me as if she'd waited nearly thirty years to say that.'

'Yes, I know what you mean. Poor Hattie.'

'She killed her baby brother, Gwen!'

'When she was six years old! She can't have known what she was doing! Perhaps it was an accident. I can't believe Hattie would commit murder. Not *Hattie*. She's such a gentle soul.'

'She is now. Maybe she wasn't then. Thirty years of guilt could change anyone's personality.'

I thought of Marek, then strained my ears for sounds of shouting or crying, or footsteps on the stairs. There was nothing and the silence was unnerving. I said, 'Do you think the family know what happened?'

'They must. It would explain why they went to such extraordinary lengths to keep Alfie alive.'

'Maybe Rae didn't know. Perhaps it was all a plot to protect her as well as Hattie.'

'Maybe.' After a pause, he said, 'Will she be OK, do you think? With Tyler?'

'If anyone knows how to deal with what she's going through, it will be him. He used to be a psychiatrist, remember.'

Alfie said nothing for a while, but I knew what was coming. Without meeting my eyes, he said, 'So... are you and he—'

'I don't know *what's* going on, Alfie... I suppose I should call you Tom now.'

'No. Nobody does. Not any more.'

'I prefer Tom. It suits you better.'

There was another uncomfortable silence and then he let out a weary sigh. 'I can hardly claim that you owe me an explanation, Gwen, but I would like to try to understand... what happened.'

'It's hard to explain. I'd suspected you were some kind of an impostor. And then I found out that you *were*... I was very upset. Well, that's putting it mildly. I was in a bad way. And Marek listened.'

'There must have been something going on between you for you to turn to him.'

'Yes, there must, but I don't know what it was. Mistrust of you was a lot to do with it. The knowledge I was being deceived... You should have told me, Alfie! *Trusted* me. I would have accepted you for who you really were.'

'Would you? Even if I was nobody? You think I'd take that risk?' I didn't reply and he continued. 'I had a lot, Gwen. The flat in London, the car, the family mansion, a certain amount of celebrity status. But none of it was *mine*. It all belonged to Alfie. Even my girlfriend wasn't mine. She was Alfie's. Why would I choose to be Tom when I could be Alfie? You see, it wasn't just a part I played, I wanted it to be true. All of it! Rae and I had that much in common. I wanted to *be* Alfie. And I was. Tom died years ago. How could I have told you that? Maybe if I hadn't cared whether or not I lost you, but I *did* care. Very much. And it wasn't Tom you liked. It wasn't him you slept with. It was Alfie. Everyone liked Alfie. Even me. Well,' he added with a shrug, 'I liked him more than Tom.'

I gazed into Alfie's sad, brown eyes. I no longer felt any sexual attraction towards him but my heart – or some other organ – turned over with a sickening lurch at the thought of losing him as a friend. Perhaps that was all he had ever been. A friend I happened to sleep with. But he had been a *good* friend.

And a good son.

'I remember now, something Rae said the other night, when I took up her tea. She was rambling on and half of it didn't make any sense to me, but I realise now, when she was talking about Tom, she wasn't referring to TDH, she was talking about *you*.'

'What did she say?'

'She was telling me about filming the documentary. What a dreadful experience it had been. She said she didn't know how she'd got through it.'

'A film crew invading your home isn't a pleasant experience. A herd of elephants would show more sensitivity. Rae was pretty upset by it, even leaving aside the conspiracy element and her fear of exposure.'

'She said something rather odd. I dismissed it at the time because I thought she was talking about TDH. She said, "Tom saw me through it... He was the hero of the hour." She was talking about you, wasn't she?'

Alfie nodded. 'I sat and held her hand and cracked jokes to cheer her up while they were setting up lights. She was terrified. But she was also very proud. Proud of her "son". She kept looking at me and smiling. You could see her dream had come true, a dream she'd cherished for eighteen years. She kept touching me, as if she was trying to convince herself I was real. It gave the film a particularly poignant quality, the whole mother-son thing. The director just lapped it up. They made me much more of a feature than we'd expected.'

'That's what Rae said. *Tom* was what the film makers

were really interested in. She said they loved him. And the viewers loved him. Loved *you*. That's what she meant, didn't she?'

'That's where things started to go wrong. I made too much of an impact. People sat up and took notice. And when they realised I was an actor, well, one thing led to another. It was hard for me to walk away from all the... possibilities.'

'I do understand. I just wish you'd told me.'

He smiled sadly. 'So do I, now. I think I did try. Well, I almost tried.'

I got to my feet. 'I'm going to make some breakfast. I feel as if I'm fading away. Do you want some?'

'Please. I don't remember when I last ate.' He rubbed at the fair stubble on his chin. 'God, I'm tired.'

I put the kettle back on the hot plate and cracked some eggs into a bowl. Alfie opened the fridge and handed me a packet of bacon and put plates to warm. It was all so domestic and familiar, I felt a lump in my throat and dreaded I would start to cry. I'd expected him to be angry, to be jealous, not sweetly reasonable. But as I turned rashers of bacon in the pan, it occurred to me, Alfie would have been angry, but Tom wouldn't. Tom was used to losing things. Tom was used to rejection. My eyes did fill with tears then and I was careful to keep my back towards Alfie as he laid the table.

He suddenly said, 'Do you think I should go and see Hattie?'

I rubbed at my eyes and thought for a moment. 'I don't really know. I would have thought Marek would come and get us if he thought it was a good idea. He'll do whatever he thinks best for her.'

Alfie stood beside me at the Aga, staring down into the frying pan. 'None of this was in the script, you know. Losing my girlfriend to another man... Hattie being a child killer... What was it I said about promising you your second-worst Christmas? That wasn't meant to include me. Or Hattie...'

~~~

Marek knocked softly on the door. 'Hattie? Can I come in?' He put his ear to the door and heard muffled sounds of crying. 'Hattie, unless you tell me not to, I'm going to come in.' He waited a moment, then turned the handle and entered the room known to the family as Hattie's Bazaar.

Marek had never seen the inside of Hattie's room, which served as study, sewing room and bedroom. A kaleidoscope of colours, shapes and textures assaulted his senses. Every inch of dark, wood-panelled wall was covered with quilts, wall-hangings, pictures and pin-boards, on which hung swatches of fabric, drawings, cuttings from magazines and postcards. A sewing machine was set up on a table by the window and a pile of quilt blocks awaited assembly. On a side table, spools of thread, arranged by colour, lined up in regimented rows. A bookcase was so overloaded, the shelves bowed. More books and craft magazines lay in haphazard piles on the floor where faded rag rugs sat incongruously on threadbare Axminster. Folded quilts were stored on shelves and the doors to a large cupboard hung open revealing Hattie's fabric collection, carefully ironed and folded, stacked according to colour and forming a textile rainbow.

Hattie's dressing table displayed little in the way of toiletries. Instead it served as a mirrored stage on which dressed dolls posed: fairies, sea nymphs, Harlequins, princesses, fantastical creatures fashioned by Hattie's imagination. In a corner of the room stood a single bed with a red and white quilt folded at its foot, the red faded almost to pink. In places, the wadding showed through holes worn in the fabric, like wounds. Hattie lay sobbing on the bed, her face buried in a pillow.

On entering, Marek scanned the room and made a professional assessment. The curtains were drawn but he assumed the window would be closed. There was a glass of water beside the bed. He removed it and placed it on a high shelf, but the sewing table was a nightmare: a pot held rotary cutters of various sizes, a scalpel and a Stanley knife; a fearsome pair of dressmaker's shears lay on a cutting board; a china jug stored scissors of various sizes, which Hattie no doubt kept sharp.

He pulled up a chair beside the bed and sat down. 'Hattie, I'm here as your friend. Not as a judge. Or a psychiatrist. Just a friend. I'd like to help if I can.'

She didn't lift her head from the pillow, so her words were indistinct. 'You won't want to be my friend now you know what I did.'

'It doesn't change anything. Not for me.'

'You're just saying that.'

'No, I'm not. Look at me, Hattie. Look into my eyes and see if I'm lying.' After a moment she turned her head and scraped back her hair to peer at him. Marek's face was a blank, but his dark eyes bore into hers. She found it hard to look away. His eyes continued to hold hers. 'Have you ever talked to anyone about... what happened?'

'No.'

'Do you remember what happened? The details?'

'No.'

Marek felt his spirits lift but his face betrayed nothing. 'But you remember the baby dying? Were you there?'

'Yes. I was there... I was in Rae's bedroom. And I shouldn't have been. It was getting dark and I felt frightened. But I don't remember why... Alfie was lying in his cot. I watched him. For *ages*. I wanted him to wake up. But he didn't. He didn't move. Not even when I poked him through the bars... He didn't wake up because he was dead.'

'That doesn't mean you killed him. He might have died of natural causes. Or an accident... What did Rae say about it? Or Viv?'

'It's never been discussed.'

'Never?'

'No. We've never discussed Alfie's death, just how to keep him alive. For Rae's sake. And mine.'

'So... how do you know you killed him if you don't remember what happened?'

'My sisters said I did it.'

Marek was thrown by this statement but his voice betrayed no emotion. 'They might not have been telling the truth. They could have said that to hurt you.'

'Oh, they didn't say it to *me*. They've always tried to

protect me. They've never even let on that they know. But I heard them. I was in the garden and they didn't know I was there. They were talking about how Alfie died. That's how I found out. That it was me. *I* did it.'

'Are you sure, Hattie? You were very young. Perhaps you misunderstood.'

She sat up, propping herself on an elbow. 'Why has it never been discussed then? Why has no one in my family *ever* talked of how Alfie died? Why haven't they ever mentioned meningitis or whooping cough or something that could have killed a baby?' She lay down again and covered her face with her hands. 'It was me! I did it! My sisters *said* so.'

'To you?'

'No. But I heard them. Talking to each other.'

'And they didn't know you were there? Could it have been some sort of game? A terrible sick joke?'

She rolled over to face him, her eyes red and puffy, her face stained with tears. 'They weren't children! Viv was a grown woman. And Deb and Fanny were teenagers. It wasn't a game, they were having a serious talk. They told me to go away and then they went into the garden, so Rae wouldn't hear them. I followed them and hid on the other side of the hedge, so they wouldn't know I was there. They sat on a bench, all three of them, talking. Talking about Alfie. And *me*. I kept really still and listened... Then when I started to cry, I crept away. So they wouldn't hear me.'

'And you never told them what you heard? Not even Viv?'

'No.'

'Can you remember what they said?'

'Yes...' Hattie closed her eyes and turned away. 'I don't remember anything about— about Alfie dying, but I remember exactly what my sisters said.'

'Can you tell me what you remember?'

Marek watched Hattie's face as she struggled to speak the unspeakable. Her head rolled back and forth on the pillow, then she sat up suddenly and swivelled round, so she perched on the edge of the bed, her shoulders hunched. Her eyes swept round the room, avoiding Marek's, but he noticed

229

her breathing quicken. Her gaze settled on her worktable. He felt rather than saw the muscles in her legs bunch, then she launched herself at the table, lunging for the scissors. But he was ready. As her fingers closed around the pair of dressmaker's shears, Marek circled her wrist with one hand and her waist with his arm, clamping her to him.

'Let them go, Hattie! Please. You don't have to say any more, not if you don't want to. Look at me, Hattie! *Look at me!* Drop the scissors.' Then, in a moment's inspiration: 'You don't want to get blood on the quilts.'

She froze and the scissors fell to the floor. He released her wrist and loosened his grip round her waist, but didn't let her go. She went limp in his arms and started to wail. Supporting her, he half-dragged, half-carried her back to the bed where she sat, then, with Marek's encouragement, lay down again. He pulled the folded quilt over her, took her hand and held it loosely while she cried. He knew there was nothing anyone could say that would quiet the mind of someone who'd killed a child, so he stroked her hand and whispered soothing words, Polish phrases he hadn't heard for almost forty years, which, when his father used to utter them, had the properties of magic charms. Even when he knew she slept, he didn't leave, nor did he let go of her hand. When she whimpered in her sleep, he stroked her tangled hair back from her forehead, murmuring.

Hattie didn't wake, but her sleep was troubled.

Deborah broke a long silence. 'Who'll tell Ma?'

'I will.'

Vivien and Deborah stared at Frances. 'What will you say?'

'I'll tell her I saw Hattie do it. I'll tell Ma I know what happened... I know how the baby died.'

'Poor thing.'

'The baby?'

'No, Hattie.'

'Oh, Deb, don't be ridiculous! Hattie need never know I've told Ma! None of us will ever mention it.'

'But Rae will never forgive her,' Deborah persisted.

'Rae's never forgiven her for being born. I can't really see this makes much difference,' said Frances.

'Poor Hattie...'

'Oh, do shut up, Deb! Ma's sanity is at stake here! She must face up to the truth. She has to accept that the baby is dead! For <u>all</u> our sakes.'

'I know you're right. It just seems so harsh... I mean, you're actually going to tell her Hattie killed her brother?'

'Yes. But she didn't know what she was doing. It was just a game, a child's game that got out of hand. Hattie wasn't really to blame. A six year-old can't be held responsible for murder.'

'Not in the eyes of the law perhaps,' Vivien said. 'But Ma might not see it like that.'

'Yes, she will,' Frances said firmly. 'Once she's got over the shock. Ma will see reason in the end. But she has to be told. We can't put up with this charade any longer. It's driving us all crazy.'

'Poor Hattie,' said Deborah and started to weep.

Chapter Twenty

Gwen

I was alone, loading the dishwasher, when Marek came back into the kitchen, his coat pockets bulging. He handed me a glass, then emptied the contents of his pockets on to the kitchen table: dressmaker's shears, scissors, knives, knitting needles, a tin of pins and a needle case. I stared uncomprehending and watched as he took a cornflakes box from the worktop, discarded the inner packet and re-filled it with all the hardware. He opened the larder door and placed the box on a high shelf, behind some packets of kitchen towel.

Then I understood.

I sank into a chair, my stomach churning. When I was sure my breakfast wasn't about to make a reappearance, I said, 'Did Hattie try to—'

'Yes.'

'But she's all right?'

'Yes. But she probably shouldn't be left alone for too long. She's asleep at the moment and I think she'll sleep for a while now.'

In the silence that followed I heard the first notes of the dawn chorus: a solitary bird, sounding tentative at first, then obscenely cheerful. I swallowed and said, 'Do you think she did it?'

'*She* thinks she did. And she says she heard her sisters talking about a cover-up. She believes that's what's behind the whole Alfie/Tom scenario.'

'But you don't.'

'There's a condition called *pseudologia phantastica* where the patient concocts elaborate, sometimes fantastic stories. But they can seem quite plausible, so it can be very difficult to be certain they aren't telling the truth. But it's really not my place to have an opinion.' Marek's face was calm. Inscrutable. Infuriating. 'It's not even as if I'm family,' he added.

'Well, neither am I. Nor is Alfie. I'm asking what you think as Hattie's friend, not her psychiatrist.'

'As Hattie's friend, I'd say she couldn't bring herself to kill a slug, let alone a baby. But as a psychiatrist, I have to acknowledge such things are possible. If Hattie is now the soul of kindness, it could be because she's spent thirty years atoning for an unspeakable crime. But...'

'But what?'

Before answering, Marek took off his coat, hung it on the back of a chair and sat down beside me at the table. 'I have my doubts whether this murder actually took place. We're dealing with an entire family of fantasists here.'

'But Tom isn't Alfie – I think we can be sure of that, can't we? So where is he? And what happened to him? You have to admit, Hattie's story does add up in a way. It also explains her *strangeness*. And Rae's mental frailty.'

'Oh, yes, it all adds up. I just don't believe it.'

'No, neither do I.'

He laughed, then took my hand and raised it quickly to his lips. I leaned over and laid my head on his shoulder. I felt a protective arm go round me and was glad of something strong and certain. As the songbird continued to warble inappropriately, I said, 'Could a six year-old kill deliberately?'

'It happens.'

'But why would Hattie have done such a thing? What possible motive could she have had?'

'Several. Sibling rivalry. Being very angry with Rae, who seems to have ignored her. A six year-old would be conscious of rejection, emotional neglect. And Hattie might have understood that this baby was the longed-for son. She could have killed out of spite. Or revenge.'

I suddenly remembered a conversation I'd had with Hattie in the attic. I debated with myself whether or not I should mention it to Marek. She hadn't said she was speaking to me in confidence (given her lack of discretion, I wondered if Hattie had any understanding of that concept) so I decided

I would tell him. I sat upright again and said, 'There's something about Hattie which you probably don't know. I think it might account for her sense of guilt. Well, some of it.' Marek looked at me and waited. 'Hattie told me she'd had an abortion. When she was a student. She made it sound as if she'd got pregnant without really knowing how. Then she had an abortion. I think it was one of the things that contributed to her chucking her musical career... So she could feel guilty about that, couldn't she? Hattie with her childlike way of thinking might even have seen *that* as a sort of murder. Do you think she could have got confused?'

'Yes, I think she could. She certainly seems confused now, but thirty years of living the lies this family has imposed on her would confuse anyone. The point is, even if Hattie had nothing to do with the baby's death, he's still unaccounted for.'

'If the baby had died of natural causes, Hattie would know, wouldn't she? It would have been discussed.'

Marek shrugged. 'She says it never was. She's adamant about that. She said, "We never discussed Alfie's death, just how to keep him alive".'

I thought for a moment and came to the inevitable conclusion. 'That doesn't sound like death from natural causes, does it?'

'No, it doesn't.'

'Which means Hattie – or someone else – killed the baby. Doesn't it?'

'It appears to. But...'

'But what?'

Marek shook his head. 'I don't know... Something just doesn't feel right.'

'Are you basing that on your professional experience? Or your affection for Hattie?'

'How would I know? But if you're asking for my considered professional opinion, I'd say the whole thing stinks. To high heaven.'

'But if what she believes happened, *didn't*... and they *know*... that would mean the family had used Hattie as some kind of scapegoat... Oh, God, that's appalling! That seems to me even more incredible than the idea of Hattie being a child murderer! I don't believe Viv would be party to such a thing.'

'No, nor do I. And I like to think I know Viv pretty well.'

'Dare we say anything to her?'

'In the light of Hattie being bent on self-harm, I think we have to. I presume Alfie won't carry on with his impersonation now?'

'No. I think he's as stunned as we are. He's fond of Hattie.'

'And he's also dealing with being dumped by his girlfriend. How much does he know about us?'

'Only what he guesses.'

Marek's smile was lopsided, ironical. 'Everything, then.'

'I suppose so.'

'Look, Gwen, I'd make myself scarce and leave you to sort things out with Alfie, but I imagine you'd like me around to deal with Hattie when she wakes up.'

'Please. And I think it had better be you who explains to Viv. She'll be down soon. I can hear movement upstairs. Someone's up and I doubt it's Frances or Deborah.'

'Somebody should go and sit with Hattie.'

'It has to be me then.'

'If she wakes up, just try to stay calm. And keep *her* calm. We have to guard against impulsive behaviour. Take what she says seriously, but try to act normally. If things get difficult, yell and I'll come and deal with it.'

'What are you going to do?'

'I'm going to wait for Viv to make an appearance.'

'And then?'

'Then I'm going to ask her what happened to her baby brother.'

'You think she knows?'

'She must. She was in her twenties when he was born. If Rae ever knew what happened, she's probably forgotten. And Deborah and Frances were just teenagers. But Viv will have the answers. If there are any.'

'And you think she'll tell you?'

'Not necessarily. But I'll know if she's lying.'

The kitchen door opened. I hoped it would be Alfie, but Harris and Lewis trotted into the kitchen followed by Viv, bleary-eyed in her dressing gown and slippers. She saw us both seated at the table and stopped in her tracks, smiling uncertainly. 'Tyler! What on earth are you doing here so early? Is there a problem at the mill?'

'Good morning, Viv. I'm here because... Gwen needed some help.'

Viv turned to me, surprised. 'Oh, my dear, why didn't you come and wake me? What was wrong?'

She smiled at me affectionately, then went over to the back door where both dogs waited patiently to be let out. I turned to Marek, feeling helpless and unaccountably guilt-stricken. He put an arm round my shoulders briefly then, as Viv closed the door behind the dogs, he said, 'I think you'd better sit down, Viv. We need to talk.'

'Oh dear, that sounds ominous! I hope it's nothing serious.' She turned an anxious face to me, then back to Marek. 'Oh... It *is*, isn't it?'

'It's potentially very serious,' Marek said, in a quiet, reassuring voice, totally at odds with his words and the cereal packet of lethal blades he'd so recently hidden. 'I'm concerned—' He shot me a sideways look. 'We're both concerned for Hattie's safety.'

'Hattie? Why? What's the matter with her?' Viv sat down at the table facing Marek and me. 'Where is Hattie?'

'She's asleep in her room. Or she was when I left her a little while ago.'

Viv's eyebrows shot up. 'What were you doing in her room?'

'He was making sure she didn't do anything stupid,' I said, leaning across the table, quick to defend Marek who, despite his calm demeanour, was beginning to show signs of strain.

'What do you mean, "stupid"?' Viv asked.

'Trying to harm herself,' Marek replied.

'But why on earth would Hattie do such a thing? Please tell me what's happened.'

'I need to go back and explain, Viv. Then...' Marek paused. 'Then I think *you* need to go back and explain.'

As realisation dawned, her bright brown eyes clouded

over and her shoulders drooped. 'This is to do with Alfie, isn't it?' Marek nodded. Viv bowed her head and stared at the table, then, straightening her spine, she looked up. 'How much do you know?'

'About Alfie? Everything, I think. He's back at Creake Hall now. He talked to us at length. Very frankly. He explained... the set-up.'

'Why did he do that?'

'Because Gwen had guessed he was an impostor.'

Viv turned to me. I can't say she actually looked surprised, more like resigned to the inevitable. 'The photographs?'

'Yes. But I'd also read Alfie's letters home. Bits of them. They were sewn into Hattie's quilt top. I read them when I was working on it. Alfie was supposed to have written them, but I found out that he had no idea of the contents.'

'No, he wouldn't. He didn't write those letters. I did.'

There was a scratching noise at the back door and Viv got up to let the dogs in. They trotted through the kitchen and took up their customary positions in front of the Aga, for all the world as if this was just a normal day. I suppose for them it was.

When Viv had sat down again, I said, 'Were Freddie's letters to Rae genuine?'

Her eyebrows shot up. 'You've read those too?'

'Only bits. They were also in the quilt. They said the baby died. That Freddie left Rae because he couldn't cope any more with all the pretence.'

Viv nodded. 'It was all very sad. Heartbreaking, in fact... And you say you confronted Alfie with all this?'

'Not exactly.' I looked at Marek, uncertain how to proceed. He gave me a slight nod and I continued. 'We were trying to get the truth out of Hattie when Alfie came back. He'd driven through the night. He told us who he really was. And he explained the part he's played in... all this.'

'I see. But why is Hattie so upset?'

Out of my depth now, I turned to Marek who leaned forward and said, 'Hattie sees herself as responsible for the baby's death. She appears to have lived with a lifetime of guilt. She didn't need to tell us about her part in what happened, but she chose to. Then she left the room, in great distress. I followed and sat with her for a while. We talked and eventually she fell asleep. But I thought it best to remove certain things from her room – tools and so on. Things she could use to hurt herself.'

Viv closed her eyes. 'Oh, God...'

'Did Hattie ever have any counselling, Viv? For what happened?'

She opened her eyes again and looked at Marek, puzzled. 'You mean the accident?'

I pounced on her words. 'So it *was* an accident?'

'Yes, of course. No one thought Hattie had done it deliberately! Not even Rae.'

Marek resumed. 'Hattie believes she was responsible. She claims to have heard you talking about her as if she was the culprit. She sees herself as nothing less than a murderer, Viv. She always has. And she believes the Alfie business is a cover-up – not just a consolation for Rae, but something to protect the family from Hattie's "crime".'

'How extraordinary! Are you sure that's what she thinks?'

'Yes, I'm sure. Hattie says she has no memory of what happened, but she seems to have a clear recollection of a conversation in the garden that she overheard: you and your sisters discussing whether you should tell Rae that Hattie murdered the baby.'

Viv's face turned grey. Never in my life have I seen anyone look so dreadful, apart from my mother when I found her on Christmas morning. All life and colour drained from Viv's face, leaving a mask of horror. After a moment, she opened her mouth to speak, but no words came. Eventually, in a hoarse whisper, she said, 'Hattie *overheard* that conversation?'

'Yes. She said she was hidden in the garden. Behind the hedge.'

'And Hattie believes she murdered the baby?'

'Yes.'

'So... when we asked her to play the game that Alfie was

238

still alive... she had to pretend the baby she believed she'd *killed* was still alive!' Viv clapped a hand to her mouth. I think in that moment she was struggling not to vomit. I got up quickly, moved round the table and put my arm around her. I looked up at Marek but he was watching Viv, waiting for her to compose herself. Eventually, he said, 'I take it Hattie misunderstood? There was no question of her having murdered her brother?'

When Viv finally answered, her voice was faint. 'No... Absolutely none. You see—' Her large brown eyes filled with tears and I took her hand. She clutched at mine and said, 'That poor girl! What have we *done*?' Moistening her lips, she said, 'There was no question of Hattie having murdered the baby because— because there never *was* a baby!'

Chapter Twenty-one

Hattie stood shivering at the end of her mother's bed, watching her sleeping form. The room was dimly illuminated by a shaft of grey light that entered through a gap in the heavy curtains. Hattie had stood in the darkness so long, she could now discern familiar features of the room: the sampler she'd made; the patchwork cushion covers fashioned from the floral chintzes Rae loved; the framed portrait on the bedside table of Rae and Freddie on their wedding day; all the other family photographs – the girls at various stages in their lives and snapshots of the boy – or rather, boys – they'd always referred to as "Alfie".

Rae stirred, then rolled over in bed. Hattie looked away to a corner of the room by the window. She appeared to stare at vacancy since there was nothing in that part of the room. She continued to stare until Rae, awake now and struggling to sit up, said, 'Viv, is that you?' She switched on the bedside light and blinked in astonishment at the figure standing at the end of her bed. 'Hattie! What on earth are *you* doing here? You gave me an awful fright, standing there like a ghost. What do you want?'

Hattie said nothing. For a moment, her body appeared to sway and she clasped the foot of the wrought iron bedstead. The metal was colder even than her hands. She clung to the iron frame and said, 'Do you know what I did, Ma? Did they tell you?'

Rae stared at her youngest daughter, unnerved by the harsh note in her voice. 'What are you talking about? Really, Hattie, couldn't this wait? What time is it?'

'I want to know now. Did they tell you?'

Rae began to feel alarmed. This wasn't a Hattie she recognised. Hattie was simple, but harmless. A kind, affectionate girl, just not all there. But the woman standing at the foot of the bed was grim-faced. Her eyes bore into Rae, accusing. But accusing her of what? She had no idea. Rae reached for the buzzer on the bedside table to ring for Viv, but Hattie leaped forward and snatched it from her hand, holding it aloft.

'Tell me! Do you know what I did? Is *that* why you always hated me?'

Rae cowered against her pillows. 'I don't hate you! What on earth are you talking about? I don't understand!' Her eyes darted around the room as if she was looking for help, even escape. 'I know I wasn't a good mother to you, Hattie, but I've never *hated* you! How can you think such a thing?' her eyes settled on Hattie's face, pleading. 'You must understand, I couldn't be expected to cope after... after my breakdown. I left everything to Freddie and Viv. Viv was so very capable! *They* looked after you. And I—' Rae looked away, unable to meet Hattie's eyes. A querulous note crept into her voice as she stammered, '*I* had to look after Alfie.'

'No you didn't! Alfie *died*. You *know* he died. You've always known. But we had to pretend he was alive for your sake, because you couldn't face the truth!' She approached the head of the bed and bore down upon her mother, implacable. 'I want to know if the truth you couldn't face was really about *me*.'

Rae began to whimper. 'Hattie, I don't know what you're talking about. Please – go and fetch Vivien. You're frightening me! I *insist* that you get Vivien!'

'Not until you've answered my questions about the baby.'

'The baby?'

'Yes. Did they tell you it was me? My fault the baby died?'

'No one needed to tell me. I knew it was you. Who else would have left toys lying around? Frances was fifteen. I knew immediately it was you. But I never *said* anything. I never accused you! You were only six. You couldn't possibly have understood.'

Hattie put a hand to her temple and rubbed, as if her head was hurting. 'I remember you screaming at me... Screaming and screaming. I stood at the top of the stairs with my hands over my ears... Then Viv took me away to my room.

She said you had to go to hospital. That Daddy was going with you... I remember looking out of my bedroom window and seeing an ambulance drive up... and men carrying you out on a stretcher.'

'You *remember* all that? But you've never talked about it. Ever.'

'I thought you'd died! I thought you'd *burst* with anger! I was so frightened.'

'Oh, my dear – I didn't realise! I wasn't thinking of you, I was only thinking about myself. And the baby.'

'What did I do? Tell me.'

'You don't remember that?'

'No. I remember being in here. And I knew I shouldn't have been. Daddy said I wasn't allowed in here until Alfie was stronger.' Hattie looked round the room as if she could see the scene she was describing. 'There were no lights on and it was getting dark... The cot was over there.' She pointed to the empty corner of the room by the window. 'I don't know where you were. You weren't in here. I was alone... With Alfie.'

'But Hattie, you're getting confused—'

'No, I remember all this very clearly. I stood beside the cot, watching Alfie. He didn't wake up, he just lay there, quite still. I remember that I... I *hated* him. That I wanted him to go away. Back to the hospital... I remember that I wanted to *hurt* him... So I put my hand through the bars of the cot and I poked him. I poked him as hard as I could. But he didn't move.'

'Hattie—'

'Then I started to drop things into the cot. My teddy. My shoes. The jug of water from the bedside table... I remember throwing things into the cot, trying to *bury* Alfie. I think he was crying, but it might have been me, I don't remember. One of us must have been crying, because Daddy came rushing into the room and picked me up. He took me away, out of the room. He wasn't angry with me, he was just frightened, I think. Or upset. I couldn't tell. He put me to bed. He sat with me and held my hand and said everything would be all right, he would sort everything out.' Hattie's expression changed as another memory came to her. 'He called it a *mess*. He said he would "sort this mess out".'

'And he did,' Rae said softly. 'Freddie sorted it all out. At least, he thought he did.' A calm had settled on Rae and she reached for her daughter's hand. As Hattie let her take it, she noticed Rae's agitation was gone. Her eyes were focussed now, clear, but infinitely sad. When she finally spoke her voice was quite steady. 'The next day, Alfie was gone, wasn't he?... Do you remember that?'

'Yes. Daddy told me Alfie had been taken to hospital. He'd stopped breathing. Daddy said Alfie's lungs had never been strong and they weren't working properly. Then a few days later he told me Alfie had died and gone to Heaven... None of that was true, was it?'

'No, it wasn't.'

'But I believed him. I believed him until I heard my sisters talking in the garden. They were talking about what *really* happened. Then I realised... I killed him, didn't I?'

'No!' Rae clutched at Hattie's hand. 'You didn't! Dear God, forgive me—'

'I killed my baby brother while he lay in his cot. I suffocated him. Or I crushed his skull by dropping things on him. Which was it? I want to know what I did, Ma! I want to know just how evil I am. You've all protected me long enough. I killed a baby. I drove you mad with grief. I broke up your marriage. And I drove my father away. No wonder you hated me!'

'Hattie, stop! I can't bear it! Stop this at once!' Rae threw back the bedclothes and struggled out of bed. Staggering as she made her way across the room, she lurched towards an armchair and clung to it until she regained her balance. Turning her head, she addressed Hattie over her shoulder, gasping, her words coming in short bursts. 'Stay there. You hear me? You're not to move. I have to fetch something. Something you must see.'

Rae tottered across the floor, opened the door to a dressing room and entered. Hattie heard a groan and the sound of something being dragged across the carpet, then the sharp click of two metal catches. There was a long exhalation from Rae, followed by silence.

Panic overwhelmed Hattie and she ran to the bedroom door. She'd grasped the handle and was pulling the door open when Rae's voice – strange, high, unrecognisable – said, 'Hattie, don't go... I have something to show you.' Hattie froze in the doorway, her back towards her mother.

'Look... Please look, Hattie.'

She turned. By the dim light of the bedside lamp, Hattie saw her mother's bent figure, standing at the end of the bed. She was cradling a baby wrapped in a shawl.

Gwen

I stared at Viv – open-mouthed, for all I know – as I struggled to take in what she'd said. After an eternity, Marek got up from the kitchen table and made a pot of tea. The rattle of spoons and the clink of crockery sounded deafening to me. He set mugs in front of each of us and sat down again. I was sitting beside Viv now and studied her profile. It was such a strong face – devoid of beauty, but there was integrity there, a fundamental honesty. This was a plain-dealing woman, surely someone you could trust. Yet she was party to a lifetime of lies, party to the destruction of her sister's mind, nearly her life.

I thought of Hattie asleep in her room and wondered if I should go up and check on her, but at that moment, Viv started to speak again.

'If you're to understand what happened – what we did and why we did it – I have to go back a long way. A very long way. Back to Rae's childhood... She was an unwanted child. My grandfather thought little of anything other than his own status and material possessions. Children fell into the latter category. He was a successful businessman and he wanted a son to train up as his successor. But he got Rae, an only child. She was christened Rachael, but she was always known as Rae. She believed that was because her father liked to imagine her as the son she should have been... You might think that as Rae herself had suffered from this dreadful sexual discrimination, she'd be the last person to perpetrate it herself.' Viv looked up at Marek with a faint smile. 'But it doesn't work like that, does it?'

Marek shook his head.

'Rae desperately wanted a son. As a young married woman she thought it was her last chance to redeem herself in her father's eyes. If she presented him with a grandson, she would be forgiven, her life would somehow be validated – not just in her father's eyes, but in her own. You have to remember that in those days – I was born in 1957 – equality of the sexes was a new and not very popular idea. It was still very much a man's world. The birth of a son was something to boast about and the more Rae produced daughters – four in a row – the more she felt the pressure to produce a son. It was the thing she'd always wanted – wanted to *be* and wanted to *have*. And it was the thing she believed she never would have. Until she fell pregnant with Alfie.'

'So there *was* a baby!'

Viv turned to me, her expression grave. 'It depends on your point of view. There *was* a baby, for Rae. But legally, Alfie never existed.'

'I don't understand—'

'Gwen,' Marek said, very softly. I turned to look at him but his gaze was fixed on Viv. 'Go on.'

'Rae and Freddie were thrilled about the pregnancy. Hattie had been yet another disappointment – Rae made no bones about that – and she was forty-three. This was her last chance and she knew it. She had the best medical care and she charmed – possibly even bribed – an obstetrician to tell her the sex of the baby. It was a boy. Well, you can imagine... Rae worked herself up into a frenzy of anticipation. She kitted out the nursery as soon as she found out. She bought blue baby clothes. She decided on the name Alfred, after Freddie, and the baby was known as "Alfie" when it was just a bump. Rae was so proud of this pregnancy. She put on maternity clothes long before she needed to. I simply don't know how to convey to you how much this baby meant to her. Well, perhaps I don't really need to try. I just have to tell you that when she lost the baby, she lost her mind.'

My voice was a whisper. 'She miscarried?'

'Yes. At twenty-three weeks. That's too early to qualify as a stillbirth. Legally, Alfred Donovan never existed. But Rae gave birth to a perfect baby boy, too immature to survive.'

'If he was perfect, why did she miscarry?' I asked.

'That was the most tragic part... Rae fell downstairs, here at Creake Hall. She fell down the hall staircase, from the landing to the stone flags below. She fell because she didn't see there was a toy on the stairs – a little wooden horse on wheels that Hattie was forever dragging around behind her. I imagine Rae didn't see it because she was dressed in her billowing maternity wear, like a galleon in full sail. She wouldn't have been looking down at her feet. She must have trodden on Hattie's little horse, slipped and then fell. She was on her own when it happened, but she screamed the place down and Freddie and I came running. I think Hattie was there too – standing at the top of the stairs, looking on. But I don't think she knew she'd caused the accident. None of us knew then. And when we'd worked it out, no one said anything to her. She was only six. It was just an accident. A tragic accident...

'Rae stayed in hospital for a week. We didn't dare to put the cot or baby things away. I realise now we should have done that – it might have helped – but I was twenty-two. All this was outside my experience. Freddie didn't know what to do either. He was grief-stricken, naturally. He was waiting for a lead from Rae, or from a doctor. He didn't tell Hattie that Rae had lost the baby or why, because he didn't want her to feel responsible. He told her Rae had had to go to hospital because the baby was coming early. His idea was that we would break the news to Hattie gently, when the time was right. She was his only child and he was very fond of her. It really didn't seem such a bad idea at the time. She'd been terribly upset by what had happened. She'd thought Rae was going to die, so we were trying to reassure her. Protect her, in fact. But when Rae came home she talked about Alfie as if he'd *survived*, as if he was in the nursery, asleep! She talked like that in front of Hattie, so there was no way we could tell her that Rae had lost the baby. The poor child would have been so confused. We fudged it by saying Alfie wasn't well and had to be protected from germs, so Hattie couldn't see him. Then, when I could finally face going into the nursery – Freddie asked me to put away the baby's things – we discovered that Rae had found an old doll...' Viv faltered and took a sip of her tea. 'I think it was one of Fanny's. One of those squishy baby dolls. Quite realistic, actually. Rae had dressed it up in the blue baby clothes and put it in the cot. She'd tucked sheets and blankets around it and placed toys at the end of the cot. It was... *heartbreaking*.

'I told Freddie and he confronted Rae, but it was useless. She was living in a world of her own where Alfie hadn't died. The proof was lying in the cot in the nursery... We didn't know what to do. Nor did the doctors. We all agreed she shouldn't be forced to confront the reality of her situation. She wasn't a well woman, mentally or physically, and her GP thought this could be a natural process, a form of grieving. His policy was to wait and see, give Rae time to come to terms with her loss...

'So that's what we did. Freddie moved the cot into Rae's bedroom so Hattie wouldn't see it and she was forbidden to visit him.' Viv gulped down her tea, which must have been cold by now. 'You know, I think that was the beginning of Hattie being shut out, sidelined by everyone. She was the only one – apart from Rae – who didn't know the truth and she was the only one who wasn't preoccupied with Rae and her mental infirmity. We forgot about Hattie and left her pretty much to her own devices. I can see that now. I should have taken better care of her and let Freddie look after Rae. But it was very hard for me. My mother had gone mad! *I* was frightened too. And there was no one for me to turn to. No one at all. Freddie wasn't my father and he wasn't exactly a tower of strength, kind though he was. My sisters looked to me for guidance. *Everyone* did.'

'It was a lot for a young woman of twenty-two to deal with,' Marek said.

'Yes, it was. And I didn't make a very good job of it.'

Marek shook his head. 'You acted for the best, Viv. With compassion. For Rae. Freddie. Hattie. Everyone. You just couldn't see the big picture. Not until it was too late.'

She looked at him and smiled gratefully. 'That's not much consolation when you discover your little sister has spent her whole life believing she's a murderer.'

'But why *does* Hattie think that?' I asked.

Viv sighed and appeared to brace herself. Staring down into her empty mug, she said, 'Hattie must have overheard a conversation I had with my sisters... The family wasn't coping with the pretend baby. Rae was, but we weren't. And I knew it was only a matter of time before Hattie found out there was no baby, just this pathetic doll. There was no sign of Rae snapping out of it, as the doctors had hoped. On the contrary, Alfie seemed to become more and more real to her. She'd give us progress reports on feeding and broken nights! Things came to a head when we found Hattie alone in Rae's bedroom. Freddie had heard her crying and he'd gone in and found her hurling things into the cot, crying and shouting at the doll. She was hysterical. That's when Freddie decided to put a stop to it. He had to choose between his daughter and his poor mad wife. And he chose Hattie... He confronted Rae with the truth. I wasn't there but I heard the fallout from several rooms away. It was pitiful... The cot was removed. The baby clothes and toys were put away. He allowed Rae to keep the doll on condition that no one ever saw it. I don't know what she did with it. I wouldn't be at all surprised if she still has it somewhere.

'Freddie told Hattie that her brother had been rushed into hospital, that he was very ill and might not recover. After a few days Freddie broke the news to her that Alfie had died. She appeared to accept this. Accepted it very readily, in fact. I think I see why now... If she'd actually heard what was said in the garden... And if she'd only heard *some* of it... Yes, I can see now how Hattie came to think she'd killed Alfie... She must have thought we were protecting her, that the story about Alfie dying in hospital was just a cover-up.'

'What exactly *did* she hear, Viv? Can you remember?'

She turned her head to look at me. 'Oh, yes. I can hardly bring myself to tell you, it's so appalling... Hattie must have overheard us plotting. Plotting shock tactics, out of sheer desperation!' Viv was struggling now to control her voice and, as if reading their mistress' mind, the two terriers in front of the Aga raised their heads and looked up at her. One of them let out a high-pitched whine and trotted over to Viv, who bent down and fondled his ears absently. 'Hattie must have heard us planning to use her as a way of making Rae accept Alfie was dead. If Hattie believes she murdered Alfie, then she can't possibly have heard everything! But she must have heard enough to—'

Viv broke off, covered her face with her hands and burst into tears.

'We could say Hattie smothered him,' said Frances. 'Threw him out the window in one of her awful tempers.'

'It wouldn't work. Rae would never swallow it.'

'She might. After all, she swallowed the idea that the baby exists!'

Deborah broke a long silence. 'Who'll tell Ma?'

'I will.'

Vivien and Deborah stared at Frances. 'What will you say?'

'I'll tell her I saw Hattie do it. I'll tell Ma I know what happened... I know how the baby died.'

'Poor thing.'

'The baby?'

'No, Hattie.'

'Oh, Deb, don't be ridiculous! Hattie need never know I've told Ma! None of us will ever mention it.'

'But Rae will never forgive her,' Deborah persisted.

'Rae's never forgiven her for being born. I can't really see this makes much difference,' said Frances.

'Poor Hattie...'

'Oh, do shut up, Deb! Ma's sanity is at stake here! She must face up to the truth. She has to accept that the baby is dead! For all our sakes.'

'I know you're right. It just seems so harsh... I mean, you're actually going to tell her Hattie killed her brother?'

'Yes. But she didn't know what she was doing. It was just a game, a child's game that got out of hand. Hattie wasn't really to blame. A six year-old can't be held responsible for murder.'

'Not in the eyes of the law perhaps,' Vivien said. 'But Ma might not see it like that.'

'Yes she will,' Frances said firmly. 'Once she's got over the shock. Ma will see reason in the end. But she has to be told. We can't put up with this charade any longer. It's driving us all crazy.'

'Poor Hattie,' said Deborah and started to weep.

'No, we can't do that,' said Viv putting an arm round Deborah's shoulders. 'It would be wicked! Worse than that, it would be criminal. I'm going to talk to Freddie. I'll choose my moment... He's got to make Ma see reason. And if he won't, then I will. I'll tell her the baby's dead. That he never lived. And that this... this wretched fantasy is over.'

'Viv's right,' said Deborah, wiping her eyes. 'Someone has to confront her with the truth. I mean...' She laughed nervously. 'What's the worst that can happen?'

'She'll go barking mad!' said Frances.

'She's already mad!' Viv exclaimed. 'Maybe if we remind her what actually happened Ma will go sane!'

Chapter Twenty-two

Gwen

When Viv had composed herself I got to my feet and, for something to do, drew the kitchen curtains. The sky was light and clear now. Snow still lay on the ground, but it looked as if it might be a fine day. Somehow, that made me feel even more depressed. I turned away from the window to find Marek watching me. He regarded me, unblinking, with an intensity I'd come to realise was characteristic of him and which reminded me – briefly, but long enough to bring a flush to my face – of our lovemaking the night before. I felt a sudden surge of happiness then, of *rightness*. I thought how very glad I was Marek had been here, in this kitchen with me, witnessing the family's story. His support, though mostly silent, had meant a lot to me. To Viv and Hattie too, I suspected.

I made Viv some fresh tea and persuaded her to eat a piece of toast. She chewed dutifully and said, 'I presume Tom told you the rest?'

'Hattie told us her version of it. And then Tom arrived... and he told us how he came to be involved.'

'That was a disaster,' said Viv, shaking her head. 'A complete disaster. Though I must say, Rae seemed much happier once she had a real person to pin her fantasies on. I suppose what I'm saying is, she was happier once she'd finally retreated into her delusions. She'd hovered between two worlds – fantasy and reality – for years. Freddie had tried to put a stop to it, but he couldn't. Rae just wouldn't let go of her dead child. Her determination that he should exist wore us down. In the end we all gave in and accepted Alfie. Colluding with her seemed the easiest thing to do.' Viv nibbled at her toast, swallowed and then continued. 'Rae set out the toys in the nursery again. She'd go and sit there every day – sometimes she'd ask me to sit with her – and she'd talk to this imaginary child. Read stories to him. Sometimes she'd make up stories for him... I think that was probably the origin of the Tom Dickon Harry books. Alfie – or the *idea* of him – seemed to spark her imagination. Rae had only ever written adult fiction before and she'd never been very successful. Her novels were all out of print and the literary establishment had forgotten her. She was quite bitter about that and had been looking for a new direction. So I suppose there was a plus side to the Alfie business, in a way. The death of Alfie led to the birth of TDH and the rebirth of Rae as a writer.'

'How on earth did Hattie cope with having an imaginary brother?' I asked.

'We told her the family had to play a sort of game to help Rae get over Alfie's death. Hattie had an imaginary friend, the way children do, so it wasn't too much of a stretch for her to imagine that Rae had an imaginary child. Of course we didn't realise then what we were asking of Hattie. I shudder to think now... Deborah was away at university, so she wasn't affected that much. Then Frances left home and went off to college. She'd always kept herself pretty aloof anyway. Freddie was the one who found it hardest. He felt as if he'd not just lost his son, he'd lost his wife as well. He was convinced Rae would never get well all the time she believed in Alfie. He waited, hoping she'd make a full recovery, but of course she didn't. For years she lived a kind of dual existence. At one level she knew exactly what had happened – she remembered the miscarriage, she knew there was no child – but at another level, the fantasy was completely *real* to her. And therefore unassailable.'

'A fantasy life can be lived as intensely as real life,' said Marek. 'In some cases the fantasy can seem more real.'

Viv nodded. 'That's exactly how it was for Rae. She wasn't interested in her real children. She wasn't even interested in Freddie. He found that very hard of course and he— well, he looked for consolation elsewhere. Can't say I blamed him. Mental illness is absolutely exhausting to deal with. It casts a shadow over the whole family. There's no normality. You can never really relax. And eventually you run out of compassion.'

'From the sound of it, Viv,' said Marek, 'I don't think you ever did.'

She waved a hand dismissively. 'Oh, I did my best. I had to keep going, for Hattie's sake. The poor child looked on me as a surrogate mother. But Freddie reached the end of his tether and he left. It wasn't a marriage any more, not in any real sense. And Freddie was still an attractive man, not even fifty. He went abroad, so I decided to have one last stab at laying the ghost of Alfie to rest. I told Rae that Freddie had taken Alfie with him, that Alfie had wanted to go and live with his father. She was very upset and confused to begin with, but then she appeared to accept the news. She actually used it to develop her Alfie scenario! She concocted this story that faithless Freddie had deprived her of her only son on the grounds she was an unfit mother. That's when the photos started to appear. Rae cut photos of boys out of magazines and newspapers and stuck them in frames. She said they were photos Freddie had sent her from abroad. Fanny couldn't bear to see these awful things scattered around the house – they were so obviously clipped from magazines – so she took some photos herself and gave them to Rae. I suppose that was another mistake on our part. But Fanny was so clever. Over the years she managed to photograph boys who looked similar to each other *and* similar to Freddie – blond and brown-eyed. But their faces were never very clear, or the boy was photographed at a distance, so it wasn't immediately obvious they weren't the same child. Though I gathered from Tom,' said Viv, turning to me with a rueful smile, 'that *you* spotted they were fakes.'

'I happened to notice one of the boys was left-handed. And Tom isn't. That was the first thing that made me wonder about him.'

'We put up with the fake photos to keep Rae happy. I even sent her fake letters from Alfie. She went on and on about how she never heard from him, not even a Christmas card, so I started to send a monthly letter home, supposedly from Alfie away at boarding school in the north of England. Deborah, bless her, faked his school reports! I remember she made Alfie good at sport and English and hopeless at maths. I'm ashamed to say that, after a while, Alfie began to seem almost as real to me as he did to Rae. I used to quite enjoy writing those letters. And they gave her so much pleasure! It was hard to believe what I was doing was wrong, but now I look back, I can see it was. But we didn't have a master plan, we just made it up as we went along. What else can you do if someone simply won't accept a death? The only advice we'd ever been given was to play along with her. So we did. Rae just wore us down – me, especially. Alfie's existence made everything easier somehow. *Calmer.* Because Rae was calmer. And of course happier.'

'What happened to Freddie?' I asked. 'I think Tom said he was dead by the time they filmed the documentary.'

'He died of a heart attack in 1989, when Alfie would have been about ten. I wasn't sure how the news would affect Rae so I kept it from her for a while. When I finally told her, she took it fairly well. Disappeared into herself, in fact. She talked less and less of Alfie and spent a lot of time alone in her room, scribbling in notebooks. One day she presented me with a stack of them and said she'd written a book for Alfie – would I type it up for her? That was the first of the TDHs. *Tom Dickon Harry and the Haunted House.* I read it and realised it was rather good and – just to humour her, really – I suggested we send it off to a publisher. Well, the rest is history... I thought this new interest would be marvellous for Rae, stop her mind wandering back to Alfie. I didn't bargain on her claiming her non-existent son was the *inspiration* for her boy hero! Nor did I bargain on the books being a runaway success. I suppose Tom told you how we came to approach him?'

'Yes. He mentioned his relationship with Frances.'

'Tom was another of Fanny's bright ideas. Seems lunatic now, but at the time it looked like the only way to save Rae from public humiliation. By then she was a literary figure of some standing, with seven or eight TDH books under her belt and a huge fan base. There was a lot at stake, one way and another. So we did what we thought was best – best for Rae, best for the family. But looking back now, it seems like a series of disastrous misjudgements. Tom's impersonation – good as it was – was directly responsible for Rae's second breakdown and she's never really recovered. I don't think she ever will. She's nearly seventy-three. Old age is taking its toll. God knows how she'll cope if Tom pulls out, as I imagine he will now. There was a time, early on in his career, when he needed us – needed the cash and needed the kudos of TDH – but I think that's long past.'

'I'm not so sure,' I replied. 'Tom also needed a family. He's attached to you all, in his way. Especially Hattie. I think he might find it quite hard to make the break.'

'You think so?' Viv was thoughtful for a moment, then said, 'But he *will* make the break, won't he?'

'Yes. If I know Alfie – and I'm not sure now that I *do* – I think he will.'

Viv didn't reply. She sat still, gazing into space, her face tense with worry. I felt a sudden impulse to give her a hug, but self-consciousness and common sense held me back. I loved this family, but I didn't understand them. I suspected I needed them more than they needed me, so I held back. When Viv finally met my eyes, I simply smiled and said, 'If there's anything I can do—'

'Thanks, Gwen. You've been a great help, just listening. It was high time all this was sorted out. You've given us the kick up the backside we all needed.' She stood up, cinched her dressing gown at the waist and said, 'I'm going to go and see Hattie. The poor girl must be put out of her misery. Though God knows how you break news like this.'

Marek said, 'Would you like me to come with you? I wouldn't want to intrude, but if you're concerned about how she might react...'

He left the sentence hanging in the air but the relief flooding Viv's face answered his question. 'Oh, *would* you? I'm worried what might happen if she goes off the deep end.'

'I'll leave all the talking to you. But if things get out of hand,' he added vaguely, 'you can leave her to me.'

'Thank you so much.' Viv's eyes were bright with tears – whether of gratitude or fear, I couldn't tell. Both probably.

As Marek followed her out of the kitchen, I decided I

would go up to my room and finish packing. I switched out the kitchen lights and made my way along the passageway to the hall where I found Viv and Marek standing at the foot of the stairs, gazing upwards. Rae stood on the half-landing in her dressing gown. One hand clutched the banister rail. From the other hung a doll dressed in a blue babygro. A few paces behind her stood Hattie, her face pale, but composed.

Rae drew herself up to her full height. 'Vivien... I have something to say to you.'

'Ma—'

'It's over. Do you hear? It's finished. Alfie's dead.' Rae shut her eyes and leaned on the banister for a moment, steadying herself. 'He's *always* been dead...' She opened her eyes again and continued. 'I have explained – explained *everything* – to Harriet. And now, I'm feeling very tired. I would like to go and lie down.' She looked over her shoulder as Hattie took a tentative step forward. Rae turned back to Viv, and said, 'Would you please look after Hattie for me?' Her voice failing now, she added, 'I want you to... to take good care of her.'

As Rae crumpled, Marek launched himself up the stairs, taking them two at a time and caught her just before she hit the ground. Hattie shrieked as the doll fell from Rae's hand, tumbling down the stairs, its limbs jerking, until it landed at Viv's feet.

Upstairs a door opened and heavy footsteps pounded along the hall. Deborah's head appeared over the banister and she leaned forward, panting. Her eyes widened and a hand flew to her mouth. 'Good God! Is Ma *dead*?'

'No, she fainted,' said Viv.

Deborah stared as her sister bent down to pick up the doll. 'Oh God, Viv, that isn't— is it?'

Viv gazed into the doll's serene and glassy blue eyes. 'Yes, I'm afraid it is.'

As Marek passed her, carrying the unconscious body of her mother, Deborah's lower lip began to tremble. She looked down at the group of anxious faces below and said, 'Would somebody please tell me what's going on?'

~

Marek carried Rae back to bed and Hattie went with him to make her comfortable. Viv took Deborah back to her bedroom, leaving me standing at the bottom of the staircase, feeling useless and dreading the descent of Frances or, worse, Alfie.

A door opened and closed quietly and Marek appeared on the half-landing. He'd only been gone a few moments, but I felt as if I hadn't seen him in an age. I hadn't looked at him properly for hours, not since we'd come back to Creake Hall, so it felt strange, watching him descend the stairs – this man with whom I was barely acquainted, this new lover, so very much older than me, with his silver hair and disquieting navy blue eyes.

When he reached the foot of the stairs, he stood facing me and said, 'I think I'd better go.'

'Must you?'

'I think so. The family needs time to settle down again. They won't want outsiders. I'm going back to the mill. I've told Viv she can give me a call if she needs me, but I think Rae will be OK.'

'And Hattie?'

'The worst is over. They just need time.'

'And kindness.'

He smiled. 'Yes. That too. Viv will look after them all.'

'And who will look after Viv?'

'I'll keep an eye on her. Were you planning to leave today?'

'If I can. I don't know if there are any trains on Boxing Day.'

'You won't drive back with Alfie?'

'No.'

Marek hesitated, then said, 'You know you can come and stay at the mill if you need to get away.'

'Thanks, but I think that would just confuse me further. I need to be on my own for a bit. Sort out all that's happened... And I have to talk to Alfie when he wakes up. Attempt to explain.'

'Under the circumstances, I don't think you owe him anything.'

'No, I know. But I'd still like to try and make a good ending.' I looked up at Marek and said carefully, 'He wasn't just a lover, he was a friend.'

His expression didn't change. 'Perhaps he still is. Or could be.' He laid a hand on my shoulder. 'You don't need to close all the doors and bolt them, Gwen. You might feel differently when the dust settles. When you get back to Brighton.'

'Differently about you, you mean?'

'Yes. And I'd understand if that was the case.'

'Do you think *you'll* feel differently when I'm back in Brighton?'

'No. But I still think you should take some time out. A lot has happened and a lot of it happened to *you*. You maybe rushed into something because— well, just because I was there. Because I listened.'

'I never realised just listening could be so exhausting.'

'It depends what you're listening to. Listening – *really* listening – to pain is very hard. And you waste energy trying to think of ways to help. But the best way to help – often the only way – is just to listen.'

'I do want to take some time to think. Mainly because how I feel about you now is exactly how I felt last night. That's the point, really. I think I want to stop feeling what I feel about you and do some *thinking* about it. I mean, for a start, I live in Brighton and you live in darkest Norfolk. It will require quite an effort to even see each other.'

'And I imagine you're not wild about returning to the vicinity of Creake Hall in the immediate future.'

'No, I'm not. You see what I mean? It will be *complicated*.'

He nodded. 'I'm not saying "no", Marek, I'm just saying— oh, I don't know what I'm saying! Especially not when you look at me like that!'

'Like what?'

'Like you looked at me last night.'

'Looking's not a crime, surely?'

'It is the way you do it.'

'In which case, I might as well be hanged for a sheep as a

lamb.' With that he bent down and kissed me.

All thoughts of an early return to Brighton evaporated as Marek's long arms enfolded me. His long arms made me think of his long legs and one thought led to another, so that I briefly considered dragging him up to my attic bedroom, but a door banged upstairs and I heard brisk footsteps move along the corridor.

Marek extricated himself and said, 'I'm off. You know where I'll be if you need me. My number's on the board in the kitchen. I'll wait for you to ring. If you decide to, that is.'

'Of course I'll ring you!'

'I hope you do. Take good care of yourself.'

'You too.'

He turned and walked away in the direction of the kitchen.

As I watched his retreating figure, I called out, 'Marek!'

He spun round, his brow furrowed, his dark eyes concerned. 'What's wrong?'

I hesitated, then feeling very foolish, said, 'I'm missing you already.'

He grinned and said, 'Good. See you in Brighton... Maybe.'

I made enquiries about Boxing Day trains and drew a blank. Alfie offered to drive me all the way to Brighton, but I declined. The thought of sitting side by side in awkward silence for several hours was enough to reconcile me to spending another night at Creake Hall, which is what Viv and Hattie wanted me to do anyway. I knew Marek was right about the family needing to close ranks and bury their figurative dead, but they weren't ready to do that yet. Everyone was braced for Alfie's departure and none of them believed they would ever see him again. I would provide some distraction at least, a reason for them to hold things together for one more day, so I agreed to stay another night. Viv insisted she would drive me to Norwich the next day and from there I could begin my train journey home.

Hattie and I spent much of the day sewing, saying very little. We were both exhausted, but the silence was companionable and I kept a watchful eye on her. I sensed that, as she sewed, she was piecing her life back together again in the light of her new knowledge. Every so often she would heave a great sigh, but I thought it was probably a sigh of relief.

I was aware that, elsewhere in the house, goodbyes were being said, some undoubtedly painful. I kept my head bent over my needle, dreading the moment when it would be my turn to say goodbye to Alfie.

~~~

Hattie made her way to the nursery and stood outside the door, listening for noises within. She could hear Alfie moving about, so she raised a tightly bunched fist and knocked on the door.

'Alfie, it's me. Hattie. Can I come in?'

He opened the door. Over his shoulder, she could see an open suitcase on the bed and clothes lying on the floor. It was what she'd expected but she nevertheless felt dismayed.

She took a deep breath. 'Viv says she's explained to you. About me. Me and the baby.'

'Yes, she did. I was very relieved. Gobsmacked, but relieved. I can't imagine how *you* felt.'

'Numb. I don't think it's hit me yet. So I wanted to see you, before it does... You aren't staying for lunch then?'

'No.'

'Is your flat habitable?'

'It's not mine, it's Rae's. It always was.'

'Are you going to give it back?'

'Yes. I hate it anyway. Hate it because it isn't mine and because I keep getting bloody burgled. I'm going to get myself a grotty bed-sit, somewhere so dire, burglars won't sully their fingers breaking and entering. I shall sleep soundly at night and my conscience will be clear.'

Hattie laughed to keep tears at bay, then said, 'I suppose this is goodbye then?'

'I suppose it is.'

'You won't come and see us any more?'

260

'If I did, it would be as myself, not Alfie. And I don't think that would be fair on Rae, do you? I think a clean break is best for her. For everyone.'

'Will you revert to your own name now?'

'I can't. Equity names are for life. I'll always be Alfie Donovan professionally, so that's what I'll have to stay. But I've promised Viv I'm not going to do any kiss-and-tell stories for the papers. I'll remain Rae's son, nominally. But I'm about to become Rae's *estranged* son.'

'Oh... I see.' Alfie sensed she wanted to say more, so he waited while she shifted from one foot to another. 'Alfie, are you and Gwen—'

'I don't want to talk about that, Hattie. It's none of your business, in any case.'

'Sorry. It's just that I liked her so much!'

'So did I. That's why I don't want to talk about it.' He turned away and began to fling clothes into his case.

'Alfie—'

'Yes?'

'I want to say something to you. Something important.'

He looked up from his packing, registered the expression on her face and straightened up. 'Go ahead.'

She clasped her hands in front of her as if she was about to burst into song. 'I just wanted to say... you may not be my brother, but... you're the only brother I've ever had. I've loved you, Alfie. Loved you for the wrong reasons. Gratitude mainly. Your existence meant mine was somehow less shameful. But... I *have* loved you. And I really, really don't want to lose you. Please, can we still be friends? *Somehow?*'

Alfie bowed his head and appeared to study the floorboards, then he looked up and said, 'Oh, Hat... You're a complete bloody pain in the arse.' He opened his arms wide and Hattie flung herself at him. He held her for a long time, saying nothing, then, when she was calmer, he put his mouth to the tangled curls at her ear and murmured, 'I think I might have missed you anyway. The way you miss a wart, once it's been removed.'

She hugged him with a force that drove the breath from his slender body. He staggered, then laughed and Hattie started to laugh too, her face shiny with tears. 'You were a rubbish brother anyway.'

'And I'll be a rubbish friend.'

'Don't care,' she replied. 'I need all the friends I can get. I can't afford to be too picky.'

'Bloody cheek! You might at least put on a show of being grateful.'

She grasped his hand with both of hers. 'Oh, I am, Alfie... Believe me, I *am*.'

Gwen

I was alone in the sitting room, sewing, when Alfie came and found me. He stood in the doorway and said, 'I'm leaving now.'

'Oh... Have you said goodbye to the others?'

'Yes.'

I secured my needle in the quilt top and laid it aside. I stared down at my lap and noticed a tangle of threads. I gathered them up, rolled them into a ball and dropped them into the waste bin beside my chair. When I looked up Alfie was watching me.

'I feel bad leaving you here on your own. Are you sure you won't—'

'No, Alfie, I'll be fine here. I'm leaving first thing tomorrow. I think the family will be glad of a bit of distraction after you've gone. Everyone begged me to stay another day. Even Rae.'

'You've been a big hit.'

'I suppose so. They've all been very kind to me. I thought it was the least I could do.'

He took a step into the room. 'Look, Gwen, I don't want to prolong the agony or the embarrassment, but I just wanted to say, I'm very, very sorry things ended this way. I wish I'd told you what was going on. And I wish you knew how close I came to telling you. How hard it was *not* to tell you.'

'I think I see that now.'

'It wasn't as if I could ever offer you anything more than

Alfie. Alfie is all that's left now.'

'Oh, I don't think so.'

'What do you mean?'

'Alfie's just a part you play. It isn't *you*. I always knew it wasn't you, right from the start. I could sense the discrepancy. The man who agreed to bring me here, against his better judgement; the man who listened to the sad tale of my mother's death... That wasn't Alfie, that was Tom. The angry young actor who's fed up with playing fops and wastrels is Tom, too. You only let me get to know Alfie, but I *sensed* Tom. He was always there. It was unsettling. Exciting in a way, I suppose, the contradictions in you. But in the end, it became frightening. I felt I couldn't trust you. And trust means everything to me.'

He was silent for a long time, then said, 'Will you be seeing more of Marek?'

'I hope so.'

'So there's no way we can... start again? You won't give me another chance?'

'If I didn't want to see Marek, I'd give us another chance. But I don't think it would have worked. I think of you as a friend. I think I always did. A friend I slept with. And you were lovely to sleep with! But it wasn't love. I don't think it was ever going to be love, do you?'

'And what you feel for Marek – is that love?'

'I've no idea. It's very different. It isn't anything I've ever felt before.'

He smiled. 'Sounds wonderful... Well, I wish you both luck.'

'Thank you... Would you like to keep in touch? Or would you prefer—'

'I don't know, Gwen. I don't know anything about anything any more. Can I give you a call now and again? I'll really miss talking to you. You were a good listener.'

'Yes, call me whenever you like. I hope we can stay friends, but I'll understand if we can't. I betrayed you, Alfie. I'm not proud of that.'

'And I was deceiving you. I'm not proud of that. Let's call

it quits... May I kiss you goodbye?'

He stood waiting for an answer, so I murmured, 'Yes, you may.'

I stood up as he approached, steeling myself to meet his large, brown eyes, sad as a Labrador's. A little smile played at the corner of his mouth. He raised a hand to my hair and removed a piece of thread. He held it between his fingers, regarding it fondly, as if it was something precious.

'*This* is what I shall remember... Pieces of thread. On your clothes. And in your beautiful hair... Goodbye, Gwen.' He leaned forward and kissed me on the cheek.

He was gone before I could bring myself to speak. I stood, staring blindly at the door as it closed behind him.

~~~

Alfie had arranged things with Viv. There was to be no fuss. Farewells were to be said privately and he was to take his leave of Creake Hall with no ceremony. As he descended the stairs for the final time, he took a last look at the portraits on the walls and derived some small satisfaction from the knowledge that they had no more right to be there than he had. Perhaps less. What was it Rae had said? It had almost unmanned him, as had the old lady's pitiful tears and the quiet dignity with which she'd eventually said goodbye. Alfie didn't remember his own mother, but the woman he'd almost come to think of as his mother had said, 'You've been more of a son to me than I was ever a mother to my girls. You put me to shame, Tom.' Then she'd taken hold of his hand, grasped it firmly and said, 'I want you to know, I'm very, very proud of you! I couldn't have wished for a better son. I could only have wished for my *own*. Goodbye. God bless...'

Alfie arranged his belated Christmas gifts on the hall table, setting Gwen's apart from the family's. He picked up two carrier bags containing presents intended for him, then set them down again. Reaching into his jacket pocket for a pen, he leaned across the table and pulled one of the gifts towards him. He struck out the word "Alfie" on the label and wrote "Tom". He repeated the exercise with each of the remaining parcels. He put his pen away, picked up the carrier bags and struggled through the unwieldy oak door for what he believed – and very nearly hoped – would be the last time.

Chapter Twenty-three

Gwen

I hate goodbyes. They feel like little deaths to me. I had to endure a minor holocaust of sad farewells at Creake Hall, some sadder than others. Deborah hugged me to her ample bosom, as if I were the daughter she'd never had. Frances took my hand in hers and regarded me thoughtfully, her elegant head on one side, as if I were the subject of a particularly challenging portrait.

'It was a pleasure to meet you, Gwen,' she said, unsmiling. (It occurred to me that Frances had perhaps trained herself not to smile to discourage wrinkles.) 'I'm sorry it didn't work out between you and Tom. Really, I *am*. He's a nice guy and I think you were probably rather good for him. And good to him. He needs that, poor lamb.'

Anxious to change the subject, I said, 'It was nice meeting you too. Perhaps we'll run into each other in London.'

'I've got a website. Get in touch if you're in town. Perhaps we'll do lunch. That would be fun,' she added, still unsmiling. 'Really,' she added, her beautiful eyes earnest now. 'It *would*.'

I decided I liked Frances after all. Alfie had said she was an acquired taste, like Guinness or Marmite, and he was right. But I liked both. And Frances.

Hattie insisted on accompanying Viv and me on the drive to Norwich station, so it only remained for me to say goodbye to Rae who'd kept to her room since her fainting fit. After I'd said goodbye to Deborah and Frances, I made my way upstairs, knocked and entered Rae's room. There was a heady smell of hyacinths now and I caught sight of vivid blue spikes in a china bowl as I made my way to her bedside. Rae didn't speak but waved me to sit down.

She'd aged. Yesterday had clearly taken its toll, but Viv said Rae had refused to see a doctor. Now she lay back on her pillows, evidently weak, but her eyes remained alert. Her hands scrabbled at the bedclothes, as if she was anxious to sit up. I smiled and laid my hand on one of hers. It became still beneath mine, so I left it there.

'I've come to say goodbye, Rae.'

She took several deep breaths before she was able to speak. 'Must you go so soon? I've so enjoyed your company.'

'I'd like to get back home.'

'And where is that? If you told me, I'm afraid I've already forgotten.'

'Brighton.'

'Oh dear, that's a long way! Is Viv taking you?'

'No, I'm going to catch a train. Viv's taking me to Norwich station.'

'I do wish you could stay another day. But I expect you're anxious to get away... A fine sort of Christmas you've had here! I am *so* sorry, my dear.'

'Please don't be! I've had a wonderful time. I feel as if I've made lots of new friends. In fact, you almost feel like family to me. Everyone has been so kind. There have been problems, I know, but in some respects, this was the nicest Christmas I've ever had. I shall remember it forever. And I shall remember all of you very fondly.'

Rae struggled to lift her head off the pillow. 'But will you come back? I do wish you would! I would so love to show you the garden in spring. That's the best season. Come back in the spring, my dear, and Viv will show you round the garden. There's such a lot to see at that time of year. The bulbs, the blossom in the orchard, all the trees breaking into leaf. It's glorious!'

'I'd much rather *you* showed me round the garden, Rae.'

Her smile faded. 'Oh, I very rarely go out nowadays. But I can see it all from my windows.'

'But you don't smell it. Or touch it.' Speech failed me as I suddenly remembered something Marek had said, his voice unsteady with emotion as his hands had stroked my naked body. *Like the petals of a magnolia. So smooth... and firm.* I took a gamble and, fixing Rae with a look, said, 'When was the last time you touched the blooms on your magnolia, Rae?'

Her mouth formed a startled "O", then she made a little tutting sound. 'Some years ago, my dear. Far too many,' she added sadly.

'Well, I'd like to come back when the magnolia is in flower. Will you show it to me? And will you show me round your garden? If you aren't up to the walk, we'll get a chair and I'll wheel you round.'

She hesitated, then a mischievous light appeared in her eyes. She narrowed them and said, 'I do believe I'm being bullied!'

'No, not bullied. Cajoled.'

'Nagged!'

'All right then – nagged! But do we have a deal?'

With what looked like a superhuman effort, Rae hauled herself away from her pillows and leaned forward, offering me her large, knobbly hand. 'It's a deal!'

I took it and we shook. She sank back onto her pillows, laughing. As her laughter subsided, she sighed and looked at me. 'You've been good for me, Gwen. Good for all of us.'

'Please don't mention it. We're friends now.'

'Indeed we are! Now don't let me keep you, if you need to be getting along. I wouldn't want you to miss your train. We don't need to say goodbye, do we? Not a proper goodbye at any rate, because you'll be back in the spring!'

I looked at my watch. 'I've got a little while yet. Viv said she'd give me a shout when she's ready... Rae, before I go, can I ask you something? Something rather personal. You don't need to answer if you don't want to.'

She smiled. 'I don't think I have any secrets left, my dear. What did you want to know?'

'I wanted to know – I wanted to understand, why you wanted a son so very badly.'

Rae looked surprised, but not shocked. 'That's a very good question. One that nobody's ever asked me before. Perhaps if they had – well, there's no point in speculating now, I suppose.' Her gnarled fingers clutched at the covers. On a sharp intake of breath she said, 'I had a brother. And he died... My father never forgave me.'

My heart in my mouth, I said, 'Was it *your* fault he died?'

'Oh, no! Not at all. My mother gave birth to twins, you see. My brother Raymond and me. Neither of us was a large or healthy baby – we were several weeks premature – and poor Raymond didn't survive. He lived for two weeks, then died. It must have broken my parents' heart, to watch me grow and thrive, while Raymond struggled for life. And then to see him lose the fight...' She turned to me and said, her voice quite matter-of-fact, 'The wrong child died, you see. That's what my father said. I heard him say it to my mother when I was unfortunately old enough to understand what he meant.' She looked away towards the window and her breathing seemed to become laboured. 'I felt as if I'd been turned to stone. Looking back now, I think my heart *was* turned to stone. My father had wished me *dead*.' She waved her hand in a hopeless gesture. 'I was just a little girl, I didn't know what to do. I couldn't bring Raymond back. I knew I hadn't been the cause of his death, but somehow I felt responsible. As if I'd stolen something that was rightly his.

'I decided to do the only thing I could. I resolved to try to be something like the son my parents had wanted instead of me. And when I grew up and married, I dearly wanted to present my father with a grandson. I saw it as making some sort of reparation... But of course that didn't happen. Then, when I finally lost my own son, I understood just what my father had gone through. I felt as if I was being *punished* – punished for a second time because, Heaven knows, my father had never made any bones about my being a disappointment to him! He punished me for not being his beloved son and when I lost mine, it just seemed like the last straw. Something snapped. It seemed so terribly *unjust...*

'They tell me I went mad. I ignored my husband and my other children and I reverted to a world of make-believe where I could be what I'd always longed to be: the mother of a son. It seems so sad and foolish now. To have turned my back on all that I had. Four healthy daughters. A loving husband. It *was* madness.'

'But a madness brought on by grief.'

269

'Yes. But also by a lifetime of living in the shadow of Raymond. The child who might have been... And Raymond would have been the perfect child, you see! In my imagination, he was a paragon! Everything I could never be!'

I considered Rae's words for a moment, then something occurred to me. 'Tom Dickon Harry was based on *Raymond*, wasn't he? Not Alfie!'

'Oh, yes! How clever of you to realise. I claimed TDH was based on Alfie, but that wasn't strictly true. The idea was already there in my head – had been for my entire life – in the form of my dead brother. I'd wanted my son to be an incarnation of my brother, so that the long shadow he'd cast would no longer fall across my life. And when I lost my baby, I refused to accept that was my last chance... to be free.' She shook her head slowly. 'It was many more years before I found a way to be free of Raymond.'

'Writing the books?'

'Yes. I re-created Raymond – my *idea* of Raymond – as the boy-hero of my books. This strangely old-fashioned, heroic little boy, who isn't very strong but who's clever and resourceful. That was how I'd always imagined my twin brother, as he grew up alongside me, in my head. He was my hero, and he became the hero of my books... But of course, by then, there was another long shadow.'

'Alfie.'

'Yes. My own lost son... It all became very muddled in my mind. I felt free of Raymond, but I couldn't let go of Alfie, my imaginary son. He was always there in the background, the other boy who might have been. *Should* have been... Then one day Frances introduced us to Tom. Tom Wilson. He was *just* as I'd imagined Alfie! He even looked something like the photographs she'd chosen to represent him. Tom was all I could have hoped for in a son: charming, intelligent, articulate. We talked about books and the theatre and we discovered we shared a passion for certain poets.' Rae lowered her eyes and smiled. She looked positively girlish. 'I'm ashamed to say, I think I fell a little in love with that boy... He reminded me of Alfred, you see, my second husband. He'd also been a blond charmer and was a very cultivated man. I was besotted with Tom, even before they filmed the documentary. And *that* dreadful experience was only redeemed for me by his presence. He was so kind and attentive. So funny! I knew I couldn't bear to live without him in my life. So once again I retreated into a make-believe world where Tom *was* Alfie. So I could *keep* him.'

She sighed and clasped her hands in front of her. 'They tell me I had another breakdown after the documentary was filmed. I don't really remember. I recall it was a very bad time. I remember feeling utterly confused – about Tom, Alfie, Raymond, TDH. It was all *such* a muddle! I could no longer keep all the stories straight in my head. All the lies... I had ideas for books, but I couldn't sort out a logical sequence of events. That's when Viv stepped in. She helped turn my ideas into proper stories, with a beginning, a middle and an end. You know, I think Viv's the real writer in the family, not me.'

'Have you ever told her that?'

Rae thought for a moment. 'No, I don't believe I have.'

'You should.'

'Yes, I probably should... Oh, there's so many things I should have done!'

'You still have time to do some of them.'

'Yes, you're right. You know Gwen, you're a lovely, lovely girl but...' She lifted her hand and wagged a finger at me. 'You're also the most fearful *nag*.'

'I know. It's because I'm used to looking after people. Dippy actors who've lost their shoes and ageing designers who've lost their confidence... The homeless at the night shelter in Brighton... And my poor deceased family, who had to be organised, sobered up, occasionally *found*. I've had a lifetime of looking after people. And if they don't co-operate – you have been warned, Rae – I *nag*. Without mercy.'

She was laughing now and a wheezing sound was coming from her chest. 'My goodness, I think I've finally met my match! Hurry back, Gwen. Come back in the spring and tell me more about your family.'

'I will. Goodbye, Rae. Give my love to the garden.'

'I will.'

'In person?'

'In person.'

'Promise?'

She laughed. 'Oh, you dreadful girl! Away with you before you miss your train!'

I stood my ground, pressing my lips firmly together, the way I clamped pins when doing a fitting. I've been told I look fearsome in this pose. Sure enough, Rae caved.

'Oh, all right, I promise!'

I leaned across the bed, kissed her papery cheek, mumbled 'Goodbye' and fled from the room before my stupid tears could overwhelm me.

Rae

That's the car. I can hear it going down the drive... They've gone. Viv and Hattie and Gwen. But she said she'll come back. In the spring. To see the magnolias...

Alfie won't be coming back. Not now... He said goodbye and he meant it was for good. But Vivien says I shall still see him. When he's on the television. And I shall hear him when he's on the radio... He said he'll let her know when he's going to be on, so she can mark it in my diary. I wouldn't want to miss it. Not now...

Frances said the next time Alfie's in a show in town, she'll take me to see it. She said we'll have dinner and the best seats in the house!

So I *will* see him. He just won't be coming back to Creake Hall. Not any more... That's what he said. I thought perhaps his eyes said something different, but I was probably imagining things... Wishful thinking...

If wishes were horses, beggars would ride.

He told me to look after Hattie. He made a particular point of that. I promised him I would. That we *all* would. He looked pleased when I said that. No, *relieved*.

He didn't stay long. He said he didn't want to drag things out. I think he meant he didn't want me to get upset. I tried hard not to. I don't think I disgraced myself. I didn't blub until he'd gone. When I remembered what he'd said... How he'd said goodbye. He said, 'I'd better be on my way' and then he bent and kissed me on the cheek. I touched his hair... So soft! Just like a baby's... And then he said, 'Goodbye, Ma. I'll miss you.'

Ma.

He didn't call me Rae. He said, 'Ma'.

He didn't have to say that. Not now it's all over. He could have called me Rae. But he didn't. He said *Ma*...

I think Alfie might come back.

One day.

He *might*...

Endings and Beginnings

Gwen

Rae was persuaded to leave her room and eventually she ventured out into the garden, cautiously at first, then every day, sometimes several times a day, so that she became fully involved in the maintenance of the garden, taking on some light chores herself. Before he left, Marek suggested Viv had a conservatory built, so Rae could enjoy the garden in all weathers. Now even on cold, wet days she sits in her conservatory, notebook in hand, making plans for the garden.

Viv engaged a new gardener after Marek left – an energetic young woman called Sally. They've become good friends. In fact I think they might be more than friends. Viv certainly seems very happy, but complains she doesn't have time to write any more TDHs. She claims the next one will be the last book in the series. (But that's what she said last time.)

Deborah took early retirement and, with great misgivings and a handbag full of valium, went to India on her own. She didn't come back on her own. She met Trevor, a retired Cambridge academic and a widower. They fell in love, she says, on a beach in Goa. Deb says it isn't hard to fall in love on a beach in Goa, depending on how many cocktails you've drunk, but the miracle was, she found she was still keen on Trevor in England, in November, in the rain. So she's cautiously optimistic about their future together, to the extent that she's put the Beccles house on the market and moved in with him. She says her son Daniel couldn't be more pleased and thinks Trevor is 'a great bloke'.

Frances joined the AA. Not the four-wheeled version. She'd always said that if she ever woke up in bed with a man whose name she couldn't remember, she'd admit she had a drink problem. Apparently the young man in question was very nice about it, but Frances took it badly. She hasn't had a drink for over a year now but says every day is 'a bloody awful struggle.' But I think she's winning.

Hattie is teaching *City and Guilds* Patchwork and Quilting and exhibits her work at the mill, which she's turned into a studio where she teaches and works. She's sold some pieces and now has a commission for a wedding quilt. In her spare time she makes tiny quilts for a charity that donates them to the parents of stillborn and miscarried babies. The baby is wrapped in a quilt and brought to the parents who can hold their dead child and begin their grieving process. Some parents decide to bury their baby wrapped in the quilt, but most decide to keep it as a memento of the precious time they spent with their child. Hattie says some mothers claim they can still smell their baby on the quilt and, for that reason, they'll never wash it.

Alfie gave up the London flat and returned the keys to Rae. He now rents a large, rather seedy bed-sit in Notting Hill. He loves it. He says what he likes about it most is that he knows he'll never be burgled. (He lives next door to a professional burglar who has assured him this is the case.) Alfie's acting career took a surprising upturn when he played criminal twins in a TV drama series. He won a BAFTA award for his performance (perhaps I should say performances) and he's now offered a much wider variety of rôles, most of them criminals, but this appears to delight him. He refers – gleefully – to Tom Dickon Harry turning in his literary grave.

Marek left Creake Hall and now works as a family therapist in London. He visits the Holbrooks regularly and Viv – who misses him dreadfully – always sends him away with flowers, fruit and jars of home-made preserves.

Marek and I are expecting our first child, so we've decided to marry. Viv insists on providing a grand reception for us at Creake Hall. Hordes of Polish and Scots relatives are expected to descend for the event, to welcome me into their family. I suspect some of them – especially the children – are more excited about meeting the creator of Tom Dickon Harry than meeting Marek's new wife. (TDH is very big in Poland apparently.)

Marek and I have asked Alfie if he will be Best Man.

He said he would be honoured.

~~~~~

ACKNOWLEDGEMENTS

I'd like to thank the following people for their help and support while writing this book: Tina Betts, Liz Broomfield, Amy Glover, Philip Glover, Ruth Howell, Gillian Philip and Elaine Reid.

I'd like to extend a special thank you to Sue Magee of *The Bookbag*. www.thebookbag.co.uk

Blankets of Love is an initiative started in Australia in 1992 by two sisters, one a midwife and one a quilter, to offer beautiful small quilts as a lasting memento to parents of babies who have died at or around the time of birth.

For more information see www.childbereavement.org.uk

Made in the USA
Lexington, KY
30 June 2014